B. CATLING

The Cloven

B. Catling was a Royal Academician, poet, sculptor, painter, and performance artist. He was professor emeritus at the Ruskin School of Art and emeritus fellow at Linacre College, University of Oxford. The author of the Vorrh Trilogy, Catling made installations and painted imagined portraits of cyclopes and landscapes in tempera. He had solo shows at Serpentine Gallery, London; Arnolfini in Bristol, England; the Suermondt-Ludwig Museum in Aachen, Germany; Hordaland Kunstsenter in Bergen and Museet for Samtidskunst in Oslo, Norway; Project Gallery in Leipzig, Germany; and Modern Art Oxford. Additionally, he was the creator of six large-scale installations/durational performances for Matt's Gallery in London. He died in 2022.

The Cloven

The Cloven

➤ A Novel

B. CATLING

VINTAGE BOOKS
A Division of Penguin Random House LLC
New York

A VINTAGE BOOKS ORIGINAL, JULY 2018

Copyright © 2018 by Brian Catling

All rights reserved. Published in the United States by Vintage Books, a division of Penguin Random House LLC, New York, and distributed in Canada by Random House of Canada, a division of Penguin Random House Canada Limited, Toronto.

Vintage and colophon are registered trademarks of Penguin Random House LLC.

Library of Congress Cataloging-in-Publication Data
Names: Catling, B. (Brian), author.
Title: The cloven : a novel / by B. Catling.
Description: New York : Vintage Books, [2018] | Identifiers: LCCN 2017048950 (print) | LCCN 2017052234 (ebook)
Subjects: | GSAFD: Fantasy fiction. | Science fiction. | Occult fiction.
Classification: LCC PR6053.A848 (ebook) | LCC PR6053.A848 C58 2018 (print) | DDC 823/.914—dc23
LC record available at https://lccn.loc.gov/2017048950

Vintage Books Trade Paperback ISBN: 978-1-101-97274-8
eBook ISBN: 978-1-101-97275-5

Book design by Jaclyn Whalen

www.vintagebooks.com

147028622

In loving memory of Rebecca Hind

Where is the soul of a termite, or the soul of man? . . . Someone once said that all behaviourism in nature could be referred to as hunger. This saying has been repeated thousands of times yet is false. Hunger itself is pain—the most severe pain in its later stages that the body knows except thirst, which is even worse. Love may be regarded as a hunger, but it is not pain.

EUGÈNE MARAIS,
The Soul of the White Ant

Nebuchadnezzar was living in his palace in peace and prosperity when he had a strange dream that troubled him. None of his diviners and magicians were able to explain it for him, and he called for Daniel, chief of all his wise men. This is the dream: The king saw a great tree at the centre of the earth, its top touching heaven, visible to the ends of the earth, and providing food and shelter to all the creatures of the world. As the king watched he saw a "holy watcher" come from heaven and call for the tree to be cut down and his human mind changed to that of a beast for seven "times."

Summary of Daniel 4 based on the translation of C. L. Seow in his commentary on Daniel

A man without a moral code is just an appetite.

PETER BLEGVAD,
"King Strut"

The Cloven

PROLOGUE

Noontide repayeth never morning-bliss—
Sith noon to morn is incomparable;
And, so it be our dawning goth amiss,
None other after-hour serveth well.
Ah! Jesu-Moder, pitie my oe paine—
Dayspring mishandled cometh not againe!

RUDYARD KIPLING, "Gertrude's Prayer"

*E*ugène Nielen Marais had sat silently for more than an hour watching the ground, sheltering under the long veranda, tucked into the blind spot of the house, not yet wanting to be seen. If the farmer had poked his nose outside and seen the fatigued man, he would have concluded that he was locked in deepest thought again, because that was what he was famous for, often while wandering in the bush around Pretoria. He had just made his way up from the Prellers' farm. His daily supply of morphine had not been replenished and he was miles from anybody who could help, if indeed those people existed at all. This was not a surprise, he had seen it coming like the constant squalls of rain that saturated the land. He wondered if it was but part of his subconscious plan. There was nothing here to help him; he enjoyed the remoteness of the farmhouse, knowing that too much contact with humans might deflect his purpose now. He needed the clarity of ants and the passion of baboons to battle the cramps and shout down the sweltering cold pain.

The black ants that made the ground writhe were not the kind that he had studied. They had not yet entered his brain, which would literally happen before the present hour was spent. But now, while watching, he let his sight go deeper—the tethers to actual meaning stretched beyond need. He saw a movement beneath the ants, a movement in the earth itself, as if the very particles were alive or infested with something of great power and invisibility. A kind of focus that lived independently. Like water that had seeped into the matrix of solidity. This wild scrubland seemed to seethe with a force that would cleanse or bleach every living thing, giving a whiteness to all, forcing all nuance and ingenious time into submission. The idea chilled his blood and sent an involuntary shudder chasing after the ghost of the morphine. For a fraction of a second he remembered a child's dream of a terrifying whiteness. He stood up and walked to the other side of the house. His bones ached and he could barely climb the wooden steps. He knocked on the sun-faded door that was now sodden with rain. The farmer took his time answering. Eventually he appeared at the threshold and glared at the gaunt figure of Eugène Marais: lawyer, poet, drug addict, who would one day, years after this meeting, be hailed as a visionary and a genius.

"There's a snake in the thorn tree," said Marais, trembling.

The farmer just looked at him.

"At the rondavels, it's eating the birds."

The sound of the long rain hissed between then, amplified by the corrugated tin roof of the simple building. The farmer stared a little deeper.

"Do you have a rifle I could use to kill it?"

"Take a shotgun. You can't shoot a snake with a rifle, you should know that," said the farmer.

The men looked at each other for a long while with no more

words to say, before the farmer turned back into the house to retrieve the gun from its rack, which bristled with others. It was one of his best, a handsome well-used double-barrel 12-gauge. He loaded it as he slowly returned to Marais. They nodded and the gun was exchanged.

They walked together for a short while into the wet, sour grass. Marais had missed the path and the farmer understood. He stopped and turned back so that Marais could walk on alone. Alone with a vision that confirmed his regret about humanity, a vision a millionfold stronger than his own human frailty.

Marais walked less than another hundred yards before he closed the shotgun and cocked its hammers. He turned it in his shaking hands, holding it like a paddle, gripping the oiled barrel, keeping the butt end of the stock away from him as if ready to row and steer his way along a stream that only he could see. He straightened the gun, resting the twin holes on his chest, and put his thumb in the trigger guard. Some part of him smiled at it as the sun poked out of the clouds and he turned sideways into its light. He hoped that the farmer would ignore the shot and that by the time they came looking for him, most if not all of his earthly remains would have been removed by wild dogs or hyenas. Under his feet the wet ground dipped. A previous subsidence in the tunnels of other creatures had caused the surface to smoothly hollow. He stumbled a quarter pace, slithered the barrel, and fumbled the trigger, sending the resounding thunder glancing through the side of his rib cage. The heavy fist bludgeoned and ripped at an inch or two of his lung and sent splinters of bone to dart and embroider the skin and silk that had contained them. The gun fell away as he spun backwards into the soaking knee-high grass. The morphine ghost shrank, hiding away from the pain as Marais groaned and wrestled the bloodstained gravity and terse plants, crawling through them to try to find the gun. And suddenly he remembered Cyrena Lohr and the letter that he had written to her. Saw it on the table curling in the sunlight next to the empty box that he was going to gift the mechanical crown in. He had been delighted in finding her dream object, her halo of insects. He had found it inside one of the most treasured magical artifacts that survived the Possession Wars. A great sickness of pain and guilt rose up in him. He knew that his servants would find the crown, the box, and the letter and send them to her. And he knew the terrors that could happen if she wound its motors and placed it on her head. He now had another reason to die quickly.

The sound of the shot echoed out and over everything with ears, and a few without, for miles—their keen activities and their shallow sleep halted for a second or two. Heads lifted to gauge the distance and direction. The scavengers moved first. The farmer looked out towards the shot and the place where the visionary had disappeared into a blurred focus.

Marais's sticky fingers touched the barrel again, dragging it closer. One shot left, he knew he did not have the strength to miss again. Half sitting, he edged the gun closer until he could bite onto its end, tasting the fresh cordite, gun oil, and gritty earth. The shaking white hand seeking the shaking black trigger, which waited alert and as sensitive as the antenna of an ant.

The remote farm Pelindaba where he took his life is now unrecognisable. In Zulu, Pelindaba means "the end of the business"—although the more common interpretation is "place of great gatherings."

Pelindaba is derived from the words "pelile," meaning "finished," and "indaba" meaning "discussion." The whole area is now dominated by the 2,300 hectares of the Nuclear Research Centre. The home of South Africa's atomic bombs.

➤ *Part One*

CHAPTER ONE

The patience of the Sea People was about to be rewarded. They sacrificed and prayed in their homes and temples and at the estuary's mouth, where the waters changed colour and taste. They conjured the return of the magic creature that lived among them before. It had been called Oneofthewilliams because there were many. Some had black skin and silver hair, some were as white as fish. It was even told that some had feathers. One had carried a bow. Another had one eye.

Sidrus knew little about and cared less for these pagans or their beliefs. He had killed the Bowman Peter Williams, and years later had been tricked into eating his shrivelled head, which seated its longing deep in his marrow and its waking in the empty ventricles of the monster's leather soul. Now it was waking up. But this he did not know. All he knew now was revenge, as he ravenously sought Nebsuel—the shaman who had dared to attempt to assassinate him, who left him diseased and weakened. But the head had cured him, made him strong again. He was saved, he thought, by his beloved Vorrh. He truly believed that his destiny was his own. His only immediate task and pleasure was to take his revenge. He had sworn an oath to this fine fury before leaving Essenwald. His destruction of Ishmael's whore, and his blame and execution for the crime, were as nothing to what he was going to do to Nebsuel.

Sidrus's anger blinded him to the being growing in the quieter part of his cells. The transparent one that basked and clenched and responded to the call of the Sea People.

Sidrus was being pulled. And he didn't know it. His slender boat veered in a graceful misdirection that notched a degree east every quarter of an hour. So that by the time the sea flowed under the river it was dark again and the implicit Cheshire moon showed nothing, with a modesty that was fiercely believable.

Sidrus made his camp and lay down to sleep. The remains of the head slid silently inside him while ghosting itself into every fibre and energy of its host, grafting its being into the nerve tree, bone, and blood.

Sidrus awoke just before dawn covered in ants. He rubbed his eyes and stretched, brushing their activity from his face and clothing. During repacking he noticed that the sun was bedraggled in the thick vines of the wrong kind of trees. He walked like a somnambulist to his boat and found it facing a dribble of tide that had dropped several feet, and worse, seaweed had decorated its mooring rope. This was all wrong. He sat on a fallen tree, bewildered and for the first time anxious. A flight of black swans thrashed against a thick and cloudless blue sky. All these clear signs and impossible readings meant only one thing: that this place was utterly different to the one that lived in his head and, even worse, his instinct. It did not fit into either and meant nothing to both.

He was lost.

He rummaged madly in his pack, finding his compass, staring at it and shaking it in disbelief. At the height of his infuriation he bellowed out what should have been a roar of frustrated rage. But something in his throat realigned it, bending the vocal cords to mimic a harp instead of a war horn. The sound shimmered through the trees, towards the sea—high, resolute, and profoundly clear. Sidrus grabbed at his throat as if seizing a traitor, but it was too late. The eloquent call dashed ahead, tumbling in its sleek surety and need to be heard. Through the hissing bamboo and the dark sucking mangroves, its shredded velocity leaving all the verticals and diminishing towards the beach. Its last quiver feebly touching the inside of the fair-haired child's hollow cranium.

Tyc, her rumpled ear wedged tight against the ear of the cold infant, heard the strangled cry. Over the years her name had shortened, indicating her venerable, wise status. The young had very long names, some up to fifty-two syllables. This was to hold them firmly in the world. To tie and bind them to this side of eternity. As they got older and more firmly instated, they needed less, so mother Tyc's single syllable indicted that she was prepared and unfettered, ready to make the slip into the next kingdom. In reality she had no intention of passing over for a good while yet, especially now that the sacred one was arriving. The future of the tribe had changed and she wanted to be part of it. She even considered recalling some of the shed parts of her name to make her plans to the tribe more obvious, but after consideration she thought that it would be ridiculous and without necessity.

Now she staggered back, shaking the low altar in her haste. She rushed from the temple hut with the excitement of a girl, bursting into the breeze and sound of sea, its low waves rejoicing with the bright palm leaves and the fluttering birds. She shrieked and turned towards the village and sang out with all her might that he was near. He was alive and near. At last returning. Everyone ran towards her and looked in every direction for a sight of the sacred one returning.

➤—→

Sidrus was out of their range but moving towards them. He had left his canoe in the mangroves and was now on foot. The matted roots and swollen mud made it impossible to paddle forward, so the land was the only way. He did not trust it and had the Mars pistol stuck in his belt and his machete in his hand. His eyes flickered ahead watching for movement. He could smell the sea and knew he would find his bearings when he reached the coast.

The scouting party heard him approaching, cutting through the bush. They stopped and waited, crouching in the spindly grass. They carried a charm Tyc had given them, a delicate contrivance of substance that held the power of the entire tribe. It twitched in the young warrior's fingers, matching the footfall of the approaching stranger. Sidrus walked into their midst without ever sensing their presence. They all stood up together, holding their arms and spears above their heads, laughing and saying the words of welcome.

Sidrus snatched the gun out of his belt, cocked it and aimed it point-blank into the chest of the first warrior before him. In a quick stab the young man pushed the charm snugly into the pistol's massive bore. Sidrus pulled the trigger. The gun roared. Its horse-stopping power was no match for the twisted strands of leaves and fair human hair. The pistol's heavy slide bucked back against the restraining bolts and sent them asunder. The shock wave travelled down into the slenderest part of gun and wrenched the trigger guard away, its brutal velocity and brittle snapping hardness ripping off two of the fingers of the hand that held it. The slide of the breach kicked through Sidrus's abdomen and disconnected his solar plexus, the last membranous web that had held Williams, the Bowman, trapped inside. It continued and shattered his spine, crushing him out of consciousness.

They carried the broken man back into the core village of the Sea People and placed him before the wise woman. Tyc placed her wrinkled hands over the body. Every inch of her visible skin was tattooed. Many of the designs had lost their sharpness and definition. Age had folded and smudged the insignia while increasing the power of their meaning. She was annoyed by the wounds that he had sustained but was too busy to apportion blame and the necessary punishments. Greater meanings were at hand. She had no doubt that Williams was here, but he was enfolded in the bleeding, wounded body of another. All her skills would be needed. She must release the sacred one from its imprisonment inside this other man, the soul of which she knew was cantankerous and vile. But right now the sacred one needed the blood and the nerves of this monster to stay alive. She must stitch and pray him back into health. So she began on what remained of the right hand, finding that miraculously the three remaining digits still worked. She bound up the other wounds and structured some of the circulation back into function. The splintered spine she could not touch. There were no painkillers in her wide arsenal to quieten its fury; every time her fingers slipped into its disaster zone, the body shook and screeched in agony. She had it strapped down against movement and never again attempted to heal that part of its damage, hoping that in time it would settle and heal over. She and the tribe would have to wait for some primal healing before the true cleaving could finally take place.

Tyc and her neophytes and servants constructed an elaborate frame that worked as a series of adjustable splints and resting platforms, so that the shattered body that held Williams could not move and damage itself further. Feeding and bodily waste could thus be dealt with in a more convenient way. The device also functioned as an altar. Once the body had healed closed, Tyc would start the complex and exhausting work of speaking to the sacred one trapped inside the foreign devil. She intended to enter his unconscious condition and awaken him to gain direction on how the other might be peeled off. The rot and vileness dissected. The Sidrus part eliminated.

➤→

Sidrus awoke in the middle of a star-filled night, a warm breeze flowing over his near-naked body, which ached intolerably. He tried to move but nothing happened. He closed his eyes again and opened them more slowly. The same result. He squeezed them tight shut and clicked them open and shut like a camera, as if to paddle away the bad dream with his lids, but it would not go. His head was fixed down and felt strange, as if it had been extended upwards, elongated like a snake egg. A cold, bald, fragile one. His body was also immobile. He was restrained or paralyzed, and he could not tell which because he could not move his head and catch sight of the rest of his body. He could only stare straight up at the infuriating sky. He remembered nothing and feared the worst. He closed his eyes again. He could hear the sea. He was not in the Vorrh. He opened his eyes again. Of course, the sky was so big because there were no trees to obscure it. He became aware of the taste of fish in his mouth. Who had been feeding him and why? His tongue and mouth felt burnt and dry, and his voice sat in the middle of it like a bald chick in an empty, prickly nest.

"Help me," he feebly said. "Help me."

There was stirring beneath him and to his left side. Suddenly a face entered his vision. The face of a young boy. He instantly noticed how large and white and mercifully unfilled the youth's teeth were. The boy ran away shouting, and he waited and prayed for survival or a quick death. It must be remembered, however, that the Sea People are a patient folk, and Sidrus would be given neither.

CHAPTER TWO

*A*fter any execution, the city always became a party, and it was no different after Ishmael's.

The great theatre was over and the city and its horde sank back into normality and quiet. The mechanical tree and the wooden figure of Adam were disconnected from the stark verticality of the state guillotine. The handmade leaves of the tree were lovingly packed away, their wires unhooked and coiled to wait for the next time, when they would turn the velocity of the wind into the tug that would trigger the falling of the blade. The sliding muscles and the locked jaw of Adam's sculpted face were oiled and reset. The wooden apple extracted from his wooden teeth with a noise like a rusty hinge. All the small sounds had come back after the intimidation of the bellowing crowd and the parties that followed the execution had worn out. The beer halls and street counters did more trade in those few hours than they did for the rest of the year, and the guttural tide of noise had touched the real leaves at the edge of the Vorrh, so far beyond the city wall. Now the tiny fleeting shadows of sparrows and mice darted and pecked at the emptiness of the main square. It had been the greatest spectacle so far, because it had sacrificed a hero on its bloody stage. A man called Ishmael Williams who had saved the city by finding and bringing back its lost workforce. A man who had been held aloft before falling from grace, charged with the butchery of a dancing girl and sentenced to be cut in two in the hunger of the public eye.

Ghertrude Tulp had left the celebration early and now sat absentmindedly holding the hand of her servant, Meta, in her bedroom in 4 Kühler Brunnen. Ghertrude had lost all perception of Meta. It was only when she touched her that Meta became real, visible and tangible again, and Ghertrude knew this was some kind of perverted miracle, and that its strangeness and mystery now seemed less than any other in this old dark house. The loss of her daughter, Rowena, overshadowed all else. In some way she was able to share the aching hollow of it with Meta, especially after her return from the warehouse on the other side of Essenwald. She had never been there and never wanted to go, but knew that it was tied to her life through Ishmael, the Kin, and even Mutter himself. Nothing had been said after Meta's return, but Ghertrude knew Meta was also seeking the beloved child.

Ghertrude held Meta's hand. This also had the added advantage of heightening the clarity and pitch of the world. They discussed Rowena, and who could have abducted the infant from under their noses. Meta was grinding her teeth and increasing her grip. Ghertrude tried not to think about Ishmael, her former lover, who had just had his head cut off. Meta tried to comfort her companion. The execution had been over for more than an hour now and soon she would release herself and make them both tea. Which would help clear the way to the conversation about the path of the rest of their lives.

Then they both heard the latch of the street door. Someone was turning a key and coming in. Very quietly. They heard the soft footfall in the hall below and strained to hear more without admitting and acknowledging the fact to each other. The sound stopped for a while, as if whoever was there was also intently listening for their movement.

It was not Meta's father; Mutter could never be so careful. His clumping arrival was a long way off spilling in the taverns. Ghertrude's father also had keys, but Deacon Tulp would never make an entrance like this, and even when creeping he dented the air in a different way.

The only other person with keys to Kühler Brunnen was Cyrena Lohr and she was defiantly elsewhere, struggling with the traumas of the day.

The unknown entity below stopped listening and moved through the hall to the basement stair. It was going deeper into the secret parts of the house.

Ghertrude abruptly jolted into action.

"I am going downstairs. You must not come, wait for me here. If there is a problem, find Mutter and tell him."

Ghertrude moved quietly across the room to the door and the stairs below. The whole house was quiet and bathed in bright energized light. The vast and ragged sky outside was filled with luminous gigantic clouds that rolled soundlessly around the buffeting wind. Each carpeted stair suddenly seemed to have a voice, and she hoped that the active wind that occasionally rattled the house might conceal the sound. She passed the hall stand where she kept the crowbar and retrieved it on her way down. Her hand automatically stretched out to where the key to the basement door was hidden. It was not there. Nobody knew about its hiding place. Nobody went down there anymore except her. The door was open and she stepped through it and descended.

➤→

Quentin Talbot had his trembling arm around Cyrena Lohr's rigid shoulder in the upper room with its view across the square. They both held small glasses of brandy in their limp hands. He wanted to say something to comfort her but could not find the words. She had not cried when Ishmael was decapitated. Even though he was once her cherished lover, the opposite of tears had happened. She had spoken his name once and it was astringent. As if alum had been applied to the moisture of her bountiful soul—the inner shrivelling making her taut, parched, and brittle. She wondered how Ghertrude felt.

They had both tasted and loved Ishmael's body and heart, and both been repelled by what should have been his soul.

She had not even noticed Talbot's nervous intruding arm, and when she did, she certainly did not want or need it.

"I have had enough of this place, would you please take me home, Quentin," she eventually said, standing and putting the untouched brandy down on the silver tray.

"Yes, of course, this very moment." His arm sprang back, as if slapped.

They remained speechless on the drive back to her grand house. She had no intention of inviting him in. She wanted the horrors of this day sealed with him outside her home, until she saw Guixpax standing on the front steps. He looked dishevelled and confused.

She leapt from the slowing car and called to him as she approached. "Guixpax, what's wrong, what has happened?"

His crisp diligence seemed to have been doused in vagueness.

"The door was open, madam," he said, explaining nothing.

She moved past him, with Talbot quickly following. The house seemed normal. She moved from room to room. Everything was the same. Nothing was touched, nothing stolen. She went into the kitchen; the cook and housemaid were asleep at the table—their mop-capped heads resting on sprawled arms. This was most unusual. Cyrena sped back to the hall and then up to her bed and dressing rooms. She removed the concealed jewellery box from its new secure place of hiding. Nothing was gone, nothing had been touched. She quickly checked the other rooms and found them secure and void of intruders.

Talbot stood with Guixpax in the hall and both looked equally confused.

"The door was open," Guixpax said again. His eyes were bleary and his speech was slurred. In any other man this would have been a sign of drink. But with him that was impossible.

The three of them sat in the living room without any refreshments because the kitchen staff was out cold.

"This is all most peculiar," said Cyrena.

The men nodded. Guixpax was about to explain again about the door when Cyrena announced that she needed rest, which instantly dismissed her companion and sent the old butler back to the kitchen. She saw Talbot to the door.

"Thank you for being so supportive today, Quentin. I am sorry my homecoming was dramatic and meaningless."

He bowed and almost clicked his heels together. The moment he was gone she ran up the stairs to recheck all her possessions, after which she picked up the internal phone and called the garage. It was instantly answered by the chauffeur, who was obviously not under the same influence as the rest. She explained the situation and told him to come over to sleep and guard her house. He grunted a reluctant consent, and she went to bed fully clothed after locking the bedroom door.

By nightfall the big parties were breaking up. The crowds were settling into their clans to continue more serious reveries and talk about the day. Only in the gullies and pits of the Scyles did the bacchanalia remain, where the decadent and downtrodden of all races and tribes and religions interbred and mingled.

The noise of their festive parties could be heard well outside the crumbling boundaries of that infested community. The drunken glee shuddered and bellowed by the old city gate where the pale wooden execution suit hung in the cooling breeze, flapping lopsidedly like a crashed gull dangling stupidly from a tree. Only fizzing was heard in the sack where the headless body of Ishmael Williams lay. The porous open weave of the material was already encouraging the reaction between the white lime and the vacant flesh. In the corner of the hastily filled-in pit the wooden masked head lay upside down. Lime and dry earth sucking the cold blood in the darkness.

➤→

Farther west the rabble's songs rattled the windows in the small, almost decent homes ten streets away, where in one Thaddeus sat glumly on his bed looking at his hand-drawn calendar that was pinned on the wall of his narrow room. The machine being in the warehouse had said: *Bid your father well, our sympathies we give. His work is ours and five more moons he has to dwell and hereby live.*

Today's date was one of many that had been circled in red pencil. One of the days that he had calculated might be his father's predicted last day. He stared at it while the rich smell of homemade oxtail stew levitated up through the thick and absorbent floorboards. Nothing was wrong. His mother was busy and happy. His sister, Meta, even though disturbed by recent events, was back with Mistress Ghertrude. His baby brother, Berndt, was in the front room, stacking and toppling coloured bricks that he could hear fall in the quiet, normal, secure house. And his father? Well, Mutter was where he wanted to be, snugly settled among drinking cronies in a post-execution discussion about the niceties of this particular day compared to all the others. He knew his father was going to really enjoy this one, and it saddened him. But the condemned man probably was as bad as Mutter had said. So why should he care? His father was going to have a happy day and there was nothing on the horizon to suggest his demise.

CHAPTER THREE

*F*ifty percent of Anton Fleischer's plans had been successful. Fifty percent had failed miserably. The problem was that he did not exactly know the proportional divisions and the positions of their weight and balance. True, the main outcome had been achieved and the lost workforce of the city had been returned, and their previous dwelling of the old slave house was now cramped with their mournful occupancy. But they showed no desire or intent to work, instead spending their time sleeping or staring at the peeling walls.

Fleischer's rank in the Timber Guild depended on his scheme to find and return the Limboia to active service. The first part of which had been achieved not by him but by the recently executed murderer Ishmael Williams. He had stolen all the laurels of the expedition before his most unexpected downfall. So great had been his triumph and demise that the glare of it had blinded everyone to the fact that the genesis of the expedition was indeed Fleischer's original concept.

Only now when the Limboia refused to work did the guild start to look towards him for an answer to *his* problem. The secret of Ishmael's success had died with him. Whatever he had said to them to make the Limboia willingly leave the Vorrh and return was totally unknown. Fleischer's only answer to the growing monotonous accusations was to busy himself in the day-to-day workings of the constipated system. He had found the kitchen staff and restarted the gruel machine that fed the vacant mass. He had advertised for overseers and a warden to supervise them, desperately seeking anybody who might kick them back into action.

Fleischer had spent the morning in the slave house looking at each one of the Limboia until he was convinced that these hollow beings had never been men at all. The fearful depressive weight that they gave off like a miasma had saturated him, making all his hopes and previous achievements nothing but limp and insignificant doubts.

He now stood outside the featureless confines of the house and deeply breathed the air that did not taste of mortal rot. He had just spoken to the herald of the Limboia, the only one of their number who even attempted to engage in language. The terse and sullen creature had said little that made any sense: odd words so divorced of content that they left Fleischer with a sense of impossible isolation. He took another deep breath and walked across the fenced space that sloped down towards the modest proportions of the overseer's house, which looked like a child's toy or a model next to the monolithic three-storey slave dwelling. He unlatched the wooden gate and walked into the domestic enclosure, stopping briefly to take some interest and solace from the small garden that was showing signs of early flowering among the unkempt rows of overgrown vegetables. He squatted to examine them and out of the corner of his eye saw that he was being watched. A man and a tall woman were standing on the other side of the house. For a brief disconcerting moment, he thought the worst. Then his sense and his focus locked in and he recognized the man who was waiting for him. The only man who had a good word to say about Ishmael at the curt trial.

"Sergeant Wirth," said Fleischer as he walked towards them, trying to regain his affable manner.

"Herr Fleischer, I have come to talk to you about the position of overseer and the future of the Limboia."

"Please come in," said Fleischer, fishing the keys out of his pocket and opening the door into the musty house. He stood back while the tall, lean woman guided Wirth forward using only the tips of her fingers on his arm. She came very close to Fleischer, her proximity completely ignoring him. He had no choice but to look into it and smell the radiance of her purple, blue-black skin. He shivered and knew without a doubt that he was in the presence of a human who was his natural superior. She never once looked at him or acknowledged his open stares. He marvelled at the shape of her head, so clearly seen because she was almost bald, her hair having been cropped to a shadow. Her ears were long and deformed, reshaped at childhood to hold the silver pendant jewellery that hung there now and shone against her smooth skin, as did the white beads and pearls that collared the longest neck he had ever seen. Her strangeness rewrote beauty as her silent authority and her grace glued him to the spot. He unexpectedly placed himself back with the Limboia, being closer to them than this vision that passed before him. His curiosity suddenly felt lecherous and voyeuristic, especially in the presence of the blind Wirth, who obviously owned her in a way that he could not imagine.

"I want to apply for the position," Wirth bluntly stated. "I have worked with them before and have some experience of Bill Maclish's tactics of control. Also I am a survivor, as you know. Herr Ishmael and I were all that was left of the retrieval party."

There was a lull, a quietness in the air after his Transvaal bluntness. It put Fleischer in his place. He knew without Wirth and Ishmael the Limboia would still be lost in the Vorrh, and he might be rotting in there with them. He lifted his downturned face to look directly into the strength of Wirth's face. It was speckled and pinched by the scars of dozens of wounds. Most parts of his body had been stabbed and torn, but he had survived when so many of his men had been mutilated. The small spinney of trees that he and his men had charged into with their bayonets were thorn trees, an unknown kind of black honey locust, their dagger-shaped spikes as resilient as steel. Things grew that way in the Vorrh, indifferent to mercy and unique in their cruel perfection. The entanglement of the men was brutal; the more they struggled the deeper the foot-long thorns punctured. Ishmael had said that some of the men had struggled so much that they had been drawn upwards and were found almost crucified in the branches. He said that Wirth had frozen on this side of panic, and it must have saved him, but only after both of his eyes had gone. Fleischer smeared his staring away from the horror of the soldier's blind scars. Eventually he found his voice again.

"But, Sergeant Wirth, would not your injuries make it very difficult for you to complete such strenuous duties? And you already have a pension for your significant contributions in the field."

"I am no good at being a lame man. I am not built to sit around and do nothing. I need a task to exist. Besides, I have Amadi here. She will be my eyes."

"Yes, I can see that, but I think the position might be too taxing, even for your exceptional capabilities."

A small quiet shuddered and gradually unfolded between them. For the first time Amadi's eyes moved from Wirth to Fleischer, and while he was transfixed by them Wirth said, "I know about the fleyber."

Fleischer was hearing the word *fleyber* for the second time that day. First in the awkward mouth of the herald of the Limboia. He had no idea what it meant and assumed it was pidgin or one of the hundreds of native tongues.

"Fleyber?" said Fleischer far too calmly.

The woman sensed his disquiet and moved her hand on Wirth's arm.

"Fleyber, what is it?"

Wirth turned his blind stare at the young man. "It's a child born dead."

Wheels and cogs started moving inside Fleischer, as if a brake had suddenly been released and the obscure engine of the obvious chugged into motion.

"Babies . . ." he said, almost to himself.

"It's what they want, the price to make them work. Ishmael promised them one and they followed us like sheep."

"Dead babies." Now Fleisher really was talking to himself.

"It's how Maclish controlled them, he and his doctor friend," said Wirth, seeming to be enjoying a distant joke.

"Hoffman," said Fleischer.

"That's the man. I think he supplied them and Maclish handed them over."

"What did they do with them?" asked Fleischer without hearing the normality of his question gather in the wheels of the machine that spun in the back of his mind.

"Fuck knows, man! It's disgusting."

There was a pause while each adjusted his position.

"How do you know all this?" asked Fleischer.

"I was there when the Limboia broke cover. They came right out to us. One up front and talking, holding the dead baby out to us, wanting to exchange it."

"For what?"

"For another one, a fresher one. The creep who had it in his hand said it was worn out."

"Then what happened?"

"Don't really know, there were shots. After it was over we all went back to camp and some days later I had a talk with the speaking one and kinda understood some of the things he said. I was pretty fucked up and high on morph and booze, so it all sounded sensible to me. Anyways, that's what they are waiting for. For their promised corpse. If you want 'em to work, you gotta pay up."

For no apparent reason the woman changed position, moving to the other side of Wirth and guiding him into the nearest chair. Fleisher was about to apologize for not offering a seat before, but his mind was far too full of possible solutions and their monstrous necessities.

Fleischer found the words to ask, "How can we do that?"

Wirth heard the "we" and closed in.

"With your influence we could make inroads into the infirmary and maybe find some there."

"Some?"

"We are going to need a constant supply to keep them working in the Vorrh."

"I am not sure I could get involved in such a business," said Fleischer, suddenly backing away.

"Maclish, Hoffman, and Ishmael did. That's how it works, man." Wirth was losing his moment of subservience and was now showing his true undiluted purpose. "It's the only way you're going to get them creeps out of their beds and chopping wood."

Fleischer had run out of speech: He had been given the solution that he so deeply craved but it involved a level of moral turpitude that he had never experienced before. The dilemma was immense and he felt very alone in it. Until the mechanism of the obvious again lurched at him.

"If you became the overseer, Sergeant Wirth, would you help us in this matter?"

"Sure. That goes without saying, it's what I would expect to do."

"Then I think that we might be able to work something out," said Fleischer.

"I even have a few ideas of my own," said the now-excited Wirth.

"What ideas?" said a cautious Fleischer.

"Most of the business that bypasses the infirmary comes out of the bars and brothels of the Scyles and the old town. Well, if we set up our own house, we could farm the kids directly and also make a few shekels on the side. It would be no problem finding the girls; Amadi could help us collect them." He squeezed the woman's thigh and she looked up and smiled a weird crooked grin that was as innocent as a child's and as knowing as an eternal courtesan's. "Or maybe you could get some advice from that dirty old bastard in your ranks?" Wirth chuckled.

"Who do you mean?"

"The old fat fucker who has probably tasted every whore between here and Kilimanjaro."

"Krespka," said Fleischer in resigned agreement. Ludvik Maximilian Krespka had never liked Fleischer. The old-school tyrant saw him as an upstart and a snivelling youth. Krespka's influence in the Timber Guild was monumental. He had barely approved Fleischer's scheme of retrieving the Limboia, and when it was achieved, he complained about the high cost of lives, even though everyone knew that he cared about nothing except his own wealth and personal pleasures, which were legendary. Wirth's blatant statement declared his knowledge about the old man's corruption, and Fleischer liked the tone and vehemence of its disrespect. Of course it was preposterous to even think about consulting Krespka about such matters, but it did turn up other possibilities of advantage and future leverage worth considering.

They talked for another twenty minutes or so, Fleischer becoming more convinced of the need to bend a few laws to obtain what everybody wanted. Perhaps Wirth really was the man for the job, if he could be trusted to work under Fleischer's supervision and control. There might even be some sense in his idea about brothel breeding pens. Under the right supervision such a thing might prove beneficial and lucrative, and only a select few would ever need to know. Fleischer might even gain favour or obtain something over Krespka and finally get him on his side. He could prove to be a much more powerful ally than Quentin Talbot ever had.

Fleischer finished the meeting with Wirth and Amadi and asked them to return after he had made a few enquiries. His planning was now seriously engaged with the machinery of the obvious, and he was musing on whom he knew in the infirmary and how he could persuade them to smuggle out the necessary material.

CHAPTER FOUR

*T*he scratching at the window could not be heard above the storm that rattled its casements and the teeth of the solid door in the thickness of its stone mouth. It was a thin bony clawing that sounded like a long-dead branch fallen in the wind. The storms that came up and across that coast were famous in their intensity. As were their infamous echoes that came out of the Vorrh. Freak climatic conditions produced by the enormous area of transpiration, and the broken mountain that rose up through it, took the approaching sea storm that had grumbled inland and spun it around its own vortex, often sending it flying back into the panting sea. Those storms, which passed over Essenwald, shook the city to its core, causing spiralling winds that grabbed at roofs and picked up anything loose to toss into the ragged sky. Sometimes the spires of the cathedral shivered in St. Elmo's fire, which spurted jagged sparks from one to the other. No one dared to enter its interior at such a time. Ball lightning would form and prowl the aisle and naves, frightening sheltering images of Christianity into reclusive shadow. The storm would finally wear itself out mid-ocean, where it collapsed in unwitnessed cold rain.

Carmella and Modesta had not been outside their home in three days. Nor had anybody else in the desolate village. They feared for their lives, exposed to such a tumult. This storm was outside the circle of seasonal rains and too fierce for the few remaining villages to attempt to collect precious water in their wells and cisterns. When it cleared, the sun peered through a yellow sky, shutters opened onto a wet morn where vast puddles blinked with the last few drops of rain.

Carmella opened the bolted, sodden door, putting her weight behind its swollen resistance. The air smelt good and she walked into the rising temperature, leaving the house open to air. Every scent of the earth was rising, the olfactory kaleidoscope rippling in the primal reptile brain. Strongest from her animals in the inner courtyard, which were also vocal in their joy of the fresh day. Modesta was still sleeping as Carmella circumnavigated her property. Rare optimism warmed her muscles as she stood and saw the solidity of her portion of the world. The rest of the village could be heard peeling open, encouraging the warmth and the perfume of the sea to enter their stuffy rooms. She completed her cycle and returned to her door, stepped in, and gave an involuntary shriek.

Such an adolescent reaction should have been beyond her years of experience. All the dealings with the dead and dying. All the intercourse with the other world and its denizens of strangeness. What had stopped her in her tracks and made her cry was something different, something out of time or meaning. A different kind of impossibility.

"It will come to lead you," the voices had said, "you must follow the seraphim's chosen pathway without question or hesitation. Its silence and presence will guide your way to paradise."

The voice had shaken Carmella's trembling bedroom while she had lain prostrate before its majesty and the piebald Modesta had stood erect, smiling, her eyes gleaming with joy.

"Wait for the seraphim, prepare for its coming. We will never speak to you again."

And every day Carmella looked along the winding track that led to her house and every night kept an eye on the dark door, while Modesta looked firmly into the depth of the blue sky, even at night in the black window of stars.

It should have been a child who asked the old woman what a seraphim was, but Modesta was no longer that. She should have the earthly body of a child, but it had tautened into a sinewy womanhood. The mind and soul that seethed inside her lithe patchwork skin was of an age and perception that was beyond comprehension. Most of Carmella's questions were ignored or answered with a curt "You already know," so it was a shock when Modesta held forth in her answer to the old woman's simple question.

"The seraphim are a legion. Only one will come for us, a single seraph from the first dawn. We will know it by its otherness. It will have wings and hands to pray and to cover its face."

And again Carmella turned towards the door. Nothing was there, but both of them knew that it was already flying to be with them.

Folding and unfolding in and out of visibility on her kitchen table was a creature that she had no reference for. True that some part of it resembled a bat or a bird that had been broken in half by the storm. But its animations seemed to come from light itself, flickering between black and dazzling silver, almost as if it still carried the pulse of the storm in its stencilled ligaments. A haze of shimmering blue flicked in and out of all its thin parts. Carmella approached cautiously, picking up a sturdy broom in the process, ready to beat it and shovel it off her table and out of her house.

"The seraph . . ." hissed Modesta from the darkness of her room, her pale speckled body standing in the doorway. "It's the seraph."

The old woman drew closer to the table and looked at the mangled slithering thing that was gently steaming as it tried to right itself and aim its pointed head at its audience, which now stood side by side, waiting. It opened its beak-like mouth and let out a blue light that dented and chipped the room and their ears with a sound like a cold chisel attacking a solid block of glass. They covered their ears until it ceased. Then Modesta raised her hand flatly above her head and made a circular motion while sinking to her knees. She tugged at Carmella's dress, urging her to do the same. They both knelt, now with their heads below the level of the table. The seraph hitched itself to the edge of the scrubbed plateau and pushed its beak and eyes over the brink, staring down at the women. It made a softer mewing screech and they both bowed farther. After a few moments it closed its eyes and appeared to be sleeping. The women shuffled backwards to the far side of the room, where they watched it and whispered.

"Are you sure it is the seraph?" asked Carmella nervously.

"Of course it is, look at it. It was foretold. What else could it be?"

Carmella was still doubtful but packed her travelling things anyway and stacked them by the door. She then made food for their departure.

The seraph sprang awake and fell from the table, spilling outside through the doorway and onto the track, where it made its gristly noise and jerked forward, without any care about who was following. Modesta was after it in moments, calling to Carmella to follow. But slowed by the lopsided weight of the bundles and bags that she had roped about her, Carmella quickly lost sight of the piebald girl and the angelic emissary. She hastily pulled the gate shut and latched the heavy iron padlock.

"Come, come, we are leaving the village," cried Modesta at the end of one of the blank lanes. All three were united again in a narrow fenced pasture.

"This is wrong," said the old woman, adjusting one of the bundles that had slid around her body, making her look vastly pregnant. "This is Horacio's land."

The seraph ignored her and flutter-leaped like a spastic hen across the carefully organized rows of vegetables. Modesta picked her footing warily behind it. Carmella looked for another way.

"Where is it taking us?" she implored.

Suddenly there was a clumsy commotion as the creature became entwined in a string of netting connected to small cowbells, empty tin cans, and shards of broken mirrors. The jangling array made the seraph squawk as it slid through the dancing strings. The door of the nearby house flew open and an ancient man fell out shouting, a long-barrelled shotgun in his shaking hands. He did not even look to see who the intruders where. He just rushed and fired as he lurched forward. The recoil sent him spinning and corkscrewing like a child's top, leaving him sprawled and groaning in a pile of scattered melons. The shot had been wild and nobody was hit.

"Quickly, leave!" barked Carmella, and all three departed the defiled garden.

It became clear that the instruction to follow the celestial herald was not to be taken literally. After the incident with Horacio it led them in a series of half circles back and forth around the perimeter of the village. It must be the general direction that should be followed. This was decided when they were eventually making progress towards the sea and the coastal track. With each footfall Carmella doubted the ability of their guide and the virtue of its supposed origin.

By late afternoon they had started the slow gradient of the

winding cliff path, often having to stop and wait while the seraph flapped up and down, fell and skidded off the steep sides, or scrabbled outside of the range of human visibility. Its shrill voice would often be the only sign they had about which of the many dividing tracks they had to take. The light was fading fast and they were getting higher, the sea wind buffeting their nimble footsteps on the narrow ridge.

"We should stop soon and get off the track so that we might find a place to rest for the night," said Carmella.

"But we are almost at the highest point," said Modesta. "We can stop and sleep on the other side."

The seraph, as if in response, squawked and tumbled sideways, looking like the wind was tossing a matted ball of sticks.

"See. He is pointing towards the inner path, the one to the left, it must be shorter." And with that Modesta scrambled up the loose pebble path, which looked like little more than a goat track in the dying light. Forty minutes later a luminescence was coming off the land to meet the depth of blue in the twilight sky. The sun had been gone fifteen minutes and its last echoes were clinging to the edge of every surface. They were near the top and capable of looking straight down to the crashing sea and the slender worm of the lower path that inched below. The guide had vanished again and the child was holding her hands out in front of her in a crouching low wander, a movement that looked like a cross between tightrope walking and blindman's bluff.

"We should stop now," said Carmella, looking down at the child, who seemed to be where the track turned downwards. The seraph flew up above the child, calling impatiently, so Carmella stepped forward, expecting a gradual progressive slope, but it was a steep step and she stumbled down sideways into it, the weight of all her bundles swinging to one side of her faltering body.

"Seraph," she beseeched as the combined inert momentum unbalanced her and twisted her sideways off of the path and crashing down the cliff. She clawed and screamed at every rock and shrub on the way, trying to dig her heels into every ridge and crevice. She knew in her panic that there was only one chance. If she could catch hold of the lower path, she would fall no farther. As she skidded and tumbled and her skin was ripped from her hands, she saw its thin line of hope rising towards her. She hit it shoulder first and it splintered her collarbone and broke her arm. Then as she screamed and tried to stop, the weight of the falling bundles was moving faster than she was and they sent her cartwheeling over the edge into the roaring darkness of the sea in the granite wadi below.

CHAPTER FIVE

On one of the endless grey afternoons of London, Nicholas was lying on his bed listening to his radio when Dr. Barratt poked his head around the door. He immediately sat up and pulled the headphones off. Tinny sounds of audience laughter could be heard escaping.

"Good voices?" asked the doctor.

"My favourite," said Nicholas.

Barratt came into the room and pointed at the single unused chair. "May I?"

"Please do, it's nice to have a visitor."

Nicholas swung his legs around so that he sat side-on, looking and waiting for his guest to start the conversation. Barratt was not a blunt man, but he had little time to waste with the formalities and niceties of polite conversation, especially while working inside the less-than-normal confines of the Bethlem Royal Hospital. He was wearing his usual rumpled white coat over another of his tweed sports jackets and grey flannel trousers. Nicholas noted that he must have been in a rush that morning, because there were several tuffs of unshaved skin on his face where the hasty razor had missed its target. Nicholas was fastidious about shaving, never missing a single hair. He could take up to an hour shaving one of the inmates. Especially those that twitched and jumped about unexpectedly. He had never nicked a patient in all the years that he had been there, and nobody knew how many years that had been. He had never had to shave himself, because hair had only ever grown on his head and eyebrows. Not a whisker or a curl occurred anywhere else on his smooth neotenous body.

"Nicholas, what do you know about Dick and Harry over at Spike Island?"

"Do I have a full minute on that question?"

"As long as you want," said the already frowning doctor.

"Well . . . I have never met them, but I knew that they were there because we are alike, the three of us. I know that Hector Professor Shoe-man went to visit them. He told me. And that while he was there, there was a bit of trouble. That's all I know. Oh, and the fact that they came from France. Why do you ask?"

"I ask because I have just received some new information about them."

"When?"

"Today. Dr. Hedges, who was looking after them, rang me this afternoon."

"On a telephone?"

"Yes, on a telephone."

"I would like to see and use a telephone. I imagine it's a bit like my radio, but I could talk back. Maybe I could answer some of the questions or even set a subject myself. Maybe I could—"

And here Barratt interrupted him. "I am not here to talk about telephones, Nicholas." His snappy tone silenced the room for a few minutes. The man and the Erstwhile sat and gazed at the shrunken, ailing plant in a dented enamel pot that was the only ornament in the room. A few moments later Barratt said, "How do you know anything about them?"

"Um, that's a difficult one. I just know they are there and then people tell me the rest, I suppose. I remember that some of us came. Me and another here. Them in France. Some in Denmark. And you told me the rest."

"I did?"

"You said that two like me had come to the Spike."

"When?"

"Some years ago."

Barratt was just about to repudiate that he'd had any part in the fuelling of these fantasies about angels and animated corpses, when he remembered the auto-interning.

"I said they were like you because they buried themselves."

"Exactly," said Nicholas, pleased that their communications were going so well. "And of course we must not forget the two new ones in Germany. Do they have names too?"

"How did you know about them?"

"Hector told me all the details."

"No, I mean before he arrived."

Nicholas suddenly made a face of total blankness, the colour instantly drained and the eyes fixed in innocent moronic surprise. The immediate mask was so acute and theatrical that it made Barratt begin to smile and he had to compose himself to continue in a sterner tone.

"Somebody in London sent a box of insects to the address where the German ones were being kept. The retirement home where Schumann lived. They reacted wildly."

Nicholas kept the same strange face without moving a muscle. It was very familiar. Barratt had seen it before, but not here and not attached to patient 126.

"Well?" he demanded.

Nicholas just looked at him with the same raised eyebrows and expressionless unblinking eyes. Barratt had had enough. He stood up and started to leave the room.

"Please, Doctor, why did you ask about Deek and Hari?"

Now he was using politeness and funny pronunciations to irritate Barratt even more.

"Because they have disappeared, vanished, done a bunk."

"Oh, that's no surprise."

Barratt stopped in his tracks. "Do you know where they have gone, did anyone or 'thing' tell you?" he asked in an annoyed tone.

"Not yet, I thought that you might."

Barratt grunted.

"They must be full right up with all the parts they have gleaned in that sad hospital. Too heavy to go in the ground. Now they must split up to find another two Rumours to make a plural with. That's the problem when we are found in pairs or brought together in the same cage. Much better like me, on my lonesome."

Barratt went limp, allowed his gravity to slump in the direction of the door.

"But, Doctor, you forgot to ask the important question."

Barratt's face started to take on the same look of incongruity as Nicholas's comic stare.

"All right. In for a penny in for a pound. What question is that?"

"For points, not money," he said seriously.

"Yes, very well."

Nicholas changed his face into a beaming smile.

"Why did we all leave the great Vorrh and come to see you here, of course."

"Vorrh . . ."

"Yes, I have told you about it before. The forest in Africa with the garden of paradise at its heart."

"Oh yes, that," said Barratt in peeved resignation.

"The answer is that we came to try to understand why you

are all so stupid." Nicholas then clapped his hands and stood up. Barratt made for the door. "And to protect the tree of knowledge from you."

Barratt was in the corridor when Nicholas called after him.

"Would you like to see one of its cuttings?"

He turned to look just for a second or two at Nicholas framed in the doorway, waving the miserable plant in his direction, with the same set expression of startled imbecility on his face. Then he turned his back and stormed down the passage.

Barratt began to slow as recognition seeped in. He stopped dead when it arrived. The face that Nicholas had adopted was that of the silent Hollywood comedian Harry Langdon. Where had patient 126 ever seen his films? How could he produce such a perfect copy? Barratt slowly turned to go back and ask him, but sluggishly halted at the thought of the kind of answer he would get.

All conversation with Nicholas was exasperating, with his constantly turning the tables on the normal condition of question and answer and cause and effect. Of course this was not unusual in Bedlam, but Nicholas's technique seemed designed to get under the good doctor's skin. It was driven by what looked like a self-righteous disrespect for all that Barratt stood for. It was never offensive, just intensely irritating, especially when Barratt tried his hardest to understand the Erstwhile's point of view. The time before last had been the worst. In an attempt to deepen the communication Barratt had started talking about William Blake and had asked Nicholas to explain one of the paintings of his ol' man, as the Erstwhile called him. Barratt tried with three different pictures and each time got the same answers: "I don't know" or "I wasn't there for those ones."

CHAPTER SIX

Ghertrude crept forward and opened the second door that only she had entered before.

She slipped along the wall towards the old kitchen, the crowbar sweating in her determined hand. As she got closer she could hear voices. She recognized them. It was the Kin and they were talking to somebody. She slowed and strained her ears.

"Sit still, little one, the blood is still flowing freely," said Luluwa.

"*Little one.*" The words barked in Ghertrude's head. It must be Rowena! Her stolen child. They'd had her all along! She was back! They had her! Ghertrude's heart missed three beats and punched her ribs with the fourth.

"*Blood,*" she heard next, as if from a separate sentence from a separate universe. Her heart swallowed her brain and adrenaline roared through her body. She charged into the kitchen. Seth stepped in front of her to slow her stampede, embracing her and turning her on her own axis like a dramatic and passionate dancing master. Nobody else moved. She regained her stance and saw Luluwa daubing the face of the seated figure that she held lovingly in her stiff brown arms. It was not Rowena. As the bloody cloth was taken away, the figure turned towards her and spoke.

"Hello, Ghertrude. You missed my execution, so I decided to come to yours." Ishmael gave her a sickly grin and she jolted into shock when she saw him alive and again with only one eye. The other had been gouged out, the scarred socket empty and streaming with thin tearful blood. His words eventually bypassed his appearance and she saw the sleek black pistol dangling at the end of his arm.

In the grief of her disappointment, she did not hear herself say, "Ishmael . . . how . . ."

"With the help of an old friend, a *real* friend."

Luluwa still had her hand on his shoulder. She was watching Ghertrude with an expression that for the first time seemed baleful and accusing, even though Ghertrude knew that the Bakelites had only one fixed set of facial movements. Luluwa removed her gaze and continued to daub at the rend in her patient's face, speaking as if addressing the wound itself.

"Ishmael has come home."

"This is not his home, he no longer belongs here."

"And you do?" said Ishmael, lifting his arm and levelling the slender wagging gun at Ghertrude's heart.

"Ishmael will stay with us until the humans stop looking for him," said Seth from behind her. And there it was, for the first time. Her inclusion with them and her spoken separation from the rest of mankind. She felt cold and horrified; a clammy distance enveloped her life.

"I'm not one of you," she barely murmured.

"That's not what they have been saying," said Ishmael, quivering exhortation in his voice. "They say we are brother and sister, you and I. Both made with their help in this very house."

Ghertrude clamped her hands over her ears, but his voice still got through.

"Brother and sister, different mothers maybe. But the same unknown father. Brother and sister who fucked like rabbits. That kind of makes our offspring very special, don't you think?"

She ignored the gun and rushed at him, crashing him out of the chair and Luluwa's arms.

"You monster," she screamed, "you foul monster! Don't you talk of Rowena that way. She was never yours!"

She was going for his eye. The gun skidded across the floor, hit the skirting board, and fired, the bullet going through the wall. They both rolled in a tangled fury, punching and screeching, crashing into Luluwa's ankles and bringing her down, whistling shrilly, on top of them. They slithered on the floor, Ishmael shielding his eye and trying to kick out at Ghertrude. Luluwa's flailing limbs were getting in the way. Seth rushed at them and with his fearsome strength tried to yank Ghertrude away. There was a sickly muffled sound and she bellowed in pain as he dislocated her left leg. Aklia also tried to grab part of the writhing mass. Suddenly all the Kin stopped moving, their heads swivelling towards the door in unison. Luluwa was instantly upright and shrinking back with the others. The fight on the floor continued unaware: Ishmael had Ghertrude's hair wrapped around his fist and was pulling her head backwards. She had sunk her nails into his face. Their feet kicked in all directions.

It was only when the gun went off and they were splashed with the sticky, hot, creamy fluid that they stopped and came apart. Ghertrude saw the pistol floating in space, smoking and moving slightly towards them. Then she saw Luluwa, who was shaking her head from side to side like a dog worrying a bone. A stream of white fluid pumped from her abdomen in a constant rapid flow. It had splashed all over them. Everybody was frozen; the white torrent and the automatic head were now the only movement.

Ishmael saw the squat young woman whom he did not know standing with his gun in her hand. There was something famil-

iar about her but he did not know what it was. She had closed
the door behind her and moved into the room, grating her teeth
as she approached. Her eyes were set and ferocious. He did not
know what was driving her, but he knew better than to get in its
way. So did the remaining Kin, who shrank back. Ghertrude was
still on the floor fearing to move because the pain in her hip was
agonising when she shifted her weight.

Meta liked the Steyr Mannlicher in her hand; it fit her new-
found vengeance perfectly. For surely these disgusting creatures
were of the same family as the shapeshifter that had so ill used
her in the warehouse. The sleek metal had automatically cocked
itself and was primed for action. Ishmael dithered in front of its
awesome sniffing barrel.

"Who are you?" Ishmael spat.

"Get back," said Meta. "Mistress, can you hear me?"

There was no response. Meta jabbed the gun harder at the
space before her and they all slithered backwards away from
Ghertrude. Meta grabbed Ghertrude's hand and materialised
before her.

"Oh, Meta, it's you, oh thank God, it's you."

A sound from above, as if somebody on the upper floor had
changed direction noisily, caused them to freeze. They gripped
each other tightly.

"Are there any more of you here or upstairs?" Meta demanded.

No one replied. Meta remembered a Wild West film that
she had been taken to one Christmas. She always remembered
it because her parents could never forget. In one scene a band
of desperadoes entered a saloon where a troupe of dancing girls
had been high-kicking in fast, loud black-and-white. The ruffi-
ans took out their guns and fired endless smoking rounds above
their heads. Outraged and confused, the young Meta had said,

"Mama, those ladies were dancing, then the horrible men came and killed the ceiling."

Her parents laughed about it for days. For years. At every Christmas.

"Are there any more here?" she demanded again.

When nobody reacted she lifted the pistol and fired for effect above her head. The crisp plaster of the ceiling cracked like old bone. It was a satisfying feeling until she heard another distinct response from above. She crossed the room, waving the gun and grinding her teeth at the cowering group. She still held on to Ghertrude and tried not to pull against her pain. She leaned down and said, "Hold still, mistress, I will save you from these."

As she said it, Ishmael made a move towards the door that led down below, towards the well. Meta turned the gun on him as the other door behind her splinted and started to crash open from a great force that was pushing through it. She spun the impatient gun towards the sound. This was the creature from the warehouse, the one that had defiled her, she thought, come after her again. As the door shattered, she aimed and pulled the trigger again and again with the hissing brass cartridges flying over her head and merrily dancing around her feet, while the deafening reports closed down her senses. Fired until the gun steamed jarringly open, locked back and gutted into its empty position. Everything went quiet. And now she could see it was not the creature from the warehouse that lay groaning on the floor but Mutter, her father, torn apart and dying.

The gun fell from her hand as she slipped the other out of Ghertrude's and walked towards the leaking bulk of Mutter. The Kin and Ishmael had bolted for the lower stairs. Ghertrude groaned at her pain and the shock of what had just happened. She looked up at Luluwa, whose head was now just gently flinching, the last spills of her cream oozing down her flat brown body, between her thighs, and pooling with the rest on the floor like a white atoll in which Ghertrude now sat like a besieged, hopeless sovereign. Her eyes glazed and locked on the atrophied statue that showed no sign of falling and had once been so full of life. Meta stood over her father. A faint gurgling sound could be heard somewhere deep inside him.

"Poppa," she said with the last trace of hope left in her concaving body. "Poppa?"

She knelt into the pool of his blood, which surprisingly was much smaller than the white one that surrounded Luluwa. She touched his hand, but there was nothing, he was gone, just cold. Cold and gone.

After what felt like hours or even days, she returned to Ghertrude and knelt in her puddle, the red and the white making swirls and eddies of interlaced colour. She grasped the leg and with a power and a knowledge that was never there before rammed it back into place. Ghertrude passed out and Meta dragged her like a broken flag out of the room, leaving a smeared trail of red and white. Luluwa was empty and still, her dead body standing in locked amazement.

CHAPTER SEVEN

*N*ebsuel broke into Sidrus's house after the execution, being absolutely sure that the monster would have fled. After thoroughly examining the small house, he made himself at home. He found all the booby traps and deactivated all the locks in minutes. Nobody was a match for his cunning instinct and experienced logic. Here, he was waiting for Ishmael, but time was waning. "No more than two days," he had warned the cyclops. He wanted to be gone and free of the growing oppression here. He looked around the stark interior and felt the loneliness and mania that saturated the walls. He would wait another few hours and then leave alone.

Nebsuel was still amazed at the total success of his plan. He sprang into action the moment he heard the sickening news of Sholeh's death. He knew Sidrus was the only man capable of such an atrocity. It certainly wasn't Ishmael, and when news broke that Ishmael was sentenced to death, Nebsuel made his way towards Essenwald. He found a rat hole in the Scyles where he spied on the monks, following them each day to watch their work with the executioner and jailers. He found the loophole quickly and knew that the key to their undoing would be fashioned in speed and brutality, not cunning and finesse. No one would expect a friendless misfit like Ishmael to have a saviour lurking in the cells under the scaffold. It was clear from Ishmael's trial that everyone despised him, even the women whom he trusted and had been maimed into normality for. When Nebsuel stepped out of the shadow bristling with knives and drugs, none of the slow-witted jailers had a chance.

The most difficult part had not been the slaying and chloroforming of the guards and the executioner, or even peeling off their clothes and forcing the dazed body of one of them into the pale wooden suit of death. It had been trying to raise Ishmael from his torpid lethargy. He sat motionless on a low wooden stool, blood dripping from his face onto the straw that lined the stinking cell.

"Help me, boy," demanded Nebsuel as he manipulated the dead weight of the unconscious man. Ishmael did nothing. The old man dropped the body and spun round, taking a handful of Ishmael's jacket and dragging him abruptly to his feet. Staring into the good eye for traces of medication and finding none. The old man was disappointed to see Ishmael's face so damaged, shocked when he realised that it was self-inflicted. Upset to see his fine handiwork torn out. Especially when he had tried to persuade Ishmael against the operation in the first place. He was a cyclops again. But best not to think about that now. He had come a long way to save his young friend from the woeful miscarriage of justice. He pulled the executioner's mask up onto his forehead so that Ishmael could see his furious need.

"*Wake up,*" he bellowed at him and then cuffed him squarely across the mouth. "I need your help, quickly."

Ishmael fell back into reality and the disbelief of what was happening around him. The executioner's black costume now wore another head under its leather mask. A face that meant everything to him.

"Take his arm."

Ishmael bolted into action, the sting of the blow making him forget about his drooling eye. They worked together and closed the wooden suit of execution about the dim naked body of one of the guards. Nebsuel filled the still-unconscious man's mouth with pieces of torn blanket, to remove any coherent speech. He then clamped the mask into place and they dragged the new victim behind the canvas screen and strapped him into the waiting guillotine. The old man pulled his mask down and stepped from behind the screen into the audience's waiting applause. With theatrical deliberation he released the brake. Adam Longfellar came awake, his fingers twitching, his wooden eyes slyly following them as they fled the scaffold and the square, Ishmael leaning on the wiry arm of Nebsuel while the old man grinned at the mildness of the wind.

The cyclops had all he needed, Nebsuel had seen to that. He had visited the Lohr house during the hours of the execution, inserted gas into the kitchen, and chloroformed the sluggish butler. He had collected Ishmael's satchel with his desired possessions and met him in the nest of alleys outside of Kühler Brunnen, where Ishmael said he had unfinished business. Nebsuel had tried to dissuade him, saying that every second spent here after his apparent death would expand jeopardy and infuriate the Fates. But the bitter youth would have none of it. Deaf to all but his need to punish those who had betrayed him, even while the remnant of his savaged eye still dripped.

There was a spectral, paternal bond between them, and after saving the young man's life it strengthened for Nebsuel. He had enjoyed meeting the strange otherworldly youth again and only wished that Ishmael had stayed intact and savoured his uniqueness instead of being constructed into the normality that he so desired—the very condition that so earnestly wanted to destroy him. They had only had a short time to talk, while the old man tended to his face and Ishmael regained his strength and sanity, and his desire for revenge.

"And after all this business is over, meet me at this address," Nebsuel said, handing him a piece of paper.

"I will, after I have been back to the Vorrh."

"I can take you. What do you still seek there?" said Nebsuel, genuinely surprised.

"Origins."

"Whose?" snuffled the old man in distaste.

"Mine, and I think everybody else's. That is what the old tales say, isn't it?"

"And you believe that and still find it important?"

"I have not yet met all the occupants," said Ishmael, deflecting the question. "There still might be a voice with an answer there."

"The Erstwhile," said Nebsuel.

Ishmael nodded and turned his head away from the daubings and stitchings.

"We have spoken of them before."

"We did, but you never really told me anything." Ishmael's tone had changed. Hurt and a whisper of anger was rising in him.

"I told you nothing because you were incapable of understanding back then."

"And now will you tell me? Tell me how I might get to their wisdom and knowledge?"

"Wisdom," chortled the old man, and the cyclops became tense at the jest, wearing the word like a hand in a boisterous glove puppet.

"Yes, wisdom. Are they not the servants of God? Celestial beings?"

"They were," said Nebsuel, all of his glee suddenly drained. "But that was a long time ago and they have been forsaken and alone in their lost garden for thousands of years."

"All that time making them wiser."

"Making them insane, becoming lost and mad."

"*How* can you know that?" yapped the distraught cyclops, hearing his last vestige of hope being discarded by the only human being he trusted.

"One hears things."

"You can know nothing about them from lies." His anger was shifting colours. "What have you heard to make you speak of them so badly?"

Nebsuel emptied his hands of needles and gauze and washed them in a simple copper bowl. "They are . . . disconnected." He said the word carefully. "Separated from the power that commanded them by their failure. They dare not even look at that failure in the eyes of their own kind. They dwell alone, seeking death, perpetual sleep, or dissolution in the Vorrh—or under it. Hiding from the very time that you think makes them wise."

"Why would they do that?" Ishmael frowned.

"Because it's not the time that we live in. If it were, they might gain the sediments of knowledge that we all acquire bit by bit to build some kind of foundation of understanding. They exist in all time at once. All the flows and tides of before and after washing away at any grain of gathered memory. That is the nature of immortality. Everything at once. All directions equally meaningless. Especially if you have botched the only task that you were ever entrusted."

The cyclops was confused and disturbed.

"Their wretched temporal disconnection adds to the predatory amnesia that shelters in the forest and keeps them imprisoned forever."

"Not all," said Ishmael, his eye locked on his miserable friend. "Some have left and entered the world of men."

"Oh, you have heard that one, have you? Those that got away."

"Is it true?"

"So many stories."

"*Is it true?*"

"Calm yourself, you should be dead and your ghost knows it. This is not the time to be shouting and becoming deranged."

Some part of Ishmael wanted to lunge out and hurt the man who had saved him. But the rest held him back and saw the sense in the old magician's words.

"I just want to know," he said dejectedly.

"And you will in time. The only thing I can tell you is that you must heal. Shock has separated your ghost from you and it must melt back before you even consider entering the forest and seeking those forlorn rejects."

"They are all the same, then?"

Nebsuel looked long and hard into the young man's despair. "Very well. The last thing I will say on this: No. They are not all the same and some have escaped and gone into the world, but they are crazier than those who stay behind. It is said that they have given up grief and immortality and attached themselves to a single time. They think they understand the world of men, because they know that this world was never made for them, never made for them to dominate and reconfigure."

Ishmael's face flushed with pain just before another layer of drugs settled in.

Nebsuel waited and then continued.

"The men who walk and build all over the world are an aberration. They were never meant to be anything more than all the other animals who know their place. It is believed that God gave them clever thumbs and a few folds in their brains so they might tend the gardens and be skilful servants to all the things that would eventually grow there. The Erstwhile were made to contain and train them, but they failed and men tasted knowledge that rippled through their brains and made them grow sideways into the opposite meaning of all other beasts. Our so-called intelligence might just be a wild cell. An abnormal growth that reshaped the entire species once it escaped the confines of its intended enclosure."

"Do you believe this? That men are not God's chosen ones, just another animal?"

"What I believe is for me. I tell you these things because you insist on subjecting yourself to the company of those desperate creatures."

Ishmael ignored this and wanted another answer. "Men must be the prime species—look at all they achieved."

"Yes, for themselves. What value are their inventions and ideas to any other living thing? Are they not a totally selfish lifeform? Are they not totally alone in the arrogance of everything they believe and think they own?"

Ishmael was without words.

"Don't be like them, you might be something else. Don't be like *us*, like me locked in a spiral of deceptive awareness. *And don't be like them*, insane and envious, living an eternal exile of sham. I tried to explain before that you are something different, something unique. When you made me operate on you and add that cosmetic eye, I had to move your real one slightly, to nudge its cradle of muscles and nerves to one side. I could not resist examining your optic nerve and its tight passage into your skull. It was then that I was certain that you are not made in the same way as us. I have opened many men's skulls and seen brains of all shapes and sizes, of all dimensions and numbers of folds, but one thing they all have in common is that they are divided. Split down the middle, only a thin joining holding them together— twin halves snuggling in a nest of bone. Men's eyes have two optic nerves that cross over before they mate with the brain. Left eye to the right side of the brain and right eye to the left. This slingshot draws an X in the brain and some men think it marks the seat of the soul. But you are different, I believe your fine brain is undivided, uncloven and whole, and that your single optic nerve is a straight, untwisted line into its core. *Unique!*"

Ishmael was shaking his head. "I don't want to be that. I want to be dissolved in the many." There was a pause of gagged silence and then the cyclops said, "And I don't care of what. Everything I have met so far has tried to hurt or kill me. Only the Erstwhile and the Kin remain."

Nebsuel changed the position of his listening. "You have said much about those machines, their care and their teaching. But never explained their origins."

"I have no idea where they come from, all I know is that they came for me."

Cautiously Nebsuel asked, "Would you give me permission to seek them out and try to discover who or what made them do this?"

Ishmael snorted and trickled a sneer. "Since when did you need my permission to do anything? I never gave you sanction to rummage about in my brain. When did I ever ask for that?"

"When you forced me to butcher the perfection of your originality, under the threat of that malign bow."

The silence was now made of lead and flour.

Ishmael stood up shakily and looked about the room as if for his possessions and the closest door. Nebsuel held out his hands to support the hesitation.

"Anyway, I don't want to talk about that, I want to know

about those other ones. They must have something for us, for me, a way of explaining men and my place among them."

"O my son, don't you see they have nothing to give to you or anybody else? And some of them use human contact as another way to hide, to bury themselves in the imaginations of men. It is said that some actually think they can become them. Do not go near such beings. They will ensnare you in their glamour. Their mesmeric wrongness must be overwhelming." Nebsuel looked into Ishmael's face and saw in its straight light of his single eye that he would not listen. So he turned away and gathered his anatomical herbs, curved needles, and surgical charms and started to end the conversation, but in his manner, he could not help adding one last stitch to seal his argument.

"Do you know what the Erstwhile call humans?"

Ishmael shook his head and prepared to be told.

"Rumours," said the old man, his smirk knotted behind careful eyes. "*Rumours.*"

Ishmael was looking at his hands when he spoke again. "It's not just the words written by men, there is proof. I have seen the garden where they say God walked on earth, seen the remains of paradise where the great tree of knowledge grew, waiting to explain all things, so that man would know his natural place."

"Why do you imagine that the tree of knowledge was for men?" said Nebsuel in a jarring, amused breath.

"Because the Bible says so."

"Which Bible?"

Before Ishmael could answer the old shaman continued.

"It does not say that in any Bible. Because it does not dare, you have to look elsewhere for a truth that you will understand. *The tree* was made for trees. Its leaves and branches semaphored the first language, constructed of the spaces made in time and shape, the vivid utterance running between shade and light, wind and rain. And that was only the surface conversation. Deep below, the white roots worked hard to expand their territory and drink from the waters that are so full with the memories of futures and pasts. The root tree is twice the size of its surface self and its contours follow the twigs and branches of those above, forcing the crust of the earth and the forest floor to be the dividing plane. Man was told to keep clear and ignore it. But instead he bit into its fruit. An act of blasphemous stupidity. The first crime between the kingdoms."

"But Satan caused that crime."

"Satan caused nothing, he was nothing then, just another kind of Erstwhile, a mistaken failure."

"But now he is a god and abroad in the world."

"What makes you say that? What makes you think he ever left the Vorrh?"

"Because he is everywhere now, the cause of evil all over the world."

Nebsuel spluttered and laughed out loud and then said, "This is why I have separated myself from humanity. Why do you think the Erstwhile call them Rumours? It is they that carried evil out of the forest and have evolved its huge spectrum and power. Satan could never have done that. He is no more or less than gravity, a weak force that is constant in all things. There are worse things to fear than his slender dimension. Have you heard of the Black Man of Many Faces?"

"Yes, but not in detail. I assumed it to be a tribal myth about one of their lost gods."

"It is not that," said Nebsuel, an uncomfortable weariness meeting a dread in his voice that seemed to blunt all the previous cut and trust of his diatribe.

"This is a new entity on this earth. A man unwound and remade in the knowledge and likeness of the tree. Something to step forward when the Rumours have gone. The Black Man of the Forest will write the new Bible, and not a trace of wood will be found in its paper nor in its ink. If it has physical form at all, then it can be made only of human skin inscribed with human blood. And it will be buried in the deepest, driest earth, so that its passing will never touch an atom of water and the great memory of the sea will forget everything about the moment of the Rumours."

Now Nebsuel sat alone. On the other side of Essenwald the cathedral bell sounded the hour. It was hours past the agreed time of Ishmael's return. Their conversation had dried up before the old wizard had time to explain more about water and its properties of memory and how one of the great unspoken prophesies told about a world without men; all the Rumours obliterated to leave a future where the forest stretched and was imagining in endless time and the oceans, seas, and rivers reinforced all in the distance and depth of its memory.

Ishmael was not coming; he had given up on Nebsuel.

"You must be getting old," he said out loud to himself and started to prepare to leave. A sadness rumbled inside him as he stretched his bones in the house of his sworn enemy, ready for departure. He looked about the tight rooms as he stood up. This was truly a horrible place, he thought, and he would take nothing from here.

He left the house silently, trying to disperse the clinging image of Ishmael by his side. He had so much more to tell him.

CHAPTER EIGHT

Sidrus saw Tyc looming above him. He closed his eyes. Seconds later she pulled one open and stared into it, a flaming torch being held close; he could feel its heat scratching his sight. She mumbled something. The flame was gone and he started to move. Not on his own. He floated up and forward on his frame of handcrafted wood, being carried into the row of huts where the ceremony had been prepared and was waiting.

She had been inside him three times before this night. But her rummaging had been confused. She had not found the clear instructions she wanted. His injuries had produced a resonance that distorted her seeking. The unconscious state of the host was also blurring the definitions between him and the secluded sacred one. Tyc had been praying for an awakening and now it had happened. She was ready, shaking off the residue of her sleep, where she had been dreaming of a running horse. She had only ever seen one once, when she was a child. It came with a party of invading forces, who had no real interest in her or her village, they were just passing through into the interior. The rider and the horse had walked in the surf, cooling the animal's hot hooves. At first she believed that the man and horse where one creature. The horse of her dream was a very different beast. It was made of shadow and flickered as if seen through windy foliage. It was kept captive in a wheel where it ran in circles, its hooves never touching the ground. When the boy had arrived shouting "Mother Tyc!" the horse had vanished as if a flame had been blown out.

The frame was carried into two of the huts that had been restructured into one. It was placed on an angled trestle of the same wood. The eyes of the damaged man were working wildly, as were the flaming torches that illuminated the dancing walls and the hoard of effigies and talismans that looked from there towards him.

"We will wait till dawn this time," Tyc said to the men who lined the room. She then crossed the space to the frame and placed her rough, lined hand gently on Sidrus's head. She leaned close to him, but her words were not for Sidrus.

"Very soon, sacred one, very soon we will have you free and in the heart of your people."

She moved her hand from the forehead to the back of his head, where she had previously removed the bones at the back of his skull. It was there that she squeezed her hand into his brain. Slowly, so as not to tear and injure the soft tissue. The swellings that had distorted his head had occurred because of her intrusions and the softness of his previously diseased anatomy.

Sidrus prayed again to his savage God to whom he had given so much. He had understood nothing of what the hag had said and hated her sickening touch. If ever he slipped this obscene pantomime, he would butcher her, break her idols, and raze the village to the ground. The other inside him was weary and angered by this continual hubris, the bile of which poisoned their shared blood and left him feeling exhausted.

Tyc wallowed out a stream of sung commands as the daylight slanted through the gaps and windows of the long hut. The men who lined the walls standing between the staring deities changed the dirge that they had been singing for days. This one was faster and swayed layer upon layer of sound. Sidrus felt sick as his frame was lifted and turned into the sun. He felt even sicker when Tyc began sliding her hand into his brain. She did it with the very slow caution of a nervous lover, easing her fingers between the folds and layers where she had been before. The limp light that would soon roar filled his eyes with a yellowness that he would never forget.

Tyc knew that Oneofthewilliams was in there waiting, that he was shivering under the brain and sleeping in the long bones, even though they had been dented and bruised. She knew she had to gather and assemble him and that he would know how. Know what could be taken from where and how.

By her hand she had tools made of steel and iron, but most important she had tools made of grass, hair, and feathers. These were the ones that would do the real work after the metal ones had slit the tough fibres. She would feel the whisper lines and be told where to grip and pull the brain apart. To cleave the two minds, one precious beyond gold, the other to be sealed back to boil and rage in its own vile juices.

She needed all the strength she could muster. What she had been asked to do would take at least two days and nights and the fingers of many strong hands, entranced and guided by her. She assembled her assistants and supplies. She took a mouthful of a slimy substance from a sealed jar and put a reed to her lips. The other end she slid into Sidrus's brain where her hand had been. Slowly she blew the substance into the folds, knowing that her own charmed mumbled spittle would enhance its potency. When it was absorbed she lay down to sleep, waiting for it to take effect. Some hours later she was awakened by a faint high whistle that seemed to be coming from the prone figure's eyes. Her helpers had stepped back from the frame, terror seizing them by the throats, their own eyes staring and whatever hair they had standing upright on their shining heads. Now it was time to bind them to her will and begin the operation.

All the signs and omens were right. It was just after midday and the sun outside was ferocious. Everybody in the long village that bit into the contours of the beach and coastline was silent. The day-to-day chores had ceased. The Sea People sat in the shade without speaking. Some smoked palm-leaf cigars, others chewed crimson nuts. Even the children were quiet, infected by the weird concentration of the adults. They listened to the continual murmur of the sea, occasionally looking at parents and elders to check that all was well. The only sound in their world now came from Tyc. She sighed and grunted with the effort of her labours and gave commands to those close by. All were covered in blood and the smell of warm open flesh filled the room, only suppressed by the pungent vehemence of the scorching irons and the high burning note made by their intermittent usage. Cauterisation and the binding spell were the only methods she had to contain the fleeing blood and lymphatic fluids.

At the end of the next day they separated the frame, having to make some new cuts along its axis. The sawdust fell to the hard ground like innocent snow after what had leaked and pumped across it before. The two halves were taken to two separate huts, each with their own attendants. Tyc collapsed and slept for another two days only after giving strict instruction that should anything go wrong she was to be awakened immediately. It was unlikely because great sleeping draughts had been administered. The tribe slowly began to go about its normal daily business of fishing and talking, mending nets and cooking the fruit of the sea. It seemed odd to all of them after the weeks of waiting. The hourly chanting and the smoking sacrifice. Each time any one of them passed either of the huts they could not help but squint inside. Only the very old, with few syllables, averted their eyes completely. Even the great ocean stayed quiet and poised, not allowing the winds to rise and trouble its lingering swell. The fishes flopped into the nets without conflict or struggle as if they too were so engaged in listening that they had not noticed their incidental drowning in the thorny air.

A week or so later chaos broke loose when Williams crawled out of his restraint and dragged himself to the ragged door of the hut. His sleeping attendants quickly lifted his bandaged form and carried him between them into the sun and instantly rising wind. Tyc waddled up from the sands and the children followed her. A great crowd came to meet their saviour and the fact that he was only half a man did not concern them. They were overwhelmed to have him returned, finally to live with them forever.

The occupant of the other hut slept longer and remained passive and silent. There was more to mend and the length of him was now grafted onto bound wood. When he did awake he was unable to sit up because he did not understand the form and asymmetry of what once was his body. So he rolled back and forth on the surface of his world, attracting the attention of his attendants, who heard the shuffling grunts and the rudimentary words (which was good considering he had been given the vocal cords and one of the lungs). The anger that drove him forward identified him clearly as what had been called Sidrus. The wrath and memory had been contained exactly where it could be easily determined. The body that had grown so strong, and renewed into a virile healthiness that could have competed with his brother, was now gone. The bandaged shard was an invented slither nailed to a permanent ingrown splint. He was now a kind of puppet, a scarecrow: a head and rib cage supported by an invented spine and a semi-working leg. A turnip on a stick. With the help of the shy attendants who well understood his evil self, he was propped up dizzily on the frame, which now looked like a rudimentary bed. He twisted his tightly sutured neck and lifted his arm to touch his head. But no arm came to do the work where the ghost one probed. Nothing was there on either side. He no longer possessed arms. He looked down to the numbness in his legs and found he had only one and that it had been modified and changed beyond recognition. They gave Sidrus a new name. He was now Wassidrus, and he was alive and as well as he was ever going to be.

CHAPTER NINE

*U*p in their Heidelberg garret, V.Ess.43/x and V.Ess.44/x, commonly known as Hinz and Kunz, were sitting in high-backed leather wheelchairs. Their hands and heads were now fully pink with the innocent inflated blush of infants. Their lips, eyelids, ears, noses, and fingernails were yet to develop and take on a more human appearance; these had obtained only a grey crispy quality that seemed more like the rest of their bodies, which still remained in the jet-black atrophy of the forest bog in which they had been found preserved. They enjoyed or endured long days of static silence and long nights of unimaginable sleep, and possibly dreams. Some of the more dedicated night staff had observed movement behind the grey eyelids, indicative of mind activity in slumber. There had been some reports of whispering. But nobody had actually seen or heard them talking. As the months turned into years, Superintendent Capek, the medical administrator of the Rupert the First Retirement Home, became less and less interested in their inactivity. Their attendants, monitoring, and care were running like clockwork and that was the way he liked it. Even the officious Himmelstrup had stopped visiting and sending memos, his Department of Internal Affairs having been renamed and its growing profile in the rapidly changing politics becoming far more important than before. The dawn of the Third Reich came with greater and greater powers being given to Himmelstrup, his powers expanding under his beloved Führer.

All conversation about the disappearance of Professor Schumann had long since ended. That subject was an embarrassment to them all, and Capek suspected that the old meddler had simply died somewhere in London. It would be better for Schumann if he had. Schumann's mission in London to find another Erstwhile, one that had been fabled to have a voice and a working intelligence, had failed. Patient 126 turned out to be just a lunatic. The other two, Dick and Henry, or whatever their names were, had vanished. Compton, the London overseer of the project, had been attacked and grievously injured. Some said by the decrepit old Jew himself. Himmelstrup found this difficult to believe. Compton had been a large, solid man who could have swatted the frail old man at will. Then there was the dilemma about the money. Schumann had found a way to withdraw the entire allowance he had been awarded to complete his task. Every pfennig had been drained from under Compton's nose, even before it had been sliced off. Himmelstrup's immediate response was to send a posse of his elite to find Hector Schumann and drag him back. Himmelstrup knew how to treat such treachery, and his growing power and the evolution of his department into what soon would be called the Gestapo had both the means and the desire. But ultimately his name was pinned to this minor disaster, and it would benefit his ascent to have it known. Fortunately another shift in emphasis was coming from the Führer himself. There were greater issues at stake in Africa than a few shrunken corpses. It was time to unite the German domain in all its colonies. Especially in the vastness of Africa. Finances were changing direction, gaining magnitude and velocity. Best to write off and forget one thieving Jew until after the triumph was achieved.

A week later and Capek's complacency was dumbfounded and

overturned when Hinz and Kunz also vanished from the indifferent scrutiny of his staff and their shuttered attic ward. How would he tell Himmelstrup and what would be the consequences?

During his last infuriated visit, Himmelstrup had mention that all his other researches had paid off and that he had received excellent levels of intelligence about every other subject dealing with Africa. When he was asked why Africa was suddenly so important, he had turned on Capek.

"Because it will be ours soon! We already own four colony states and have control over the mineral wealth of another three. Africa will be the storehouse for the Reich's war machine. We are sending troops there now and nothing is in our way."

"How did Professor Schumann's contribution help in this conquest?" asked the baffled Capek.

Himmelstrup had no answer because he had no idea. The Führer's own vision had guided this ridiculous quest. What a few living corpses and a crooked old Jewish professor had to do with mining the wealth out of a continent, he never knew. So he responded in the only way he could and bellowed into the superintendent's quaking face, "*What fucking contribution!*"

He then stormed out of the retirement home and had not contacted them again. So perhaps the whereabouts of the "living corpses" was no longer of interest; perhaps Capek did not even have to report the event. The recent news of ships full of troops being sent to Africa had verified everything that the officious little man had said, and his growing rank may have even moved him into a more important position. Capek was beginning to think he was off the hook; then he reminded himself that Hinz and Kunz might be human. In which case his moral Christian duty was to care and, even worse, to set about finding them. Three days later news of their whereabouts came to him via one of the female nurses who had access to the upper floors.

"Standing about on the corner they were, just awaiting like."
She sniffed through a long winter cold, her red nose and wet
words snuffling into a soggy handkerchief.

"But why there? Where do they think they want to go?"
Capek asked himself via the coughing nurse.

"Don't know, sir, but they are there or abouts all the time,
day and night."

It took Capek almost an hour to cross the misty damp city. The
recent snow had turned into frozen slush, which made walking
slow and hazardous. There was more than the usual amount of
military activity in the streets. The weather had given permission for them to use their more robust vehicles to carry troops
and goods into civilian territories. Monstrous half-track cat-
erpillars crunched and groaned their way through the frozen
snow, leaving black oiled lines gouged into the silent streets. The
marshalling yards seemed to be the focus of all the efforts.

Is this what had attracted them? Made them leave their comfortable beds in the retirement home? Because this is where they
had been seen.

Capek went to the exact spot that the nurse had so clearly
described. They were not there. Only a bustle of soldiers and
the continual clanking movements of goods and cattle trucks.
He had never seen so many. Probably another ridiculous and
extravagant military exercise, he thought to himself. He looked
at the closest wagon, one in a tethered line of twenty or more
rolling stock, and noted that it and all the others had been fitted
with strengthened locking levers and new shiny padlocks. Such
a waste of money, he mumbled to himself. All the heavy wooden
sliding doors were open and expectant except one. He walked
up to it and peered inside: In the far empty corner crouched

tight in the apex they sat. Somewhere they had found two identical trench coats that disguised their strangeness.

"What in God's name are you doing in there?" he barked.
Hinz or Kunz—he could never really distinguish which was
which—raised an arm and beckoned him inside. He tutted
while finding a foothold to climb into the wooden wagon.

Once inside he also noted that the slit-like windows that
allowed the cattle to breathe had also been modified with steel
bars. Kunz was still flapping his arm, so Capek approached.

"What are you doing in this stinking boxcar? You must come
back home with me."

They both started shaking their heads, which also made
their bodies and overcoats shudder.

"You will freeze or starve to death in here."

He took another step closer and was about to more forcibly
persuade them when Hinz pointed a bony finger at him and then
turned it towards his own crusty heart. Capek froze in his tracks.
Something about the gesture terrified him, more than if it were
made with a loaded gun. All his words, care, and responsibility
faded to nothing. Kunz then held up three fingers and nodded.

"Three what?" asked Capek.

The fingers were shaken.

"Three hours, three days, weeks, months?"

Hinz nodded in agreement and Kunz shook his head too.

They both then waved at the confused administrator as if
saying goodbye. They did it until he left the wagon, looking back
for no apparent reason. There was something very touching
about the gesture, like children leaving home. He walked away
feeling lost and foolishly sad. As he left the yards he saw a small
group of workers and a soldier loitering by the gate.

"There seems to be a lot of activity, considering the appalling
weather."

The men looked at him from under rims of their caps, eyes nervous and distrustful of such questions.

"Where is all this transport going at this time of the year?" Capek boldly asked.

"East," said the soldier.

Capek was just about to tell them about Hinz and Kunz waiting in the cattle truck when he saw something in the workers' eyes that changed his mind. With more caution he asked, "When will they be leaving?"

What looked like the oldest worker flicked the stub of his cigarette away and lifted his filthy hand up to Capek's face and shook three gnarled fingers at him. The other men smirked.

"*East*," he said and spat into the trampled grey snow.

CHAPTER TEN

*C*yrena Lohr fidgeted in her beautiful house that finally had lost the last trace of Ishmael. The signatures and stains of love and passion had evaporated or been polished away by the servants, along with the arguments and his surly presence. And it had all been so easy. The house was clear of him and she felt utterly alone. She went to her favourite balcony and sat trying to extract pleasure from the shifting view. None came. She watched the birds squawking and clattering in the nearest tree, sending leaves and snapped twigs into her garden below. She watched the butterflies avoid them and marvelled at their lightness and colour, their tiny wings pattering the warm and pungent air. She looked across her corner of the city to where it ended and the vivid land danced towards the great shadow of the distant Vorrh. He was still out there somewhere and she wondered if she had preferred the idea of him being dead. His cunning guile that had hurt so much when she discovered that she had been tricked again suddenly took on a note of nostalgia. An almost pleasant recollection of the cleverness of his perfidy. The birds rattled again, dislodging even more foliage, and she snapped off the taste of sweetness in that memory. She needed to do something positive, to aim herself at a task.

A far-off wind rattled very different trees and she was back in her childhood, when she was blind and happy, with her father and brother far away on the open plains. She sat and closed her eyes and let the memories rise up and flood in. They always started in the same place. On a journey towards the south. It was almost as if she had been born there, awakened on the visit to the cape, and the seven years previous had been dissolved or evaporated by its vivid potency.

When her father, who had spent most of his life in Holland, came to Africa, they had all gone on hunting trips to the Transvaal. She had greatly enjoyed the excitement of the bush camps. The violent purring odour of the wilderness and all that lived there. Twice they had taken her with them onto the spoors, the actual hunting fields. She had witnessed the stealth, the adrenaline of the chase and the kill through her other straining senses and loved every minute of it. She was special then and there, where a great magnitude existed in that place and in the endeavours of the men around her. The colours of sounds were more vivid than sight could ever be. The echoing barks of the hunters' guns filled the great plains and drifted to the mountains and back, describing a vast and harmonious distance that seemed to throb in the percussion. The smell of the cordite chiselling the air. The far-off roars of the game. There was always a party after the shoot. The servants would erect tables under the shade of the trees. The men were loud and happy and a great business filled in all the spaces. The next day they would travel back to one of the smaller townships, tired but exhilarated by the wildness of it all.

The details were becoming brighter while her eyes were closed. Scenes constructed of scent and sound uncurled.

They were in the library of her father's friends talking about the potshots that they had taken at a tree full of baboons. She could smell the books and hear other children in the garden.

"What are baboons?" she casually asked.

Her father seemed surprised by her question and explained

that they were a kind of large and ferocious monkey. Towards the end of the description his voice became a little uncertain.

"Err, it's best if we don't talk about the shoot when Eugène arrives."

She had been told that he was arriving in the afternoon and that he was very special, a poet and a scholar, and that she was to call him Oom. Because although he was not a real uncle, he was the closest thing to one: her father's oldest friend.

"Doesn't Oom Eugène like baboons, Father?"

There was an embarrassed silence for a short while; then her brother spoke.

"He doesn't like us shooting them. Just don't talk about it when he's in the room."

"How will I know when he's in the room?" she asked.

"You will know," was all they said.

And she did, they all did. Eugène Marais was not yet famous, but there was a presence about the quiet-spoken man that filled the room. She first thought that he had an extraordinary voice. Softer and more resounding than the rest, who yapped and growled like playful dogs. He had stillness and dark in his voice, like the sounds in an ebony piano when it is not played but just listens, upright, to other sounds in the room and murmurs them back—rich, dark, and sensuously hollow.

He was different from all the other grown-ups. When he spoke to Cyrena and the other children, he did not pretend to be interested, did not fake being a child in their company or an adult above them. She became aware years later that he had that rarest of gifts: engagement. Whatever he became interested in absorbed him totally during the time of his commitment to it. It was that strangeness that made him close to children. He could talk to them with ease and share the wonder of their under-standing. When he asked them a question, he meant it. It was easier than the chitchat of adults, where she thought she could hear him becoming a little lost.

She remembered how he had asked her to search for sight. It had been on the veranda of another of her father's friends after a long lunch, where much of the conversation was about the possibility of new war in Europe. Marais had sickened of it and walked outside to smoke. She understood many years later that a previous war between the Boers and the English had left him saddened and damaged inside. The heat of the sun was waning on her face. She followed him, followed his tobacco smoke to the side of the house where all was quiet, away from noise of talk and the servants washing pans.

"Oom Eugène," she said into the pink whiteness that described the boundary of her blindness in the quiet light. She heard him turn, the surprise in the swivelled dust of his footsteps.

"Cyrena?"

"Yes, Oom."

He walked over to her and cautiously offered his warm bony hand.

"Come sit with me, child, you should not be wandering about, away from the others, there might be snakes here."

She held his hand tighter and he guided her to the trunk of a fallen tree nearby. They sat quietly for a while enjoying the light breezes of evening that guided in the difference of birds. Above them, she heard the swallows carve the brilliant air.

"Do you like it here, Cyrena?"

"I love the sounds of the bush, the way it touches and runs away and then comes back again from afar."

"Little one, you are a poet."

"That's what they call you, Oom!"

It became quiet again while the man looked at his hands and ran one of them through his thin hair.

"What is a poet?" she asked.

The quiet became louder and the distant pots and pans being washed somewhere inside the house sounded important.

"It is somebody who sees our life in a different way," he said.

"But I can't see anything," she answered.

"You see it in your soul, not in your eyes," he said, "and through your other senses."

"I don't really understand *see*, but I know I don't have it," she said carefully.

"What do you think *see* is, Cyrena?"

Nobody had ever asked that question before, and it was hard to hold it in her head. But she trusted her father's friend more and more.

"I think it must be like my head touching things, becoming happy and sad like my ears do when music and other sounds get inside them."

"Well said, Cyrena, you understand much of this invisible world," Oom Eugène said, with great happiness in his voice. "Many people with sight see only the surface of things, it's all they want to see. I think you have the gift of imagination, which makes some of us question the interior of things."

"What, like the interior of the baboons? I heard Joshua say he wanted to keep some of their innards—he meant interiors, I think."

Then she remembered that she must not speak about these things with him.

"Did they take you on the shoot with them?"

Cyrena did not know what to say; she had broken the only rule she had been given. He saw her drastic change of expression.

"Did they tell you not to speak to me about it?"

She stared hard at the ground and felt a stone growing in her throat.

"It's all right, my dear, I am not upset, you've done nothing wrong."

She strained her senses to find out if this was true.

"I don't hunt anymore. I spend my time living close to the animals. I think they have more to teach alive."

"Do baboons have imaginations?" She started up again.

"I think not, my dear, only us humans are cursed with that splendid gift."

She ignored his paradox, which sounded like a mistake to her, and pressed on.

"So that's why animals can't see with their souls, because they don't have them, the pastor told us that."

She heard the discomfort of his movement and the distance between his next words.

"The church is not always right in the wisdom of its proclamations."

She did not understand "proclamations" and said so.

"Well then, in all the things it tells us are true," he said a little breathlessly.

"So you think they might have souls but no imaginations?"

Again he shifted. "They are lower animals than us, is what I meant."

"But that's what the pastor says."

Oom Eugène stood up and moved about. When he spoke again he was facing away from her.

"I think you can have a soul without an imagination." These words were very slow, as if congealed in his mouth, without spit or water. "Shall we go and find out what the others are doing?"

He put his hand close to hers so that she could find it, and then she knew that their conversation was over, he had moved on to something else. She found his hand and also understood that he really knew where she was. Most people grabbed at her from out of the casual comfort of their own direction. Making her jump or flinch against the abrupt interaction. He had given his hand to be found and the difference was overwhelming. It was the same as his questions and answers. She held it with firm gratitude and began to weld a friendship.

The next day she was with him again in the shade of the backyard tree.

"Tell me, Cyrena, again what you think about seeing," he said.

He smelt funny today, a strange lingering heavy rub about him.

"I don't think about it, but sometimes I think that it thinks about me," she said.

"Child, you are a wonder."

"Why?"

"Because you see the world the right way around."

"Which way around?" she said, perplexed. Her small brow furrowed.

"The way that you know about the interiors, the innards of understanding. Your way of seeing things is so clear, it's a miraculous gift."

"Like in the Bible?"

"No, not like that at all." He sounded as if he had just nibbled a grumpy seed.

"But they say you are like that, like in the Bible."

"Whatever do you mean, child?" Adultness had taken him over.

"They call you a miracle worker. The doctor of miracles."

"Oh, that," he said in a dismissive way, "that's just a job I did once."

"Making miracles?"

"A lady got sick, sick in the heart, and it made her head tell her legs that they did not work. So for fifteen years she never walked. Had to be pushed around in a wheelbarrow. Imagine that."

"How did the miracle fix her?" asked Cyrena, moving forward.

"Well, I put her to sleep a little bit each day, and then one day while she was deeply asleep I told her that she could walk again. I then woke her up and she could."

"So *you* are the miracle?"

Marais said nothing. After a while Cyrena said, "Can you put me to sleep and make my eyes work?"

He hadn't seen this question coming and answered it with a speed that sounded like harshness. "No, it's different."

"Because it's eyes, not legs? Jesus did miracles with all kinds of sick people. The blind and the lame, they were called. Some had caught the Travail."

Marais's face perked into attention. "The what?" he said.

"The Travail. It's a kind of sickness that poor catch from the world, a bit like the TB. I think."

"Out of the mouths of babes." Marais chuckled with glee.

"I am not a baby," snapped Cyrena.

Marais suppressed his mirth. "No, you are not. You are a wise woman. An old soul."

She thought he was being cruel calling her a baby and now an old woman. She no longer wanted to talk, he was laughing at her. He was just like the others after all. She shrank away from him into her private dark.

"Cyrena?"

She ignored the miracle worker, pretending to be deaf.

"Cyrena, I was serious. It's a way of saying that some people are born with more knowledge than others. That they come into this world already knowing important things."

This made her open her ears.

"Some people think that they might have lived before, here or in some other place. That they see this time through the understanding of another."

"Do you mean because I was adopted? I know all about that, Papa explained it."

"No, child, I don't mean that."

"Did you know I was adopted, Oom Eugène?"

"Yes, Cyrena, I helped your father with it."

"It's a kind of secret to most people."

"It's easier that way," he said, and then steered the conversation back to his previous questions. "Do you think that sometimes you might have memories from another place, see things from a different time?"

"But I don't see anything," she said flatly.

"We could try talking about that."

"We are."

"No, I mean can I ask you when you are asleep?"

"Like the lady with the forgotten legs?"

"Yes, I will put you to sleep like her. It's a way I learned when I was studying medicine in London. It's a way where you go to sleep but still talk to me."

"When I am in bed in the dark?"

"No, child, here and now."

"Will it hurt?" she said, shading her closed eyes with her hand so that she could hear his face more clearly.

Marais smiled. "No, not at all, why should it hurt? Sleeping doesn't hurt. Not for you anyway."

"You said medicine, and medicine always hurts."

Marais laughed again, quieter this time, and moved closer to her. "I promise you that nothing will hurt, little one, and that you will enjoy the magic of this."

"It sounds funny," she said.

"Your poppa asked me to ask you to try the magic. So what do you think?"

While she thought about it, the birds in the trees became interested, and some of them watched and made small comments.

"Yes please, Oom, I want to try the magic."

"Very well," he said in a jaunty manner. "May I touch your head for a moment?"

She nodded and he put one of his hands across her forehead; it felt cool and gave her more shade to think in. His other hand held hers.

"I want you to imagine you are in your room lying down by the open window. It's raining outside and you can hear the water dropping on the leaves and the roof of the house. Very gradually the sound will fade as you become more tired and soon the rain will sound a long way off. Soon. Soon."

Cyrena's breathing changed and she slumped slightly.

"It's far, far off now, and you are in a warm, cosy sleep."

Now all the birds were quiet.

"Tell what is inside you, what story lives there."

Cyrena instantly began to talk. "It's a tall sky in a closed room with everybody sleeping next door."

"Is it light or dark there?" he carefully asked.

For a moment she looked like she did not understand the question.

"Do you know what light and dark are?"

The corners of her mouth twitched. "Of course, dark is the inside, the deepness. Light is the outside, shifting, the forever. Now it's sort of in between, as if the shell of me lets them in and out."

"Very well, Cyrena. This is what sighted people call transparent."

"Glass is transparent," she said eagerly.

"That's true. How did you know about glass?"

"I broke one and Mother said not to move until she found all the pieces, and they were difficult to find because they were transparent. She explained that it was like invisible, which is like not being there."

"Did any of this make any sense to you?"

"No, but I do know that glass is different because it's colder and quicker than the other cups."

Marais shifted and came closer to her. She was thinking hard where she was supposed to be dreaming and he was a little worried about her expression of concentration. He had never seen it before in a hypnotised subject.

"I think I can understand 'sight' now," she announced.

"Tell me, child," he said softly.

"Sight is like part of the me shell, it lives between light and dark and keeps them separate. In most people it must be cold and hard, but in me it's transparent. Which means that it makes things invisible and lets them pass through. Isn't that right, Oom Eugène?"

Marais was mesmerised and just stared at the child, who had opened her eyes on speaking his name. He stared through her with her wisdom ringing in his ears.

"Oom Eugène," she said into a space that he had never conceived of. "Oom Eugène?" Fear had entered her voice and her remarkable eyes moved as if searching for him, but why? Why did those defunct beautiful orbs attempt to catch his trace?

"Yes, Cyrena, I am here."

Her face softened, the eyes resting on him before the lids closed. In that moment he felt them touch him, as if an infinitesimal pressure had emanated from them in a physical ray onto the surface of his being, his position in the world being held and defined by the beam of her tangible sightless gaze. It jolted his concentration and he felt his control of the session slip.

"Cyrena, can you hear the rain? It's getting closer again."

"Yes."

"It's coming towards your window and pattering on the leaves outside."

"Yes, I can hear it."

"Soon it will wake you from your refreshing sleep, soon, soon . . . Now you are wide awake."

Nothing happened, there was no change in her position and she said nothing.

"Cyrena, are you awake?"

"No."

"Why not?"

"Because I think I just saw something."

This had never happened before. All of his "subjects" had responded instantly to his suggested commands. Unease had entered their session.

"Cyrena, it's time for you to wake up, the rain is on the roof. Can you hear it?"

She did not answer but turned her head sharply to the right and opened her eyes again and strained them towards the tree full of silent birds. Marais was trying to hold down the anxiety that was welling up inside him.

"Cyrena, close your eyes and sit back as you were before."

"I think I can see something," she said with curious dispassion.

Was this possible, he asked himself. Had the hypnosis unlocked her vision? Undone some knotted causeway in her bright mind? Was it possible?

Cyrena had been born blind, and that was the least of her tragedies when her father found her. Her malnutrition and exposure were as easily soothed as her lack of social awareness.

The Lohrs' wealth, love, and commitment shaped her back into normality before her first words came. But the blindness remained, seeded deep in her infant soul and body. The nature of the malady had never been accurately diagnosed, even though all the family's riches and influences had exposed it to some of the best specialists in Europe. There had been wildly disparate and disappointing opinions about the cause of the problem and very little solid evidence to form the basis of a cure. One of her father's and Marais's old friends from London had suggested surgery. But the proposed operation sounded vague and exploratory, and Lohr had no intention of letting his precious daughter undergo the hazards of anaesthetics and infection without the balance of cure and recovery being heavily weighted on their side.

"Cyrena, what can you see?"

"I think it's sight, but I don't know, Oom."

"Describe it to me."

He knew he should not be going in this direction; he should be fiercely trawling her back into full consciousness.

"I think it's the invisible living in that tree, where the birds are quiet."

"What?" Marais barely said.

"The invisible and it's coming closer."

She lifted her arm and moved her flat hand in a circle above her head, as if describing a halo. The obscure gesture galvanised the gently spoken man. A cold chill ran through the warmth of the day and hid itself in his blood.

"Close your eyes, Cyrena. Close your eyes."

"But, Oom, it's coming."

"No buts, Cyrena, close your eyes now, it's the rain that is coming closer."

"But the sight."

"*No buts, close your eyes.*"

The cold in his blood had strengthened into a furious ice, so that now his muscles copied it and his slender body knotted into the purpose of pulling her back.

"*The rain* is getting *closer*, you are in your tall room with all your people sleeping next door. You are home and the rain is getting closer, do you hear it?"

After a pause, which seemed to span an eternity, she turned her head back towards him and closed her eyes.

"Yes, Oom, I hear it."

"It's getting closer and you are waking up."

"Yes, Oom."

"Now you are awake."

Her eyelids opened and her face set into a beaming smile. The weight and tension fell from his bones like a suit of rusted armour. She looked straight at him and her radiance told him all was well. Her sightless eyes gleamed in anticipation.

"When are we going to do the magic?" she asked.

The next morning Cyrena wanted to talk more to him about the "magic" of the day before, but there were so many people at the breakfast table it was difficult to attract his concentrated attention. Later, before he left, she spoke to him for a few minutes, but he seemed distracted, as if he were already travelling.

"You said I talked in my sleep."

"Yes, Cyrena."

"Tell me again what I said, the bit about the tree."

She heard him fiddle with the catch of his suitcase, heard its weight scuffle the planks of the wooden veranda. He seemed to be taking too long to answer, as if he forgotten the question or was distracted by something else. She started to ask again and he began speaking.

"You talked about something in the tree, something that you thought you could see." His mouth sounded dry.

"Did I say *see?*"

"In a way, yes, Cyrena."

They sat quietly for a few minutes and then Marais spoke. "You said you saw the invisible."

"Yes, I think I did, but not with my eyes, I saw it inside my head."

"And you made a strange movement."

"You said I touched my head."

"Not exactly." He sounded tired. "You held your hand out flat and moved it over your head."

"Like this," said Cyrena, lifting her arm and waving her hand in a boneless kind of way.

"Not exactly. May I take your hand and show you?"

She grinned and nodded approval. Marais stepped forward and took her hand, unfolding it gently, and rotated it in the circular motion that he had seen before. He then let go and stepped back while she continued.

"Feels funny," she said, the grin vanishing from her confused face. "Like I am wearing a halo."

He said nothing. They were interrupted by the car that was to take him away pulling into the dusty yard. Marais spoke a few words to the driver and put his suitcase on the backseat before returning to Cyrena, who had stopped making the movement.

"I have to go now."

"Yes, I know."

"If you dream the answer will you write it down and send it to me in Waterberg?"

"Yes, Oom."

"Write to me about anything, stay in touch, especially about the invisible," he prompted.

"It's gone now, I used the lemon juice."

"Lemon juice, what lemon juice?"

"It's something I heard my brother and his friends say."

Marais was looking at her the way he did yesterday and she could feel it.

"They said it about the invisible, so I did it. I put the lemon juice in my eyes and then looked at the sun to make them hot, and then the invisible was gone. But I won't do it again, it hurt."

"Yes, I think you'd better not," said Marais as he walked to the car, opened the door, and joined his case on the backseat. He was laughing as he waved goodbye.

That had been so many years ago, when she was a child. Only Christmas cards and formal family notes had passed between them through the years of her growth into maturity.

CHAPTER ELEVEN

*T*hey had been forced to flee the house, when they ran from the terrible child with the gun. Their only way was down and Ishmael led the descent, going lower than the cyclops had ever dared to before. At the mouth of the well they stopped and he doubled over, fighting for breath. Seth saw this and knew what he must do. He looked at Aklia, and she nodded and put her hand deep in her mouth. Seth brought his tight Bakelite fingers down onto the coughing Ishmael and pinched his neck hard. The cyclops passed out. Seth turned him over and unbuckled the belt of his trousers. Aklia brought a thick paste out of her throat and applied it putty-like to Ishmael's mouth, nostrils, and gaping imitation eye socket. While it was setting, her brother turned Ishmael over and lovingly wormed his long brown finger into his anus. After a moment or two he found the conduit with the fleshy switch and turned it off. Ishmael instantly stopped breathing. Together they lifted him and dropped him into the well and then slid down after him, grasping the sinking body as it swirled, spiralling like a heavy meaningless pebble through the thick black water.

Below the meniscus of the water in the deep cold well, the tension changed. Seth and Aklia were holding Ishmael between them in the pitch-blackness that flowed between the well of Kühler Brunnen and the centre of the Vorrh. They kicked against its resistance and crawl-swam farther and farther from the city.

The pool that was embedded in the heart of the Vorrh was fed by the twisting river that passed through it. It also gained dimension and substance from underground waters that streamed from the unnamed core. And who would dare attempt to classify the interior of that compacted heart that still tastes the impact of the violent planetary bodies that wandered into the earth's sluttish gravitational lure? After so many millions of years the core still remembered the impacts and passed them on in stutters to all its waters. The myriad capillaries and veins wormed their way upwards to meet the fault lines that run web-like in all directions. The most profound of the enclosed channels was the muscular aorta that led into Essenwald. The one that ended in the well beneath Kühler Brunnen. The one in which two swimmers propelled a sagging weight inch by inch through the tight water, scraping and clawing against the irregular pitch-black sides where roots forage but obey the laws of this uninfestable water. They do not intrude but grip around the conduit, creating riblike enforcements that have strengthened its intention over the millennia. Even the inquisitive nibbling hairs at the foraging roots' farthest tips dare push not any deeper, dare not fulfil their ultimate purpose. They have learned that intrusion here would wither and perish all the patient wood that creaks above to semaphore the stars.

The dense root mass that cups the pool and strains towards the old heart is thicker than the earth that it drinks from. The tangle of blind suction has dug deep and grabbed all substance with its anchoring fists. Even the roots of the tree of knowledge are down there. The tree itself is long since gone; it had started to wither before the sons of Adam had populated the world. Its husk hollowed out, choked and leached by the vines and strangling figs until it fell away, leaving only a circular stump. But a stump that was not entirely dead. It thick dark mass had been fed by the trees around it. Tendrils of mercy seeking its lostness and insisting on sustenance. The black cap got darker and hid what was happening below ground, the roots having copied its primary form. An albino structure of florescent grey echoing what once was above. So that each bough, branch, and twig is mirrored in the dark moistness. Each contour and gesture locked in the earth where none may see or disturb it ever again. The tunnel of water passes beneath it and at that place a vibration was felt in the working cream inside the Kin. They knew they were near their exit as they dragged their burden towards the surface. The darkness in the water-filled tube was changing as their vibrations travelled ahead to the open waters of the forest pool in the straining realm of turgor.

When Seth rose up and punctured the air, a great wave of water spread across the pool's surface. His polished brown head looked around for signs of danger, steam rising from his temples; when he made the erroneous assessment that nothing malign was in the vicinity, he bobbed back down to fetch Aklia and Ishmael. The moment his head went below the water, a chattering whistle was spat out between the dense foliage. Small smears of yellow could be seen in the stubborn bushes moving closer to the pool. The anthropophagi where there, and they were hungry.

CHAPTER TWELVE

*B*efore Father Timothy stepped into the jaws of the Sea People's home, he had climbed a high rock to look down upon them and understand something of the layout and occupation of their realm. The great mass of Vorrh and the vastness of sea was joined by a meandering serpent of a river and the tribe existed there in the mouth of the estuary, their huts and temples like so many ragged and broken teeth on both sides of the splintered mouth. The right shore was for dwelling, eating, and fishing; the left shore for prayer, surgery, and containment. He watched people come and go and smelt their charcoal of fish and incense, labour and strangeness. When he walked into their presence he did so with a fearful heart, holding the box above his head and speaking the words of visitation that he had learned. He said he had come for the sacred one. He said he had been told to come by a young majestic child named Modesta. He said the box was for Oneofthewilliams and should be opened only by him on his long-awaited return.

The Sea People thanked him and gave him fish and comfort. He told the story of Modesta. He was encouraged to speak of her dreams and his visions, and when these were believed, he was invited to speak to Tyc. She had no time for Men Without Substance, finding their bleached anaemic skin both offensive and unnatural. They had no place here.

But this one carried bounty in his mouth. Something had been put in the hollow of him and floated towards her and perhaps Oneofthewilliams. Could the child he spoke of be the sacred Irrinipeste, come back to life?

Tyc was impressed by the way he held the box and would not give it up to any but the sacred one. She could have taken it at any time, chopped his hands away from it, but there was a foretelling in his puny will and little actions. Such things once perceived should never be violated, no matter how weak or disgusting their host. During the night of the squid moon she questioned Yuuptarno, who had been making the translations of the little white man's words. She wanted to know of the accuracy of their meaning and how much was guesswork on Yuuptarno's behalf. When she was satisfied, she called for her neophytes to bind the white creature and shelve him beneath her bed. She literally wanted to sleep on the matter.

In the morning he was taken out and washed in the sea. The box put within sight of his ablutions. Once cleansed, a leash with a collar of shark's teeth was put about his neck and given to Tyc. She thought such a thing necessary because Men Without Substance could not be trusted and she did not want an unpredictable animal close enough to Oneofthewilliams to be able to cause harm or injury. She demonstrated the choke-chain effect of the collar while he was still standing in the sea and some of the droplets of blood splashed into the warm eddies that giggled about his ankles. Yuuptarno explained that he was now allowed an audience with Oneofthewilliams and that he must behave quietly and with veneration, and that any signs of disrespect would not be tolerated by Tyc, who held the other end of his leash. And that any signs of threat or violence by word or deed towards the sacred one would be dealt with by a muscular yank of the lead, which would stop him and eventually remove his head. When it was clear that he understood, he was allowed to pick up the box and walk slowly behind Tyc and her troupe towards the brightly painted hut. Inside, his eyes strained and watered against the dark and stench, eventually tuning themselves to the atmosphere. Tyc prompted him forwards and slid a small patch of twigs and woven seaweed aside to reveal a slit of a window. The light fell directly on the open hands of the sacred one. Father Timothy let out a sigh of relief at seeing their normality. A sigh that was quickly sucked back and ingested when the slit revealed the entire personage of Oneofthewilliams. The hands, arms, and shoulder were human, but they were balanced in a shallow bowl. The legs were gone, as was indeed the head. Only a lopsided sack extended from the neck and hung boneless and swinging like an animal's nose bag. Several large veins or nerves or arteries clung to its exterior like ancient vines. The hands made one more gesture towards him before this world strobed into black and white and vomited him into unconsciousness.

When he came to, Tyc was furious: This act of disrespect had nearly cost him his life. Indeed, she had the leash double knotted around her hands within seconds of his swoon. It was only the raising of the sacred one's hands that prevented his exhaustion. When Timothy finally recovered, he was eventually allowed to gift the box. Its contents were a colony of sleeping ants that instantly came alive. The sacred one felt inside it and they crawled and niggled, stitched and inflicted their long and complex messages. It was as if Modesta were whispering in the ear that he no longer possessed. Tyc watched closely and became aware of the change that was taking place. The inner locked part of Oneofthewilliams had become undone. The ants had brought it out. There was a new fluency in his motion, a concealed dance in the legless, faceless body.

Timothy was taken away. The collar carefully removed. He was now cherished and fed, even against the piety of his will.

After the meeting, Tyc prepared Timothy for departure. He was given his robe back with a pack of dried fish and a new staff freshly cut from the forest. He was escorted along the coast by the three men who had guarded and caressed him. He left without ever seeing Oneofthewilliams again. A mile after he left the Sea People, the charm that Tyc had implanted in him took effect. And a great longing and remembrance of home flooded back. And at its core stood the beautiful vision of Modesta, waiting.

On Father Timothy's way back home, the journey seemed enhanced, more vivid than any other. The high cliffs and jagged spurs were the signature of a different geology, a more ancient and alien shard of the mountain peeking out of the waves. Father Timothy's long journey had been forced up over these sheer faces, following the goat tracks from the gentle sea edge, where he had walked in the surf to cool his aching feet, onto the high precipitous stone. The advantage there was its view. He could look out over God's good earth as he had never done before, cast his imagination across the billions of waves and fathomless splendour of the sea. The wind tugged at him in the dazzling light as he rested from his panting climb. Gulls and kittiwakes sang against the ozone, and he marvelled at the strength of the beauty before him. He had completed his task, delivered the box to the savages on the beach. He had met the abomination called Oneofthewilliams and understood nothing of the meaning. He was pleased to leave that place and its confusion and return to his parish. He had earned his promised respite from the intrusions that had so shaken his little life and now wanted only a simple day-to-day existence.

He hoped to return to his meagre duties and solitary life without the intrusion of commanding visions, insistent old women, and unnatural children to spoil his peace and sanity of mind. He undid the strap of his hat and removed it, holding it hard against the sun-filled tugs of the wind. He wiped his sweating brow and let its saltiness dry, his eyes closed tight against the glare. He turned and look back towards the estuary, which had become lost in the curve of the distance he had travelled. That place and the Sea People were beyond sight and he hoped never to see them again. He estimated he must be halfway on his journey and turned to look into the future and his return, dreading the abnormalities that might still be hovering around Carmella and Modesta. There was a slim hope that they might have left. They had said that a messenger would be sent to escort them out of the village forever—a seraphim would conduct them to paradise, where they might shelter beneath the tree of knowledge forever. He looked along the winding goat track and imagined them tottering on its unstable distance. He prayed for their departure, for their continual absence from his life. He also wondered in a nagging afterthought if he might really meet them on this, the only track. He strained his eyes and his anticipation, unconsciously looking for a trace of movement, and then smirked and frowned at his foolishness. He shook off all thoughts of them, pulled his hat back on, finding its wetness reassuring. Its leather strap was now cold with chilled condensation. He picked up his staff and continued his journey home, wanting to spend as much time in the optimistic shining air as possible.

The only blemish on his journey was the bundle being sucked by the tide, in a crevice below the highest part of track. His mind had been singing in the bright clear air when the loose pebbles began to slide under his feet, sending a gritty cloud plummeting over the edge of the track that was near precipitous on its outer side. He grabbed on to the wild thyme growing on the cliff walls on the inner side, tearing into the spiky tightness to steady himself while he made his slippery foothold more secure. It took his breath away and his heart beat in his mouth as his staff clattered down into the boulders below. He waited until he was calm and the ground stopped trembling, then edged past the loose scree and onto firmer ground. Once secure, he sat back on the solid rocks to gain his full composure. That's when he saw the black mass moving back and forth in the wadi below. He could not tell if it was an animal or a bundle of rags. It certainly wasn't driftwood or seaweed. It was more compact and rolled bent over in the shallows. A nub of white flopped in and out of focus, and at one point he thought it might be a face. But on its third roll it looked more like featureless foam, merely stuck onto the bundle's matted surface. He convinced himself that it was just his imagination turning a perfectly normal incident into a sinister event. He grew tired of his surmise and started the slow descent off of the sheer rock face, back onto firmer ground and flatter lands that banished the unpleasantness from his thoughts.

He pushed on, wanting to be home by night, and as he got closer to his homeland, to the depopulated lands, he started to recognise features in the landscape. Thoughts of Carmella and Modesta returned—by now they were separating. All of the odious and unnatural things flocked magnetically to the old woman, while thoughts of Modesta became cleansed and even pleasant. With each strenuous step, the memory of the girl warmed and matured until he felt a great anxiety about not seeing her again. He wanted to see Modesta, wanted to breathe the same air and watch her limbs move in it. On his way back the memory of her beautiful sarcastic face had been replaced by the conjured glimpses of her growing body, of her nakedness and the fertility that pulsed inside it. He knew he was becoming obsessed and that it was wrong. He knew he wanted to see and touch her and also knew he never would, because deep in his heart of hearts he expected her to be gone. Departed without a thought of him. But hope clung like the dusty soil to his boots as he rushed and stumbled through the terraced fields and made for Carmella's house. The sand and stones ground to a crunching halt as he stopped, black-clad and defeated, a bent shadow in the blazing sun.

He sobbed one clay-grey fist of a sob when he saw the chain on the door of the closed house. He stood trembling without being able to make the decision to touch the weight of the padlock that ignored him, as it ignited a merciless flame in him, that began the inverted alchemy of transforming passionate longing into torturous despair.

Eventually he gathered himself enough to walk up to the house and peer through its shutters into the dark interior, half expecting to find a note that she might have left for him. Nothing was visible. He was wondering who the miserable old woman had trusted with the key to tend her animals in the inner courtyard when he saw a brightness in the air unfold. Close to one of the windows a warm light dappled the bricks and a halo of white flames (or were they feathers?) spun. He rubbed his eyes, then stared again. It was still there trying to attract the attention of those within. There was something about its gentle unworldliness that propagated a great peace in him. He wanted to touch it and bask in its glow. As he hastily approached it faded until only tiny sparkles, like willow ash, dotted the lazy air.

He looked about for the apparition; everything was still until he spoke.

"Hello," he said foolishly.

Then the breath of his word caught fire, as if each particle of water vapour or sound had become separately ignited for a fraction of a second. It was wonderful and without a glimpse of terror. When he realised that the illuminations were fed by him, he blurted out a muddled sentence.

"I am Father Timothy, friend and protector to those who live here, and I have returned to find them."

The air lit up and swirled next to him, and he was instantly reminded of the sea phosphorescence that he had witnessed when first he came to this exotic land. It too had been in twilight on a beach nearby. He had been attracted by the sounds of children playing in water, laughing and shouting with glee. Then he drew closer and he understood why. Every movement of their feet, hands, and body in the water was glowing, a quick pulsing light silhouetting each of their actions, the very water alive with light. He too plunged his hands in the low waves and millions of normally invisible bioluminescent creatures throbbed around them. This moment was like that, but in the air. He laughed out loud and the brightness unfolded again, showing that it also had its own form. Then it spoke in a voice that was wrong in the face of its wonder. It spoke in a slow drab whisper, like a wet biscuit.

"You are not they who must be taken," it accused. "Where are they who must be taken?"

Timothy's ears were forsaken by its miserable tone, while his eyes stared in wonder at its light.

"They must have gone."

"They must be taken, not have gone themselves."

"Are you the seraph that was foretold?" stuttered the priest.

"I am of those that bear message and direction and have come for those who must be taken."

"Yes, but they have already gone, even though they were waiting for you."

Something like feathers were fluttering in the darkening air, their majestic beauty tilting into something else, more like the fluffing up of the lank plumage of irritated poultry.

"They who should be taken must await my coming."

"Yes! I know, you said that before."

"I was not in the before when they went."

"Something else must have taken them."

"What else, there is nothing else to do the taking."

"A mistake, some kind of mistake?"

The feathers bristled and the light made a faint sizzling sound, and ozone could be smelt.

"Mistake is not known, we are without mistake."

"No, not your mistake. A mistake by them, those who were awaiting you."

"Those who must be taken?" the seraphim asked again.

"Yes! Modesta and Carmella."

"Do not speak given names without them."

Timothy was becoming annoyed with the apparition and said nothing. A slight breeze ruffled the late light, and sounds of the animals in the courtyard could be heard. A goat bleated above all else.

"It be they! They who must be taken."

Timothy said nothing.

"Hark, it is they. Come hither, my children, it is time to be taken."

"It's a goat," Timothy said bluntly.

"Do not speak their given names without them," said the seraphim.

"It's just an animal, wanting feeding, it's not them."

"Who?"

"Carm—! They who must be taken."

"Yes, those who must be taken, bring them forth."

It was now dark and the tired priest was beginning to understand that not all of God's "higher beings" have the same intelligence as humans. Suddenly his modest room and the warmth of his village seemed an urgent need.

"I don't think I can help you."

"I have been foretold."

"Good, I am sure if they were here you would be most welcome."

"But those who must be taken."

"Yes, those. I must go now."

"I shall come hither with thee."

Timothy's heart sank at the prospect. "No, that is not possible, I live alone."

"The taking is foretold, it must become, I will live with thee until then."

The exhausted little priest was just about to shout at the divine light when the goat did it for him. He quickly took advantage.

"There it is! They who must be taken." The plumage awoke with new brilliance. "Praise be!" it exclaimed.

"They are on the other side of this wall in the courtyard, you must go there."

"They must come to me."

"They are caught there by the mistake, do you see, you must go to them."

"Those who must be taken."

"Yes, those on the other side of this wall."

"I must go over?"

"Yes."

There was a moment of thinking or the growing of moss in the air and then a great noise inside the inner courtyard. A crashing and slithering that made all the animals speak at once, a tremendous cry in the stables of celebrations or panic or fury. Timothy did not wait to hear or see more but sped up to the track that led to his village, grabbing his rucksack that he had left by the gate. He looked back twice as he stumbled onto the well-worn homeward track. He was moving faster and faster.

He paused for a breath only when he reached the serrated crest of the village boundary. Nothing was following him and he regained his composure enough to let another doubt creep into his fatigue. What or who had lead Carmella and Modesta away? The thing below composed of a single purpose and shadows was obviously the seraph. And he knew that the resolve of the two women was implacable. They would have let nothing prevent their journey with this angelic form. But something had. Its purpose and action must have been malign, and he feared for the souls and bodies of his departed wards.

$\mathcal{M}$odesta had watched as the old woman fell over the cliff, hit the path, and then sprang into the crashing dark water below. Why had she done that? It was impressive and fast and very effective, but she thought that she would keep her life, at least until they had reached their destination. To hop, skip, and jump it away now seemed silly. The impatient herald clacked and scuffled, wanting to go on.

"All right, I am coming," she said and left the steep rock face, going down on all fours, down towards the sea and the softer path along the shore. She looked over the edge and saw the bundle of food that Carmella was carrying bob up and down next to her in the lively waves. One of the loaves of bread had already escaped and was moving out to sea, being propelled by nipping bites from a shoal of small fish swirling under it. Modesta pulled herself up and called out to the seraphim. Two minutes later she had forgotten the village and all that had happened there. She never thought of the old woman again. But occasionally, very occasionally, her tongue remembered the fish soup that steamed in brown bowls in that old house, somewhere back in her forgetting.

Seraphim are curious things, she thought, but the eminence of this one seemed curiously tarnished and broken. She knew its random ways and scruffy flight must have meaning and that those shards of wisdom were always obscure or impossible and were constantly shielded from the eyes of men. The true magnificence would blind them, for hadn't the seraphim sat under God's throne and bathed in his light while they sang his eternal praise? That is why they were called the fiery ones. This manifestation seemed a long way from that. Its dismal spastic tumblings looked more like a village drunk than an angel of God. She grew tired thinking of it and shouted ahead that she intended to sleep, finding some soft ferns among the thorns and wiry thyme of the escarpment.

That night she had her first dream, and when she awoke, she did not know what to do with it; pictures and scents and a heart-bruising ache that might be memory spilled into the overly bright day. And as it was fading, a great hollow of loss was nudging into every vivid crevice of where the dream had been. Its still-fresh and setting mould was filling with astonishment that yearned to be actual and sentient. A wriggling nascent awareness that was tangible only in pressure. For a precious, delirious, and terrifying few moments it filled her mind and was as real as everything else. For the first time in her short life she was knocked off guard, and it shifted all her outlines in the world that she thought she understood and so domineeringly owned. As the last wisps of the dream vanished, she realised that she had no means to hold it or call it back. Its great gift was stolen by the sun as it flooded into the hinge of her sight. The reality of the dream was gone, leaving no teeth of the image to focus on. But its unseen gums gnawed all day, slowly pulping and dissolving the contours of her implacable lucidity.

This was the moment that the Vorrh spoke to her. The first touch of its forever vastness. High on the cliffs above the sea at the peak of oppositeness. The trees came to her with the taste of the baptism water that filled her mouth. Its memory coming like an embrace, she raised her arms above her head to let the wind feel her contours. Goose bumps nibbled her mottled skin and she shifted again into a body of familiarity.

What seemed like many days later she finally lost the seraph and entered the new world of vertical sounds and dappled majesty where she knew that she was home, amid the shaven tides of wind and the rampant voices of the birds and the monkeys that cascaded between the echoing trees. This was not a subject of dreams but a gigantic reality that gave her sleep a physical dimension. Her Vorrh that was growing her in its proportions. She was thinner now but had grown older, and her spotted skin was taut over her lengthening bones. She had dreams every night, and their enigmas were making her grow upwards to match the trees, a different realm of turgor contained within the walls and pressures of her consciousness. Her footfall was light and its quietness surprised animals in her path. She stopped to drink in a startled clearing, enjoying the bright taste of the cold water and defining a change in flavour. She ate little, being unaware of food. All the proposed sustenance for their journey had gone over the cliff with Carmella. Modesta was now eating berries and clawed-up roots, chewing leaves and occasionally the grubs that clung to the shade of their undersides. She was unaware that the gradual starvation was affecting her mind as well as her body, and that the increasingly vivid dreams were feeding on her hunger. A great tiredness came about her on the fourth day in the forest and she lay down by the fast waters, incapable of anything but sleep.

The dream that came in dappled light was softer than the others. A Man Without Substance came to her and told her he was of her blood, that he was her grandfather. He had visited her before but never in a dream and never in sight. His name was Eadweard and he told her that he had always known she would arrive on the other side of the world and that he had dug into the ground on his side of the world to send gifts to her. She said they had not arrived yet, because the time was thick between them. So was the land, he said, and it was making him thin in this the last year of his life. He tried to smile at her when he said this, but his face was not made for it and got stuck halfway. They were standing in a strange place that he called a garden, and he was pointing at many rough-dug holes that were filled with water and looked like eyes. At the edge of the garden, houses had been piled one on top of the other, so that a wall of windows looked down. A rag behind one twitched and she knew they were being watched. Then she woke up.

CHAPTER FOURTEEN

*M*eta was sleeping on the stairs and hiding from everyone. After they took the remains of Mutter away, she shifted among the rooms of Kühler Brunnen, never in the same one for more than a few hours. She hid when Thaddeus came to speak to her. She hid from the one visit of her mother and she hid from the police. She did not have to hide from Ghertrude because Ghertrude could not see her. Not even when she lay on the stairs or sobbed in the same room, absorbing a bit of her mistress's unique inability to see her. But mostly she was alone. Ghertrude had told the family and the police that Ishmael had shot Mutter and then run away. At first the police did not believe her, being convinced that the criminal had been executed some hours before. It was only after her continual insistence that they dug up the wooden masked head and peeled its cover off before the lime had done any real damage. It was not the head of Ishmael Williams. Indeed, one of the diggers recognised the bloody thing as a man called Cranz, a prison guard who had volunteered for execution duties that week. After the shocking and humiliating discovery, they came back to ask Ghertrude more questions and then began their manhunt in every quarter and rat hole of the city.

After they had gone, Ghertrude ran through the empty house, her bare feet pattering on the wooden floors, calling out to Meta and telling her of her safety and how she would never be blamed and that nobody would ever think she had been guilty of this terrible mistake. Meta didn't care about the authorities and the law. They meant nothing compared to the cost to her family and the look in her father's eye that she never saw but dreamt of every time she closed her eyes. The truth was that the old man never knew what hit him. The hail of bullets and the splintering door had spun and fogged him so that he died with his fist clenched and furious that he never got his throttling hands on the villains, whoever they were. There was a tiny balm as he was extinguished: the voice of his beloved daughter calling to him, from very far away.

At night Meta would go into the kitchen to drink cold water from the old iron pump that connected directly to the well. She had not eaten in days, and hunger and the tortured lack of sleep were beginning to take their toll. The glow and roundness had gone; the apple complexion and the wide happy eyes had paled. She was changing in her solitude and starvation. She used the pain of her shrinking stomach and aching limbs to drive the nail of vengeance in deeper. It had never been there before, but now its bitter iron tasted of blood and its cold resistance gave her hope. She was not going to die in this house, not going to perish of heartbreak and let her enemies escape. She was going to change, to split and knot into something else. The water and the stairs kept despair at bay. Their indifferent hardness and chill would chisel her softness into angles that the hunger would sharpen. This process had begun without her knowing, outside of her will. But now all of her was involved. What had once been her beaming optimism had been snatched up and cuffed into a dirty shape that cherished the lean hollowness of her passion. The bleak stair was a vindictive mould and Meta was reshaped in its stiff pressure.

Thaddeus had visited every other day, but not even he could find Meta. He inspected the scrubbed floor where his father died, where he had been murdered by the man whom he'd once had a little sympathy for. Ghertrude left Thaddeus to reflect in the room with the shattered door, and his remorse was always overshadowed by guilt. He knew this was going to happen. His father had died within one of the red-ringed circles that he had scrawled on the calendar after the prediction he had been given in that gloomy warehouse. He hadn't really understood it but made the calculations anyway. But he never saw it coming like this. He watched for signs of illness or fatigue. He visited his father in the stables, and when the old man wasn't looking, he would test the endurance of things: overhead racks and mis-placed tools and the strength and good repair of all the wheels of the carts. He even looked deep into the swivelling eyes of the horses, seeking indications of frothing madness lurking beneath their tranquil indifference. How was he ever to expect murder, by his own sister no less? The shock was that it happened here in the safety of Mistress Ghertrude's home, a house that had always meant kindness and stability to his family. After his short vigil he would return to the hall, where Ghertrude would meet him and offer tea or coffee. Their conversations were stilted at first, but with practice they became more fluent. They said the same things each time, almost the same words. He would ask about Meta and she would say that nothing had changed. He would delicately enquire about her daughter, Rowena, and she would appreciate his care, which jolted her in its sincerity. And she would explain there was no news, which was an act of repeti-tion, a device to keep the daily horror and agony separate from who she must be to others. She said these things by rote. The words were able to hold her formality if others were listening. In the sanctum of seclusion she would fret every hour, gnawing at the gap between her child and her until she bled white tears and amber blood against her bed and clothing. It was easier for her to recount her notions of the world outside. In relief of her anguish she again went through the detail of Mutter's murder and the escape of the evil perpetrator. Mutter had had no comprehension that the floating gun that had split him apart had been wielded by his daughter, her trusted but invisible servant. Thaddeus was bewildered and without words as he shuffled his nervous, bashful hands under his hat, which sat on his lap. These rituals were becoming important to them and neither questioned why. Thaddeus was becoming Ghertrude's only contact with the outside world. He had immediately adopted some of his father's duties. Especially with the horses, which gravely missed the old man's touch and smell. Concealed behind the lace curtain, Ghertrude would watch him working in the stables. The sight and knowledge of his being there gave her a settling reassurance.

Ghertrude was in despair. Rowena was still missing. Yet Ishmael was alive. She had to tell Cyrena, but how would she react?

Of course Cyrena had visited the moment she heard about Rowena's abduction and insisted that Ghertrude return to her house and stay there. Ghertrude would not go. She explained that she needed to be in her own home in case of Rowena's return. But it was more than that; she also pined for Meta and needed to play the vile scene over and over in her memory, standing where it happened in her house. Nothing was going to take that away from her.

Cyrena was also in shock. She had witnessed the execution of Ishmael at the hands of Adam Longfellar, saw him die, allowed herself a portion of grief. And then to find that it had been another trick, a guileful substitution, and that he was alive and laughing at her and the rest of the world again. Her disbelief was matched only by her fury, and Ghertrude did not

want to share in either. There was also something else, a growing shadow between them, as if some part of Ishmael or something was cleaving them. She came to recognise that perhaps it
had always been there and was generated from Cyrena's strange
and magnificent heart. For is it not so that the greater feelings
always require a counterbalance, a parallel other if not an exact
opposite? Ghertrude had always sensed some resentment in her
closest friend. Some difficulty about her knowing Ishmael first.
It was also there at the birth of Rowena and now she sensed
it forming again. Ghertrude had been the only witness to Ishmael's survival and in some way it made her implicit to his
deceit. She feared that Cyrena was brooding on her hurt and
saw her as the frame in which it was held. The ornate frame that
had always contained some part of Ishmael, which she had never
seen. Maybe even his sincere side, if anybody could ever believe
in that. Thaddeus's calls had become important to her. The
kindly young man offered a gentle stability against the random
violence that seemed to be erupting and filling her life. He also
shared her sadness without ever weighing it against his own.

During Thaddeus's most recent visit she unexpectedly told
him more than ever before and no longer feared the consequences.

"Meta is still here, sometimes I think I see her out of the corner of my eye. I still talk to her. Did you know that?"

"No, Mistress Ghertrude," said Thaddeus as they both stood
in the hall looking up and down the empty staircase.

"Well, I do."

"Yes, ma'am. But I don't know where she could be, we have
both searched the house. Twice now."

"Do you think me unstable, Thaddeus?"

He looked at the floor and his large shoes, scuffed and often
repaired.

"It would not be surprising if I were."

"No, ma'am."

"So many terrible things, one after another. It's enough to make anyone go mad." She looked at him, her lip trembling, her throat tight, her insides turning to grit and dribble. Then suddenly he seemed different. Standing in a different space. He was most unusual, different from anybody else she had ever known. He was quite simply the most normal person she had ever met, despite his weird self-conscious hands. The alarming speed of this revelation had thrown her off guard. She had never understood normality and now it flowed over her. Not as the tiresome, boorish shallowness that she as always suspected it to be. But as a reassuring tide of warmth. How could this be? In this one moment it was revealed. She looked again at the tall, stooped young man who fidgeted his bruised felt hat in his embarrassed hands. He was his father's son, but without the width and solidity. In its place was a willowy carefulness, like a slender tree growing inside a hollow oak. His long jaw, nose, and ears were set in a listening cast. His brown eyes were the same shape as Meta's and had the same smoulder of kindness in them that once so illuminated her expression. Ghertrude had never really examined him before, and she found that she was enjoying the act. Then the clarity of it made her blush and totter. He was the exact opposite of Ishmael in every conceivable way. He seemed to want nothing and offered benevolence shyly as a path or a prayer mat.

"I don't think you are mad," he said, still examining his shoes and not seeing her flushed interest. "It has been you that has kept us all sane." There was a tiny crack in his voice and he cleared his throat to glue it together and wedge back the emotion that was solidifying under it.

She saw his plight and acted without thought or word. She crossed the space between them and took the hat from him, put it on the hall stand, and then held both his hands in hers.

Nobody had ever done that, nobody had ever held them. Not even his mother, who had helped him wash and dress when he returned from his alteration. Ghertrude had grasped them, and while he did not know what to do, she had brought them to rest chastely across the warmth of her bosom. He was instantly and overpoweringly in love with her. He dared not move. Tears were hurrying to form a great geyser inside his awkward size and he feared offence by the unmanliness of such emotion, lest his touch might insult her, even the accidental brush of the back of his trapped paws. But mostly he feared that his reaction would wake the dream that he was now in and send it skidding away into the reality of nothing at all. For surely this must be a dream, what else could it be? He lifted his gaze and she ducked her smiling face to meet it halfway. It was everything, far too much, and it doubled again and he was lost in her forever.

Meta could hear their stillness from the stairs. Hear that they were silent and unmoving in the passage below. She dared not creep down to see why. She wanted to thrust her head between the banisters and look down upon them, but instead she put her head on the polished wood and pressed her ear hard against it, trying to sense the house and be sure that they were not in danger. She had no more fear left for herself; it was not used up but converting: compressing itself to temper her resolve.

Ghertrude moved closer; she parted his arms and folded them about her as she pressed into his stiff embrace, tilting her head to rest it on his beating chest. He enfolded her and felt her weight give in to his arms, a strength filling them with a confidence he had never possessed before. Levels of transformation were moving inside the whole house, different vibrations fingering its old walls and blushing its whispers. They shuddered between them and in the small compacting body of Meta lying above.

They slept together without making love—or better and

more accurately to say, love made them without any sexual congress. They held each other fully clothed in a most unusual bed, where tears and grip bound them in a wordless union. Exhaustion and relief wove them together, so that as dream and surprise, wakefulness and slumber exchanged, they became one unique body. By dawn a new being arose.

Meta had seen it all. At first watching from the stairs when the tension dropped, and then, without a trace of voyeurism, she tiptoed to the bedroom door to sense the alchemy that sweetly churned within. A great burden fell from her aching shoulders at the same time that she also became invisible to Thaddeus. For in their union one of the last parts of her worldly responsibility faded. Benevolence had slipped its leash. In the radiance that flooded from the quiet room, she had become untied from that great compound that had so ruled her heart. Now her brother could take care. He was obviously much better at it than she. All the care that was needed for those she had so cherished was now his. He was suddenly so strong in this, and her pride in him had bit through the umbilical that kept her kind. It was on the carpet by the door that she transformed. Curled there, she shifted from opaque to translucent, then to transparent, her gentleness evolved into a clarity that had nothing to do with the emotions and visions that had governed her previous life. Those painful qualities had solidified into something greater: a nameless strength that had been gifted equally by all those who had loved and abused her. The demons and angels had clashed together and she was at the matrix of the collision, where sublime knowledge is silently forged.

By dawn she was already washing on the lower floor. Singing quietly to herself under the warmed water. Knowing that her task in the world was delineated. Now that her brother was protecting Ghertrude, she was free to find Rowena in her own way. And she knew where and how to look. She stood steaming, wrapped in a large towel, and all the fear and trepidation that filled that horrible warehouse dispersed. Her teeth were quiet and her purpose sang.

CHAPTER FIFTEEN

*C*yrena trusted Marais with her life, or, more important, with the meaning of it. She had trusted him when she was a child and blind, and she hoped that he would be there for her all of his days, even with the fierce cruelty of physical distance between them. And with the diminishing of his fragile health.

She would never forget their meeting at the time of her father's funeral. She saw him with her vivid eyes, which saw the world anew, without the long filter of time to numb the harshness. She also knew something else had grown between them at that time, now that she was a woman.

And she also saw his vulnerability and stubbornness, especially when she tried to warn him about entering the Vorrh.

He had stared at her across the crowded room with a recognition that strained too far. He saw her shine in the sombre darkness of that day.

He could not wait to draw her aside and talk about her gift of sight.

"How did it happen? Was it a slow accumulation or did it happen in one startling moment?"

Before she could answer he spoke again.

"Forgive me for being so blunt, so crude, but I never expected this. When your father wrote to me saying that you could now see, I imagined a slightness of vision, not a complete, perfect condition. I don't think I have ever heard of such a thing. And certainly the doctors in London that we consulted never suggested that such a thing was possible."

"It was a miracle," she said quietly.

They talked for hours, he asking many questions, which she happily answered without ever mentioning the existence of Ishmael, whose touch had restored her vision with no explanation. It wasn't. Then it was.

Before he left they again swore to keep in touch and again she let her promise slide, this time for a different reason. Because in that sad day she had sensed two things about the great man which scared and surprised her. Firstly, the weird detachment that he had from the world that all else lived in. What she had thought to be only a misunderstanding held in place by her vivid childhood memory proved to be an actual tangible fact. Even while they spoke about her father and dined and drank with others at the funeral feast she sensed a division in him, as if some part was elsewhere or listening to something that was far off and remote. It never affected his warmth or engagement with her; in fact it strengthened the latter, no doubt because it was as if they were the only two people in the room. The second thing which surprised and unnerved her was their powerful mutual attraction. He of course was double her age, but this made no difference. His presence and the uniqueness of his mind illuminated his heart and how she imagined him physically. She could hear that he too understood this, and the flattery made him falter and question what he was feeling in such a place and time. Their departure had been unexpectedly painful. Each holding a great longing for the other without the nerve to dare to believe it to be true, shocked by the speed and momentum of its sensation. She had even suggested to him that he stay on for a few days after the other guests had gone.

"That would have been such a pleasure, I wish I had considered it before. Now my travel plans are firmly established. It's very generous of you to offer. I know little of this part of the country and you would have made such an excellent guide."

Cyrena smiled and took his arm.

"I have arranged to meet another friend and travel back together after visiting the Vorrh."

"How do you plan to do that?" she asked.

"We thought we might hire horses and travel through its lower territories. My friend has some business at the garrison on the far side, in the kraal of the True People."

They had been gently walking as they spoke, and she now stopped.

"But that's not possible, you would be in the forest for more than four days. It's much better to take the eastern route close to the river, which leads straight to those troubled lands. But even that is fraught with danger." Her grip on his arm had changed.

"Cyrena, my dear, do you believe in these witch-doctor tales of monsters and malicious forces in the Vorrh?"

"Yes, Oom, I do, we all do. There is something not right. Something malignant in the great forest; a condition that seriously affects the memories of men. Any amount of time in there will begin to erase parts of the mind. My family has harvested it for two generations and all our relations with it are at extreme arm's length."

"Now you are really interesting me." Marais grinned.

"I am in deadly earnest. Ask any member of the guild. Ask anybody in this city."

"All right, my dear, I am listening and taking you seriously. I think I'd better do my homework first." He placed his hand over her arm and they started walking again.

"Well, at least talk to Quentin Talbot before you set one foot in that direction. Or his protégé, a young man called Fleischer, who has made notable studies of its folk history and collected many stories of past travellers."

"Those that remembered what they saw," he joked.

"I believe in some of those stories, that they tell the truth about that place."

"Yes, I am sure they do in some way." He saw that his attempt at humour was producing the opposite effect, so he quickly reversed and joined in with a parallel comparison to her sincerity.

"Do you see any value in these stories?" she asked with a splinter of distrust in her voice.

"Many scientific facts are hidden in the dull purse of village fiction and even the stupefying effect of the Vorrh might be explained."

She said nothing.

"And it is more than possible that such a vast mass of vegetable growth might affect a human mind."

Cyrena was now paying close attention to Marais's words.

"How is that possible?" she asked.

"Certain toxins exist in the bark and leaves of many species of plant. And some saps can be hallucinogenic."

"Could they take memory?"

"No, not exactly. I use these examples to say that the vegetable kingdom is not necessarily on the side of mankind."

"You make it sound like an enemy."

He looked deep into her peculiar eyes. "No, I say that trees could fight back if they had reason to do that."

"How?"

"Transpiration would be my guess. If they became tired of men, they could starve them of oxygen or change the consistency of the air we breathe. Do you know how little change it would take to wipe out all breathing creatures?"

She shook her head.

"It's been estimated that a change of three percent in oxygen levels would be seriously felt. Ten percent would choke all mammalian life, and fifteen percent would finish us forever."

He was getting excited with these ideas and a slight tremor attached itself to his energy.

"If trees were really clever they might mix the low oxygen levels with other gases, to turn men's minds, so that after a number of years or even generations they might become insane and more violent, and eventually annihilate each other. That potential and condition has been demonstrated from the beginning of humankind and in lesser ways in most other species in the animal kingdom."

Cyrena was aware that his mind was speeding, rushing through a forest of questions and conclusions.

"Of course that is the astonishing difference between the two kingdoms that flourish and populate the earth. They live in different times and understandings, side by side. The vegetative being lost in a long thinking that communicates across all its species, sharing the common purpose of reproduction and survival in union. While the animal realm is driven by conflict and violence to achieve the same ends. Species against species in the gory imperative of the food chain. Mankind would happily butcher and devour every other living thing to expand its domain and keep its sex drive overactive."

He suddenly looked up and grinned at her expression of shock. He swallowed and decided that she might just have had enough of his darkening speculation.

"But tell me something else about your part of the world."

Her eyes refocussed on him.

"The True People, are they calm these days?" he asked.

"Yes, as far as we know. The uprising was many years ago

now. We have some trade with them and our agents report nothing sinister."

"Good, then I shall take your advice and go straight to them. They made some wonderful artifacts during their famous Possession Wars."

"Please take care, Oom, you are very dear to us." Her father's death had still not truly settled in, and her speaking for them both made her affection seem even greater.

"Don't worry about me, my dear, I am solid Afrikaans."

The next morning he was gone and her life changed direction and depth.

Soon after, Cyrena inherited her father's house and esteemed position in the family business in Essenwald, while her brother returned to the lowlands of Europe to protect their interests there and run the receiving yards of their highly valued wood. The Timber Guild would never allow her a seat at its meetings. But respect was given to her by all its members after the unexpected death of her father.

Marais had left Essenwald with Cyrena's eyes still burning in his head. And some part of him feared the intensity. He forcefully switched his focus to the expedition ahead, knowing that the vastness of the forest would overwhelm such emotional disturbances. The concentration it demanded and the plain common sense of his travelling companion, Koos Nel, would establish a very different landscape of sensations. He had met up with Koos Nel at the De Bruck stables, chosen their horses, and now followed the directions suggested by the pompous young man named Fleischer, whom Cyrena had so enthusiastically recommended. Much of what Fleischer had said about the Vorrh was obviously nonsense, but his understanding of pathways and topographic features seemed sound. Marais had said nothing about the meeting he was hoping to have in a place near the western chapel path. A meeting in which he hoped to purchase some artifacts that had survived the Possession Wars.

They left the rim of the city, all sight of it devoured by the enclosure of trees.

They found a gully between the trees after an hour of searching. Koos Nel spurred his big, reluctant bay onto the path that they supposed was a track, with Marais's smaller filly following.

Koos was a farmer and not the sharpest knife in the drawer, but a man who could be trusted in a squeeze. They had known each other since late childhood, and renewed their comradeship when the poet had returned from Europe. Koos had never held a moral opinion about his friend's addiction. There was no difference in his mind between morphine and gin. He had even accepted Marais's weird ideas about hunting and how to treat the Kaffirs. When Koos had been invited along on this trip up north, he had jumped at the chance to leave his wife and sons and their greedy farm for a few days' "sport" with his old pal the scholar. While Marais had been in the grandeur of the Lohrs' mansion, Koos had been sampling the backroom pleasures of the Scyles, disposing of a good deal of his "travelling fund" in the process. He now hoped to top it up by joining in Marais's treasure hunt. They were an incongruous pair, trotting tightly between the enormous trees. Marais's spare leanness was stiff and agile against his mount, his long bony face and rampant eyes shifting to catch every movement around him, while Koos sat back in his saddle with the ease of a bored ploughman—large, muscular, and reserved, in the sense that he never wasted energy but held it contained, ready and waiting. He negotiated his way through the world with instinct and quick active response. In his youth those "talents" had been ill used by bouts of violent anger, often fuelled by excessive drinking. His broken nose and irregular knuckles still bore witness to those far-off days of thrilling scallywaggery. Solid farm work and management had slowed and matured him, but never really tamed his deep animal power and his delight in testing it. He was a foot and a half taller than Marais, as was his horse, which meant that he continually had to duck under low branches as they rode farther into the sumptuous depths of the gigantic forest. Where the trees were thicker, they dismounted and trudged ahead at a more cautious pace. Marais held a green army compass in one hand and kept a careful watch on the sun. The light was dazzling against the great trees and the solitude was growing as the slow horses snorted a steady passage.

He had recently heard of a German called Leo Frobenius who had just arrived in Africa and planned on staying for years to dig and destroy—another adventurer looting Africa, this time for cultural artifacts. During Frobenius's excavations he started to ask his workers what they thought of the objects "he found." He started to collect those explanations and stories. The rumours and myths that have verbally recorded the history of all tribes across the surface of the earth and their attempts at manipulating the planet's powers. Many of the stories had doppelgängers in other parts of the world. Impossible coincidences of narrative invention that echoed in opposite continents. One of the stories that came to light was identical to a pre-Christian tale found all over Europe, that of the green man: a creature of the forests and wild places that is the spirit of the earth and vegetation, all that is not human. Frobenius became obsessed with the Black Man of the Vorrh: a fiercer, darker being of the eternal night and depth of the jungle. There were also versions of something like this in the complex pantheon of Hindu myth.

Perhaps, Marais thought, he could find this Black Man himself. He was a storyteller, after all, and what better story than that of creation?

"I think we should go for two hours and then turn and follow our tracks back out," said Koos. "Then we can skirt around and find your dealer of illicit goods."

Marais groaned a good-natured ascent. Troupes of monkeys called from the canopy, brushing flights of loudly coloured birds swirling among the branches.

"Magnificent," said Marais, who greatly enjoyed the contrasts to his own beloved plains.

"What's the game like in here?" asked Koos, patting the polished butt of his saddled carbine.

"Nothing you would be interested in."

Ten minutes later they met a fork in the path, one that ran at right angles westwards. Marais was already consulting his compass when Koos asked, "Do you think this might be a shortcut, a way of flanking towards your meeting point, save going all the way back?"

Marais looked doubtful. "We could give it a go, see where it takes us for a bit," he responded, trying to ignore the buzzing in his head and the empty ache in his empty veins. They mounted and turned the horses, who sniffed at the new path as they entered.

"What's that?" Koos said, pointing up into the trees.

Marais saw it too: a large mottled creature had slid from its camouflage and was shifting its position, hanging high in the trees.

"Maybe a sloth or a . . ." He faltered, not having a name for what he saw. He did not recognise or understand the creature that was moving at a snail's pace, crossing the branches.

"There's only one way of finding out," said Koos, the truncated rifle already in his hands.

Marais had long since learned that arguing with hunters was a waste of time. Anyway, he was curious to see what the creature was and there was only one way of reaching it. Koos worked the bolt, aimed, and fired three times in quick succession. Each round found its mark with a hard thud and a shiver. After the third the animal ceased moving with a slight whimper that might have been only the sound of the vines receiving its lifeless weight. They stared upwards, waiting for it to drop. Leaves and twigs tumbled languidly onto their upturned faces; each danced momentarily in the quiet bright sun that sent lazy spokes through the canopy. The beast held its position until the birds forgot the shots and began singing again. Then it twisted around. But instead of releasing its grip and falling, the creature peeled, like an overripe banana, from the head down, its body splitting and unzipping before them.

"Christ, what is it?" said Koos, shielding his eyes with his large hand.

Marais did not have an answer. He realised he was watching an unknown species die before him. After an agonising and silent time, it fell from trees in an asymmetrical, sodden parachute of skin. Koos dismounted and gave his reins to Marais, who watched as he approached the collapsed mass. He held his rifle out before him, knowing that not all prone creatures were defenceless. He walked around it and kicked it.

"Well, what kind of thing is it?" asked Marais.

Koos was very quiet and bent down to look even closer. Something in his sturdy gait had changed. He looked back at his comrade with strange eyes.

"Well?" insisted Marais again.

"I think it might have been a man," he said quietly.

Marais dismounted and pulled both horses behind him. As he drew closer they resisted, stepping backwards, pulling against the reins in his firm grip.

"Take them, let me look," he commanded.

Koos happily complied, walking away from the split fleshy pod. Marais knelt close to it and smelt its strange aroma of cinnamon and seashells. He peeled its fibrous winglike flaps away and saw the fragments of a rib cage smothered in its density. He poked inside it with his crop, moving the wrecked cranium that was elongated to look like a stalk. He rolled it over and saw that a dense black-brown mass like stiff hair protruded from its back, following the ripples of a knobbly spine. The horses were still shying backwards, neighing and shaking their heads against the tight reins.

"What the fuck is it?" said Koos, shouting over his shoulder while arguing with the nags.

"God knows, I have never seen anything like it before. We should take it back for dissection."

"You are joking," said Koos. "It's already spooking the horses and stinking the place up."

"We could make a sledge and pull it out."

"You could. I want nothing to do with it."

"But, Koos, this is unique."

"Look, man, the day is wearing and we have got other business here. If we cart that fucking thing with us, we'll never make the west side before dark."

Marais looked at the sun, already forked in the high branches. He realised that his friend was right and stood up and walked away from the prize specimen and back to his mount.

"Perhaps we might come back for it tomorrow?"

Koos ignored that and said, "Let's go back the way we came."

With great reluctance Marais mounted his sweating horse and turned it back the way they had come. After twenty minutes Koos stopped.

"Have we missed it?"

Marais's head was pounding and his veins were aching for their fix, but this was far too early. He hadn't expected his need to come barking and scratching for at least another five hours.

"I said have we missed it?"

"What?" groaned Marais.

"The turning, man, the spoor back."

They were gullied in a gently curving track, thick trees on either side.

"We must have missed it."

They turned the horses again and slowly rode back the way they had just come. No junction appeared and they stopped only when the horses started to object. They were at the spot where the mysterious creature had fallen. Except that it was not there.

"It must have been taken by scavengers," said Koos.

Marais said nothing. They turned the horses again and took five paces before Koos spat-whispered, "Christ." He was looking through the interior trees.

"What?" whispered Marais, instantly infected by his friend's sudden violent quietness. Koos just pointed. It took Marais's bleary eyes moments to focus onto the dappled and vine-crossed interior. Then he saw it. The thing Koos had shot, standing upright twenty feet away and appearing to be looking straight at them. It was one again, its limp skin zipped up, back in place.

"It can't be," said Koos, his hand already on his carbine.

"Is it another one?" Marais was rubbing his aching head. The watching pod appeared to bend as if looking more intently. As it flexed, two of the wounds in its smooth mottled skin opened and closed like kissing mouths.

"Christ," said Koos.

Then the horses bolted. They charged through the curved channel in the trees with both men furiously yanking their reins and demanding the animals to halt. But nothing would slow them and they were now running at full tilt. Both men were experienced bush equestrians, but they were finding it difficult to stay in their saddles, especially as hitherto unnoticed low-hanging branches and thick swaying liana were threatening to snatch or wipe them off the horses. The forest sped past with a new intensity that made the riders' flesh creep under the spray of their sweat and the thin paper cuts from the hanging, whipping leaves. Suddenly they were in a clearing; the horses spun and reared, kicking dust from the perimeter road, and finally stopped. They were back where they had begun, panting outside the vast forest. The Vorrh had spat them out. They continued on their way to a chapel where they were told "goods" would be on sale.

➤—→

Never trust the Men Without Substance to tell the truth, especially about the power of their gods. The True People would never be fooled again. The white men were pilfering all their sacred artifacts and instruments of divination in exchange for crossed sticks, thick books, and too many clothes, and that would never be forgotten. None of the old deities of their forefathers would ever leave the village again. The Possession Wars had reestablished the old gods back in their rightful home. And some of the sacred objects that came into being before the great conflict were equally prized. One such was the roughly circular block of dried mud called "the crown." It was not unlike a thick heavy cow pat. Straw and root fibres mixed with the mud to hold it in one piece. Charms and amulets were woven into its tightness. Its name came from the regular gold-coloured protuberances that made an elliptical pattern on the surface of the block, each sticking out an inch above the sunbaked earth. The rest of the surface had been painted and drawn with the story of the crown. Pictographs and glyphs telling how the crown had once belonged to the prized Irrinipeste and was worn by her legendary mother when she gave birth in the depth of the Vorrh. Nobody knew who had inscribed the object thus, but its status was unquestionable.

The Irrinipeste cult had caused a fracture inside the unity of the tribe and this had been deepened by the Sea People's claim that Irrinipeste had imprisoned their messianic saviour, whom they called Oneofthewilliams but who was her lover, the Bowman, Peter Williams.

So the sanctity of the crown was held solid by most of the elders of the True People. Some said that it had been made of rare mud taken from deep and holy wells. Others that Irrinipeste's mother had brought it from the other side of the world. Some believed it was sleeping, some thought it dead. Most were afeared to touch it.

It lived with other lesser objects of power in the longhouse of the the zealots of the Irrinipeste cult, protected by the Tarpfa family, one of the oldest clans of the True People, until Kweki Tarpfa stole everything and ran towards the dwellings of the Men Without Substance, who were said to be buying such things for a small fortune. Kweki was running low and wild. The small bag that was strapped tight to his chest was not heavy, but its irregular load frayed and scratched his worried skin. He had stolen the sacred crown and the joined coconut shells that were called the head bones and an armful of lesser trophies and was heading towards the edge of the Vorrh, where he knew men would meet to buy these things.

He was running out of his history, his tribe, and his life. He reached the place of barter by the old broken chapel before the bidders arrived and sat on the scuffed fractured wall until they came. The loud man who was there collecting for Leo Frobenius arrived first. Then another, who was there for Nebsuel, and a tall silent man who watched everybody else with great care. They observed one another with anxious, controlled eyes. Tarpfa said he was not ready to begin the auction but wanted to rest and wait for the allotted hour. Frobenius's man seemed irritated. Sometime later, when they were just about to begin, a squat, very black man in a green robe appeared, apparently out of the forest. He said he was called Iron Engine. Nobody laughed or passed comment. Iron Engine did not look the type to share a jest about his name. The sound of horses broke the tension, and Marais and Koos Nel rode in and joined the group.

"A rough journey, bwana?" said Lupo, the richly costumed emissary of Frobenius. Everybody ignored him and looked at Tarpfa, who got up from his squatting position and started to unwrap his bundles. He laid out the prized objects in a ragged line on the low wall, touching each as if it were precious Meissen. Three of the bidders scurried forth. Marais sauntered behind them, demonstrating a dignified curiosity. The silent man just watched. Lupo was acting like his boss and elbowed his way to the front, being the first to touch the crown and barking his bid. The auction had begun: each man bidding for his chosen object, each in his own currency. Tarpfa sat back to watch them squabble and started calculating the various values in his head. The crown was the prized item. All had placed bids on it except the quiet man who now held the halo of dried mud in his careful hands. Nebsuel's man had made a minor bid because he was interested only in a dull leather bag that contained mangled and besmirched charms. Lupo wanted everything and had no difficulty in pushing the stakes higher than most others could afford. He stood proud and defiant, just saying *"All"* and giving his price.

"A bit selfish to want everything, couldn't ya leave something for somebody else?" said Koos automatically.

"Money or be gone," said the bidder to Koos, and Marais put a restraining hand on his friend's wrist, holding back his tense fist and riding crop.

"Leave him," Marais hissed.

Koos unclenched at his friend's request.

"It's all fucking mumbo-jumbo crap anyway," he said, turning away and fishing in his pockets for his cigarettes.

It appeared that the auction was over and that Lupo would bring Frobenius a king's ransom. Not that Lupo would have ever mentioned his master's name. He would own these goods himself for a day or so and then sell them to Bwana Leo for twice the price. Most of the other bidders just stood around, dejected and gloomy, still admiring the line of ugly objects. Iron Engine stepped forward and held out his round polished fist. Then he dramatically placed a single irregular brown object on the crumbling wall next to the coconut shells that he so wanted.

"Head bones, one possidum," he said.

There was an intake of breath and the expression on Lupo's face changed utterly. None of them had ever seen a possidum, but everyone knew what it was and that it was more valuable than anything else on the slumped wall or all the coins that the other bidders had called out before. Tarpfa walked over on stiff, unbelieving legs and stared at the dirty-brown octagonal lump. All began to move towards it, except Lupo, whose jaw had locked with rage and humiliation.

"What's a possidum?"

It could have been only Koos who did not know. He was whispering, again looming over Marais's shoulder.

"May we touch?" asked another bidder.

"Sure thing." Iron Engine beamed and made a magnanimous gesture, displaying an alarming array of gold teeth.

Marais took Koos aside. He was very excited and anxious to explain.

"It's very valuable: a fabled ancient treasure, truly a handmade enigma, very rare and never seen in these parts."

"Where's it from?"

"That is a very good and almost impossible question, only matched by 'where's it going,'" said Marais, a fierce twinkle in his clear eyes.

"Don't riddle me, man, just give it to me clear and simple."

"It comes from a place that most people think never existed. A land of another god where all was perfection. A land that vanished beneath the sea thousands of years before Jehovah was conceived of."

"Christ!" said Koos.

"And a hell of a long time before him," Marais continued. "That chunk of pure gold is the only known artifact from that fabled land. Every scholar and witch doctor has heard stories about its value. It was some sort of currency. For buying not property, goods, and chattel but knowledge in its purest form. One of those is the key to absolute gnosis."

"Christ," said Koos, not really understanding.

"They are very rare and some say they can give one the ultimate truth. Can you guess it?"

Koos looked blank.

"The soul's journey. Existence itself." And here he pointed to the hushed men who held the metal object with enormous reverence.

"One of those might be the key to eternity. Beyond heaven itself to the other side of everything. There are men all over the world who would give their right arm and more for that thing."

"Christ," said Koos. "But why is he wasting it on that broken tat?"

The question was never answered because it and all the concentration and respect of the little group was broken when Lupo pushed his way in between everybody and snarled.

"Take your wretched head-bone shells. I will buy the rest. All else."

He glared down at the jet-black man with the gold teeth, who made a gesture of contempt, showing that he would endure no more of this upstart's insults.

"You will own nothing today," he said, turning his back on his new, angry, overdressed enemy. Iron Engine then retrieved the possidum and addressed Tarpfa directly, putting the small heavy weight in the thief's hand and forcibly closing his fingers around it. "I will buy all with this. I will take the head bones myself and give all else to these good fellows." He waved a thick black hand in the general direction of the assembled gawping men.

"But," he said, "he gets nothing." And here he pointed into the furious face of the man who had just lost Frobenius everything.

While the tension sizzled, the thief agreed, with the proviso that if anyone here wanted the same thing, then they would have to bid again and that he would split the profits with Iron Engine, who laughed back.

"You keep all," he said. He carefully picked up the broken coconuts, wrapping them like a newborn child in brightly coloured silk. He then said his salaams and walked back into the forest. All but one applauded him as he disappeared with his back to them, waving.

When he was finally gone and the clapping had ceased, they turned towards the objects and the snarling, defeated bidder. They ignored him and debated quietly among themselves.

Lupo knew that he had lost not just the auction but also his job and the trust of the man who had changed his life. There were hundreds, thousands who would have done anything to gain Bwana Leo's patronage. His failure today meant that he would be replaced instantly from the queue of eager, devoted young men who sought his place in the world. He decided that now the arrogant fool was gone he could deal with these dithering men, could win them over and start the bidding again, and if it did not work, he would kill them. If not here and now, then later. After that he would track his enemy back into the Vorrh and slit his fat throat and take the broken shells for himself.

"Gentlemen," he said. "May we begin again. My sponsor only seeks two of these goods, so shall we agree on one artifact each?"

Before any of the bidders could open their mouths, Koos stepped forward.

"You must be deaf, man. You ain't getting a goddamn thing. Make tracks."

"*I have the right to buy!*" shouted Lupo, suddenly enraged by the insult of this obviously penniless white lout. He demonstrated his full height, taking long steps forward and puffing out the breadth of his shining black chest, adorned in golden chains.

"You have the right to fuck off before you get my boot up your arse," said Koos. He was beginning to enjoy himself.

Then the emissary made the biggest mistake of his life. He kept coming, and as he did so, he drew an ornate curved dagger from his waistband. Everybody flinched except Koos, who dropped his cigarette and then made minor adjustments to every part of his body. Three fast steps away and trapped in his own growing momentum Lupo knew he had made a terrible error. He saw it in Koos's eyes and in his grin, just before the Boer launched himself low and horizontal, his stiff muscular leg pistoning out. The heavy steel-tipped boot smashed sideways into the running assailant's leading leg, just below the kneecap. The force stopped the lower leg in an instant, so that the whole, full-speed weight of the man toppled over the static knee and ripped it apart against the joint. He fell in the dust screaming as Koos moved aside and stood up, brushing dust off his shorts. He thought about kicking the sobbing fool in his stupid mouth, but couldn't be bothered when he saw Lupo's wrecked leg swelling to comic proportions. He fished in his pockets for another cigarette as he walked past the buyers who stared up at him, but they were already thinking about dividing the goods. The grovelling man had stopped crying and passed out, his fine gown covered in the loose dust. He lay in the scratched composition of his own expressive agony that was drawn around him in the thick, dry earth.

Before each man had begun to decided which fetish they wanted, the silent man stepped forward again holding the crown of mud.

"This must be yours," he said with great solemnity, holding the thing out to Marais. For some unknown reason, nobody seemed to want to argue or disagree with him. They turned away to paw over the other fragments that remained. Marais looked closely at his benefactor.

"Thank you," he said. "Who are you?"

"Another white man called me Seil Kor."

"Where are you from, Seil Kor?"

The tall man's dignified face broke into a beaming smile. "That, Herr Marais, is a more difficult question. Shall we just say I know the Vorrh and the god that walks in its inner garden. These are my lands and they have held me well."

"You know my name?"

"Yes, but not you."

"Why do you give me this and what is it?"

"I once was lost with a white man in this forest. He spoke only French and could see only with his imagination, which lived at home. We were lost together in two different places. This magical thing is from the True People, who know that all seeing is without doubt or meaning. Is this not the way you understand this country of mine?"

Marais was speechless and Koos, who was listening, started to make noises of irritation. Marais turned to placate his confused and impatient friend. When he turned back with more questions brimming, Seil Kor was gone. Marais turned the ring of encrusted earth in his hands and started to walk away from the gathering.

"Truly a thing of wonder. A gifted enigma."

"It ain't much to look at," said Koos as they walked towards the horses.

"True," said Marais. "But it has a heart of gold."

Koos laughed out a warm cloud of smoke and they mounted and turned towards the city. It was an hour before nightfall and the voices of the forest had changed. The other men had already left, each going their own way with their new possession.

"We are skirting the Vorrh, right?" said Koos.

"For sure, it's the only way," said Marais, adding: "What about him?" He looked down at the mangled Lupo.

"He's sleeping like a baby," said Koos.

"He's mercifully unconscious, he will never be able to walk away from here or defend himself."

"That's his lookout, man: Behave like a cunt, die like a cunt."

The long, plodding night seemed to dissolve the memories and effects of the day, so that as Marais and Koos neared the outskirts of Essenwald, all recollections of their journey and adventures had faded. Nothing of the unknown creature, the buying of the crown, or the crippling of Lupo remained in their wandering minds. Their mounts took them back to the stables. The owner then ferried them to the aerodrome where their plane had been waiting for twenty hours. After a brief wash in a corrugated hut both men opened warm bottles of thin beer while their possessions were loaded aboard the plane. Marais prepared his hypodermic and Koos smoked. Thirty minutes later they slept and rattled all the way back to the cape.

CHAPTER SIXTEEN

*T*he yard of Kühler Brunnen seemed desolate and empty. It was unswept and seemed to lack its previous size and authority. The gate was unlocked and on her way across the yard Cyrena quickly looked in at the stables without knowing why. It too was different, had become less. It was Mutter's large and taciturn presence that was so startlingly absent, as if the flask of the place was now three-quarters empty. She shuddered slightly and made for the door, ringing it until it opened. Not by its new mechanical contrivance but by the strange hand of Thaddeus.

"Good morning, Mistress Lohr," he said politely and stepped aside so that she might enter.

"Thank you, is your mistress at home?" She had assumed his status of servant without a second thought.

"Yes, mistress, I will fetch her." Thaddeus showed none of the swirling new sensations that were now welling up inside him.

Cyrena went into the reception room and waited, peeling off her chamois gloves and lightly testing the gentle dishevelment for dust. She knew something had changed the moment she heard her friend's footsteps descending. There was a new quick lightness there. The previous sullen weight had dispersed. The speed, the patter of happiness's footfall. Her instinct, perceptions, and sensibilities were all still intact, no matter how much they had been trampled by Ishmael.

"Dearest Cyrena, I did so hope that you would call."

Ghertrude was beaming with a quiet joy that seemed to have removed all the stress lines and knotted muscles from her much slimmer face and body.

"Have you found Rowena?"

It was the only thing that Cyrena could think of that would have produced such a distinctive change in her friend. Suddenly some of the lines and angles returned and the banished years connived in her face.

"No. No, we still wait and pray."

Cyrena crossed the room to Ghertrude, putting her arms about her in a warm and sincere embrace. As she did this she saw that they were not alone, which stifled her affection by making her aware of it mid-hug. Looming just inside the doorway was the long, drab presence of Mutter's son. Cyrena stepped back from her friend and said, "Yes?" The tone of the word spoke volumes.

Thaddeus said nothing in return, his eyes flickering between the two women and the floor. Now Cyrena became more emphatic, the honed edge of Lohr authority qualifying her voice. "Thank you, you may go."

Thaddeus received its full weight and started to turn away.

"No," said Ghertrude in a very different voice that seemed totally out of place. Her single negative word resounded in a warmth that filled the room and stroked Cyrena's command into total submission. Ghertrude held out her hand sideways and said, "Thaddeus."

After a moment of total incomprehension between him and Cyrena, he crossed the room to Ghertrude's side where she lovingly grasped his hand and pulled him a little closer. The look of absolute disbelief and astonishment on her friend's face was so extreme that it provoked an instinctive single laugh from Ghertrude, who quickly turned it into speech before it offended.

"My dearest Cyrena, don't look so shocked, you can be no more surprised than we." She gave a darting glance to Thaddeus that was more than a kiss. "We had no idea that so much joy could grow out of so much horror, and this quickly." She gave him her other hand and looked from his glowing eyes into the beautiful cool and mystified pools of Cyrena's.

The women sat while Thaddeus went to fetch drinks, not as a servant and certainly not yet as the master of the house, but as something awkwardly displaced in between. The moment that he left Cyrena said, "Are you mad? Mutter's son, a peasant boy?"

Ghertrude did not even flinch, but was firm and clear in her answer. "Saner than I've ever been. He is genuine and kind, and who is there left to care where he comes from?"

"But, Ghertrude—"

"Do you believe that Ishmael came from nobler stock?" inflicted Ghertrude.

The comment hit Cyrena like a slap. Hammering her countenance out of gawping disbelief into hurt shock, but only for a moment because her defences were up and the agile adrenaline that so liked the elegant corridors of her sharp mind was now coursing and speeding there.

"There is no comparison."

"Why not?"

"Because . . . because Ishmael came from another world and fooled us all."

"Thaddeus isn't fooling me, he is genuine."

"I know you want to think that, but what can he really offer you?"

"Love."

And there the conversation stopped because Ghertrude had won the first round flat out and Thaddeus had appeared at the door with a tray of drinks. Ghertrude insisted that he stay and held his bent hand throughout the strangled silences around their loud sippings and Cyrena's announcement that she was going south for two weeks or so.

After she eventually left, Thaddeus did not know what to say, so Ghertrude took command.

"It's all right, my dear, she will get used to us. She's a funny old stick, a bit set in the formal ways of the Fatherland. But she has a heart of gold. It will take time, that's all."

"I don't want to come between you and your best friend," he said.

"Much worse has come between us before, don't worry. When she gets to know you, we will all be friends."

Thaddeus severely doubted that but said nothing as Ghertrude put her arm around him and took him back towards the unfinished drinks.

➤——→

Outside, Cyrena was fuming.

"How dare she, how dare she!" she said out loud while storming towards the cathedral, where she had told the chauffeur to bring the car to collect her. How dare she compare what had been between her and Ishmael and this inane infatuation with Mutter's idiot son. What kind of life did she expect to live now? And what about Rowena, had she forgotten the poor stolen child while she billed and cooed with this dolt?

"I give up," she said loud enough to make passersby turn their heads.

The car was not there when she reached the great door, so she waited and paced up and down. She had never really noticed how out of place the cathedral was baking in the meaninglessness of the constant sun. How silly its European proportions in this vast primitive land. The folly and monstrous arrogance of the city fathers, including her own, whom she had loved so dearly. Again she thought of Marais and wished he were here now. She must see him, talk to somebody who had intelligence enough to share and dissect her growing turmoil and disappointment in all things. The car arrived, and after lambasting the driver she returned home, knotted silently in her anger and ludicrous envy.

After the painful visit to Ghertrude, she was even more convinced to visit Marais and the glorious south. She should have invited him to her house there years ago. Especially after she had heard of the death of his young wife. If she met him now, they could talk about pain on equal terms. She wanted to look again into the face of that genuine man and explain the growing misery between her heart and her eyes.

She wanted to spend some time in Marais's strange warmth and charismatic wisdom. He might be the only person alive who could restore or galvanise her faith in humanity. She knew he was still in South Africa and working because the business about his book being stolen was all over the press. It had even been reported on the radio. There was nothing to keep her here. She would tidy up her family affairs, appointing Talbot to supervise them in her short absence. There was little chance that he would decline, his hesitant flutterings had told her that. Her quick and easy insight suddenly appalled her. "My God, I am thinking like Ishmael," she almost said out loud. But perhaps that was also part of his reluctant gift to her, though earned rather than given.

She would take a plane or a train down to the cape. It would take the same time as a letter. She need to know more about the *tree* and let this extraordinary man enter her heart and mind again.

The three-engine plane was waiting for her after her first enquiry. Talbot had made it possible, as she had so wilfully predicted. The white-and-red Fokker F.12 sat high and proud on the landing strip. It rested at a fifteen-degree angle because of its large fixed front wheels that made its polished rectangular body point alertly at the sky as if impatient to leave the binding earth and embrace the upper breezes. Cyrena left Talbot at the steps and thanked him with a kiss on his happy cheek. Inside the plane were three metal reclining seats that were capable of being turned into beds. They had an alarmingly surgical quality about their design. Thoughtfully, one had been made up for her, cushions and a plaid blanket added in an attempt to give it a homely feeling. One of Talbot's personal touches, she thought, and smiled. She looked around the walnut-veneered interior with its little kitchen and bar at the back. She was to be the only passenger. The two pilots were busying themselves with preparation for takeoff while the flight attendant was carrying supplies into the tiny galley. Cyrena made herself comfortable just before the engines choked and spluttered into action.

Everything in the thin metal box quivered and shook violently. Now she understood why the seats were so stoically functional. Her doubts about the journey surfaced as her immaculate teeth rattled in her beautiful head and the freshly picked flowers that lolled in a tiny wall-mounted vase leapt up and down and tried to escape their elegant confinement. Another of Talbot's little touches. The plane sprang forward and galloped down the runway, jumping into the singing blue sky. When it nudged between the low puffs of cloud, the rattles ceased and the flowers sighed back into their ornamentation as the plane glided the gentle buffers of rising air. The land below rolled over to expose its magnificence as they banked and circled the vast and forever canopy of the Vorrh. Seeing it from above and at such an acute angle displayed the complexity and depth of its ancient volume.

Cyrena strained at the window, wanting to see more. The

gleaming Fokker turned again, with the sunlight polishing its wings, and the forest curved away, the dark shadow of the Vorrh sliding to the horizon behind them as they veered south. The landscape that now opened and flowed forward was breathtaking—great broken rills of colour and vast expanses of mountain with a far shimmer of desert to the east, all focussed and held by the purest light that she had ever seen. She found it hard to keep all this in her head, so much space and distance. A land that went on for days. The only other thing that she had to compare it to were the echoes of gunfire rattling back and forth from the mountains to the plain in those early years on safari. But this was greater. The sun cut apertures and highlights across the broken land. Herds of wildebeest and gazelles ran between the shadows; rivers and lakes shone and winked out of the dry ochre ground; and the flooding gallons of light washed in through the cabin and danced under the stiff upper wings. A huge joy seized her heart and cleansed the last remaining shades that were folded there. Tears came to her eyes and she started to gently sob as a flock of great birds flapped windward far beneath the silhouetted aircraft's black static wings.

Eventually she slept as twilight drained the last colour from the settling sky. The shuttle between vision, sleep, landings, and further hours of magnificent landscape lolled her into a deep, sumptuous visual world in which she felt submerged and expanded. The flight attendant brought her coffee and brandy and opened the thick embroidered curtains. A bluer light slanted in.

"Two hours, madam," she said.

"Yes," said Cyrena gleefully.

She smelt the difference in the air the moment she walked down the plane's metal steps towards the waiting car. Thirty minutes later it pulled up next to a low, slightly soiled wooden colonial building. A red-faced man in an antiquated safari suit stood outside it, grinning at her arrival. "Welcome to the Transvaal and Jackari's Lodge. I am Wolfgang Steiple, a friend of Herr Marais," he said.

She suddenly knew where she was, and her old blind memory of this place slid beneath the visual structure of the lodge, giving it solidity, meaning, and association. She had stayed here before when she was a child. The smell of the place crashed in and pushed aside the insignificance of the peeling paint and the uncleaned windows.

The next day Steiple would drive her forty miles to the smaller community where Marais had chosen to live for a short time.

"I think you have known our celebrity friend for many years," he said in an accent that she greatly enjoyed.

"Yes, Herr Steiple, since I was a child."

They chatted about the Transvaal and the cape, about mutual friends and the journey tomorrow, which would be in the late afternoon when the ferocity of the sun was spent. Just before they arrived in Waterberg, he asked a question in a different tone of voice. "How long has it been since you last met the good advocate?"

"Too long, not since my father's funeral," she said wistfully. The canvas-sided car bumped relentlessly across the rough track.

"You may find him much changed," said Steiple carefully for such an openly spoken man.

"Oh, we have all been changed by time," she said, staring across the jagged land towards the great plateau that was absorbing the setting sun.

Steiple left her on the steps of the white wooden house that had turned pink in the twilight. A grinning young man whose black skin was also weirdly glazed pink held her bags as Steiple drove away. Marais had been told that she was coming. Now all she had to do was wait. The guesthouse was one of those used for arriving safari members—it was at the top of the range and almost empty. The season had not yet started. The weather was still unsure, the breeding season almost over. She sat just inside the veranda behind the fly screen to avoid the mosquitoes that were rising from the marshlands, and the moths and beetles that wanted to taste the artificial lights. She sat and waited with her eyes closed.

His footsteps came hurriedly in from the right. She was not sure it was he until he walked onto the broad white wooden steps. He saw her there, slightly hazed by the fly screen.

"Cyrena," he said as he pushed open the door and she opened her eyes.

He was indeed "much changed"; changed from the man she had wanted to give her heart to. The firmness of his confidence had gone, the brightness of his charisma had changed colour and dimmed. He seemed to have lost the buoyant aloofness and sharp elsewhereness that gave him a sense of mystery.

This man had been rewritten in doubt and unease and something else that she could not place in the fraction of a second before they embraced.

She felt his bones through his once elegant light suit.

"My dear, how wonderful that you have come." He offered his arm in exactly the same way as he had before, when she was blind. She took it and looked deeply into his eyes. Had he forgotten their last meeting at her father's funeral and all they had said about her gaining of sight?

Suddenly the questioning force in her eyes stopped him dead

in his tracks, and he looked at her in shock, trying to find an answer rather than a question in her gaze, looking for the mind to engage with its splendour and warmth. Now it was seeking him, directly beaming out and illuminating some of the darkness that sat behind his cringing irises. In a second she saw the scars of entangled damage and the brilliance like cave paintings scratched on a wall that only a given neophyte had ever glimpsed, crawling through the tunnel of ritual, burning torch in hand. But there had never been a neophyte. And those flickering signs had only ever been read continually by him. Something in him took a sharp intake of breath and she did not know if it was actual or psychic. They were both paralysed, their eyes locked, holding each other on the edge of the parlour as the house servants moved discreetly past.

She broke the spell, or rather the interrogation of shadows.

"Oom Eugène, shall we go in?"

He had no words as the pressure of his weight answered her and they glided towards the high-backed cane chairs adorned with the pelts of fine beasts. She let her eyes retract and looked at the surface of the man. He smiled and said, "Tell me about your life, Cyrena, tell me about what you have been doing in the great dark heart."

For the next two hours they exchanged tales of wonder and pain. She could finally talk to him about Ishmael. To admit to her failings under his spell. Something she had never done with another person, not even Ghertrude. She had "seen" only what she wanted to and it had made her more blind than before. She allowed herself to verbally balance and gush the ironies of perception on a stage of revelation and betrayal. But the tide of sadness that had recently so filled Cyrena's life seemed but a trickle in relationship to her friend. She had no idea how much life had chewed at him, gnawing away the foundation of hope. She had wanted to talk about his articles on the baboon and about the fragments that her brother had translated for her from *Die Huis-genoot*. The journal came in a great bundle every month, following her father's lifetime subscription. She of course did not read Afrikaans, but understood a little of its speech. Marais's ingenious and breathtakingly original thesis *The Soul of the White Ant* was electrifying to her. After the second reading she found a schoolteacher in Essenwald who could translate and read it to her, her brother's infrequent visits being far too lax for her appetite. The way Oom Eugène told the tale and shivered the questions of consciousness was an absolute delight. The resounding meanings stirred deep and significant thoughts in her. After the third session the well-paid teacher insisted on also reading each article in its original Afrikaans, saying that the translation lacked some of the rhythms and sounds of the unique language. She did not object because in those moments of meaningless words she heard the veldt rise up and the guns thunder from the mountains to the plain. She heard her childhood. But mostly she heard him.

"I read your treatise on the white ant," she burst out.

The rudiments of happiness that had been growing on his face during their conversation were snuffed out.

"Oh," he said, the sound draining.

She knew why. The papers had been full of it. The stealing of his wisdom by an eminent European intellectual.

"Surely all that miserable business with the despicable Maeterlinck is over and settled?"

"Far from it."

"But everybody knows that he stole your work," she insisted.

"In this country, yes. But abroad nobody has ever heard of Afrikaans except the Dutch and British, and they know it only as an enemy tongue. Nobody cares about obscure dilettantes choosing to speak and be published in the language of African stockmen. No, far better to trust in the much-awarded poet communicating in a civilized voice."

"But, Oom—"

"Just Eugène, please, we are now both too old for nursery names," he interrupted and for the first time she heard vinegar in his voice and some of it had been splashed her way. "I am tired of the whole business, he can have the fame. He can finish my book if he likes. I have lost interest in the spite of grown men. And the ants can take care of themselves."

The iron in his voice was sinking in a desperate well. She put her hand on his arm in the gentle, hesitant way that he had always offered his to her. She felt the muscles harden under the slightness of her touch. Draw back. It was not against her. It was against all that had spurned and refuted his offered wisdom and the wisdom of the ants.

The servants moved meaninglessly across the room, their motion rearranging the tension of their dilemma, dislocating the awkwardness. Marais cleared his throat and rubbed his arm, and Cyrena sat back in her chair.

"Do you remember when you first tried to help me see?" she said in a tone of voice that surprised them both. Marais accepted the change in direction and used it to shrug some of the greyness from his eyes.

"Yes, we used hypnosis."

She perked up at his description of their joint adventure and carried the brightness of it like a vanguard into the changing tide of their next conversation.

"I think it helped me understand for many years, in a way that I can never explain."

"Really, I am surprised," he said regaining his place in the celebration of their company.

She watched the change in him and closed the circle around them in the prospect of a similar future.

"Do you think that we might try it again tomorrow?"

He seemed confused for a moment. "You mean hypnotism?"

"Yes, but this time I would like you to ask me about blindness."

CHAPTER SEVENTEEN

*T*he hunched man-thing bent backwards to look up. An act that its anatomy was never designed to do, having no neck to flex, its head and face growing directly out of its upper chest. He and his tribe of the anthropophagi had been distracted from their task by the droning of the stiff red-and-white metal bird streaming high in the clouds, far above the treetops. They had been hiding in the undergrowth that fringed the great pool near one of the hearts of the forest. They had been watching three figures that floated to the surface and came ashore. They watched very carefully because something was wrong here. They had the appearance of humans and the sweetness of their meat was a great allure. But they did not smell like them. Only the one that the other two dragged out of the water onto the warm mud had a faint whiff of ammonia, fat, musk, and salt that so marked the man species. The others that had brown shiny skin smelt like nothing they had ever known before. The strangeness of it warned them of bad danger. The bird moved away and the yellow tribe peered back at the trio. The brown ones were holding the other between them. One sucked at his face while the other probed his anus. Both hammered and punched his chest. Some kind of mating act easily recognised in all species. This one looked much simpler than the complex entanglements of the anthropophagi. There was a one-in-three chance of being savaged or infected hideously in their procedures, and some-times dying from blood poisoning caused by their sexual clusters becoming knotted and turning septic. These hazards in breeding functioned as a unique form of natural selection and stopped the Vorrh from being overrun by the constantly hungry and famously ferocious predators. The most human of the trio started coughing violently and the yellow tribe sank back away from the noise. The brown ones stopped their manipulations and started to talk to the other one.

"Ishmael, Ishmael, talk to me, talk to me," said Seth.

"Come on, little one, awake," said Aklia.

Ishmael rolled away from them. He had a terrible pallor: a white-grey that gleamed unhealthily in the dappled light. There were minor lacerations and bruises all over his face and some bleeding under his clothing. The socket of his lost eye had turned black around the paste that Aklia had smeared there, and his original eye appeared shrunken and wild. He was not responding to their voices because he could not hear them. In their hurry to resuscitate him, they had only removed the paste from the nose and mouth. His ears remained blocked. He stumbled over onto all fours, trying to find the balance that he'd had knocked out of him somewhere in the underwater tunnel. As he panted like a maimed animal, the anthropophagi came closer, their hunger and the sweetness of human flesh testing their fear of the strange other two. There were nine of them, armed with wooden blades and long barbed spears. The one that smelt good was obviously too weak to fight at all. The strength and ability of the brown ones was unknown. Gradually their aching stomachs and saliva won, and the three that were hiding behind Aklia attacked, running with their spears and blades at her slim Bakelite body. She heard them before they had moved a pace, turning to catch the spear, while the others snapped against her hardness. Four more were charging at Seth, while the other two were creeping up on the

prone Ishmael. A terrible noise screamed through the Vorrh and
they saw that their weapons had no effect. They instantly turned
and ran into the deeper undergrowth. It was far too late for the
three within reach of the Kin. Aklia had put her hand through the
first one's face, grabbing out a soggy handful from inside while
kicking out at the second and sending it squealing in a broken
ball. Both of the Kin had made a high, hissing warble, which carried deep into the trees and had sent the remaining yellow pack
running and crashing through the foliage. Seth had plucked the
third attacker out of the air, snapped it, and thrown it towards
those that had dared to touch Ishmael. They fled before it hit
the ground. Aklia stamped the noise out of the one that she had
kicked and suddenly the clearing became very quiet. The birds,
animals, and insects were speechless, having nothing to say about
what they had just heard. The Kin walked over to Ishmael, who
was now trying to sit up. Having ascertained his well-being they
both walked to the water's edge, where they calmly washed the
sticky acrid blood from each other's perfect dark lustrous bodies.
For a moment it looked like Eden again; then all the silent creatures burst into song, as if having something wonderful to say.

On the other side of the great forest, Modesta stopped in her
tracks as a great tidal wave of sound rolled through the trees. It
was as if her ears had become unblocked and every living creature's voice had sharpened into a new and profound clarity. She
stood marvelling at it, bathing in its momentum that seemed to
be coming for her. Something in her face gave way and opened;
she put her hand on it and it felt like a wound or the shape of
a scream, but it was filled with warmth and tasted like nothing she had ever experienced before. Her lungs expanded and
shrank in a fast pulse that aligned its rhythm to her heart. Her
terror of malady or damage was puffed out. She was laughing.

CHAPTER EIGHTEEN

*I*n London, winter arrived with an unnecessary vengeance. Siberian iciness blew into the streets of Whitechapel, where the populace hid from its biting and relentless cold.

Snow had fallen over the compacted layers of solid ice that the wind polished black across every street. The only movement in the thick grey sky came from the smoke that poured upwards from the spikes of chimneys. Nobody in their right mind was on the streets. Hector Schumann looked down on it from his eyrie on the fourth floor.

He was restless and needed a change of scene. He had not been out for days. Solli's boys had brought him food and drink, including an astonishing bottle of brandy that he knew could not be purchased legally. Well, at least on this side of the city. The violent leader of this pack of petty criminals seemed to have a soft spot for him, thank God! Without Solli's help he would have been beaten and sent back to Germany, or worse. Hector had never met a Jew like this panther of a man, and a strange paternal attachment was beginning to form inside him. He had all he needed and yet a very virulent species of London cabin fever was causing him to become irritatingly distressed. He knew that walking outside was hazardous and that the hard slippery cobblestones would threaten his frail old bones, but it did not matter. He needed to walk, to think. It was midafternoon when the sun began to dim, and he stoked his continual fire and found an excuse there, the ashes having built up to a hillock in the last few days. He shovelled them into the empty scuttle and put it by the door, while he bustled into his overcoat, scarf, gloves, and hat.

The stairs outside were partially open to the elements; each landing had a metal-fenced veranda that received the bitter winds with stoic determination, like the prow of an icebreaking ship. The moment he opened the door onto it, the cold shrivelled his nose hairs and picked at his watering eyes. This is a mistake, he thought, as he cautiously tested the first stone stair, gripping the metal banister with the fortitude of an Eiger mountaineer. The steps were miraculously free of ice and he made his way down gingerly. On the second bend he saw the shadow on the red over-buffed step of his neighbour below: his guard dog, the indomitable Mrs. Fishburn. She was there, her door partially open, her nose or ear or both cocked against the crack, awaiting his arrival. There had been times when he had found her vigilance reassuring. The knowledge that she heard every step he made above her gave him a distasteful but necessary security to his frailty, which paradoxically seemed to be getting less and less each month. But today was not one of them. He wanted to hurry past to confront the fearful street before his resolve slipped and his cosy nest called him back up the flights of grey angular rock.

"Professor," she whispered as he reached the traverse of her landing. "Professor, come here."

He followed her command and came to the crack in the door. Her clawlike mittened hand shot out and grabbed his lapel and pulled him quickly through the crevice. To his horror she was in her nightclothes, which mercifully had been augmented by a threadbare man's overcoat, several pairs of stout woollen socks, and what looked like a tea cosy with tartan earflaps dragged down onto the metal infestation of her becurlered head. A cigarette burned in her other hand.

"Quick, quick, come in," she said, shutting the door behind him. She pulled him farther into the flat and stopped in the middle of her "parlour."

"Listen," she demanded.

To whom or what he was unsure. But he adopted the necessary stance of attention to placate the old harridan. After a few moments of soundless tension he looked at her, trying to find some clue as to what he was supposed to hear. She saw the look and responded.

"I am having trouble with me downstairs," she whispered, her mean eyes darting downwards, then stabbing back up to find his comprehension.

Hector's understanding of English had improved vastly. Even cockney was now in his reach, mixed with rich sticky layers of Yiddish. But best of all he now understood the innuendo that glued all London speech together. It had been Betty Fishburn and Solli Diamond who had given him master classes in this concealed art. The enforced conversations with the former had often centred on health and illness, she being some kind of expert on ailments and "troubles," particularly of the female variety. So that now as her eye darted down again, he dreaded the disclosure of "troubles downstairs" that he knew was about to arrive.

"Yes," he said feebly through his scarf, into which he had retreated, tortoise-like.

"It started last night an gawn right throw-a now," she whispered. She still held his hand. "Sometimes you can feel the vibrations of it."

He reached under the scarf knowing what was coming next, his hand being drawn towards the "trouble." This was too much to bear and he started to feel queasy, like a man on a precipice on the end of a thinning rope. To his horror she got down on the floor on her hands and knees, dragging him down behind her.

"You can feel it better down 'ere," she whispered through an exhalation of cigarette smoke.

"Mrs. Fishburn, please, I don't think that—"

"Listen," she said, and put her ear to the floor. She dragged the scrawny carpet farther away so that he too could listen to the floorboards.

Relieved that the subject of his enforced attention was not the troubled lower anatomy of Mrs. Fishburn's aging body but the flat below, he undertook the new task with some relish, and after he had settled and adjusted his ear, he did indeed hear a sound from beneath. The rooms on the second floor had been empty for years. Only a malign and unspecified rumour occupied their supposedly hollow interior. But now there was something moving down there: a kind of resonant, hollow thump, irregular and unpredictable like somebody moving in the dark and bumping into things. The other sound was stranger. Impossible to identify.

"There, hear that?" she whispered.

"Yes." He nodded, then found the description he so needed. "It sounds like the fluttering of a mechanical bird."

"A what?" Mrs. Fishburn half whispered, half squawked.

The sharp, diligent, animal-like mind that she possessed was not of the speculative variety and lacked imagination outside of her own anguished internal motions. This was not the time to engage in the marvels of automata, so he simplified the matter.

"Sounds like clockwork," he said.

She pressed her head harder against the floor and then agreed by nodding, darting her eyes to him, and jabbing him in the ribs with her bony finger. Then the sound stopped.

They stayed there for another ten minutes until they both

started to groan with the aches in their prone bodies. There were no more sounds, and they got up and moved into her kitchen for hot reviving tea; she instantly lit another cigarette.

"What's going on down there? No one's ever been there all the time I've been 'ere," she muttered over her hot cup, the steam and smoke gaily mingling and adding agitation to her pale, expressionless face.

"I don't know, perhaps just new tenants?"

She looked at him with total disdain. "No one will ever live down there," she said.

So empathetic was her statement that he dared not ask any more. But it did not stop her whispering things. "Some say that Jack the Ripper lived down there!" She noisily sipped at the cup. "Or it might have been one of his victims."

Over the years stories often turn themselves inside out, so that truth and fantasy get to try on each other's clothing. And passersby only glimpse the confusions. Nobody seemed to know or care for the fact that those rooms were used by the famous photographer Eadweard Muybridge, let alone that he had been raped by an African woman, who had taken his seed and cameras and carried them back to the dark continent. Whether Mrs. Fishburn would find this worse or better than the Whitechapel murders will never be known.

Hector mildly nodded.

"Somtink horrible it was," she said before sinking into noiseless mutters and quiet tutting. So they just sat for a while in her tiny kitchen, holding the emptying cups until she brought hers suddenly down on the clinking saucer. "We should go look."

It had never occurred to him that she would have taken it any further, so as they crept down the cold stairs he began to have grave misgivings.

"Should we not wait till morning?" he asked hopefully.

She was behind him, one hand gripping the iron banister, the other her iron poker. Their breath plumed enthusiastically in the freezing air.

"No, we have to do this now. I'll never get a wink of sleep until I know."

They turned the corner of the flight and saw the door below. He looked at her again for a sign of doubt but found only steely determination. She was quite a sight and he knew that most would flee an attack from her. Even some of Solli's men would shudder and run from the vision that crept behind him on the darkening stairs. By the time they reached the door she was ready for anything, any foe.

The door was firmly closed. She nodded and he tried to push it open, but the three locks inside held it shut. She pushed him aside and rapped loudly on the heavily painted wood with her sturdy poker. The sound inside was hollow and lonely.

"Come out, I knows you're there," she bellowed and held the poker aloft.

Hector took a step back so that she could get a good swing at whoever opened the door, if they dared. Nothing moved and no sound came from within. After a long while her arm grew tired and they both realised that nothing was going to happen. She started to turn away, then suddenly stopped dead in her tracks, her body stiffening and her eyes staring at the door. Hector felt his hackles start to rise, as did his painstakingly woven hair, her genuine terror having affected him instantly. The poker fell from her hand and clattered against the bitter cold of the resounding stone stairs.

"O gawd!" she wailed before her white breath was clamped over by her shaking hand.

She was staring not at the door but at its frame. Hector closed in behind her and saw what she was looking at.

"The mezuzah," she said from behind her white-and-blue fingertips.

A small rectangular patch, smaller than her little finger, was showing on the doorframe. It was not painted or drawn on. It was an absence. A new gap in the years of the over-painted surface. A wound. This impression was heightened by a deep ragged cut that inflicted itself across the tilted rectangle of the bare, exposed wood. As if what had been there had been removed by one heavy and ferocious blow from an axe or a hatchet.

"The mezuzah!" she said again and suddenly ran at the stairs, taking some of them two at a time in her determined hurry. Hector ran after her. In grave doubt of her well-being he told himself later, but it was fear. Sudden fear of being alone in a place from which she had most violently fled.

It had been a long time since he had heard that word and was unaware of his everyday association with it. Even when Solli and Mrs. Fishburn had entered his or their dwellings—noticing them always touch the frame of the door and she automatically kissing her touching fingers—Hector's orthodoxy had slipped so far away that he did not see such actions as purposeful. In fact he did not see them at all. But now he had to. The little pewter container that held the scroll, the tiny handwritten parchment that reminded every soul of the presence of God, had been viciously removed from its blessed position on the doorframe of the mysterious apartment below. He had witnessed the devastating effect that the desecration had on the trembling Mrs. Fishburn, whom he now held shaking in his arms. She was praying between her sobs and sniffles, and he was awkwardly aware of the embarrassing dampness of their intimacy. It had been a long time since he had held a woman so. His own Rachel had been delicate and modest and very different from this woman, who was so large that he could barely get his arms around her. It had been a long time since he had touched anybody other than the partially buried body of Nicholas. He felt clumsy, stiff, and unfeeling, and knew that no real warmth was passing from his wooden embrace into the shocked and pitiful mass of the once indomitable Betty Fishburn.

Eventually she pulled herself away, wiping her nose on a soggy handkerchief that she had fished out from her puffed and fragrant sleeve. She started to make tea and Hector knew he was doomed to at least another hour of her snivelling company. For such is the cost of mock compassion, the less felt, the longer the time must be spent acting out hours of morbid duty.

"Are the local police sensitive to anti-Semitic incidents?" he asked, trying to use his pompousness to offer her a sensible way back to normality.

She stopped between the table and the oven, her mouth gaping so much that he feared she might lose the cigarette that hung there.

"Anti-Semites don't come into it," she eventually said, her eyes hardening in her blurred, flushed face. "This terrible thing ain't the workings of some fucking meshuggener."

Hector was shocked. It was the first time he had heard Mrs. Fishburn swear. And he did not understand the other word she used, but imagined it to be worse. But what really shocked him were the vehemence and the direction of her language. It seemed to be aimed at him. As if he had become the target of her outrage and anger. In some way that he did not understand, his placating question had become a red rag to her snorting bovine fury. Perhaps it was the feebleness of the comforting embrace.

He must try again quickly to offer a soothing solution to her growing distress.

"Perhaps it might only be a non-Jewish family moving in."

The cigarette fell and was followed by a string of fast Yiddish words that sounded more like swearing of a magnitude that was beyond his meagre comprehension. He thought it better to now remain silent. She slowed her spiel and tried to explain, as if to an idiot.

"No one ever takes a mezuzah away, not even goys. It's schli-mazel, taboo, bad luck. Goys just paint over them." She paused to retrieve the cigarette from the floor, wiping it lovingly on her sleeve. "And did you see it, not just taken off but desecrated, hurt." She started praying again and daubing her eyes. "It's shlekht. Beyz. Shlekht. Evil."

Two hours later Hector was allowed to retreat upstairs on the strict understanding that should she scream, shout, or bang on her ceiling, he was to come and rescue her. Exactly from whom or what was never discussed. She even said that for both their protection he could retrieve the poker from wherever it had fallen. At one point during their one-sided conversation it was subtly suggested that maybe they should spend the night sleeping in the same apartment. Hector had seen it coming and dodged it, skating deftly on his supposed ill health and her duty to protect his well-being. He also told her that he was expecting Solli and some of his gang later, and he was sure that they would provide much more security than he could ever offer. That had been the only thing he said that had given her any solace since the appalling incident. She opened the door with a bread knife in her hand and quickly pushed Hector through the sliver of a gap, pulling the door to and fastening many bolts and latches.

It was dark and very cold outside. Frost was beginning to gleam in the early moonlight that picked out some of the edges of the flights. For a moment he thought about going back down to retrieve her poker and gain some confidence against his previous actions. He took one step down and stopped. Only half the stairwell could be seen where the moon shone in through the railed verandas. The other half was pitch black, making a distorted and discordant zebra pattern of the stairwell. He would have to pass through one of these impenetrable areas to turn the corner and see the door directly below him. The poker lay farther down in another realm of shadow. He changed his mind. It was more sensible to seek it in daylight or to ask Solli's boys to use one of their lamps. He moved rapidly upwards without ever noticing that he passed through an equal area of darkness without any qualms at all. Once inside, he locked his door and found that there were several bolts he had never noticed before.

Solli's mob arrived noisily on the stairs. Their boisterous clatter let both of the upper occupants breathe again, and by the time they were rapping on Hector's door, Betty Fishburn was standing right behind them.

"I'll tell ya that it's true, it's shlekht down there."

"Yes, Ma, we heard ya."

Hector opened the door and the posse shivered in with much theatrical shaking of coats and hats. Mrs. Fishburn had embedded herself at the centre of the cold flapping scrum.

"It's monkeys out there," said one of the men, making for the fire.

"There are monkeys?" said Hector, looking over their shoulders. Some of the men laughed.

The one called Albi said, "Yeah, brass monkeys, Prof."

"Yeh, taters," said another.

Hector had been caught in one of these meaningless spirals of nonsensical and apparently comic words before, and decided to leave this one well alone. The last time he had been left in the company of these three grinning boys there had been some confusion about names, which had caused great and mystifying hilarity in them. He had now caught the tail end of one of their whispered conversations.

"That makes us the three bears."

Then they saw that the old man had heard them.

"Just a story, Prof," said Albi.

"Yeah. Just a joke, Professor Barnet," said the one called Jerry, and the others sniggered foolishly.

"My name is not Barnet, it's Schumann," said Hector, very seriously.

This instantly produced uncontrollable giggles in the rough men.

"Is it Irish?" asked one.

"No, no, it's German, but I thought you knew that."

This produced even greater laughter.

"What is so funny about that?" Hector demanded.

He never got his answer that time because Solli arrived and the gang quickly sobered up. So it had been about bears and now monkeys and taters, which he knew was a kind of potato. He had no idea what these insolent young men were talking about, but took a wild guess anyway.

"You must mean it's cold," he said.

They were just about to cream the debate when Mrs. Fishburn launched in, pushing them aside.

"Tell Solli about the noises and the smashed mezuzah."

Solli gave Hector a quick hidden look of total disinterest.

"There were some very unusual noises coming from downstairs. I wondered, could it be a family moving in?" said Hector carefully.

"A family?" screeched the suddenly deranged Mrs. Fishburn. "What kind of fucking family sounds like that and desecrates a home before they move in?"

Albi and Jerry clamped their hands over their ears in mock horror of her foul language.

"Whoo, that's a bit strong, Ma."

"I'll give you fucking strong and I ain't your ma," she squawked back.

Hector retreated closer to the fire and His Nibs.

"They were very strange noises," he said, darting glances at the furious woman. "And the scroll was cut or hammered off the door."

A glimmer of interest flickered over Solli's face.

"Malki, Jerry, go take a look." He fished in his pocket and took out a ring of keys, selected one, pointed to it until they nodded, then threw them the ring. At the door Jerry put his coat over his head and made moaning noises in a music hall travesty of a haunting lost soul. Their laughing could be heard again in the echoing stairwell.

"You have keys to doors downstairs?" said Hector.

"Those are my keys to all doors."

And before any more questions were sported, he said, "And whose is this little beauty?," whipping the lost poker out from under his coat.

"Mine," declared Mrs. Fishburn, rushing forward to retrieve her valuable weapon. "He was s'pose to get it for me," she snapped, sending dagger looks at Hector, who was stroking his beard.

"It was dark and slippery out there, and it seemed the wrong time to go searching for it," he said.

"Very wise," said Solli, much to Mrs. Fishburn's irritation. "We can't have you falling arse over tit out there, specially with all the ghosts and all. Uncle Hymie would never forgive me if you got hurt." He shot a glance at the fuming harridan, which quenched her anger like a bucket of stale water.

"Now, Ma, what about a drink to warm me and the boys up?" He poked his thumb towards Hector, indicating that he too was one of the boys. It was clear that it was not a question, not a request, but an order.

She looked anxiously at the door.

"Albi, go with her."

When they were alone Solli asked Hector what he really thought was going on. Hector shrugged.

"Somebody living secretly down there? I have no idea."

"With strange noises," added Solli.

"Yes and . . . well . . . a sense of foreboding."

"Foreboding," said Solli, repeating and tasting a word that he had never said before.

A few minutes later Malki and Jerry appeared at the door.

"Well?" said Solli from his place by the fire.

"Nothing, nothing, boss," said the subdued Malki, blowing on his fingers and coming into the room.

"What kind of nothing?" insisted Solli.

"Just nothing, not a trace of anything. Nobody's been down there in years."

Jerry was averting his eyes, showing great interest in the floor, and everybody saw it.

"Key," said Solli, holding out his hand.

Jerry crossed the room with the keys and handed them to His Nibs. Solli seized his wrist and looked up into the younger man's face.

"If there's nothing down there, what's got you so rattled?"

"Nothing," said Jerry.

Solli twisted his wrist back against the joint and in that fraction of a second his entire personality switched into the razor ice of his potency. The hair trigger automatically cocked.

"Don't fucking lie to me, what's down there?"

"Nothing, boss, it's just fucking creepy, that's all."

Solli let go of his wrist so that Jerry was propelled back, away from the strain. Solli had the jingling keys in his irritated fist and turned to look at Hector, who was shocked by the speed and savageness of his guardian's reaction.

"Foreboding," he said, and was up and striding across the room and down the stairs before anybody could catch their breath. There was a nasty silence in Hector's room for the next ten minutes. He looked at the fire. Jerry rubbed his wrist.

The metal tips of Solli's heels could be heard striking the cold steps as he ran back up the flights to Hector's door. He made a darting beeline for the fire.

"Monkeys out there," he said, warming his hands.

All eyes were on him and after a while he turned to confront them.

"Nothing, fucking nothing," he said, and the matter was closed.

Two days later Hector's reading was disturbed by a thumping coming through his floor.

"Oh, not again," he said to himself, and with great reticence heaved himself out of his comfortable armchair. He huffed loudly as he dragged his coat on and made his way down to the origin of the banging. Again he was pulled through the crevice-like gap in the door. At least she was fully dressed this time. She brought him to the centre of the room, where all the worn but spotlessly clean rugs had been pulled away to expose the bare floorboards. She nodded at the floor and he turned his head to listen.

"No," she whispered. "It ain't no noise."

Hector hung limp and annoyed. "What then?" he said.

"Can't ya smell it?"

"Smell?" he said.

She nodded at the boards again and he cocked his nose to keep her happy. Then he smelt it. He quickly looked around her apartment, especially at the kitchen, where nothing was happening. He then bowed closer to the floor and knew she was right; it was coming from below.

"Cooking," he said, and she nodded violently in agreement.

It was ten thirty in the morning and the winter sun was bright and clear outside, and the "foreboding" cooking smelt like chicken.

"This is ridiculous," said Hector. He marched out of her apartment and down the stairs to the desecrated door. It was slightly open and he entered without a thought to confront this continual nuisance, whatever it was. The smell of roasting chicken filled the rooms, which he quickly observed were unremarkable and almost an exact copy of his own, even to a north-facing window, which seems out of place on the second floor. Then he heard a noise coming from the kitchen and for the first time felt a chill of unease. He gathered himself, gritting his teeth as he turned the corner. Jerry was sitting on a low stool next to the oven, his arms wrapped around his skinny knees. He jumped when he saw Hector.

"Oh, fuck, don't do that, Prof, nearly scared the drek outta me."

"Sorry, my boy, I did not know it was you. What are you doing here?"

Jerry shifted uncomfortably on the stool. "I'm cooking you a chicken."

"A what?"

"A chicken."

"But why, why here?"

"Because the boss said I had to. Said you would like it and the oven here was better than yours upstairs."

Hector knew this was nothing to do with ovens or chickens. And that Jerry's freezing vigil next to the warm oven in the bare room was no more than a ritual punishment or a test of his fibre and commitment. He knew that Rabbi Solli was enjoying the idea of his young henchman shivering in this horrible place while the roasting bird spat and hissed in the barely adequate warm iron box.

"Leave it, for God's sake, leave it," said Hector, genuinely annoyed at Solli's bullying.

"But I've got to do it."

"Consider it done. Give it to me as it is and we won't say another word about. Tell His Nibs that you achieved your objective and I will tell him it was delicious."

Jerry's confusion gradually turned into relief as he watched the professor walk towards the door.

"Let's get out of here," said Hector, turning and ready to go.

Jerry was out of his seat and turning the gas off and grabbing at the hot door in a second. He found his scarf and used it to retrieve the black dented metal tray with the half-cooked bird spitting and murmuring inside it. Together they left, locked the door, and climbed up to Hector's room, passing the nose and one eye of Mrs. Fishburn at the crack of her door.

"Luncheon," said Hector without stopping.

Jerry put the metal tray in Hector's kitchen and then said, "Thanks, Prof. This is just between us, right?"

"Yes, Jerry, let's not hear any more about it."

On their farewell the young man gave Hector a key.

"What's this for?"

"The boss said you were to 'ave it, just in case, like."

And then he was gone, tearing down the stairwell, leaving the old man with the smell of chicken and Solli's challenge in his hand.

CHAPTER NINETEEN

$\mathcal{H}$e was flushed and jittery and unaware of his lateness. Cyrena had been waiting outside, thinking that perhaps it had been her mistake. When she saw him, she knew it wasn't.

He was wearing exactly the same clothes as yesterday only now more rumpled, as if he had been sleeping in them. Also he had not shaved and smelt strongly of the Abdulla cigarettes that he continually smoked.

"Very well, my dear, are you ready, shall we proceed?" His voice was tighter and had the edging resonance of an overly tuned stringed instrument: the gut near snapping, the wood ready to warp.

"I think perhaps you'd better sit first and have some water," she said. "You seem a little fatigued by the walk."

"Fatigued, yes, a little. By the walk, yes."

They sat for a while and he became calmer, his tremor replaced by a continual perspiration. She wondered about the wisdom of "the magic" while he remained in this condition. After smoking three cigarettes, he announced that they should begin.

"About blindness, isn't it?" he asked uncertainly.

"Yes."

She took him into the stillness of her bed-sitting room and he sat her half reclining in a chaise longue facing the bright window. He pulled up a bentwood chair by her side.

As soon as he started the rhythmic suggestions of her weariness, they both relaxed. He had been speaking for less than a minute when she slumped, deeply asleep. He was amazed. It was obvious that the suggestions and preparations of their previous session were still embedded and active. They had survived all these years. The beautiful woman growing around what had been seeded in the miraculous child. He spoke softly to her to confirm the depth and saturation of her condition. Then he leant forward and whispered forcefully, "Cyrena, I want you to tell of blindness."

The words had barely left his lips when she responded, as if she'd been waiting forever to be asked.

"It's like now, it's everything balanced in the innards. The depth and colour of everything kept inside where it all belongs. Out there on the other side of my eyes it is only described, roughly modelled in too much stuff." Her voice and language fluctuated between the girl and the woman. Her words captivated him. "The blindness always meant it was mine before. Now it is shared and dirtied by others, who add nothing to it. Most don't even know it's there."

"Are you saying it was better before?" he asked carefully.

"Yes. I have *seen* too much now. People also want me to see inside them with the light they bathe in and breathe every day. Before, I chose to let people in and then felt them close, now there is no choice—my eyes are hollow with all the taking."

There was stony silence for a while.

"Cyrena, are you talking about your eyes or your heart?"

"I don't know, one might be the other. They are both pumps."

Marais was becoming excited by her answers.

"Cyrena, perhaps you should separate them."

"How?"

"You must let go of the hurt so that you may see clearly."

"I want to go back to the inside light, there was no hurt there."

"But you were a child then, the pain you speak of comes to all of us as we grow and walk towards death. It comes from life itself."

Her face moved and altered as she listened to his words.

"Cyrena, the hurt you are feeling is nothing to do with sight, it is a symptom of humanity itself."

"I wanted it healed."

"What, my child?"

"My sight. I wanted you to take it away like the forgetfulness in that lady's legs."

The impact of her words jarred him and the morphine shadow wanted to take him home. He gathered the words and started to close the session.

"Cyrena, I could never do that, it would be a sin."

"A sin." She pondered the word like a pebble in her closed mouth. He was just about to bring her out when she spoke. "I saw the tree again last night."

"Tree?"

"The same one you stopped me seeing before."

Marais had no idea what she was talking about.

"You did not want me to see the invisibility there, you made it go away."

It must have been something from their first session all those years ago. But he had forgotten the details in the time in between.

"Last night," and here she opened her alarming eyes, "we were both there, at the tree. Close your eyes and you will see it too."

Marais had nothing to say.

"Close your eyes and join me. Come here."

His mouth felt rubbery and heavy, as did his eyelids.

"The tree is waiting. Do you see it black against the bright sky?"

And he did, behind his closed eyes. Deep in his eyes the tree of vein stood proud and defiant in negative.

"Come."

He was by her side in the high dazzling fields. Under the tree with something hiding in its branches.

"Now ask again," she said.

Anyone passing by her room would have heard nothing for the next few hours. Would have seen an oddly matched couple just sitting as if in prayer or meditation. Because now they talked only inside their heads, he had entered into and joined her trancelike state, the bastion of hypnotist and patient having been breached. Both riding a Möbius strip of altered suggestion, a magnetic ticker tape that ran through the grooves of their consciousness, sending questions to answer questions to answer questions, mind reflecting mind through the blank sides of spinning mirrors. It was somewhere in there that her future was glimpsed and the purpose of imagination became simple and as fundamental as a hammer or a bowl. He could almost grasp it, but the morphine had ruined his hold, smoothed out the sucking lines of identity on his fingers, so that nothing would ever stay held again, all things would fall useless from the grip of observation that had defined his life. He began to see what was hiding in the tree and knew that for her sanity he must become blind. He opened his eyes, his eyes opened him. He fell into the room of his waking. He shuddered and let out an involuntary noise. He must have dozed off for a second or two. He was getting old. He needed to consult the needle again.

"The tree," she said.

"Yes," he barely answered.

"Last night we sat beneath it and you gave me a halo of golden living insects. It sung with their hard little wings and made my head sing too. You said you did it to turn me backwards and now you say it is a sin."

Unease gnawed at crusted cells of abused memory. In their last session something had been wrong. Something displaced.

"Well, I am not taking it off, I can feel and hear it now."

"Cyrena, I am going to count to seven, then you will awake refreshed and without the sadness that you brought here today. One."

"It's like a spinning wheel in the fairy stories . . ."

"Two."

"The spindle's going very fast . . ."

"Three."

"The bobbin sucking the light out of the tangle in my head . . ."

"Four."

"The flyer's tugging me away from now . . ."

"Five."

"The orifice sucking me . . ."

"Six."

"The mother of all hammering . . ."

"Seven, take it off and awake."

She put her hands up to her head and he instantly remembered the strange gesture that she had made before. Then she slid back on the couch, her eyes rolling and her body pumping in little orgasmic spasms as she flickered into careless sensual moaning. Marais picked up one of the loose bedspreads and placed it over her twitching body. She had turned on her side, demonstrating the swooping landscape curve of her hips. She was unaware of his presence as he turned away to mop his soaking brow and intimidated the morphine's dominance with his delicate erection. Slowly she gathered herself and again became an occupant of the same world as he. After a while she sat up and saw him.

"What happened," she said dreamily, a smile dappling her lips. The deep hot space behind them mocking in its pretend modesty.

"You told me of your troubles and said that *seeing* was not easy for you," he said distantly, as if through a telephone.

"Oh," she said, standing up and brushing the wrinkles out of her skirt.

"And a dream you had last night about a halo."

She picked at the loose strands of hair that had escaped from her sculptured bob.

"Really? I don't remember that."

"A halo of insects."

"How unpleasant," she said. "It sounds more like one of your dreams than mine."

Now it was her turn to splash some vinegar.

The trancelike session had not helped as they both supposed it might. To the contrary, it had set up a bristle fence between them. Too much had been exposed, too many roads seen and all their openings available only in a lost time. Over the next few days their meetings became awkward, his time and concentration becoming erratic, her frustration and need making her stumble. The advice she absorbed was no substitute for the love she so desperately craved, and his attachment was progressively slipping the physical world, the desires of which he rarely noticed.

He made the effort to see her off at the landing strip. Again they agreed to keep in touch, to write frequently and plan another visit soon. Neither of them believed it and sealed the untruth with a chaste and fumbled kiss, while the props from the plane caused an impatient wind that worried at her held-down hat.

He stood in the shade, his hand over his eyes, thinking only of his next fix as the plane floated away into the perfect sky and she bit her eyelids hard closed against the salty failure.

CHAPTER TWENTY

*T*he spirit voices told Tyc to split them and keep both alive. Although there was much less of their sacred one, he obviously had all the power and soul of life. The other was nothing but a head on a withered stick—a puppet, a ghost coat of a man. So she assumed that Oneofthewilliams wanted it kept alive out of pity and some unknown loyalty. But as time moved on and she saw more and more of them, she began to change her mind. Slowly, bit by bit, she suspected that it might be spite. To keep the fragment of a man alive so that it might be aware daily of its miserable demise, its worthless attachment to the world of the living.

Oneofthewilliams was quiet and powerful in his hut. He was carried out every day to the sea. To touch it and hold the sand. Or to the edge of the Vorrh where he fingered the leaves. He had the arms and hands to do so, and they were expressive and fluent even though some fingers had been lost during his arrival. He did not need legs anymore, nor did he need a mouth, eyes and ears, or any other part of the face or head that tasted and commented on the outside world. His extended neck had what it needed, swollen and solidly bound to it. Mostly hindbrain and inner cortex. The Wassidrus got the frontal lobes, all the memories, the eyes, and the facial parts that made the voice work. Unfortunately, that was the only organ that was not healing properly. The most surprising to Tyc was the heart and the spine. Oneofthewilliams had told her how to do it and it had sounded like madness, but it worked so far. The hollowed bamboo and the wildebeest heart sewn into the demon half of the rib cage. The sad human heart lived in the sacred one. It was scarred and doubtful and occasionally it needed to be massaged through the thin walls of skin and fascia that made a lumpen drumskin over it.

In an afternoon that was filled with noise the Wassidrus opened his eyes to the gentle touches and not-so-gentle probes that he had been experiencing for the last twenty minutes or so. Outside, the children were playing and the wives were laughing and shouting at one another from across the sun-bleached yard where they gutted fish, standing at separate tables. There was a great optimism, bright in the bright air. The prone figure opened his eyes, still expecting to see his imagined arms warding off the intrusions of his dream. But this was no dream. It was a nightmare of reality, because the only hands and arms he found were those that were engaged in the real act of touching him all over, and they had once been his. For perched opposite him was his bisected other half, being held on the bed by the strong arms of two servants in blinding yellow robes. There were so many arms that he became confused, and the lack of any to use himself was intolerable. For a moment, still bleary-eyed, he thought he was in the presence of some octopus being or a Shiva or Kali deity. It was only when he recognised what used to be him feeling where his genitals should have been did he become truly awake and stare at the thing before him. The servants held it because if they had let go it would have rolled off the bed. It had no legs and rested on a kind of built-in pillow under its fragment of skinny rib cage. He was reminded of a toy he had once seen in a birdcage in the house of one of the higher members of the Timber Guild. A small ivory man with a rounded bottom and a carved laughing face. It was there to keep the caged bird amused. Having nowhere to fly, nothing to fuck, and even less to sing about, the demented creature could only eat and "play" with this toy on the shit-stained floor of its gilded prison. The insane bird would continually attack the grinning effigy of its jailers, pecking the resilient bone with all its might, butting it with vicious purpose. The figure rolled over on its half-spherical weighted base and then rolled back up again, causing the screeching creature to attack again in a greater rage. This little repetition could last for hours until the bird was exhausted, the painted mouth of the figure still grinning. The thing that lolloped forward to touch him again had the same balance as the torturous toy. But no smiling face. It had no face at all. From above the oddly broad shoulders and the sickeningly familiar arms, the neck rose and thickened out to a flat lopsided appendage that looked like a badly made beret or the cap of a shrivelled mushroom. A thick binding of the same yellow material that the servants wore seemed to keep it all in place. Why did he see this all so well and recognise it as once being part of him? This thing obviously saw nothing and looked as if it barely had consciousness at all. What could possibly exist and function in that socklike vestige of brain? Why had he been given all the senses? All the memories? He groaned it as a question mainly to himself. At the sound, the servants lifted the body off the bed and set it on the ground at a safe distance. The fingers of the thing instantly sought the offered palm of the right-hand servant. They skipped across his open hand like an electrified spider, the servant nodding all the while. He then bellowed out a name. And after a moment or two an almost naked child entered the hut. The servant spoke quickly with pronounced effort. The now-serious child turned towards the bed and approached. He looked at the Wassidrus and said, "Oneofthewilliams is telling you that in some soon days you will be well enough to leave and never return."

There was a no answer to give, what could be said? The hands moved again, making forms and shapes in space, and tapped out understanding to the nodding servant, who whispered to the child.

The solemn child again turned and spoke.

"The sacred one says you will have a servant to feed and carry you from place to place and that you have already met him before."

There was a blockage of the light in the door as another entered; a large bald man came before him. He bowed towards Oneofthewilliams and the child spoke to him very slowly. The response was totally unexpected and seemed nauseously out of place. The large man started giggling uncontrollably and spoke a few unintelligible words in a voice that belonged to a young girl. All eyes now turned towards the Wassidrus. The sacred one made a final gesture of opening his hands and the child said, "This is Kippa. You once tried to kill him. Perhaps now you will be nicer."

Apart from the love of his unknown daughter, Oneofthewilliams shivered out a great mass of other information, including that of another holy man. Father Lutchen was an old man with many truths and many lies, equally skilled in the wisdom and treachery of magic, who lived in the crime called Essenwald. He had tried to harm Modesta. This man should be punished to the same level as Father Timothy should be celebrated and sent home.

Two warriors who had experience outside the tribe were given the task of retrieving Father Lutchen. Tyc explained to them that they wanted him alive. They were given the tribal name of Essenwald and a scent of his whereabouts there.

Mumt'r and Blincc took the commission eagerly, knowing the wisdom of being in praise and the penalty of being in failure. They were paddling hard towards the white man's town, without a doubt or a question. They chatted and bounced on the waves of their esteemed journey. They came in through the river that is shadowed by high gaunt cliffs. The water here was fast and occasionally ran shallow over flinty pebbles. Their sea canoe was not prepared for such inconsistencies and many times they had to step out of it and guide its considerable weight to deeper waters. They walked through the same shallows where the assassin Tsungali attacked Peter Williams. They passed under the hump-backed bridge and its row of disreputable cottages. They paddled until they smelt the city around the next bend. They stopped, holding the boat against the pull of the water with backward strokes of their oars while their silent eyes assessed the situation ahead. Then without a word they made for the shore, found a beach with long reeds nearby, and hid the canoe, fastening it with pegs and ropes and stealing charms. They gathered their weapons and found the path. The previous humour that had driven them through the bobbing water was now gone. The path still swayed with the motion of the water as they adjusted their land legs and walked to do the serious business in the alien hive of stones that loomed ahead them.

■—→

Old Father Lutchen sat gloomily looking at the model of the Adam automata that the Valdemar brothers had made to hug the city's guillotine. He touched the small model of the ingenious articulation of the wooden leaves that triggered the terrible axe. It had been instigated by his influence, the same way that he had compelled them to design and construct the cathedral window. He had also instigated and coaxed their even more sublime work in the Chapel of the Desert Fathers. And now it had all changed, their path deviated to corruption and blasphemy. True, it was he who had brought the desire of the Timber Guild and the city's authorities to their attention and consideration. But he had expected that they might have conjured and designed an instrument of compassion and calm to aid and soften the continual grim action of the municipal guillotine. He never dreamt that they would create such a device. A machine worse than the mechanical axe itself. The monstrous automata they had devised was an outrage of biblical lore that extended the sufferings of the convicted felon while dragging even greater crowds in to gawp at the sickening act. It wasn't guilt that he felt; he had given up that mockery of emotions years ago. It was how his part, his manipulation, had become so deformed. This was the work of the subconscious mind that he thought he'd had under control. After the execution of Ishmael Williams, he had washed his hands of anything to do with the Adam machine, denied ever speaking about its conception, construction, and operation.

This had ostracised him from the company of the brothers long before the abomination was first put into practice. He no longer felt comfortable with them. The last evening he had brought his singing glasses to their workshop was a disaster. Of course they let him play, but after only a few minutes his wet finger could not keep up with the innuendoes of minor notes, the inflections of doubt and pause that slid in under the clarity of his firmness. He saw the creak in the mouth of the younger brothers and knew that he had become a joke to them. The intimate resonant language of their previous exchanges were slapped aside, nothing remained, and he stopped his regular visits. Since then he had seen them only in church, where they were aloof, indifferent, and embarrassed.

Then the case came. The brothers brought it to his door.

"Father Lutchen, we have made this for you."

They removed the packing and the restraining bolts and put the wooden casing aside. The brothers opened the curved hood that protected the line of glass bowls that diminished in size as they continued along the length of the spindle on which they were threaded.

The bowls sat above a curved lead trough that was being filled with water by Ernst, the eldest Valdemar brother. Each curved glass touched the fluid. The spindle was connected to a treadle mechanism below, so that the action of the player's foot would send the bowls spinning through the water and allow both of the player's hands to finger the lubricated vibrating glass. They stood back so Lutchen could see their fine handiwork. The old man just looked at it and recognised it as an instrument of isolation. Of solo separation. He thanked them and was surprised that they did not leave.

"Will you play it?" said Walter, the younger brother.

Lutchen was confused.

"We hope you might play it with us and take up the counter-harmony."

The old man was amazed; the instrument was a crafted bridge, a way back into the company that he so sadly missed. The only intelligent company in Essenwald that he could master. This gift was an orchestra in comparison to the simple tuned glasses he had given them, and he could not wait to hear it sing in their company. And this also meant he was closer to initiating them into the esoteric mysteries of sonic prayer and the door that it opened onto the core of many different religious beliefs.

Their playing together could counterbalance the perverted quality of their last invention and reinstate his guidance on future, more spiritual work.

➤→

Mumt'r and Blincc had both been here before but not at the same time, not together. They drew strength from each other's company and tried not to show the world around them and each other their fear. For both had been abused and maltreated in this hateful place. Mumt'r had escaped slavery by the skin of his teeth and had been severely beaten in the process. But worse, he had been imprisoned underground for many days. The lightless pit was an extended cellar of one of the grain houses of the place called Scyles. The place where it was rumoured their prey was living. He who was a demon hiding in a white man's robe. The cellar was a holding house, used by the nomadic herders of men who passed with great frequency through his quarter of the city. After his escape, Mumt'r never slept in a building again. Not even the simplest huts by the all-cleansing sea. He would never wake in containment again.

Blincc's story was less traumatic but equally unpleasant. Fate had made him the only witness to the Frenchman and Seil Kor returning from their disastrous journey into the Vorrh. Deep in its interior the Limboia had mistaken Seil Kor for another and unleashed the Orm on him: a hollowing of the soul that no other creature had ever survived. Blincc had seen this dead man move, slithering back into the forest and his true identity. He had been very young when he had been taken to Essenwald by his elder brothers, who after only a few days had caught some infectious illness, making them useless for the work that they so craved. Blincc had to take up the task to find money to feed them. This he had achieved, sweeping and carrying things around the office of the lumber station. He had taken the job without a word of the language that all seemed to speak. His brothers were sleeping at the edge of the bush where the iron tracks ran. He bought and stole simple rations to keep them alive, but had no money to pay for a healer or charming to banish the demons that gnawed at their groaning guts. He was doing his best and felt some pride in his warrior-like control of the situation. He kept his head down and his eyes averted, only occasionally receiving a blow from the overseers who ran the station. All was fine until the train arrived. It had been five days before he heard it calling out from the edge of the Vorrh. The other workers laughed at him when he looked so scared. They pointed to the track and made signs of horns on their heads. One jumped and hissed loudly. Blincc tried to ignore them. But when he thought he could not be seen he touched the black metal line. It was alive. He snatched back his fingers from its trembling surface and looked around. When the screeching, hissing monster entered the station he froze, the short hair on his young head standing bolt upright, hot urine running down his dirty leg, making a clean path on its journey. One of the hysterical men lobbed a tin can at him to break the restraint of his terror. Suddenly there were dozens of people everywhere, led by the white bellowing Men Without Substance. The vast black wagon stopped like a monstrous shadow held inside clouds of smoke and steam that rolled and hissed from its massive hot interior. Nobody else paid it any attention; they were too busy with the endless line of flatbeds that were strung out behind it, each laden with massive trunks and limbs of trees. He walked along the noisy line of wood and metal that clanked and shuddered as men attacked the sea-serpent-like chains that kept it all bound together. Ten flatbeds down, the slave carriages had been opened and the blinking occupants were spilling into the chaos of the platform. He approached them for a better look, his forgotten broom dangling from his hand, his body walking in mesmerised strides. When he got close, he stopped. His misunderstanding hitting a new level of impossibility. The men, if they were men, who stood before him had no souls. They had lost the light that should live in their eyes and were attached to nothing. Again, fear and curiosity became his engine and he stretched a hand out to touch one. He had seen many of the living and the dead and knew that these were different things. All his senses said so. He could not yet smell them. The smoke, greasy iron, and bleeding trees had overpowered the air in all directions. So he stretched forward to touch one.

"Outta da fucking way," barked a voice in his ear, just before his head stung from the blow of the brass end of the whip that the overseer held in his hard pink fist. "Move yourselves," he shouted down the line of soulless ones.

All obeyed, which was not surprising because this one was another kind of beast. The whitest white man he had ever seen, it was ferocious and red-haired and called Maclish. All wisely leapt to the side of its pointing whip and shouting commands. Blincc scrambled upright, holding the demanding confusion of his minor head wound and shambling out of the way of the massive activity that was taking place around him. Cranes had been winched over the flatbeds and machines were starting up to unload the trees. He looked back to see that his slender cheap broom had been snapped under the boots and solid naked feet of the workers. He walked away from the clusters of action, farther down the train to the untenanted flatbeds that lay outside the station's attentions. The train was so long that he was almost out of earshot of all the voices that shouted around the action of the cranes. He was openmouthed and admiring the gigantic trunks and sensuously twisting ivy, each seeming more impressive than the last, as he slowly moved from one carriage to the next. He thought he could now see the end of the train and strained his eyes into the morning mist, which still held some of the cindery smoke. Then something moved. Something that he thought had been a tree. It moved again and turned itself into a small man sitting upright and holding on to a gnarled and stained branch. Blincc had no fear of this apparition because it looked more startled than he. It crawled on all fours to the edge of the flatbed and then tumbled down the side. It was another species of white man. Much smaller and dressed in the shredded clothes of the local people, which were discoloured and ragged. It could barely stand but seemed determined to make its way back towards the station. It stopped once along the track and stared at him with huge eyes that showed how lost and confused it really was. It looked at him and then turned and staggered back towards the engine, falling once or twice in the process. Blincc almost smiled. He had seen a white man who had less than he, and such a thing was unheard of.

The dazed young man put his hand on the flatbed to steady himself against such a tide of strangeness. He looked at the trees and chopped branches where the white man had nested to reassure his understanding of the meaning of the world. His eyes grazed over the twisted forms, unfocussed for a while, and then snatched back at the wood that was suddenly a man. A dead man contorted and chained down like the trees. His long filthy robe and his black skin were saturated with thick congealed sap. Blincc did not jump away from such a startling find. In many ways this dead man was much less scary and abnormal than all else he had seen since the monster smoked into the station. He brushed leaves and vines away from the face and found the startling, completely black eyes. Still he did not recoil. There was something about this lost brother that held him in fascination and not fear. He started to undo the chains; it seemed the most natural thing to do. For surely the body needed to be taken back to its people and aligned towards its ancestors. The sap was everywhere and made the process of unbinding him difficult. The mottled blue of the dead man's robe was now showing under the grime and muck that Blincc's hands and the chains were pulling off. His fingers were slipping on the chain and his strength made him slide about on the flatbed as he applied leverage and force. Eventually the chain was off and he bent the corpse over the edge of the carriage, its head hanging downwards and almost touching the track. He had it only by its feet when he felt it slither out of his hands and fall loosely down and under the wheels. The sliding weight had also unbalanced him and he slid towards the edge of the flatbed, which suddenly jolted. The train was moving, shunting farther down the track to unload more of its huge precious cargo. Blincc quickly grabbed hold of a restraining bar as everything shuddered and jolted forward. He pulled himself firmly towards the edge, looking down to see how badly the wheels had maimed the body. It was nowhere to be seen. It must be under the carriage, being mangled by the juddering movement. He began to fear for his job and the beating that might be coming his way. He should have left the thing alone, let somebody else be responsible for this accident, maybe even the dishevelled white man. He gauged the movements and stops and jumped onto the gravel and crouched down low to look under the train. Nothing was there. He walked back down the track still bent over, looking beneath the shifting carriages, expecting to find the tattered body any second. But it was not there. He scratched his head and looked up and down the line. Smoke and steam at one end and the shadow of the Vorrh at the other. He was just about to walk back to the station when he saw a glimmer in the scuffed ground. He bent down again and lifted a small silver crucifix out of the oil-stained earth. This must have been where the corpse landed. He stood up and examined the find, turning it against the sun; that's when he saw it, out of the corner of his eye. Far down the line near the distant end of the flatbeds. Something was moving. Snakelike between the train and the living trees. He knew there were giant pythons in the forest. Had heard the tales of them eating men alive. He had even seen their movement near the water. He tried to reassure himself that that was exactly what he had seen. Nothing more than a large snake moving from under the train into the trees. But he knew it wasn't, for in those few seconds he had recognized the patches of blue in the slithering motion just before it vanished into the trees. Then a question jolted him. Was this the shapeshifter that was foretold? The Black Man of Many Faces? Had the Men Without Substance been stealing him from the forest? Chained down?

He stood rooted to the spot, staring towards the infinity of the Vorrh.

"Hey, you!" bellowed the white man with fire hair as he marched towards him, an armed overseer at his side.

"Hey you, what you got there? Stay right where you are."

Blincc watched horrified as they approached. The whip was still thrashing in the loud man's hand. Then he did the only thing possible—he ran.

His eldest brother was standing in the clearing at the edge of town, looking down at the prone body of his middle brother who had died of the horrible sickness of the city. They buried him in the bush and limped out of their failed adventure in the white man's land and began their long and weary journey home towards the healing sea, Charlotte's little crucifix nesting, hidden, in Blincc's deepest pocket. The cross that the Frenchman had taken to give as a present to his native guide, Seil Kor.

But that was all in the past when he was a youth; now he was grown and hard and stood equal beside the sturdy bulk of Mumt'r. They were in the Scyles and asking questions about Father Lutchen. It took less than thirty minutes to find the courtyard and the door to where he was said to live. They had their weapons ready and the sack folded across Blincc's wide back. They had been stopped dead in their tracks by the weird plaintive music that came from an upper room. It was like the songs of mermaids that the older Sea People told of. Voices coming clear and beautiful out of the night sea, when the ripples of the full moon lulled the sleeping waves. Some of the elders believed this was where the first Oneofthewilliams had vanished, being lured beneath into the depths by the enchanting song. How could this holy man capture the song here, so far from the sea—did he have a mermaid imprisoned in his upper room? The warriors looked at each other and feared they were taking on a sorcerer whose magic was unexpectedly powerful. He was supposed to be only a Christian shaman, who also practised in darker realms, not a master of oceans and lures. They whispered for a moment and took on a brave resolve; they unsheathed their short spears and charged up the narrow staircase, kicking in the flimsy door with great force. The two ex-monks and the old priest sat close together, empty glasses in their astonished hands. Whatever spirit they had summoned was nimble and quick because it had escaped the transparent pots, which now hung silently in the hands of their immobilised captives, or spun sideways in a trough of water. Behind them stood a wooden man half covered in copper strips, a long gold trumpet in its hands. Blincc threw his spear at it while Mumt'r shouted at the monks. The figure fell backwards and the men shrank. They had been working all week on the mechanical trumpet player—a small commission but complex in its clockwork timing. It was to live on the silver bridge and spare the terror of the live musician who had the job of sounding the moon every month.

The younger two were bound and the older one led out of the house on the shark-toothed leash Tyc have given them. Should he intend to escape or run away, the lead would be yanked and the three-layered rows of the razor-sharp teeth would tear into the flesh of Lutchen's thin neck, which was already bleeding from the first lightweight demonstration. They walked out of the Scyles without anybody seeing them. They took the least-known path and soon came to the high reeds where their boat was hidden. The old man was tied sitting up between them, his hands firmly bound to his scrawny ankles and the middle seat of the canoe. His mouth was stuffed with a dried pinecone and tied in place so that he could breathe but not utter spells during his journey. They waded the canoe and their prize into waist-deep water, then climbed aboard and paddled into the fast stream that hurried towards the coast.

Two days later Mumt'r and Blincc paddled into the streams of the Sea People with Father Lutchen bound between them.

"This is he?" gasped Tyc as she looked at the dishevelled old man sitting on the wet sand, the lead back on his scrawny neck. "He is worse than the last one." She was speaking to Yuuptarno, who said nothing. "Ask him if he is the priest who told the other one not to bring the sacred child here, but to take her to him instead."

It took Yuuptarno a good while to think how to say this in the pale words of Men Without Substance. When he did, Lutchen suddenly paid attention and denied any knowledge of the accusation. This was explained to Tyc.

"Is he lying?" she asked of the translator.

"Yes," he said.

"Then beat him," she said.

Yuuptarno walked out of the surf into the village and selected a stick of the appropriate weight and brought it back to the beach.

Lutchen thought it was a staff to help him stand or walk and was about to smile when the young man swung the stick and brought it down hard across his back and the side of his neck. The stick broke and Yuuptarno walked back to find a stouter one.

After much moaning, Lutchen pulled himself out of the hollow impression he had made in the sand and started begging for mercy.

"Ask him again," Tyc said to the returning Yuuptarno, who was bearing a stick twice as thick as the last one. He stopped and tried to remember the sequence of strange-sounding words. After he said them, Lutchen started to flail his hand in air, babbling innocence and mercy.

"Does he answer?" she asked, and Yuuptarno shook his head and she then nodded hers.

This time the stick was swung into the base of his spine, just above his kidneys, and the old priest fell forward into his now-shallow impression in the sand that had been erased almost lovingly by the warm gentle sea.

Lutchen finally understood the question that was hiding under the blows that were knocking him in and out of consciousness. Yes, he said those things, and no, he did not know where the child was. He was then dragged through the village to the door of Oneofthewilliams's hut, where he was forced to sing out all his crimes again, explain all his weaknesses and all his lies without ever daring to raise his eyes. His new role in life was explained to him by a voice in the hut. He was to go and find the child and protect her journey in the Vorrh. There were to be no mistakes. He thanked his new master and was taken away, catching sight of the sacred Williams only as he passed the door. His old God or one of his new ones must have been with him then, because he managed to vomit outside the holy place without being beaten again.

The Wassidrus discovered that he could not think forward, there was nothing in his part of the brain that speculated. Nothing that imagined. Everything that happened to him now came as a surprise or a shock. All he had were memories and they were constant and stung like a paper cut. So when without warning Kippa entered the hut and lifted him up like a tattered banner and walked him out to the centre of the village, he only had the past to keep him sane. The pole that he was part of, which extended to just short of his hopping leg, was notched into a slit in the ground. The juddering jar of it chewed at all of his sutures and stitchings as he stood upright for the first time, his bent leg twisting and flapping around the pole like a furled pennant trying to find its use and meaning. He heaved and stretched to find the boundaries of his weakness and felt their thinness, but he did not come apart.

A fluttering drum announced the arrival of the sacred one on his catafalque-like platform, carried by six men in simple yellow robes. He was tied to a seat with the same yellow cloth. It held him tight and allowed his arms to move about with great expressive freedom, as if giving the crowd around him precious and bounteous gifts. The saggy sock-bundled swelling that contained the brain was decorated with a tiara of seashells that glistened in the morning light. Apart from that, the rest of the truncated thing was naked. The Wassidrus saw that it had no genitals, and looked optimistically down at its own body, being able to see there for the first time. He too had nothing. Both parts of what had once been a man were sexless. He wanted to ponder why, but that gully of questioning lived in the other half under the yellow rag and the coronet of shells. So he remembered the brutal black witch who had butchered him and squeezed his brain hard to wring a plan of vengeance out of its narrow walls, wanting to imagine getting his hands on her fat puffy throat. But he had no hands and the straining only made things worse. It pushed his gatherings backwards as if on a slippery slope. There was no purchase in the present and he retreated uncontrollably into memories of his lost resolute power, where all that came under it whimpered as they were crushed. He tried to gain a foothold in the vindictive crags and flinty edges of those recollections, to stop sliding away from now and future conflicts. But the momentum of the gravity and the sliminess of the sides held no hope of grip, let alone traverse. He slithered only into recollections of what he had been, and this was the genius of the benign paradox in the cruelty of his punishment.

There was a new face in the grotesque procession. Another white man stood towards the back and stared at him in disbelief. The sacred one lifted his damaged hands to beckon the white man closer. The Wassidrus saw the hand and remembered the great pistol exploding in it; it was the last time he'd had a fully working body. He had been ambushed and defeated. His remaining fingers were now pointing at him and attached to the mangled remnant that seemed to be worshipped here. The fingers then prodded the old priest hard in his kidneys and he stumbled forward. Father Lutchen had seen many wonders, many horrors on his pilgrimage towards understanding the mechanisms that spoke of the diversity of God's ideas. He had seen travesty and torture, ingenuity and splendour, and he had tried to master some of their techniques of existence, but nothing had prepared him for what he was looking at now. A thing that should be dead.

A contradiction to the rules of life itself. The tatter of flesh with its live eyes that should have been taken by blood poisoning, shock, and infection or from the sheer lack of bodily organs. The quarter of a man that was sewn to a pole watched him in equal disgust, contemptuous of his life and repulsion. The smaller bundle of a man again dug at his ribs and Lutchen started speaking. The Wassidrus understood some of its meaning. The mangled German and French rattled somewhere in his memory.

"I am here to talk to, to speak your language. I am also to be your keeper."

The word keeper had different words attached to it, the speaker trying them on before he finally settled. The cold grey eyes of the white man slid sideways to the gesturing bundle and its yellow-clad entourage. The fingers pointed.

"Also, also we are to travel together. I am to deliver you to the Vorrh, destiny waits there."

⇥ *Part Two*

There is no passion in nature so demonically impatient, as that of him, who shuddering upon the edge of a precipice, thus meditates the plunge.

EDGAR ALLAN POE, "The Imp of the Perverse"

Observation is an old man's memory.

JONATHAN SWIFT

CHAPTER TWENTY-ONE

$\mathcal{T}$he next time Betty Fishburn hammered with her broom he did not even stop to ask. The cold had gone, leaving drenching rain followed by the thick miserable fog that he had experienced only twice before. Up in the sanctity of his room it glowed around him, giving a peaceful and eerie hush. But outside it was a very different matter. The daylight congested and became solid and cloying, murdering every inch of space. The London particular had moved in without pity, and suffocated the city. It even muted Whitechapel. The staircase was glowing yellow-grey and his footfall sounded stolen and purposeless. Mrs. Fishburn's door creaked as he passed it.

"Yes I know, yes I know." He coughed against the phlegmy light that eased out of the crack. "I am going to look."

At the door below he paused, the long skeleton key in his hand. Thinking that perhaps another of Solli's henchman was being tested, he knocked on the door to give warning to them and himself. Nobody wanted unnecessary surprises in this place. The knock was hollow and without response, so he fumbled the key in the lock and opened the door. Eddies of smog came in with him and he quickly shut it out, slamming the door, its spring lock closing without the use of the key. The noise signalled to Mrs. Fishburn that he had gained access.

The three rooms and kitchen were evenly lit, all the windows having the same illuminated blankness that he was enjoying in his rooms upstairs. But here the still, even vacuity gave the bare rooms a quality of waiting, of suspension that he did not much care for. He decided to ignore that and examine the rooms in some detail—something he had never done before. It was obvious that nobody was here. There was not the slightest sound, scent, or vibration of life, especially human life, which gives off so much of those even when it's trying to be unnoticed or hidden.

Apart from the kitchen furnishings, a stool and a chair, the only other thing in the locked space was a solid bench that occupied the end of the first and largest room. This was an unusual feature for a domestic dwelling, and he assumed that like many in this labyrinth of secret trade, the previous occupant had conducted a business here. Maybe a tailor or cloth cutter, seamstress or leatherworker. He remembered the machine noise that he had heard before, the sound that seemed to come from this very room. Didn't that sound like a sewing machine or some other such cranked apparatus? For the first time the mystery of the place engaged him. He would conduct a Holmesian investigation of the empty apartment before he was disturbed by troublesome flatfoots and harridans.

He told himself that those noises had always come from somewhere else, having been distorted on that evening to give the impression of emanating from here. He knew that the first-floor occupants were engaged in some clandestine trade. Bulk parcels were often taken in and out of their premises. Presumably the large family that lived there were the workforce of some less-than-legal business. This was Hector's chief suspect, but as none of the furtive family spoke English, the task appeared daunting and he had no intention of wasting his time trying to find out. The only other suspect in the block was the shop selling cat's meat and string on the ground floor, run by a couple of a sour and miserable disposition. He was pondering this as he roamed the spaces, examining doors and windows, opening cupboards and built-in shelves. There was little of interest or meaning here, and he found himself again at the bench, looking at the scars and abrasions in its dark surface and fingering the holes that pierced it. He looked beneath and saw that there was some kind of metal holder attached there. And that from it extended what had once been electric wires. These had been sheared off and remained unnoticed to the uncurious mind. He was on his hands and creaking knees examining these when a small patch of light seemed to move in the far room. It must be a discolour or a dapple that could be seen only from down here. It was gone in seconds and of little interest compared to what he had just discovered on the underside of the bench. Hector was enjoying himself, and when he found the scuffed track where cables had previously been, he got excited. He followed them to where they stopped in the wall near the window, just below the shutter casement and the built-in cupboard. It was all solidly nailed shut. He found his pocketknife and dug and prised at the wood until a small gap was opened, big enough for him to get his slender fingers in. Then with all his might he tugged and it flew open in a shower of cobwebs and dust. His investigation was successful, for inside were even more elaborate remains of more sophisticated Victorian mechanisms. He recognised the porcelain conducting terminals and brass fittings of high-voltage management. Here in a house block that had no electricity and was still lit by gas. With more effort he prised open the cupboard door and found a large and pungent stain. White salty encrustations had grown around copper screw fittings. He started salivating uncontrollably, and he knew he had found the storage place of a once very large voltaic battery. This was indeed a mystery worthy of his consideration. The thick, tarry wires hidden here had also been truncated by the same brutal clipping that had severed those beneath the bench. He tried to peer in deeper but the dimness defeated him. Then he realised why. The light was going outside, leaving the smog to feed and swallow the growing darkness. It would be lighting-up time in less than an hour. But never fear, he had a torch upstairs and could continue his investigation. The game was afoot. He crossed the room to the street door and twisted the latch. Nothing happened. He tried again; it was solidly locked shut. For the first time Hector indulged in the guttural end of the parlance that surrounded him, born aloft continually by his new young friends.

"Fokking door," he spat out, and attacked it with all the sudden spite that he must have been storing or generating secretly for quite some time.

The door remained resolutely closed. He gathered himself and searched for the mechanism, finding no keyholes on the inside. He banged on the stout wood, calling to Mrs. Fishburn and demanding to be let out. He hammered on the walls and stamped on the floor, hoping that somebody, anybody might come to his aid. This was infuriating. This was Solli's fault. Solli and that damned Frau upstairs and those stupid boys. When his hand became tired and sore, he gave in, knowing that his cries and bangs would only be added to her ever-growing anthology of supernatural phenomena drifting up from below; that Mrs. Fishburn would be chain-smoking, her yellow fingers clamped over her terrified ears. He slumped back into the dimming rooms and collected one of the portable stools and brought it over to the bench. At least it was not as freezing as before. Eventually Solli or one of his idiot boys would turn up and get him out.

An hour later. An hour darker, and he tried again to make himself known, hammering all the walls to get somebody to hear him. He was standing near the entrance to the little kitchen, pounding the wood-panelled walls, when one of them moved and slid aside.

"Ah, more secrets," Hector said out loud to the quiet room. He thrust his hand inside the narrow, dark space and touched something that was hanging there. He grabbed it and lifted it out; a small folded scrap of paper came with it and fell to the dark floor. He ignored it and concentrated on the disproportionate weight of the thing in his hand. It was a small tight leather sack with a loop to hang or carry it by. He examined it closer in the poor light. It was robustly stitched along its flat pear-shaped form. Whatever was inside it was meant to be there forever, so it was not a kind of bag or purse. The weight was immense for its size. It must be lead inside, he thought, maybe a kind of clock weight, but with a carrying strap? Then as he held it in both hands he knew exactly what it was. The foreboding crept back into the room with the shadowless darkness. In his hands he was holding a cosh, a cudgel, whose sole purpose was to inflict pain and unconsciousness on its unfortunate victim.

He bent down to pick up the paper and took both of his finds back to the low stool. He put the strap of the instrument of misery on one of his wrists so that he had both hands free to unfold the paper and was surprised how reassuringly old and brittle it felt. He opened it carefully and stared at the message scrawled there. It looked like it had been written in haste by an untutored hand. He turned it this way and that to make sure that he was reading the dim letters correctly. On his third attempt he knew it to be gibberish:

> *tell them its this gin thats making them*
> *do it there is no jack no leather apron*
> *they are all doing it to themselves*
> *look at their fingernails*

When he lifted his eyes from the paper the room had gotten darker. His eyes adjusted so that when he glanced back at the writing he could no longer see the idiotic words. He was irritated and musing on this when his situation and the desire of his imminent release flooded back into his reality. His cosh arm felt heavy, and he started to remove the inert object when he saw the patch of light again, low against the wall in the next room. He leant forward, screwing his eyes tighter to see. Then it moved very slightly to the left. Hector looked at the window to see if a beam of light from outside had penetrated the thick fog. It had not. All remained unchanging in a sooty, milky dimness. When he looked back, it seemed a little closer. It was also now clear that the blur, for that is what it seemed to be, was in fact two. A shadow or a gap separated the two dull illuminations, which were only fractionally brighter than the dusky room. Hector watched, mesmerised, and carefully hoping that this was just some kind of optical illusion. Every time he looked away they moved, their motion never declaring itself, occurring only by a fractional difference outside of his stare. The longer he stared at them, the darker the room became, as if they were devouring the last atoms of natural light. With great effort he closed his eyes tight and counted to thirty, then carefully opened them. The blur was gone and he let out a tangible sigh of relief, swivelling slightly on his stiff stool. Then he saw them closer and no longer in the far room but midway in the kitchen staring straight at him. The blurs had distinguished themselves—they were eyes. Eyes made of dim foggy light and close to the floor as if some terrible creature were crawling towards him from out of the gloom. He groaned and fell backwards, tipping the stool over noisily. If it had been a cat or other mammal it would have been afeared by the sudden harsh noise, but it wasn't. It was closing in and its eyes were brighter now and began to look vaguely human. He imagined a deranged man slithering towards him. And everything got worse.

Hector scuttled across the floor, the cudgel feeling like a friendly handshake in his fear. The eyes waited for him to blink or squint aside before they came closer, in a hideous parody of the children's game of grandmother's footsteps. To his fear was added the spine-chilling horror that the eyes had no form behind them at all, they floated disembodied and luminous in space. He found his splintered voice and screamed. He was now against the broken door of the cupboard and could retreat no farther. His eyes were hurting with the strain of keeping them open. They watered and blurred as the luminous ghost eyes grew in focus and intensity, an intensity that shifted in a fierce emotional velocity that flowed between utter pitiful loss and deep, saturated malice. Hector whimpered as they stared into his soul. He flailed madly at them with the cosh, sweeping the air before him, without reaching their starvation and vicious malevolence. They moved behind him so that he could not see them getting closer but felt their attention like razor spiderwire crawling on his neck. He shuffled round, his foot catching against the prised-away wood and making him lose his panicking balance.

The unseen luminosity of eyes behind him was now the only light. The thought of it and the absolute certainly that it wanted him made him shake violently, losing all control. He covered his eyes, covered his head, and tried to roll away, to slither across the room whimpering. As he tightened into a ball, he felt the eyes sit on his spine, on his shoulders, with the lightness of a wren and the intensity of an earthquake. He felt the tug in his scarred brain, the wrench of its paralysing yank through his left side. His age, his pain, and his injury reoccurred, and he knew that all that happened to make him well, strong, and special was just about to be snuffed out.

The door opened carefully and his name was called. Then they burst in, were silent for a glassy moment, then screamed and ran at him. He folded inwards as their flailing boots attacked. They were as nothing and seemed like so many life belts floating on a bottomless ocean, bobbing above the fathoms of pitch-black nothing. Then he passed out.

Warm light sucked on his eyes and pulled him upwards on the inside of the wrinkled lids. He hung there for a moment, tiny and unsure, floating behind their enormous protection. Then the lids quivered and opened.

"Prof!" said Jerry, tears in his eyes.

Suddenly the lightness was full of men crowding around his narrow bed. He recognised Solli, who pushed past the younger man.

"You all right, Prof?" he asked, and for the first time Hector heard him speak without the cynical snarl that so marked his joyous contempt for most things.

"Yes, my boy, all right now."

"We saw it," said Malki from near the headboard.

The others shrank a little.

"Saw what?" said Hector, a great fear arising in his heart. Because that barely submerged part that most called subconscious was hoping that what had happened had been a fit, a gibber of his sane mind brought on by a quack of his weak heart or a faulty vein in the bone case of his head.

"Rabbi . . ." Jerry said quietly, and Hector turned his head to see what Solli had to say.

"Dybbuk," said a deep voice that did not even attempt to shape itself in Solli's lips. It came from behind the curtain of other men, who now again had instantly turned into boys.

"It's the dybbuk," the deep voice said again, and everybody parted, moved away from the bed so that Hector could see the bearded man in a jet-black suit sitting in his chair and looking straight at him.

He was introduced as Rabbi Weiss, then everybody including His Nibs became subdued under his authority. He was a wide man with wide square hands that rested on his knees. His white beard was also trimmed to make the base of a square with his black homburg that looked like it had never been taken off.

"Herr Professor, I believe you have been attacked by a dangerous and vindictive spirit. A dybbuk. Do you have any knowledge of such things?"

Hector answered that he did, having read about them in the Sepher Ha-Razim of the Talmudic period and a little of the Kabbalah.

Weiss looked impressed and smiled.

"At last, a scholar," he said carefully, not looking at Solli's mob, who were uncomfortable and shuffling about on the spot.

"Then it's real, what happened down there?" And again Hector turned greyish-white and lay back against his pillow.

"As real as anything in this world," said Weiss.

Hector turned his head to Solli. "And you saw it too?"

For the first time His Nibs was without words, a worrying flicker in his hard black eyes.

"We all saw it, Prof," said Albi.

"Then at least I am sane," said Hector.

"The trouble is that they all saw different things," said Weiss.

"How do you mean?" Hector was confused again.

"I have questioned each one of the fellows who entered the room and each one saw a different manifestation. Some appeared hostile and some benign."

"Benign?" The word stuck in Hector's throat.

After a while, during which it was explained in more detail how they had found him and what they thought they saw, Hector sat up, reassured in their company.

"Thank you, Solli, and thank you, boys."

Solli shrugged and Hector shifted his attention back to Weiss, who was watching him closely.

"Please tell me more about this ghost."

"It's a genie," Jerry blurted out.

"No, he said 'djinn,' " corrected Malki.

The word had an instant effect on Hector. "Gin," he said, "gin."

"I could do with one of those," Jerry sniggered.

"He don't mean the drink, you putz, he means a machine. Gin's the old word for a machine, ain't that right, Prof?" said Albi.

Hector looked totally perplexed.

Then Weiss growled at the boys. "We are talking about a dybbuk here and it's no matter for frivolity." He turned his huge square back against them and carefully addressed Hector's last question. "Dybbuk. It's not a ghost. It is a kind of being just like we are, just like animals are. Christians might say a demon, but it's more complex than that. They came about in the twilight of creation after the human being was made, right before the climax of Genesis, so that they're neither of this world nor of the other, but a little bit of both. There is a parallel association with some of the ranks of the angels, especially the Grigori. Do you know of these?"

Hector shook his head and Weiss continued.

"Some teachings say that they gather themselves from disposed parts of human personalities, shards of injury or enigma turned spiteful and malicious. They are not always bad; sometimes they appear to assist or complete a partial human."

"But why here, why choose this place to infest?" Hector asked.

"Infest, umm, infest!" Weiss tasted and mulled the word. "Because it might have been born here. Do you know anything about these rooms?"

Hector shook his head and Weiss turned his simpering glare of a question on each of the other men in turn.

"Ma Fishburn's said something about the Ripper!"

"Ughhh!"

Weiss raised a dismissive hand. "This room was rented by William Withey Gull. Do you know who that was?" He didn't wait for the negative answer. "But he never lived here, instead he gave it to Eadweard Muybridge as a laboratory to conduct experiments in what should have been only photography. But I believe that what happened here was a blasphemy and a contradiction of nature."

Now only Solli and Hector were paying close attention to what the old rabbi was saying.

"How do you know these things?" asked Solli.

"Do you really think that you are the only one who knows what is happening in these streets and dwellings? I have a network of associates and informants that goes back thirty years."

The old man's temper had risen and shuddered inside his stiff black suit. And then one last sentence escaped like steam, making the room quiet again.

"I tell you something *rsheus* occurred here."

To Hector none of this sounded unusual anymore. After what he had seen and heard in Heidelberg, Bedlam, and Spike Island, it all sounded quite normal. A rational explanation.

This was not the case for Solli and some of his men, who scuffed the floor with their boots like worried goats and gave fleeting glances at the door.

"Solomon, would you care to ask that woman downstairs if we might have some tea?"

Solli cringed at Weiss's use of his full name and said nothing. Malki jumped in.

"She's gone, Rabbi, packed her bag and left when she saw you arrive, gone to her sister's, she said."

Solli realised that he had missed his chance, the exit clause that Weiss had given him on a plate. Hector's colour came back. He had been secretly flexing his arm and hand under the bedspread. It all worked. He touched his face and flexed his foot. They had not become twisted, wretched, and numb; the stroke had not returned.

"Are you all right, Herr Professor?" asked Weiss.

"Yes, yes, please continue."

"Some . . . some say it may be the restless soul of a damaged personality who refused death and is seeking a residence in another body. But most believe it is far beyond such a simple explanation."

The restlessness increased in the room.

"The most benign form of this possession is called *ibbur*. Do you understand Hebrew?"

"Yes, *ibbur*? Yes, to generate, I think," said Hector.

"Not exactly. Impregnation is more accurate."

The male occupants of the fourth-floor room shuddered at the word. Solli had heard enough of this hocus-pocus and wanted a way out. As if in answer to the prayer that he was about to make, another of his gang arrived panting at the door. A much younger one.

"Rabbi, Rabbi," he said leaning in the doorway, obscured by the bulk of the standing others. They all turned.

"Yes?" said Weiss, heaving himself out of the sunken well of Hector's comfortable and slightly broken armchair. He walked, stooping, towards the door, the gang of youths parting in his blunt bow wave. "What is it?" he asked of the boy panting in the doorframe, who looked up at the old man in horror. His mouth worked for a few minutes before the limp sound came out.

"Eh! Not you, Rabbi . . . it's Rabbi Solli that I want."

The air thickened as the old man became enraged, his squareness bloating. Solli was up and moved across the room with reserved stealth.

"All right, Chaim, I am here."

This action stopped the tide of furious words that were dammed behind Weiss's fearsome square teeth. The nervous boy, whose eyes never left the gaze of the old rabbi, whispered to Solli, who suddenly flinched back into quick erectness and nodded sharply. He said one word that galvanised his entire mob into action. They gratefully filed past him, leaving the room to the old men.

"Where are you going?" barked Weiss.

Solli turned. "It's Uncle Hymie, he needs me."

And with that he was out the door and running at the stairs. Weiss followed with unexpected speed and addressed the draining, downward spiral of flapping dark overcoats.

"Make sure you are back here tomorrow. Early."

Solli almost paused, looking upwards. "Why?"

"The Lurianic *yihud*."

Solli made a slight shrugging of his shoulders.

"The exorcism!" bellowed the enraged old man down the cringing stairwell.

The moment the sound died out Solli and his khevre were gone. Weiss turned back into the flat, muttering fire and gnawing brimstone under his enraged bearded breath. For a few minutes he seemed unaware of Hector's diminutive presence that was now out of bed, standing in a dressing gown near the fire. When he did, his words whiplashed the air between them.

"What are you doing with these wretched thugs?"

Hector, taken aback by the ferocity of question, did not really have an answer.

"They are looking after me," he said weakly.

"Umph," growled Weiss.

To change the mood Hector asked the good rabbi to tell him something about tomorrow's procedures, which worked greatly by calming the old man down and allowing him to bathe in the depth of his scholarship. After an hour, the previous unpleasantness had been forgotten and the gentlemen of history and wisdom indulged in the warmth and timbre of the Old Testament and beyond.

CHAPTER TWENTY-TWO

$\mathcal{I}$t was midafternoon and a slight coolness sheltered in the dense, humid heat. Modesta moved down to the edge of the stream and put her hot feet in the water, letting the ripples tickle her toes. Her head felt light and she wondered if the thin old man in her dream really was her grandfather, because he seemed unsure himself about his meaning.

Then she saw a movement out of the corner of her eye. A long canoe with six men paddling was coming towards her. A large grinning man stood up and pointed at her. Then he started laughing and shouting like an overgrown child. But it was not he nor the paddlers that made her stop wiggling her toes and freeze in wonder. It was the other man-thing that the laughing one was talking to. He lifted the man-thing up on a pole, like a flag, and flapped him towards her in a rough boisterous way, which rocked the boat dangerously. Then a small, grey Man Without Substance that had been obscured behind the bulk of the rowers barked as the boat tilted side to side. The paddlers looked scared and worked harder to stabilise the craft. The grey one who was dressed in the tattered robe of a dissolute priest shouted again, and the Wassidrus was lowered back into the boat. Then he turned to see what had so excited the idiot who was called Kippa. The look in his eye was strange and unpleasant as it changed from shock into intent. He spoke again to the rowers and they guided the boat to the side of a round green rock that jutted out midway in the stream, opposite from where she was sitting. One of the paddlers and the grey one stepped out into the fast water. They secured the boat while the small man waded in up to his waist towards her. He clambered onto the flinty beach where the roots crawled out of the undergrowth and tried to grip the wet shiny pebbles but caught only rank foam and the skin and fur of a dead beast and the matted twigs of dead trees.

"What are you doing here?" He chewed the words like he was eating a snake and looked like he was going to strangle her. She clearly did not understand what he was saying or recognise who was saying it. He said it again and again in many different languages. She understood odd words from half of them and began to try to answer. But the pollen and dust of her kindred's dream gagged her voice. He stared at her unknowing, in what looked like distrust. Then he changed his attitude and grinned a ruthless agreement to something that neither of them had asked. It was an expression that had not found its way to his face in years, and the cobwebs in its sinews creaked in complaint. The soaking grey man then spoke and she understood what it meant and twisted to answer in a haze of instinct. The grey one became more enraged. He then stepped towards her and pushed his now-quiet hand into her face, turning it back and forward like a naked, infuriated puppet. She became confused by all these contradictions. What did he want of her? He must want her to go with him. So she grabbed the offered hand and let it guide her. He gripped back instinctively and she gave him the balance of her entire slight weight, which he held confounded as she climbed down the crumbling shelf to the loose wet beach. The paddler by the rock was struggling to keep the boat in place and called across to the grey one, who looked back and forth for a while before he swept her up in his wet arms and carried her out into the stream, calling to the men in the canoe as he waded. They moved to one side, so that he could lift her into the long husk-like canoe. The paddler with the rope clambered on board and pulled in the soggy dripping priest after him. They instantly started moving away, swiftly pushing against the stream into the Vorrh. She looked past the heavy working bodies to the back of the boat and the thing she did not understand lying there. The wet man said that his name was Father Lutchen, and that she was to sit still and say nothing, and that she was not to be frightened by the ugly thing back there. It was only a hurt man. Ugly but harmless. Sidrus had always been ugly and dangerous. The Wassidrus was worse, much worse, but without the means to express it.

Yet.

After they departed the river, the beach, and the raised lip of land, it all readjusted under the towering awareness of the trees. The pebbles lost the stain of human warmth. The water shook off its taste of sweat and the flattened grasses slowly clicked back into their vertical semblance of the rest of the forest. The breeze cleared the air and the birds changed their tune of alarm and disgust into a softer conversation about being here, there, and now. The ants and the clustering insects stopped waiting for the bodies to be still and foraged elsewhere, and the omnipresent mosquitoes reassessed their menu. In one hour all traces of the intrusion were lost and decent time settled back, oblivious to the rubbed-out moment of blight.

Lutchen watched the young woman and tried to place young Father Timothy's description of her over the frailty he saw before him. But the stories of malign power and sinister control did not fit. He questioned himself again about a confusion of identity; much fit, but some details nagged at him. This young woman seemed much older than the child of Timothy's nightmares. But he did say that she had been growing unnaturally. Surely this was her, near adulthood and of a species he had never experienced before, for what else could she be to beguile him so? She had given him her trust and he had taken it and more. He had felt her body close to him, in his care. He had even spoken to her, told her his name. And he had warned her about the Wassidrus. This was not what he had planned or imagined, if he ever met her again. He would not let her trick him further. He would watch her every minute of the journey.

The boat had entered deeper into the Vorrh, and it is at that part of the river when it is best to give up oneself: shed all notions of the "I" before it is wrenched out of the living soul. He sensed it and switched into the absence produced by serious meditation—a device that allows all men of learning and the servants of God to remain sane. He thought that the paddlers were safe because of their slavish obedience, Kippa because of his idiocy. He had no idea about the disgusting Wassidrus and did not much care, as long as he remained dormant and at the other end of the boat. But this child was another matter. She had once had enough willpower and hypnotic force to make her implacable. And dominant willpower: This place would rip it out of her if she did not offer it up. His old self smirked at the prospect that he would have the pleasure of the spectacle without ever doing a thing, ever lifting a hand or a finger in the horror of her punishment.

Modesta began her first convulsions.

Lutchen leaned forward to watch the white spittle form in the corner of her mouth and her delicate legs thrash out at the gunwales of the canoe. The paddlers looked sideways at her in consternation, recognising signs of shamanistic possession in her anguish. Kippa clapped his hands and twisted the stick so that the Wassidrus's head scraped along the floor of the boat, closer to the thrashing child. This was all that Lutchen had predicted. The very core of the part of her that had hurt him was in agony before his eyes. So where was the pleasure, the satisfaction? As it got worse, his anticipation reversed and responsibility walked in. No one else on the boat could help her and he sickened at her anguish. He rushed at her, lifting her up and almost out of the boat. He pushed her choking head into the water so that she coughed and spluttered against it and the foam in her mouth. She started fighting for her life and the instinctive reaction drove all sense of "I" out of her body. The primitive battle to survive was deeper and older than the willpower that lived in her higher brain, and it took over everything. The fit ceased as she drowned and Lutchen dragged her back into the boat, turning her facedown so that he could work her lungs through her back. He did not notice that her face was only inches away from the mangled head of the Wassidrus, who was trying to speak to her. The paddlers had slowed to see what was happening and Lutchen screamed at them to go faster, to reach the next bend and farther before twilight. They hammered at the river, splashing the oars and accidentally spooning water into the boat with their force. She spluttered, now lying in an agitated pool that seemed to be coming equally from outside the boat and from inside the rawness of her lungs. She opened her eyes wide to understand where she was, and saw that she was looking point-blank into the bloated, jabbering face of the Wassidrus, his spitting mouth spraying her. She flinched back from the proximity of his gnashing broken teeth, making a small alert sound that forced Lutchen to see that she was breathing and about to make direct contact with the snapping monster in the bilge. He pulled her back and screamed at Kippa, "Keep that thing back there, keep it away."

Kippa instantly tugged at the leglike appendages and slithered the entire thing back towards the rear of the canoe, its teeth and jaw raking the bilge.

"Keep it there or it goes over the side, now."

The old priest lifted the shivering woman into his arms for the second time that day. He grabbed one of the rolled cloaks from an almost dry cubby at the side of the boat and wrapped it around her clattering bones. He pushed her head into the warmth of his chest so that he did not have to see her eyes.

The boat was quiet as twilight approached, squeezing out of the trees, thickening in the gaps between them, and snuffing out each particle of light in the crystal air.

"Make camp," he almost whispered, anxious not to anger the gods of the dark or excite them about the strange being that was sleeping in his arms.

CHAPTER TWENTY-THREE

*T*he stillborns were easy to find, and were the side effect of the almost legal brothels that brought a great deal of unexpected money into Fleischer and Wirth's back pockets. Just as the blind overseer had predicted, their idea about the discreet establishment was greatly approved of by Krespka and a few other more surprising members of the guild. The idea of sighting them outside of the Scyles was a masterstroke. The pox-ridden hovels of that quarter had long been known by every member of Essenwald's permanent community and by its even larger itinerant tribes. Husbands who slunk off there to conduct business, even innocent transactions, were scorned by outraged wives and vilified by many others of the hypocritical elite. It had of course been Wirth who suggested building onto the ramshackle and disused stable block that sat at the back of the slave house and adjacent to his own dwelling. Nobody ever strayed into that territory. No respectable woman, citizen, or lost cat would put their dainty paws anywhere near the perfectly safe but ultimately sinister little hamlet.

Finding the girls had also been easy. Amadi had collected eleven girls in three weeks, and there was a promise of more. She and Wirth ran the first house with great success. So much so that a new road had to be constructed; the old one deterred too many clients in the rainy season. The breeding cycle now gave a constant supply, which relieved Fleischer of his less-than-legal dealings with the infirmary and the cutthroats of the Scyles. The only problem was terminating the valuable products in the correct way. The Limboia were very choosey; they could instantly smell out the artificially aborted. Such rejection would make them cease work and halt the now-constant supply of trees. Fleischer found a man to help them perfect their technique, to pinch the life out without a trace or a print being left.

Dorflinger, who had been trained as a dentist, had preferred reconstructing at other poles. He had made some notorious operations realigning and inventing genders in Cairo. He had been gaining a covert triumph until blood poisoning erased his best work and the father of the once-female victim had sought to operate on him. The desolate man was a sheikh of great wealth and influence and sent his emissaries to bring the despoiler back. They were still looking, still combing every gathering of hutches from the Nile to the Limpopo. They would find him eventually, but at the moment the back rooms of the slave house hid him well enough. And he enjoyed its cleanliness and protection and secretly admired Wirth and Amadi and the authority they worked for and administered. No one would ever go up against them. They were resolute and vicious.

The only thing that troubled Dorflinger about them was their third companion—Domino, an albino hyena. Its huge savage stink followed its masters across the entire compound. One glance into its eyes convinced any onlooker about the implacability of love and hate. The beast was totally in love with Amadi and Wirth. Everything else it despised and wanted to tear apart.

Fleischer had heard about the new girl and decided to make a detour to see her. Wirth had told him of her uniqueness, a face and body that could command astonishing prices. He had invited Fleischer to be the first to "try" her, presumably after he and Amadi had sampled the goods. He had tried to put it to the back of his mind, but over the last two days it had escaped and rubbed itself against all his actions and thoughts. So now in the sweltering afternoon he gave in and made his way towards the promised delight.

The slave house was almost empty. Less than a third of the exhausted Limboia slept and moped about its locked interior. The stables, as they had become known, however, sounded busy. As he approached he saw the car of one of his parents' best friends and decided that discretion was needed. For them both. He quickly walked to the front door of the warden's house, which gave him a blind side to the stables. As he did so, he noticed a new structure had been built, which joined all three buildings. A low platform made of stout wood that rose four feet off the ground. A walkway, he supposed, as it was just wide enough for a person to stride. A walkway to keep Wirth's boots clean from the mud and puddles in the rainy season. Probably a good idea, but he had not been consulted about it and it made him uneasy. He arrived at the door of the house and delicately knocked. No one moved inside. He knocked again and tried the handle. It was solidly locked. He thought about waiting outside but the heat was unbearable and any car coming or going to the stables would have seen him lurking about in a mindless state. Then he remembered that he still had the keys to the house on his chain. He fished them out while taking furtive looks at the road. The door opened and he stepped inside, which was cooler but stuffy, with a sickly animal musk about it. He knew that Wirth would not mind him taking shelter under the circumstances. There was a hum from a paraffin refrigerator in the kitchen and he helped himself to a beer from its pleasant temperature. He pottered about, touching things and trying to imagine the life of the alien pair in what had been the neat and tidy lives of the Maclishes' home. So far he had not entered the house proper and only examined the tiny hall and kitchen. He now stood at the threshold to the interior rooms and noticed another new structure on the far wall. It appeared to be a flap or hanging door. His delineated mind quickly realised that it corresponded with the new walkway outside. This was all becoming very odd and inappropriate. Wirth was getting out of hand, cutting sections out of the fabric of the building. And what for? Fleischer stepped forward to investigate further and as he did so part of the floor moved under his feet. There was a hollow report, as if a heavy latch had been sprung back. The sound seemed to echo from the direction of the flap and then diminish as if it had been swallowed. Fleischer's previous mild irritation was turning to unease. But he pulled himself together and stepped forward into the house to look at the flap. He lifted its weight and was surprised to find that it was partially counterlevered. He extended it with his right hand while bending down to look through it, expecting to see the outside and get a new view of the stables. But what he found himself looking into was a wooden rectangular tube, a constructed tunnel that stank of the feral musk that he had noticed before. He realised that it was the inside of the new walkways he had seen from the outside. Then from its long interior came a cry that made his blood run cold. The cry was followed by the clawed frenzy of something running inside the constructed tunnel. The cry turned into a wheezing, snarling cackle and he recognised what was hurtling towards him. He spun around and made for the door, tripping in the dip made by the intruder alarm lever hidden in the floor. He tumbled and sprawled across it, sliding on the thin matting. The tunnel behind him rattled and thudded. He reached for the door handle and touched its brassy hope when the flap crashed open. He did not want to look, he did not want to turn away from the polished knob, he did not want to see what was about to tear him apart. But he had to. It was huge, white, and out of focus. It stunk of piss, teeth, and glands. Then it slowed so that he could appreciate the horror of its pink eyes and widening grin.

Domino had arrived.

The albino hyena lowered its slavering head, its shoulders raised higher than its ears. It bent its face from side to side, which meant it was ready to rend and tear. Its lower hindquarters cringed to gain the ground to launch from. Fleischer was mesmerised by its ugliness and the certainty of his demise. He was without panic or submission as he wrapped his key ring around his fist. Domino brought her head back and sprung. He raised his hand and her wide, fanged mouth took it. The muscles in the neck and shoulders of a hyena are of greater proportion than in any other mammal, designed so that once its jaw has closed it can shake and wrench the flesh and bone from its prey. Domino did that now and the force spun Fleischer in a half circle, breaking his wrist and tearing his elbow. He screamed in pain and the hyena coughed out a giggling cackle from the back of its locked jaws. His fingers had gone, crunched into a mangled hub from which his body was twisted back and forth. The cackle suddenly changed to a shrieking whimper and the beast spat what had once been his hand and arm back at him. Domino slid back across the floor, trying to bury its head in the tiles and clawing at its own ears. Amadi appeared in the doorway, languid and unmoved, a long metal whistle held in her beautiful mouth. She shouted a few harsh commands and stopped whistling. The hyena slunk back towards her, its neck lowered and its hackles raised in submission. She spoke again in the same commanding tone. Wirth arrived carrying a sawn-off shotgun. Amadi spoke to him over her shoulder.

"Naughty girl," he said blindly towards the lurking beast and laughed.

Amadi abruptly moved and yanked at the hyena's blood-splattered mane. Wirth came into the room, put the gun down, and groped his way towards Fleischer, who lay whimpering on the floor. Wirth felt his body, quickly locating the wounds by the victim's flinching. His accurate fingers moved over the stubs and tatters of the chewed hand and broken arm.

"It's not as bad as it seems, it can be put back together. Your keys saved some of the bones."

Fleischer thought about that, then passed out. Wirth shouted back towards the woman, who had taken the colourless beast farther inside.

"Get Dorflinger. Tell him to hurry and to bring his kit."

The Masai and the hyena ran through the house, across the yard, and into the stables. It was obvious that they were both enjoying the sport.

The creature was caged and the surgeon was brought. He and Wirth lifted Fleischer onto the kitchen table and stanched the flow of blood. Dorflinger worked quickly and with great expertise, stitching nerves and blood vessels back first. He extracted the keys and the bent ring that held them and began working on the splintered bones.

"Will he be okay?" said Wirth.

"Sure, but he won't play the piano again," said Dorflinger.

"Did he play the piano?" asked Wirth, sounding genuinely interested.

The surgeon looked at him in disgust. "Why don't you keep that fucking monster under control? This is the second time I have had to stitch up its fucking shit."

"It's not Domino's fault. She is doing her job, protecting us all. It's this stupid cunt, coming in without warning."

Dorflinger ignored him and concentrated again on the mangled arm. After forty minutes he looked up. "Okay let's get him to my room. I have more work to do on him there."

Fleischer had never played the piano. Nor would he now ever learn. In fact, no act of manual dexterity was available to him again. The twisted and hanging thing at the end of his wrist had some movement, but it was bizarre and clumsy. As the years went on and the meaning of his life drained, his claw would ache more each day, the concentrated pain becoming a separate focus. Something to talk to.

But now in the fluctuating tides of the drugs and fever that held him in the dampness of the hospital bed, he sweated between wretched and sweet dreams of trivia and exhaustion. He speculated on how this wound would hinder his eminence. Slow his obvious success. And then the imp of the perverse would lick the raw bones of his crushed fingers, tickling delight out of the chewed nerves. In his triumph he derived gratifying pleasure by offering the hand to be shaken by unsuspecting juniors, disagreeable visitors, wives, and other irritating fawners. He would lock their gaze while their fingers engaged.

When he left the infirmary he returned to the slave house with three armed men and demanded that Wirth bring "that thing" outside. The overseer refused, saying that the animal was valuable to their security and that it had been Fleischer's fault for sneaking around his house unannounced. The wounded man was enraged. His eyes filled with tears and his skin became a pasty grey. He waved the bandaged remnant of his hand pointlessly before Wirth's blind eyes.

"Look what it did to me, look at my hand. I want it dead, now!"

"No. Domino is ours, we need her."

"I want it dead!" Fleischer screamed.

Nobody had ever seen the young man like this before and the onlookers tasted a bilious cocktail of pity and contempt at his behaviour. Many noted that this was the beginning of the end of the trust between the two men, who had become sewn together in their clandestine partnership.

It took some days before Fleischer was able to confront Wirth again. The meeting was arranged in the new stables on Fleischer's side of town. He would never again set foot in the kraal of the Limboia. Wirth's black sluts and the albino horror would never leave it now. All business would be transacted from his new office in the elite stables, and Wirth's presence there would be commanded at Fleischer's will. His fury had turned to disgust after the abortive to demanding the death of the hyena. His status and superiority had been shat upon by Wirth's refusal to hand the monster over for execution. Fleischer's contempt had curdled during his return; he had exposed his failure to the hunters he had hired and that flare of exposed weakness made him vulnerable. One of the guns saw this and launched into an explanation of how Wirth and the Masai controlled the hyena.

"They sleep with it, share the same bed and food bowls, that's how it stays loyal."

"You mean they actually eat and sleep like animals?"

"Yeah, and fuck too."

"You're kidding me."

"No, straight up. They fuck, shit, and eat together. It's the only way to keep one of those fucking monsters straight, you let it lick ya ol' woman's arse and fuck her snatch."

Some of the other hunters laughed.

"God knows what it does to him."

"Or them to it," said the other.

"You're joking," said Fleischer.

"That monster is a female."

"Some used to think that hyenas could change sex and fuck all ways," said the second gun.

"That's bullshit, man, like lots of other stuff said about 'em. Some of the Kafas and a few Arabs believe that they got stones in their eyes, and if you dig 'em out and put 'em under your tongue, it gives you second sight or some other bullshit."

"One thing for sure is that hyenas are tight pack animals. They live in close hunting families. This one is a whitey, very rare, it's always been a loner, outcast. They must have got it as a pup and grew it in their bed."

"Disgusting," said Fleischer.

"It works, you only seen part of that. Anyone goes near the blind man or his whore, that thing will tear them to pieces."

"I still want to put a bullet in its mangy heart."

"Then you will have to shoot all three of 'em. And it will take more than one magazine. Never go after it or them alone. It takes a pack to kill a pack. Hyenas are tough sons of bitches, I've seen one still attack with three blasts from a .30-30 in its chest. Your man Wirth looks that durable too. I don't know about his Frau."

Fleischer thought about Amadi and how far the word "Frau" was from her panther-like sexuality and its sleek muscular dominance. It would indeed take more than one magazine and maybe more than one team of shooters.

➤——→

Meanwhile, the Limboia went about their daily work without noticing that the men who now ran them had changed. They had of course forgotten that they had seen the last one die by the Orm. The Orm had lain dormant since their return, because nobody had asked for it and because the Man Without Substance who had brought them back had another inside him. They had of course forgotten that as well. At least the details of its manifestation. All he had to do was point at his heart for their measly lives to cease. The man had been unaware of it hiding inside him or the instant fear he produced when he walked among them. The only thing they did remember was that he was also fleyber. The only walking, talking, grown-up one they had ever seen. The awe it produced in them was overpowering. So when he told them to come back to the city, they did it without a second of doubt. He had also promised more fleyber for them to live with day upon day. After their return they never saw him again. Some said he had been wiped out, but they knew that was impossible. The only other man who knew about the fleyber was the blind man who travelled back with them. But of course they had forgotten that and did not recognise that he was the one who now ran them.

So they worked in the forest and cut the wood, hollowing out the shaved area that was allowed to be taken. They loaded the train and when they were exhausted slept in the carriage or back at the slave house. The days turned into months and nothing ever changed. Except that one or two of them, those that had handled the fleyber, had begun to dream. Not the vast epic stories and rolling landscapes of men. Nor the simple straight roads of food and fucking that other animals slept with. But a quarter-dimensional vapour that smelt of hope. An idea that hadn't ever been known among the entire collective. Hope had a shape. It was small, far off, out of focus, entirely black, and seemed to be shimmering in a constant haze. It was the only image of salvation they had ever known.

The dream had come after twenty-six of them had died of heat exhaustion during the hottest summer ever known to those who gauged such things. New workers were brought in and quickly joined the ranks of the bleached Limboia, who of course had no idea who was new and who was ancient. Only the herald, who collected the fleyber and had had the most sightings of the dream, kept a whimper of time in his worn-out mind. He also knew that the quality of fleyber had varied greatly, he being the first to touch them. The first was good, but later they became toxic and shrill. He would not even touch the second and let it fall out of the hands of the furious overseer, who'd had him beaten. The next one was equally sick and it too fell onto the squashing concrete floor. After that beating all the Limboia could not work again. The fourth fleyber offered was vivid and clean and accepted thankfully. After that the quality stayed the same. Not that they remembered, of course.

CHAPTER TWENTY-FOUR

*H*ector slept badly that night, even though he kept all the lights on in his flat and bolted every lock. Even though he had been told that one of Solli's boys was staying the night below in Mrs. Fishburn's rooms. He tossed and turned and tried not to see blurs or shadows that moved independently. He again read Mayhew, which had always been a solace and an entertainment when he had been unwell. But tonight it seemed hopelessly remote, even though he sat in the very heart of its subject matter. He pottered about making tea with gin, but nothing worked. Only at dawn's first feeble rays when the city stoked up did he get a little troubled sleep. An hour later he turned off the gaslights and dragged himself to his ablutions. He washed with the strange-smelling soap that he had accidentally bought and pondered again why the British liked such things. In Germany, soaps were always tinted with flowers or citrus, the bite of lime or the tang of lemons, but here? He looked at the heavy lump again and was totally perplexed as to why a nation would want to smell of coal and tar.

Eventually he began the morning ritual of twisting and folding his few strands of hair into their hirsute camouflage of many. He first combed down the nightly tangle, ready for weaving. In the mirror this normally made him look like an egg wearing a battered and irregular cobweb that flopped about his ears, but this morning it was different. There appeared to be a bushi-ness about it and stubble shadowing the worried-looking egg. It looked like new growth. But that was impossible. He turned this way and that, eventually unhooking the little brass chain that held the modest mirror on its bent nail, hanging over the sink. He took it to the window to bounce more light off his weird new head. There it was, hair. Hair sprouting this way and that, an abundance of shoots. A childish joy seized him and he heard a polka humming up from inside. He jigged about to it, hold-ing the mirror away as if it were some kind of remote dancing partner.

"This is madness," he said out loud, between the splutters of giggles that even surprised the hums. It took him a long time to become dressed this morning, seeking out things he had never worn or had not remembered he owned. He bubbled and played, trying on different combinations of garments, utterly forgetting the grave purpose of the day.

There was a weighty knock on his front door and he pulled himself together to let the boys in. He swung it open, ready to bounce mischievously with His Nibs. The square hillock of Rabbi Weiss stood unflinchingly in his path. He was still wear-ing the old homburg and the black shiny suit of many years. But now around his shoulders he wore a long black-and-white prayer shawl with many tassels. In his arm he preciously carried a dark, polished wooden box.

"Are you ready, Professor?" he said with grave earnest.

Hector said "Yes" and retrieved the closest coat. But Weiss was still blocking his way, frowning and looking him up and down. Suddenly Hector became horribly aware that in his pre-vious high spirits he had dressed frivolously. Without thinking about anything else, he had put on things that he had bought on a whim (spending Himmelstrup's money with abandon) and also the garments that he had been given by Mrs. Fishburn and Christmas presents from some of the inmates of Bethlem. What he was wearing was never meant to seen outside the privacy of his own moment of playful celebration.

"Oh, I think that I should change."

"No, you are needed now, bring the key. We must begin."

Weiss turned, beckoning him to follow, and Hector scuffled behind him, still forcing one arm into the new coat, the key gripped tightly in his other hand. As they went down, he tightened the braces of his plus fours that were beginning to sag. On the second landing he stopped. Below him was a pulsating mass of black-clad men. They were dressed identically and were equally impatient. He and the original prototype slowed and stopped a few steps above them. They all looked up at Hector and Weiss . . . The rabbi addressed them in Hebrew and then introduced the learned academic from the great University of Heidelberg. Some stared at his hair, which was trapped loose and hanging under a jaunty cloth cap. Some stared at his tartan socks and the gap where they attempted to join the cuffs of the plus fours. Others stared at his pinstriped coat, worn over the Fair Isle pullover—well, at least that was what he thought Mrs. Fishburn had called it. He had hastily grabbed the coat on his exit and desperately wished he was now wearing the rest of the three-piece suit. He looked down at them through their distaste into their purpose. One was carrying a thick scroll wound around ornamental wooden staves. Others held smaller, partially hidden things under their thin shiny topcoats. The one standing next to the door held the horn of a sheep, a ceremonial instrument ready to blow.

"Hector, the key, please," said Weiss.

He put it into the square hand of the old rabbi, who stared at the long piece of bent metal, then quickly passed it down to the seventh bearded man who stood next to the horn carrier at the door. The swollen mob shuffled forward as the skeleton key was put into the lock.

"*Oyfhern*," said a voice from below.

All the bearded heads spun round.

"Stop it. It is verboten."

Weiss, who was still three steps above them, twisted his head into the stairwell to see who dared. Solli stood ten steps below him. The old man exploded, his face turning purple.

"How dare you, how dare you speak to us like this. What do you mean by this outrage?"

Solli did not even flinch. He held his ground, steely and resolute. Behind him were three of his khevre who looked pale and jittery.

"You must not enter, you are forbidden to perform this ceremony," he said in a demanding tone.

Weiss was beside himself in speechless outrage, his skin becoming a dangerous lurid white. He suddenly held out his hands before him and pushed his way down the stairs towards the impudent, blasphemous young man. Hector fell back in his shock, his new two-tone white-and-tan brogues slipping on the stone. Weiss bustled past the others and gained the head of the stair just above Solli, who also started moving. Nobody said a word as they watched the rabbi and the thug confront each other. It started with shouting, turned into concealed asides, then into head-to-head, face-to-face violent whispers. The audience leaned forward, trying to hear what was going on. Solli's quick hand was suddenly at the back of the old man's head, pushing his ear closer to his continually moving lips. The homburg slumped askew against the impertinent violation. After being held ridged there for a moment, the solid square of the old man shrank and folded away, his astonished eyes never leaving the black intensity of the younger, slighter man. Weiss faltered, grabbing the metal balustrade, and then looked up at Hector with a countenance that was unreadable. No man had ever looked at him like that before. He had never witnessed such an alarming expression. Weiss moved like a scolded sleepwalker, past Solli and down towards the street. The rabbi's lost companions looked at one another and started to shuffle down behind him. After a few minutes only Hector and Solli remained on the stair, Solli's men having been told to retrieve the key and wait in Mrs. Fishburn's apartment.

His Nibs slowly walked up the faltering empty flights. This was not the walk of the fleet-footed panther that Hector had known from before. As he passed, Solli said, "You still got some of that kosher brandy left, Prof?"

"Yes," said Hector, grabbing the young man's arm as he lurched and plodded upwards.

Hector brought them both large tumblers of brandy to the seats by the fire. Solli said nothing: his concentration in the flames, his nose in the glass.

"What did you say to him?" said Hector cautiously.

"I told him to stop." Solli's voice was distant and impassive.

"Yes, I know that, but how?"

"I told him it was verboten."

"Verboten . . ." repeated Hector. "You told him in German."

Solli gradually came out of his stupor and stared at Hector.

"I don't speak German," he said, barely moving his mouth, like a bad ventriloquist.

Hector got up to retrieve the bottle, while the young man tried to strangle sense out of his memory.

"What else did I say, Prof?"

"I don't know, you were fiercely whispering in the old man's ear."

More brandy was poured as they struggled to find meaning in the strange event.

"Who told you to say this?" asked Hector.

"Uncle Hymie and your creepy friend."

"My . . ." said Hector, for a moment not understanding.

"Nicholas," said Solli. The name sounded distorted and looked as if it tasted like bile on the sunken panther's lips. "He wants to see you."

"Oh, when?" said Hector, trying to sound casual, trying to tether the conversation to some kind of normality.

"In a week or two, when the weather gets better. He said at St. Paul's."

"St. Paul's Cathedral?"

"That's the one, he'll tell you when," said Solli, losing interest now that his task was completed.

"Why?"

"Don't ask me," said Solli, shrugging.

Hector took his statement literally and didn't.

CHAPTER TWENTY-FIVE

*T*he children of the fatherland's military forces began to appear in Essenwald after the rainy season had finished. At first they were no more than over-clad strangers passing through with all the other itinerant drifters. Then they arrived in vehicles that nobody had ever seen before. Heavy loud monsters that became stuck and aggressively lodged in the potholes and ditches of the unmade roads, forcing their occupants to walk the rest of the distance into civilization, while the tyres shredded and caterpillar tracks squealed and sank into the dismal, unimpressed red mud. Only one such machine had ever been seen before, and it was rumoured that its occupants came from the lands of Napoleon and had been driven back there under a cursed punishment from the Vorrh.

Later, unfamiliar planes began to arrive at the aerodrome: dark birds without the red-and-white plumes that distinguished the company plane that occasionally nested there. The strangers began to settle and ask questions. On a brilliant Tuesday morning they demanded their first meeting with the Timber Guild. Their contact was Quentin Talbot, who introduced the two uniformed outlanders to the table of suspicious dignitaries. There was something different about him today. He stood more erect, was more agile, and seemed to be excited. He gleamed in their company, as did the new lapel pin in his sombre dark suit. It was the same insignia that adorned the now-requisitioned building across the cathedral square. Except there it was three overlarge flags that flapped in a heavy and out-of-place ownership. The black twisted sun wheel stamped in a rectangle of red. The military men were not impressed with Talbot and ignored his felicitations and wanted only to engage with the guild. The strangers bore distant memories to the men of the guild, reminiscences of their stern fathers and inflexible grandparents, the scent of authority worn in their tribal colours of black, grey, and silvered white, stiff in an old rigidity that had been wearing itself out here under the constant sun.

During the next three hours the importance of their city's position and produce was explained to the guild. As was their need for total cooperation and loyalty in the oncoming conflict that was only months away from their unsuspecting gates. It was also suggested that their current status of independence was a thing of the past. Most of the guild understood the situation and accepted the words of domination, knowing that this was to be only a temporary inconvenience. An expedient necessity that would last a few months, maybe a year, before things returned to as they were before, only stronger and with more markets established throughout the world. They could accommodate such a pantomime of military ownership without any real hardship. True, there might be some backlash from the tribes and nomadic visitors, but they would be kept in check with gifts and demonstrations of martial supremacy. All was going well and the sound of grinding teeth was covered by the stern smiles of satisfaction. Even Krespka concealed his contempt for the upstart officers and their absolute ignorance of this region that he owned. It was going smoothly until the outsiders unfolded their map and placed it on the boardroom table, announcing that they intended to extend the train line through the Vorrh.

To bisect the forest and make a direct connection to the Belgian Congo. There was absolute silence for a few moments. Only the sound of the crisp map settling was heard in the room. Then Krespka exploded.

"Idiots. You cannot pass through the Vorrh. You know nothing of this place."

Talbot stepped in, trying to quieten the old man and deter the suggestion, which it was obvious he had never heard of before.

"Gentlemen, Vladimir, let me try to explain."

Everyone waited. The officers had stiffened in their uniforms.

"There are serious problems about extending the track. Technical difficulties that would make such an operation impossible. However, it might be possible to build a spur that skirted the forest to the west. Let me show you on your map." He moved towards the table.

"What difficulties?" demanded the tallest of the uniformed men. The word "difficulties" sounded like it tasted unpalatable in his thin mouth.

Talbot was lost for words and nobody in the room attempted to help him.

"We have no intention of building a 'spur' around the forest," said the officer with the silver skull and crossbones winking on his lapel.

"It's not possible," roared Krespka, who was beginning to see the funny side of the present tableau. "You will fail miserably," he added with a choking laugh.

"We will not fail because you will not let that happen," retorted the third member of the party. "You and your workforce, your entire guild, will work with diligence to make this happen. We will extend your modest train and open up a causeway for our troops that will later extend your trade to new horizons."

"None of that is possible," continued Krespka.

"Buy why?" demanded the first officer.

"Because the Vorrh won't let you."

And there it was, finally spoken. Krespka had said it and it hung in the air like malice. Eventually the officer with the insignia, who recognised the relief of truth that was attached to the impossible statement, turned and spoke directly to Talbot, while clenching his elbow in an insistent hand.

"What is this nonsense?"

Talbot adjusted his collar and turned his head and the attention of the questioner away from the others. They walked to one of the windows farther down the room.

"The Vorrh is impenetrable beyond the end of our tracks. It would be very difficult to cut deeper into it from there." He paused for a deeper breath and then said in a whisper, "You should have told me about this plan, you said nothing about it before. If I had known I would have—"

"Difficult, but not impossible," continued the officer, ignoring Talbot's pleas. "With our engineers and equipment and an extended labour force we could make short work of a few trees."

"Yes, but there are other problems," added the now-deflated Talbot.

"No problem is too great for the might of the Reich."

Talbot was mumbling and twitching at his collar when Krespka again bellowed, "For God's sake tell him, or we will be here all day."

The furrowed glances of the irritated officers darted and glassily slanted at the now-passive members of the Timber Guild as Talbot gave them a potted history of the Vorrh's mythology and its "factual" influence on the industrial economy of the city. When he finished there was the kind of silence that gives the ears the ability to hear the mind ringing. After some minutes the senior officer, Sturmbannführer Heinrich Keital, stood up and growled. The other uniforms stood to attention and started to leave the room. Pathetically, Talbot called towards their retreating backs.

"If there is anything else we can do, we will all be happy to help." He darted a fleeting glance at Krespka when he said "we."

Keital stopped and turned on his polished heels.

"You and these other old women will stop telling each other stories to frighten children and build us the track we demand. You will begin tomorrow."

He then left the room; the sound of him and his colleagues laughing on the stairs was loud.

The guild members were all staring at Talbot.

"I will send a telegram to our people in Germany tomorrow," he said.

"Tonight," said Krespka.

CHAPTER TWENTY-SIX

*T*he quiet, and indeed invisible to one, Meta continued her daily chores. It gave a centre to her being now that a large part of the previous one had been removed. She laundered and cooked. She cleaned and tidied Kühler Brunnen and those who dwelt there.

The fearless Meta took a long time before she searched for the gun. She knew the others would have hidden it away to spare her feelings and she silently thanked them for their consideration. But it was a valuable tool and not an enemy. It had not been responsible for her father's death. It had been those creatures who fled below and their Kin in the warehouse. The gun would help her tally them. She chose with great precision to not ask her brother or mistress where they had put it. She wanted to find it herself. It was hers and its discovery would make that more so.

Every remnant of Ishmael had been stuffed into his leather satchel, the one that Nebsuel had taken from the Lohr house. It was lurking in the disused dumbwaiter in the old kitchen. Meta took everything to her little room high in the house, close to the singing wires. She emptied it out on the floor and placed each object in a line. Some things she did not understand but most were like prettier versions of her own or her mother's possessions. She found the boxes of bullets and the curved loading strip. The Mannlicher was still locked back in its empty position. When she lifted its heavy but perfect balance, no fear was there. No flashback to Mutter's death. The sleek animal wanted to be forgiven and to work in her hands again. She took the long teeth of the bullets out of their snug nest and held the gums of the feeding strip, questioning their relationship. She pulled and pushed the levers of the gun until it jumped back into its original form, nearly snatching itself out of her hand. After an hour she finally shot a hole in the floor and understood how the machine worked.

The meniscus of the well had only been cherished or carefully ignored. Meta's decision to use it as target practice was unique and consoling. Nobody heard the shots outside and the water spilled and spat in pain, the Mannlicher proving its perfection. Inside the well chamber the shots boomed and sent justifying echoes into the entire house, trembling the attic wires with distaste. Ghertrude and Thaddeus just looked at each other and said nothing. This was external to their concerns. It was Meta's business. And she was tempering herself to meet anything in the brooding warehouse of her violation.

"I am going to get Rowena," she thought. "I know where she is and nothing will stop me bringing her home."

Meta was grinding her teeth before she even entered the small door in the looming entrance of the warehouse. She had found the keys hanging in the stables. They were now in her small white sweating fist; in the other was the Mannlicher. Over her shoulder was Ishmael's satchel, no longer the smooth elegant sleeve but a packed and bursting bag with some of the stitching already torn. She kicked the door shut behind her with no intention of creeping about, and the beam of blinding light that had come in with her was nailed back behind the iron-braced shuddering wood. She was here and she wanted it announced.

She listened for sounds. Sounds of movement, life. Sounds

of her despoiler, the thing responsible for her father's death, the stealer of Rowena. Where else would she be taken, who else would take her? Meta listened for her enemy and the enemy of her world. Nothing moved. The building held its breath. How could they keep a child so silent, conceal it so deeply beneath their malice?

"Rowena, Rowena, I have come for you."

The dignity of absence cringed under Meta's call.

"Rowena, call to me!"

Everything listened carefully again. Meta stalked forward, swinging the muzzle of the pistol before her. She decided to work from the top down, to search every inch of this vast cavernous building. She scurried up the broad stairs, the ancient bowed wood booming under her hard-shod little feet. She was panting slightly when she reached the utmost hall, the scene of her defilement. The dusty sky was blinding and expansive in the window of the roof light. No rain shadow snakes today. Heat and dryness stifled the air. She looked around her, listening carefully, expecting to glimpse the blue mist and whirring cogs. She stalked all the corridors of the floor-to-ceiling shelves. She examined every part of the room, tapping on the numbered and labelled crates.

341. CUTTLEFISH. SEPIIDAE. SPECIMENS, DISSECTIONS, ARTIFACTS. INK & RECIPES.

It sounded half empty and distant.

342. SAND. GRANULAR VARIATIONS. ORIGINS & GEOLOGICAL SAMPLES.

It sounded solid and heavy.

And so it went until she found the door. It was just after

496 and 497. CAMOUFLAGE & MIMICRY. Examples of natural deception. Appropriate, she thought, without any sense of irony or consideration that her aberrant foe might possess a sense of humour. The door was hidden inside its own blandness and the neutrality of the wall that housed it. There was no handle or keyhole and it was the only door on the entire floor. Meta put down Ishmael's lopsided satchel and withdrew the stocky crowbar. She looked around the room again before putting the pistol down between her feet. She tried to wedge the dented blade of the iron into the hairline gap of the doorjamb. It would not penetrate. She tried again and again with growing frustration until, enraged, she drew her arm back and swung the iron at the centre of the door with a petulant squawk. The resounding blow sprung the door open and a cool, soothing breeze came from its interior. A spiral stone stair was on the other side. Meta exchanged the iron for the pistol and used its sight to look above and below. The breeze came from the roof with a smear of light. Below was silence and dark. The barrel of the stair seemed much older than the rest of the building. The roughhewn stone looked as if it belonged to another century. The rest of the warehouse must have been built onto it, she thought, like a body growing on an ancient spine, function cladding the nerves. She stepped away, deciding to investigate it only after she had seen everything else. She walked under the roasting skylight and down the wide stairs to the next floor, again reading and touching the crates. Then she stopped dead in her tracks. At the end of the third aisle a huge crate had been opened, its sides leaning askew against the others.

"Come out," she called, more to hear the firmness of her own voice saturating the space than to get a response. Nothing moved or came back. The case was much bigger than she was and she crept passed its separated sides, the nails still fresh and gleaming along the edges. Her nose was level with its stencilled label as she squeezed past. It said:

1017. EUPHONIA. A GIFT FOR MISTRESS MUTTER.

Meta stared at it in disbelief, or rather in the sudden belief of the impossible. She dragged her eyes away and stepped forward. Adjacent to the end of the aisle stood an ornate piece of furniture. Its long table form had elegant but sturdy legs with gilding that also covered the carved swags of twisting foliage that graced the table's sides. Growing out of the tabletop was a mechanism that looked like a gutted or dissected piano, its skeletal remnant elegantly engineered for another purpose. Poised on that was a frame or part of a varnished wooden cage with a large set of leather bellows hanging inside it.

But that is not what Meta pointed the quivering gun at. The long black barrel wobbled its aim at the white, sneering face that floated in the middle of the frame, peering out with a supercilious and aloof indifference. Its white snootiness was amplified by the glossy hanging ringlets of its nineteenth-century wig. It was immobile and androgynous. Meta looked into its dead glass eyes through the sights of the Mannlicher and walked forward. Up close she could see that it was little more than a papier-mâché mask with slim mahogany and brass supports and levers on its blank side. These were there to strengthen it and articulate the eyes and a small part of the mouth. She touched its apathetic hardness and laughed at her own moment of fear. She walked around the table, touching the mechanism and marvelling at its intricacy. She pressed one of the sixteen ivory keys set out like a piano and a small movement passed thought the machine. A piano stool sat nearby, a note pinned to its plushly upholstered seat. It said: *Lever A is us. Lever B is you. Lever C is her.*

Meta sat on the stool, the note in her hand. Her knee banged into something under the table-like structure. It was a long treadle bar that passed through its middle of the under space and connected upwards to the bulk of the bellows. She liked this machine, knew it to be safe. Its beautiful matter-of-fact perfection was in total opposition to the treacherous uncanniness that hovered crudely in everything else around her. She put her foot on the long pedal and found the brass lever engraved B. She slid it forward and pushed her foot down; the bellows wrinkled and compressed, sending a leathery breath through the entire mechanism. At its full extent she relaxed her leg muscles and the pedal rose up on powerful springs, the bellows sucking in a dry lungful of waiting air. Soon she acquired the exact pressure and rhythm for a constant flow. She ran the fingers of her right hand over the sixteen ivory keys and gripped the raised separate seventeenth key in her left. Cautiously she tested their functions.

"Ioooutnuuugaarrr" spun from the white-faced mask, its stiff jaw gaping in the process. It was the voice of a ghost, her ghost. Her own voice, ghosted. She stopped as goose bumps dappled her pale arms and excitement wriggled up her spine. She pumped and played again, testing each note and articulating them by changing the shape of the artificial glottis with the sliding seventeenth key. The plan of this instrument was to copy the human organs of speech, the several parts being worked by strings and levers instead of tendons and muscles.

"Ioooodooyoo," the ghosted voice hissed and yodelled as she filled with tingled excitement.

After an hour or more she had stopped looking behind her and was totally concentrated on bending the voice and finding the right pauses and pressures. She had a great affinity with this instrument, and it was warming and responding to her touch and need.

"Oo loook at meee, at meee," it sang in a voice that sounded like it came from a tomb. Its unnatural resonance had no relationship to healthy communication. More and more words came, sentences were sung through the still floors, the contents of some of the cases vibrating in sympathy. After a while she stopped and looked at the brass levers with engraved letters. She pulled back the B one she had been using and slid the A one forward. She then played the same sequence of notes and articulations. The voice that issued forth made her shiver and brought bile to her mouth. She stopped before it reached the end of the last word, a half breath swilling in the wheezing bellows. The voice of them was horrible, a ghost that you never wanted to hear. But it had been heard by the warehouse, the cases holding its resonance in their multiple dimensions. The place was waking. Meta pulled the A key back and was about to insert the one that sounded like her, but her hand, driven by curiosity, pushed the C key into place. She pumped the pedal again, closed her eyes, and played the same articulation as before. The "her" voice was very young, uncertain, and high; it made Meta want to cry. But that was not good enough; neither was the designated "her." Nor any of the other catalogues or descriptions that these monsters intended to imprison her or the child in. Her fingers flew across the keyboard and the levers. She quickly worked to find the slippery vowels for her purpose, not theirs.

"Ru en naa, roou en na, row en nar," said the thin dead face.

Meta was playing faster and faster and the name was being called out with growing emphasis, meeting its echo returning from the far corners of the no-longer-inert building.

"She cannot leave," said another voice on the same floor. It spoke like them. Meta grabbed the gun and stood up, waiting for the attack.

"She cannot leave," it said again, and this time she had it

placed. It was coming from the opposite end of the shelved hall in the east corner. She was standing in the west corner. Without a moment of doubt she scurried in a fast looping, skiing motion down the central aisle until she almost reached its end. The crates were smaller here and she stood beneath a stacked tower of four of them as they gave out a desiccated pungent odour through the dry warm wood.

1614–1618 DISPERSAL: LARGE SEED HEADS. OCCIDENT / ORIENT / AMERICAS / OTHER.

She peered around the stack's corner and was amazed to see another instrument, identical to the one she had just left. No one or thing was near it. She slunk along the shelves to get closer, the gun nibbling the charge in the air. She moved to the seat and looked at the keys. The lever A was engaged. A rueful impish compulsion made her pull it out and replace it with her own voice in B. She smiled at the conceit until the voice sang out: "She cannot leave and you must go."

It came from the other euphonia. Her instrument, the one that had been assigned to her. Something had changed places with her. Ran parallel with her. Changing ends and the lever there, altering the voice. A great outrage took hold of her common sense and toyed with it like a cat does a mouse. She felt duped, cheated, and robbed. How dangerous those little snags of pride that once let in will peck away at all worthy achievement and substantial knowledge with an eyeless ferocity defined only by their own momentum. The flock that harried Meta made her blind to the game that she had entered until the game told her in a benediction of spite: "We grow tired of your intrusion, play your farewells."

She wanted to shoot it, them, the "we" that was speaking

from the other machine, but the bullets would not rend sound like it did flesh, like they did her father. The return of those bloody bullets suddenly scared the flock of snags away and she was back with her icy vengeance at the keyboard of the instrument before her.

"I groow tired ovyour yoo, bring Ruwena to me," Meta played.

"She will never leave, be gone."

"Bwing her or I wolldestroy yoo awl."

There was a pause while both of the artificial voices settled between the rows of crates. A pause where the machines remained pumped, their swollen leather lungs separated by rivalry and thousands of night-boxed objects and explanations. During the pause Meta opened the bulging satchel and purposefully placed its contents on all the nonoperational parts of the euphonia's tabled surface. She then took out a stumpy candle and placed it on an island of screwed-up paper. She lit its thick wick. She put it on the nearest of the six Kilner jars that she had taken from her mother's larder. The six sweetly sealed containers that normally glowed with jam or chimed with pickle now only slunk, stinking and clear with petrol. She unscrewed the farthest jar and let its scent tease the now-distant flame. The Mannlicher sat next to the keyboard.

The exchanges now changed into something like a conversation, the words and questions, the threats and answers calling back and forth as the sun lolled across the sky and the shadows inside dragged themselves between the huge heated spaces that separated the talking furniture. Occasionally, between the gaps, Meta would tiptoe along the aisles to see if she could get a glimpse of the other player, but never with any success and never without the gun in her hand, vaguely wavering back at the jars as she craned her head to see nothing.

Meta was beginning to believe that Rowena was dead. Who or whatever was operating the machine refused to mention the child without its sounding like a specimen or a used commodity. What would she tell Ghertrude? Then out of the blue it said, "We will show you the child, but I will speak for it and it must not be touched."

Meta agreed, and after another moment of silence a slight shuffling and a faint, high-pitched squeaking could be heard somewhere in the middle of the stacks, equidistant to the speakers.

Someone was approaching.

CHAPTER TWENTY-SEVEN

*N*ebsuel knew that Gotfrid Droisch was complicit in Sholeh's death. The answer was simple, fierce, and impatient: Droisch and all things Droischish were to be erased. The insult and blasphemy of this man and his true-blood wife were a stain. The job of cleansing was given to the Travesty: a notable, fierce, and trusted person living in the city where such attributes were rare. Nebsuel would send him a message to explain the vileness of the transgression, and he would make his own decision about the punishment. He was to be trusted because it was known that his sense of retribution and chastisement was equivalent to theirs. Some said greater, if such a thing could be believed.

The Travesty, whose astonishing beauty was hidden beneath a hood that covered his entire body. A single piece of perfect silken cloth dropped over him, from the crown of his head to his corkscrewed ankles, eyeholes cut into the cloth, like a pantomime ghost. A wide-brimmed hat put on over it to keep it all in place. He stood in a beautiful night, in a street outside the skinners' house. The stars were extraordinary and the air perfumed with jasmine and stillness. Even the wretched silhouette of this shunned house seemed to glow against the rich celestial darkness, and the scent that seeped from inside this dwelling was contoured to something rare, like an exotic musk. Nebsuel had told him of the blasphemies that had been committed here, in his beloved Essenwald, and the consequence that they carried. The news of it had made his wrath force his splendour to the breaking point. He had known of the rumours before the crime, but he'd had no idea that the slaying of Sholeh had been the responsibility of the ugly couple that now slept here, sweetly, in their wicked bed.

How had this vile fact escaped him? He watched everything in the city, balancing its rights and wrongs, keeping its thriving people in control, touching all things in a way that was never seen. The Men Without Substance saw him only as unclean and to be shunned. Most of the tribes saw him as a prophet or holy fool and made sure that he was fed and sheltered. None of them could lift their weak eyes to his true magnificence. He saw everything, except the guilt that was living here.

The Travesty knew the Droischs by sight. He understood something of their trade. Once the husband had cuffed him out of his way, sending his battered and stained sombrero wheeling away like a deflated tyre. The wife instantly scolded her husband and apologised profusely, begging forgiveness for him on her knees. He had given her his immaculate hand and she trembled at its beauty and her need to kiss it. The husband had spat in disgust. Now it was his duty to spit back and he would relish it.

CHAPTER TWENTY-EIGHT

*M*eta had moved to her farthest position from the euphonia and the jars of petrol so far. She was approaching the end of the third row of shelving and was scared that whatever had changed position before could do it again and remove her from the threat that forced them to parley. She reached the end of the valley of shelved crates and pressed her body flush against the sanded wood that still smelt of resin. The heat of the room had made it faintly sweat. She quickly twisted her head around the case and back again. More than halfway down the canyon-like aisle and moving in her direction was an old man pushing a whinging pram. He was dressed in clothes that had once been expensive; she had seen trousers and shirts like that before, the high collar and striped material always denoting authority. He had no coat and was besmirched with grime and bits of wood. He was unshaven and his eyes looked strange. It must have been he who opened the crates, she suddenly thought, realising that no other normal human had ever been seen here. The thing that attacked her before did it inside her body, inside her soul. It had left no real impression of substance, muscular power, or weight. After all, it was her father who did all the physical moving between here and Kühler Brunnen. Perhaps this shabby old man was the only one left to do the dirty work for the monsters that dwelt here. The idea of this brought a rush of confidence into her stalwart heart. She looked back around the corner and this time it was the occupant of the pram that riveted her attention. The wheels squealed because of the weight of the being it carried. This was no baby or infant. She shuddered as it was pushed closer, then ran back to her position behind the keyboard to wait for the confrontation. A few minutes later it turned the corner and she took a deep breath. She recognised the man. She had seen him before, seen him with her father, seen him with Ghertrude. He looked worse up close, but normal in comparison to his passenger, the sight of whom made her want to run home. They stopped ten feet in front of the euphonia and waited. Meta was fixated but she did hear the bellows of the other machine begin to pump.

"What do you want?" it said, and the passenger's mouth moved in unison. The C lever had been engaged.

Meta opened her mouth to explain, then realised she had to play it. She pumped the treadle and operated the keys.

"I have come for Rowena, to take her home."

"I don't want to leave this place."

Meta kept moving her foot, her fingers frozen on the keys. The sound of the leather lungs filled the space between them like concrete.

"I don't want to leave this place," said the voice from the west end of the warehouse, and was mimed by the being in the pram.

"Who are you?" played Meta.

"You called me Rowena."

Rowena had been just over three months old when she was abducted. A pretty, warm, affectionate baby with two beautiful pale hazel eyes. The single squinting eye that glared out from the soft scar tissue of the lopsided face had no colour at all. The skin and flesh seemed loose and spongy. Tiny blue veins or bruises moved and flickered inside it. Its body was that of a two-year-old child and the hands that gripped the chrome sides of the pram looked like the stringy hands of an old woman. Meta's real tongue shrivelled with her spirit, but her fingers continued to speak.

"You are not the Rowena I seek. I want the child Rowena, the daughter of Mistress Ghertrude."

"I am the only one here and I don't want to leave."

There was nothing more to say. It had all been a mistake, or worse. The air leaked out and eventually the old man pulled the pram backwards and turned it into the long aisle. Meta sat and stared at the tight jars. She picked up one of them and the pistol, looping the flabby empty satchel over her shoulder. She walked drearily back to the other machine. Nobody was there. Only the old man could be seen near the far corner, blocking the pram with his stooping body. Mutter's daughter felt sick of heart and desolate. She turned to leave, putting the jar in the bag and her foot on the broad stair. Four steps down, just as her head ducked below the level of the floor, she heard a titter of laughter and an insect-like whirring of gears. She halted, turned, and took two steps backwards. The old man was bent farther over the pram, making smirking gurgles. A blue haze was hovering around the disgusting other figure. Meta ascended and ran across the resounding floor straight at the couple. She lifted the Mannlicher and fired. Two bullets hit the end wall and splintered the wood. The third bullet hit the old man and sent him spinning sideways. The thing in the pram was swirling; its white head and upper body covered in a swarm of blue particles, spinning gears, and wheels. It looked like one was devouring the other. The old man was thrashing about and crashed into the pram, spilling it. Meta was now standing over it, steadying the gun with both hands. She was just about to pull the trigger when she heard another sound. A whimper, a child's whimper from inside the swirling mass. She lowered the gun and grabbed the strap of the satchel, swinging it hard into the twisting body. It split into hundreds of parts, disconnecting itself from the body it had previously covered. The one-eyed horror had been its disguised form, smothering and cloaking the reality of the poor smaller child beneath. The child that she now recognised as Rowena. She grabbed at her and pulled her free of the pram, the whirring haze, and the limping man, who was now standing and moving towards the concealed door that connected this floor to the spiral stone stair. He punched it open as the swarm gathered and settled about his head and shoulders. It turned, grinning. Its wheels hissed in speed. Ticker tape spewed from its mouth like blank, meaningless laughter. Then it was gone, feeling its way downwards like a blind man. Meta was up and at the door in seconds, the jar and the gun in her hands. It was spiralling down, still in her sight when she threw the Kilner jar, which hit the wall above it and smashed, showering the escaping horror in petrol and glass. She shot into the chaos that screamed, blood spurting into the blue, cogs, and petrol. The next shot ignited it. The third spun it downwards. A normal human body cannot fall far down a spiral stair. It sticks and jams on the first or second turn. But not in this case—the blue mist in its attempt to escape the seething flames wormed around the broken body, squeezing it like a crushed sack, shrivelling inwards into the shell of the stair like a scorched mollusc. The flames, the hissing, and the screams continued until it was gone and only a rank black smoke blocked the spiral stair. Meta rushed back to the traumatised child, picked her up, and carried her down to the ground floor and out into the gentle warm street. The only movement and sound that remained in the warehouse was the fatty spluttering of the squat candle.

CHAPTER TWENTY-NINE

*D*roisch's thin white arm was pinned under the sweating weight of his wife's enormous thigh. The bedroom stank worse than the rest of the house. The radiant night had been shut out and it looked like the blessed sun had never entered. The Travesty sat in a deep chair that was covered in the skin of a beast. He was watching them sleep. He was wide awake and had no intention of sharing or catching any of their squalid dreams. He had come to take their breath, but it seemed such a kind thing to do, so he decided to take their souls instead. It would be dirtier but sanctified.

It took an hour of the "time that flies." She had been easy, but the white husband had been grudging and tightly curled, like some cur child refusing the bait offered outside the womb. And so, like a practised midwife, he cut it out. Indeed, with such skill that Gotfrid Droisch never woke. He kicked about and jabbered, but stayed unaware of the blessing that was being given to the world. It was the Travesty's intention to take the souls to the edge of the holy Vorrh and scrape them off the iron rod onto which they had slithered and coiled. Of course he would not taint the interior with such an offering, but there would be something living at the edges that would willingly feed on these morsels. On his way out of the house he could not restrain his curiosity. The smell from the "shop" lured him in to investigate.

Droisch had again been attempting to mate different species. And for the first time he'd had a limited, if repulsive, success. His previous attempts had been little more than forced couplings of different animals and a few botched graftings. He had also collected live and pickled abnormalities from far and wide. They all began to glimmer in their bottles or dance or hide in their cages as the Travesty lit a lamp. He was examining the limping and floating menagerie with great interest when he became aware of their owners standing by the open door. She like a spherical dark nought and he like an anaemic stretched I. The Travesty laughed at the sight as the coils tightened harder on the metal rod, which he carried in the way of a walking stick.

"I suppose you want to come too," he said wearily to the figures in the doorway.

There was no answer because he addressed the question to perpetual sleepwalkers who were not bright enough to know that they were dying. He knew that they would be lost after the first five minutes, unable to keep up with the pace of his resolute stride. He waved his metal stick with their useless souls sucking onto it like limpets.

"Then let it be so," he said and opened the door at the back of the shop into a street filled entirely with tall, featureless warehouses. Some were made of brick but most were fashioned in timber—the verticality of the Vorrh having been sawn into horizontal planks that made the huge walls. More meaningless buildings, he thought, as what had been the Droischs followed him. Somehow the three of them made the street look emptier than before. Something about their limp nakedness and the scale of the walls and the Travesty's detachment made the whole thing look like a minor early Renaissance painting, where the artist is unsure what is most important: the grandeur of the architecture squashed into a compacted perspective or the figures in front of it, who appear to be waiting to receive their lines. The only sound in the long high place was the soft moan of the wind and a tiny creaking from the iron rod as its occupants tightened their grip once again.

Then the wall of the building opposite exploded.

CHAPTER THIRTY

*M*eta's squat candle had been flirting with the warm dry air, the rumpled paper, and the pine-scented resins that had been sweating from the crates. And the tiny waft from the jars of petrol that sat placidly impatient, flaunting their transparency, coquettishly egging the junction on. The proximity had become too much for them all. The coy distance raked itself up to touch and pet. Ignition was struck. Once it began there was no end or containment to its wantonness. The great lust of fire undid and fucked the building to panting exhaustion, the spluttering wax vaporising in a wink under the licking tinder air. Petrol, spirits, and oils boiled and spurted over drier atrophied specimens that had always dreamed of becoming ash or cinder. Frantic wasted instructions sneezed their last remote wisdom in the grains of the splintering woods. The temperature rose until the air itself was lit, flooding the inert shelves and the long-resting crates into an agreement of fire, its virulent wave skinning the euphonia in one blast. The docile plaster faces cracked in its temper, like aristocratic porcelain. The delicate carved and turned wood became charcoal in seconds. The rasping voices roasted as the leather lungs buckled and the ivory nails of the keyboard split and peeled back in agony. The bricks and timbers of the wall shook before they erupted into the street, sucking out all the fallen specimens and examples, throwing them and their glass and metal homes through the singeing oxygen: an index of solids, a library of meaning contorted into maliciously comic shrapnel. Ancient stones and recent inventions whistled and thrummed the air. A case of fossils was ripped apart, the heat splitting the impressions of bones and filling their hollows with liquid fire. Even some of the agile blue mist was boiled through the filigree impression of feathers, just before the prized specimen were blown apart.

➤——→

The Travesty and his sad companions were lifted off their feet and bludgeoned through the shocked air. He raised his rotting hand to shield his beauty, but it was less than a cobweb to the incendiary tidal wave of hot, sharp fragments of animals, vegetables, and minerals in all their ingenious modes of existence and usage that buckled everything into shrill rags. The empty Droisch waifs were obliterated by the debris, which scythed them into the walls and interior of their own shop, where live screaming abortions were crushed by long-dead species that spat blue plumes of lit formaldehyde. Cages were dented, ripped apart, and thrown in every direction. Bricks and irregular spears of wood spun vindictively at modest uprights of napping architecture and torpid decorations. The noise tore all sound away, leaving ears boxed and bleeding. Nothing remained standing. Everything had eventually fallen in and reached its destroyed stage of burnt collapse. Then, and only then, the malicious smoke billowed, choked, and bullied into every crevice of cringing space. The iron rod steamed as the charcoal souls boiled away to nothing, as the bodies that once contained them became engulfed in the conflagration that had sped up the stairs to lick under their gloated bed.

The sound halted every action in the city. The outraged windows of the dwellings of the Men Without Substance nearby blew into sedate lives and the rest of the city looked up from its concentrated actions. All the transactions—sleeping, crimes, eating, talking, buying, and copulating—stopped while the population guessed at what had occurred, peering out into the streets and running to the rooftops. Anton Fleischer thought that it was the train mishandled into failure, but hoped that it might be the warden's house and the disgusting family within.

The Sturmbannführer, the Hauptmann, and the Obersturmführer dropped their glasses and reached for their weapons.

Ishmael and the Kin, sheltering in their lostness under the million trees, thought that the sound came from deeper in that forest, a vast entity moving there, calling them closer.

Cyrena awoke from a deep dream of cathedral-like underground causeways where the echoing sea boomed and sighed in reassuring regularity. She arose to near waking and listened, heard nothing more, and rolled over to dive and reenter the unworldly depth, before the smaller explosions would convince her that they might have been on this side of her longing.

Modesta bit her lip and clapped her hands while seeking an answer in Lutchen's stern and troubled face; he automatically crossed himself.

Kippa let go of the leash that held the Wassidrus down and he rolled facedown, hearing nothing.

Thaddeus and Ghertrude knew it must be Meta. Knew with a certainty that had no words. That is why in their deathly silence they heard the gate to the street open, heard the brass key in the lock to the house, heard the strings in the attic hold their metal breath, heard the uncreaking stair and the muffled carpet under Meta's slow footfall as she carried Rowena in her tight arms and ascended towards them in their upper room.

They rushed at Meta, falling out of the bed. Or rather Thaddeus did.

Ghertrude saw her lost Rowena float into the room alone. Meta was still invisible to her. It was only as she grasped Rowena and tugged at Meta that Mutter's child blossomed before them in pluming sight. It was her brother who embraced her in a crushing hug of babbling words.

"Meta, thank God you are safe, you have done it, you have done it, you have saved her and brought her home. How, how did you do it?"

Meta could not speak because for the first time that day she was dumbfounded. Nothing else had frightened or shocked her. She had been ready and able to tackle it all. What had slapped her into disbelief was recognition. The moment that she had brushed Ghertrude's hand she had recognised the disgusting old man with the pram, the one she had shot and sent spilling down the stairs. Ghertrude had sparked the memory. Her resemblance to the man had opened her eyes. The man in charge of the pram and its hideous occupant had been Ghertrude's father. The last living remnant of Deacon Tulp.

She mumbled a few meaningless words at her brother and tugged at his sleeve, while darting her eyes towards Ghertrude and Rowena. Thaddeus understood and they both quietly left the room, leaving mother and child to stare into each other's faces and sob and forget every other creature on earth.

The Mutters sat in the kitchen, the domestic normality making it possible to talk of impossible things. They exchanged their experiences of the warehouse and Thaddeus marvelled at his little sister's courage. They talked about the explosion that everyone had heard and about the pillar of smoke that was still rising from the gutted shell of the building across town. Their shared excitement and Meta's triumph subsided as they both became very tired. The warmth of the kitchen drew out the hollows of fatigue into a safe and now-reasonable place. Meta slid across the table and her weary brother picked her up and carried her to her high room, below the attic where the soft strings played all night to guard her against memory fisting her dream or dream recalling nightmare. So that she slept in a smooth haze of nothing, which erased everything of the last thirty hours.

➤→

In the smoking rubble and steaming glass something moved, flickered like a bird in a zoetrope illuminated by a faulty lamp. Its movements were staccato and chopped by light and shadow. It looked like a drawing made of broken dried reeds or thin metal rods, incorrectly joined and falling out of any natural delineation. It seemed dazed and tattered, trailing its bent-double body like a ruined Japanese fan. It was small and electric and half visible, bits of stone embedded between its impossibly delicate wings that fluttered in a blue residue. A half-burnt paper tag was still attached to a chunk of the stone that imprisoned one of its feet and made it impossible for the thing to escape. The label said: ARCHAEOPTERYX.

Running and calling activated the wrecked street as the first hot daggers of rain fell from the blackening storm that swirled high above the city. Anxious citizens burst into the devastation, looking for victims and answers. Some came to filch, picking among the rubble and pocketing weird treasures, while showing a mask of concern. The limping skeletal shadow stitched its way into the skinny alleys of neglect and finally shook off the remnant of stone and the label of its previous meaning. In the same crate that housed its astonishingly rare fossil was a reproduction of a drawing of what archaeopteryx, or as the Germans call it, the Urvogel, was supposed to look like. It showed a perky magpie-like creature with its wings outstretched. There was something very wrong about its appearance, something incorrect in its stance and believable existence. This can be said even in the knowledge of such awkward wonders as the duck-billed platypus, the giraffe, and the much-maligned hammerhead shark. This reproduction was one of the infant Ishmael's favourite things, and Seth and Aklia had had a great deal of trouble trying to retrieve the picture from the petulant child and send it back with the box of specimens. He'd bounced the paper around the floor of the cellar trying to make the bird-lizard hop, while emitting very convincing screaming noises. The strident sounds suited the strident image that looked like a nimble, effete dancer dressed in a feathered leotard and cape, his hands gloved in claws and head wearing a toothy beaked mask. It was a long way from the shivering tattered fist of silhouetted sticks that was flinching away under the heavy hard rain that fell into the smoking epicentre. It was a fossil of a fossil. Bent over and folded back, now wet and compressed into an abstraction. The smoke that rose from the devastation was spiralling half a mile above the streets.

A storm had come in from the ocean and been heated by the Vorrh; it now brooded in a growing vortex that would eventually suck up every particle of soot, loose glass, stone, and all else that was not welded or nailed down, including the scattered slivers of the Travesty and the squealing, animated fossil of an Urvogel. It is said that the seas and oceans are the memory of the world. The gulp of water taken from the sea to make the storm had its essence of memory twisted and confused in the vast suction and the acrid explosion, so when the broken and now-living fossil was sucked up in the maelstrom and forcefully slipped between the fluctuating plurals of continuum, when the storm spat it out it arrived in the depopulated lands at an earlier date. It rained down into a muddy puddle in Carmella's courtyard, where it was hastily and incorrectly recognised as their promised long-awaited heavenly messenger. It never had the dogmatism of the real seraphim and certainly not its unfailing sense of direction. In its spluttered passage to find its way back to the Vorrh it had lead Carmella to her death and Modesta into the mouth of the river that would lead to her destiny and Ishmael.

Part Three

Bacteria have been, are and will remain the dominant group of organisms on our planet.

Essentially subterranean, living off the chemical energy contained even in rocks, they are also sustained in the atmospheric milieu through the subterfuge of intracellular symbiosis in two unimportant superstructures: plants and animal. In this vision of evolution, even human beings are a sort of efflorescence of bacterial origin!

STEPHEN JAY GOULD

I hate Nature
this passionless spectator this unbreakable iceberg-face
that can bear everything.

MARQUIS DE SADE,
in PETER WEISS, *Marat/Sade,* act 1, scene 12

The eyes have fallen into disuse in their method of stringing them. Nor is the notch placed frontally in the middle of the ends of the bow staff. . . .

LEO FROBENIUS, *The Voice of Africa,* vol. 1

CHAPTER THIRTY-ONE

*T*hey had come as far as the great stone mount that rose out of the heart of the forest, the origin of the river and the end of their journey together. It was here that the rowers happily turned the canoe around and would let the fast stream take them back to the estuary and the healing coast, home, Oneofthewilliams, and the Sea People. Father Lutchen had been ordered to go on with the idiot Kippa and his writhing burden, the shredded man-flag of the Wassidrus. But it had never been his plan to agree to this. He still carried enough gold and charms to bribe the paddlers, who were mostly ignorant of all but their physical task to go and deliver their cargo and return, to take him with them. He would slip the boat at the estuary and find his way back to Essenwald on foot. But that had been before he had gathered the girl into the boat and his future.

They had pulled the canoe up on a shallow single beach and emptied its contents under the shade of a vast drooping tree that he guessed was a species of tropical willow. The frail strings of hanging leaves were nibbled and tossed by the slightest breeze, which gave their encampment a cool and reviving agitation. Kippa had propped up the man-flag, so for the first time since they had begun, he was vertical for a prolonged period of time. The rowers sat huddled together with their backs to the weird pair, while the old priest and the girl sat farther under the tree and talked.

"What place is this, are we going farther?" she asked.

Lutchen was silent.

"I know this is the great Vorrh and that I am destined to be here, but I did not think I would come this way."

The old man looked from the swaying dappled shadows to the bright shingle, and it made him squint.

"I did not know that you would come and take me."

"Neither did I," he said quietly.

The men were anxious to leave, wanting to be as far away as possible from the malign forest. But Lutchen insisted that they made camp here and leave early the next morning. They tried to argue, but he had been given authority over the journey. At least this far.

He wanted more time to think about the options and what all the circumstances meant to him. It would have been so easy to stick to the original plan and wave goodbye to the ill-assorted trio at the jungle path. But the sickening sense of responsibility was growing stronger every minute he shared with Modesta. All she had said confirmed it and he was beginning to accept that his fate was in some way entwined with hers. He watched her closely while the men made camp, trying to remember everything that Father Timothy had said about her in his anxious, petrified letters. But little surfaced, only a distant taste of her perverted innocence when she was a child. But there was no strength in that past: It had been obliterated by the magnetic pull towards the future. Even the Vorrh itself seemed complicit. The ragged mount, the beach, and the willow were having a powerful soothing effect on him. There was a beauty here that was unexpected and it was stilling his heart. Maybe he could stay here and accept the compromise as the best solution. There was nothing of the menace or the pressure that he had sensed before. The water seemed clear and wholesome, the sky bright, and the trees beautiful and rich in their generous shade. Fruit had fallen in and near the water and perfumed it with their radiance. And yet the path from here into the core of the mythical jungle also called. This would be the peak of his explorations, of all the reading and listening to myth and fable; God knows what real wonders he would find in its uncharted depth.

That night, while the others slept, he watched the flames of the campfire on the beach. Watched the sparks rise and the thin smoke swirl. At the height of his deliberations, Kippa appeared out of the shadow, his enormous bulk shifting from one foot to the other.

"Yes?" said Lutchen.

"It wants talk you," squeaked the falsetto voice from inside the looming fool.

The old man was about to tell him to keep it quiet and lay it down in the reeds when he changed his mind. Curiosity and instinct overcame him, so that he got up and followed the shambling mass towards the horror leaning against the tree.

Kippa had washed it down, cleaning some of the filth of the bilge from its malformed head and body.

"You have something to say?" he asked. The Wassidrus started moving up and down against the pole that held him together. The pumping motion increased in rapidity and vigour and resembled nothing less than some sort of deformed masturbatory practice. Kippa was giggling and copying the motion.

Lutchen was about to leave when the first word gushed out. He then realised that the action was a way to pump its damaged lung into a concertina action before speech.

"I've-bin-er," it said.

He had never considered the intelligence of the deformed

fragment of the man. It was a marvel that it lived at all, let alone had the capacity of even a glimmer of thought. He had seen its guttural hisses and wet mouthings as little more than an involuntary grimace being expelled from the blinding fury that obviously powered all that was left. Lutchen was here now more to keep Kippa quiet than anything else, never expecting actual coherent words to come from the wreck.

"Bufor . . . Er bufor."

Lutchen suddenly heard and understood the asphyxiated sounds. He moved closer to look into the piglike eyes for a sign of intelligent animation. Surely it could not be possible. What worse torture could ever be devised? He had helped men die who were suffering smaller injuries than this. Some residual part of Lutchen's ambition had been stirred by his meeting with the tribal witch who seemed to be responsible for keeping the two impossibly deformed men alive. He might learn something of her techniques and take them into the civilised world. There must be an extraordinary secret in her methods of surgical repair or in the herbal drugs that she so studiously protected. Whatever was keeping this tatter of humanity alive was down to her. He planned to return again to the Sea People and forcibly discover her wisdom.

The Wassidrus was wetly hissing and it brought him swiftly back to the moment.

"You have been here before?" he asked carefully, as if he had already said it.

The pole and its tenant shook horribly. "Yss."

The effort was damaging and it forced Lutchen to finally recognise it as a man, a human soul tethered before him.

"What can I do to help?" he asked.

"Go im." He pumped up and down again and Kippa joined in. "Im ver."

"In there?" translated the monk.

"Yss . . . Im ver I cun bi hild."

"It will hold you?"

Another level of rage strained the next sounds out. "Hild, it cun hil mi."

"Heal you? How can this happen, how do you know it?"

"T'hupen bufor."

"How?"

After a long pumping pause, one word dribbled out of his collapsing mouth: "Puradice." And with that he was spent, sagging back like a deflated wet sack dangling from the creaking pole.

Kippa was by his side, washing his face, prancing from one foot to the other and chanting, "Puradice, puradice, puradice!"

The last candle of doubt in Lutchen's mind about what he should do next had just been extinguished by a mighty wind. He looked back at the wretched man and saw that Kippa was feeding him tiny shreds of food from the bag that he always carried over one shoulder and never lost sight of. He had not seen the Wassidrus being fed before and never even thought about his nourishment. The overgrown child was carefully pushing the black tobacco-like fibres into his slobbering mouth. The care of the operation touched the old priest's scarred heart.

"Kippa, what do you feed him?"

Kippa turned, surprised at the question. He looked into the bag and at the stuff in his gentle hand.

"Im, bwana."

"Yes, Kippa, but what do you give 'im'?"

He grinned an enormous smile. "Im, bwana, I giv im, im . . ."

Lutchen realised that any conversation in the abstract was a waste of time with the poor soft-brained child. So he turned away, saying, "It's all right, my son, it does not matter."

Kippa was still looking at his hand when he said, "Plenty leavings over after the split. Tyc feeds im imself."

The old priest stopped in his tracks and let the words settle before his gorge began to rise.

The canoe floated off the shingle with a crunching shush as the last paddler jumped aboard after pushing it into the stream. Lutchen waved them off, but they did not respond, just paddled hard until they were out of sight. He turned back to the party that waited for him to lead them into the demented forest, searching for paradise. He looked at them and his heart sank. He was about to share an unknown path into unknowing with a fool, a young woman, and a monster or a victim. And even worse, he guessed that the ownerships of those qualities might be exchangeable. And worse still, he did not know which he would finally be allocated.

The vastness is the first thing to misunderstand. There is no space in the mind to hold it, either as a distant dark mass seen from above or in the endless labyrinthine folds of its interior. All become lost in those overlapping gaps that sometimes appear to be pathways between the trees. The vertical trunks confront and shutter all distance and any sense of volume.

But all these majestic flowerings were nothing compared to what occurred below. The root mass extended deeper and farther than the tallest tree in all directions away from the light; its iceberg proportions creaked and slithered in the ancient soil, clenching the particles of mud and stone with a relentless blind determination, while the strangeness at the very tip of the roots nuzzled and sensed all around them. There is no structure of mind or body in the animal kingdom that parallels the uniqueness of roots. There is no understanding of why or how that delicate mechanism becomes a sensing tendril and seeks out the nutrients it needs. No animal understands the process that makes it decide to turn this way as opposed to that way. To snuffle with force in its "chosen" direction. That sightless tip without any apparent organs or methods of perception moves forward to devour and conquer with a will that is outside the meagre appetites and instincts of all the blood-filled inhabitants.

Behind each moment of acute sensing lay solidification, each blind nuzzle dying back into the terse density of colourless fibre, the water squeezed through the now-inert roots and passing upwards. If the mass of the forest that lived in light was alien to humans, then the mass that lived in night was positively hostile in its indifference. Even the burrowing Erstwhile would not be tolerated. Even though their supposed purpose was a form of protecting the forest. When they dug down they never snapped or cut a root. They simply pushed them aside and squirmed in between their languid violence. But as the sleepers hid, the roots turned, often trapping them in fearful embraces. Or sent out more tendril extensions of themselves to penetrate the mothlike bodies, digging into their ribs and hooking through their faces. Those that eventually awoke often bore the scars of these intrusions, looking like ill-formed knotted arteries wandering under their jaws, cheeks, and eyes. Some no longer had eyes. The tips of the roots had found their moisture and sucked it into all the others, sugars to sprite the distant, frivolous leaves that jiggled and danced in the warm sunlit air.

CHAPTER THIRTY-TWO

*H*ector was enjoying meeting the dead in their ornate stone blocks. Great names were here under the tons of the poised cathedral. He was soberly dressed, the new strands of hair concocted into a much less elaborate arrangement than before, and it made his head feel light and strangely fresh. He respectfully visited John Donne. Eventually he found clever, subtle Wren tucked into a modest cleft in the far wall. He shuddered under the sealed black polished marble bath of Admiral Nelson and the Duke of Wellington's impregnable sarcophagus of Cornish porphyry. He pondered on the brief tablet to the absent Blake. Nicholas's obscure words sung in his memory. The voice detached Hector's vision from the vast window in the Bethlem Royal Hospital, a vision of the angel shuffling his ol' man through the streets of London, pointing ahead towards the gigantic cathedral. But the words would not attach to that vision; they preferred to cling and render to Nicholas's description of holding the old poet's head to the curved wall of the whispering gallery and demanding him to recite his last poem into the abstract depth of the stone's surface. Hector looked up, knowing that somewhere its implacable mass encircled the area above him. He dismissed himself from the company of the famed dead, many of whom he did not know. The good, the mighty, and the honoured barbaric, whose gritty bones formed a webbed foundation to strengthen the mud and hold the gigantic white cathedral aloft.

In the nave he felt a little lost. The size and the skidding echoes of human bustle shrank him. He sent fleeting glances into the dark corners and long perspectives, seeking Nicholas among the shadows. He had been looking for more than an hour now and wondered if he had understood Solli's oblique words about when and where they were supposed to meet. There seemed to be no service planned, so he walked gingerly into the great circle of the nave. The coolness was pleasurable, an escape from the surprising heat of the spring sun that had been dominating the streets outside for the last four days. Under the massive dome, he looked up into its hooded vastness and felt some trepidation about the amount of containment suspended above him. He was turning his head, bent on his twisted neck, when the first whistle sounded. A long, thin strand of sound blown from practised lips. In tune and wistful. He looked harder to trace its origin. From above, he thought, but he could not be sure. For a moment it was here or there, then it was everywhere, filling the entire dome. And now it was gone, only its memory sounding in the resonance of his head.

There were silhouettes of visitors up in what he knew must be the Whispering Gallery. Their heads and shoulders dotted the great ring of its railed-in walkway: a halo of a path, gated in stone, rimming the base of the great dome. He crossed towards the altar, still looking up. Another whistle sounded out, and as it happened, somebody waved from above. Were they waving at him? The raised hand moved until the sound faded and then dropped. It must be Nicholas, thought Hector, and made a feeble half response, his hand flapping just below his chin.

The steps leading up to gallery were mercifully shallow and wide, designed for a horse or an old man, he thought as he ascended. Two hundred and fifty-seven steps later, his heart pulsing sensibly in his throat, he arrived through the wooden door into the gallery. Its great O immediately engulfed him in the peculiarity of its size and alarm of its perspective. How could any architect ever conceive of such a space? Surely it was a by-product of the vast dome rather than a specified identity. How could any man live with this precipitous edge in his consciousness or, worse, in his dreams? Hector walked to the metal balustrade, gripping it severely, and peered over and down its high scrolled rail. The volume below seemed greater than its reverse when he looked up. A monstrous gulp of space, a concavity of dread. He shrank back from the vast hollowness to the low seat that ran around the gallery and pressed his back against the reassuring solidity of stone. A flutter of sound came off the wall, the famous ring of whispers. He looked quickly at the few other visitors to see which one was testing the weird audible phenomenon, which couple was spinning sweet nothings to each other along the ghostly curve. None of them were near the wall. They were all engaged in peering down into the sculptured abyss or craning their faces up to peer into the dome. Who was making the sound? Where was it coming from? He put his warm ear closer, nearly touching the chill stone. Out of nowhere the skidding centrifugal whisper said, "We will sleep together again to keep it tight, to make the plural, to keep it right." It was a singsong man's voice, and the words were clear and unmistakable.

Hector snatched his head back from the wall, outraged and blushing. Looking around to see who was playing this distasteful prank. He strained his eyes to look across the void to see if anyone was talking to the wall, expecting to see Nicholas somewhere on the other side of the circle. None of the other people dotted around the ring paid him any attention, even though he thought that his head must have been signalling violently, like the new orange flashing globes that were being erected all around London. "Belisha beacons," the workman had said. The ridiculous name had stuck in his mind and kept repeating like an indigestible pebble of food. For some reason it now seemed to merge with the distasteful nonsense from the wall. He shook his head to dislodge the words from his ears with a horrible feeling that it was too late. The obscene utterance was already ringing inside. It must be Nicholas, playing a trick. They had never slept together that night, never shared his bed, even though they were both exhausted. He had been alone. Playing jokes like this was dangerous. Other people might hear and think him unnatural, even perverted. He would talk to the Erstwhile about the jeopardy in this sort of thing. The whistle sounded again, but this time it was dropping in pitch, seeming to go lower than he thought possible from human lips. Then a vibrato strangled its linear directness. A quiver entered the air. He moved back against the wall for solidity and it shuddered too, and all the light in the cathedral flickered out, including the damp daylight that had nudged the windows. Time turned inside out, spilling pitch-blackness. Then a gaunt sharp flash seared every window and threw the giant statues of saints into horrid spotlight. An enormous explosion rocked the air inside the cupped dome and the hollow beneath. The orange of the Belisha plumed into the magnitude of the sun and a totally black combustion wrecked his ears and hammered his face through his skull. He was lifted off his feet and sucked through the sharp, broken iron ribs of the balustrade into the night rubble and falling sightless volume of whirlwind shrapnel. Then it stopped, instantly cut short by normality before reaching its deafening, destructive crescendo where his body would have been torn apart. Turned off mid-blast by wet sun and the hum of people below. The unaware murmur of visitors, the hush of prayer, and the timid bustle of the choir taking their place, ready to sing God's good praise. People moved quietly around and past him on the rim of whispers. A rhythmic pulse of near words chanting him towards death or life.

Hours, days, or years later Hector broke out in trembling, giddy perspiration, fearing the worse for his sanity. His back stuck wetly to the cold stone. His sensible mind climbed out of the rubble of phenomena, adjusted itself, wiped off the dust and cinders, and took stock of his body and the distrustful solidity of the building that surrounded it. He was in one piece, nothing had actually happened. The metal and stone halo of the hand-rail was still intact, the dome unbroken. This event had been another of the abnormal experiences that had so punctuated his recent life. So why should he be so terrified by it? It was only an illusion, a waking dream. He closed his eyes and breathed deeply to let all the images and sounds settle into a proper and unalarming place.

Then again the whistle sounded high, long, and thin above him. He slowly, resentfully opened his eyes, and bent his weary head upwards to look into the cupola. At its centre aperture there was a glimpse of another much smaller gallery sitting tightly above the dome. His eyes were still bruised by the frightful vision and he rubbed them hard to see if the sound came from there. A single figure was looking down at him, the whistle swimming about its head. Hector stood up to look more closely, and then it waved and beckoned. The tune of the whistle calmed him like warm milk, shushing and coating the jagged violence in his head. Removing shock and hurt. Replacing the trauma with a model of its meaning; white and rounded as if memory itself had been sculpted and smoothed by hands, gloves, and sponges soaked in tepid, discreet balm.

St. Paul's Cathedral has two domes. One inside the other. A brilliant contrivance to give exterior grandeur and interior closeness. Between the domes there is a great supporting cone of bricks pierced with oval windows, spiracles to let the dark and music breathe. To circulate with the gone-astray prayers that still drone in the unseen masonry hive. Sir Christopher's years of sucking the stars and the heavens into his eye through a tube inspired him as much as his dissected mappings of the human brain. The calculations of orbits unscaffolded in the limp tissues is reversed here. There is not a trace of flaccidity in the heights of London's most dominant church. Smoke, cloud, and the London particular are banned entrance, and even gravity holds its tongue in the space between the domes that is belted and braced against all options and opinions. Hector knew some of this. He had of course read about the building in advance of his visit, being the first customer outside the public library on that warm morning.

Dark locked doors punctuate the Whispering Gallery. A few are open to let visitors circulate to other viewpoints. Hector found the one that led to the next staircase up to the stone gallery, which is a stone balcony on the outside of the dome. He mistakenly ventured there and was quickly repelled by the hot gusting wind. He found his way around to the next ingress upwards. It was a very different matter, for now he was in the space between the great outer dome and the dynamic cone of bricks that rose up like a hidden, polished, smoothed-out Tower of Babel. The voices that swam around it came from below and outside, a litany of whispers pummelling and washing the dark air. An iron stair wound its way up to the Golden Gallery that ringed the base of the lantern and crowned the outer dome. But this was not his target. Somewhere in between lay the entrance to the Ornamental Gallery that sat on the top of the eggshell of brick and plaster of the inner dome. The iron stair sullenly rang with his footfalls as he corkscrewed his way upwards. His birdlike weight shook the iron and suggested a rhythmic sway to its length, which was mercifully broken by jutting cantilevered landings that perched gauntly like so many forged crows on the corbels that extended from the cone.

Hector did not look down nor did he look up. So that when he stopped to get his breath and saw the door open on the landing's extension, he did not know how far he had climbed. The whistles that came out from it were clear and touchable. He approached it across the squeaking iron. He gained its landing and bobbed through the door in the cone onto timber stairs that creaked at a lower and vaguely more reassuring pitch, turning to set foot onto the floor surrounding the ring. Nicholas was there leaning over the cast-iron fence, the resonance of a whistle in the air, hanging in the gritty atoms around him. The platform Hector now stood on felt the most unstable yet. True, it sat on the top surface of the inner dome and it was securely attached to the walls of the cone, but it felt thin and delicate, no more than a membrane over the long fall that he had already seen crumble in his nightmare vision into black wrenching nothing . . . His feet tried not to convey his timid weight to this floor that sounded under him, and he could not help thinking that he was walking on a stone circle balanced like a halo on the thin eggshell structure of the blind side of the dome. He held the railing as if it were the last thing on earth. He stepped forward towards the grinning nonchalance of Nicholas, who waved him on.

"Professor Schumann, how wonderful to see you, and looking so well," Nicholas said with great enthusiasm.

Hector knew he was shivering and that his pallor must be ghastly in the extreme, but he did not have the breath to debate the Erstwhile's friendly greeting.

"I am so glad to meet you here in little Christopher's great folly. Have you been enjoying the view?"

Hector was now fighting for a reply, edging around the circle towards Nicholas.

"We are very privileged to be here, the Ornamental Gallery is not normally available to the common public."

"There is nothing public or common about you," Hector spat out in a wheeze.

Nicholas beamed even more, taking the old man's venom as a compliment.

"Did you know that there are more stairs up to the Golden Gallery on the outside? From there you can see across the entire city, even to where the river tastes the sea, where we will be. And then there is a wonderful stair farther up into the lantern itself. In the old days you could even climb a ladder and put your head inside the golden ball."

The talk of ladders and further heights was making Hector nauseous. He had heard enough and wanted to find a safe way down to dogmatic terra firma.

"Why are we here, Nicholas?"

"Come closer. Look down from here, see how tiny the people are, like ants," said Nicholas, his long body leaning over the rail, standing on tiptoe.

Hector felt frost in his spine and a giddy hollow in his bowels.

"I don't want to look," he said between clenched teeth.

"Oh, but you must look, it's respectful to do so, just for one minute."

A fury was joining the frost.

"Respectful?" he snarled. "What respect is there in saying

obscene untruths for all to hear, of playing tricks, and . . . and . . . and whistling in a church?"

Nicholas turned his attention from the ants below.

"Oh, that wasn't me," he said, his beaming head turned to one side like a petulant bird's.

Hector looked openmouthed into the lie.

"Who else could it be? There is nobody else here."

Nicholas shrugged and opened his hands in a sign of unknowing. They stared at each other, locked in their gestures as the organ began to play seventy metres below.

"Whistling isn't bad. There was lots of whistling in the Vorrh."

"In the what?"

"The Vorrh, the forest that holds the garden of par—"

"Oh, that," said Hector nastily. "Have I climbed up here to talk about myths?"

"The Vorrh is more real than you. But you are right, let's not talk about it here, let's talk more about whistling. It's all foible, I think you call it. Did you know they used to have horse races in the nave here in the good old days? Between the services, of course."

"That can't be true," said Hector, outraged by the speed and change of direction in Nicholas's jabbering and yet another lie.

"It was the wooden days before the burning pies," laughed Nicholas, convulsing, taking his hands off the low rail and bringing up his fluttering fingers to cover his lips, in what Hector saw as a suspiciously effeminate gesture. The choir joined the organ and the twisting strands of sound rose towards them.

"I want to go down," said Hector flatly.

Nicholas continued to titter.

"I have had enough," Hector said, a great sadness beneath his voice.

Nicholas stopped giggling and turned his head violently backwards, his teeth snapping at his collar. Hector had seen this before and it made no sense then. He assumed it was a kind of nervous spasm but of little interest to him now as he turned towards the small wooden door.

"Sorry, Hector, the bombos must have scared you." The loose grin was gone and replaced by a sensitive caring smile. Nicholas crossed the resounding floor and loomed over the confused man, putting his arm around his little shoulder.

"Was it more semblance, is that why we are here?" said Hector again, more to his shoes than to the looming Nicholas.

"If you want to see afar it must be from high, is it not so? If you wanted to see the past it must be from below, underneath."

Hector looked dumbfounded by such an obtuse answer.

"Now you can start your undoing proper."

"I don't know what you are talking about," said Hector wearily.

"There are no words yet. Except what William told you from the wall."

"It was difficult to hear and understand. It was a poem or a hymn about a celestial wood. A great forest that covered the earth and healed all sins. He sang about the two kingdoms that I think mean earth and heaven. There were many names that I did not know."

Nicholas frowned and said, "No, Professor, you got it wrong. The two kingdoms are the multitude that live here. One kingdom of sap, the other of blood. That's what my ol' man's song was about. The healing of the great mistake, putting all of Adam's tribe back in its place or wiping it all away. The forest covering over the scars and ideas that were not supposed to happen."

"This is really difficult for me to understand. Is Blake saying that all of humanity was a mistake?"

"Not God's mistake in making it. The mistake was that it escaped from the garden and grew abnormal in one direction. Those clever thumbs were given for the tending of plants, not making cities, machines, and endless ideas of how things work, most of which are wrong."

"But Blake's song is quiet and hidden. What good is that?"

"My radio is quiet when the wires are not attached, but the voices and vibrations are still there. The tellings of the past and futures bubbling in the space around things. His song works like that, it saturates and surprises the growing wires and when his little church is laid to waste it will spin out across everything."

"Is that what the whistling and the explosion were?"

"It is important that you understand it. He heard the whistling too. I am sorry if what you heard and saw scared you, but that bombos was only a tiny part of what will be, if we don't make the plural in the river together. There will be much deviation and hesitation, many will be burnt alive."

Now Hector was completely lost, having no idea what this lunatic, angel, or reanimated corpse was talking about. Nicholas tightened his grip on Hector's shoulder in a friendly way and for a moment Hector thought he heard the whistling again, this time coming from below, somewhere inside the stairwell. But it could have been a discordance between the great organ, the choir, and the architecture. Or the wind disconnecting all three. He looked up at what now was pretending to be his guardian.

"Shall we go down?" said Nicholas.

Hector nodded.

On the sloping turns down Nicholas started talking again.

"Have you noticed any difference since the malgama, any changes in the old soma? Any improvements? The yoking will do it, you see."

Hector was just about to run out of patience when he thought he understood what Nicholas was trying to say. He stopped mid-stair.

"Improvements. Do you mean my health? Do you mean my hair?"

"Ah-ha, the old barnet." Nicholas laughed.

That's what those foolish boys had said, Barnet, Professor Barnet. There was obviously somebody else involved in all this, another senior academic that he had not yet met. Perhaps someone who might make some sense.

"Who is he?"

"Who is who?"

"Professor Barnet."

"Who?"

"What do you mean, 'who'?"

Both men stopped talking while Nicholas thought for a while, cocking his head in a studious fashion, stroking his chin. In profile Hector thought he looked like the Sidney Paget illustrations of Sherlock Holmes from *The Strand Magazine* and was surprised he had not noticed it before. He brightened at the likeness; then the tall man answered.

"Too-wit too-woo," he said energetically and was very pleased with himself.

Hector's mouth sagged open before it puckered into a livid snort. "*Hundsfott*," he spat out and stomped off, away from his imbecile protector, downwards towards the sanity of the noisy street.

In his temper he hammered the pavement, walking fast, his velocity powered by mutterings and curses on his way back towards Whitechapel. Passersby cringed and flinched out of his way: a small angry tweed cannonball parting the waves. He stopped somewhere in the hub of Threadneedle Street, a little lost but more surprised by his speed. His irritation with Nicholas had been burnt off, its vapour trail snaking through the old streets. He had suddenly become conscious of his actions and the effect of them on the crowds around him. He had not stopped to take a breath once and was now ready for more. His body felt lithe and wired by adrenaline. But this is impossible, he thought. He should be wheezing, panting, and fatigued. But every muscle said the opposite, they were just warming up. He gazed about him finding his compass point, and decided to test this phenomenon. What was there to lose? He had already given himself up for dead or dying years ago. Better to be extinguished by a heart attack while enjoying the gleam of health rather than rotting away in a bed somewhere or being blown asunder in one of Nicholas's future explosions. He turned his head towards the east and reared up into an expansive strut. Again the crowded pavement cleared and in his wake he left dozens of mystified strangers. By Aldgate he was trotting and had lost his hat, spinning below the dynamic wedge of Gardeners Corner under the hissing tram wires. The wind tore at his head, dragging at his unwoven strands of hair, pulling them behind him, trailing out like an imaginary heroic mane. In Whitechapel Road he was running full pelt, the faces and shops flapping past him, exhilaration burning oxygen brightly. A woman at a costermonger's stall screamed as he passed, dropping her paper bag of shocked bouncing oranges. Others called after him without anything to say. One of Solli's khevre was loitering outside the Pavilion when he thought he saw the hirsute Hector barrelling past. "Don't be silly," he said to himself and turned back to his halted conversation. Such general amazement is often accompanied by a sense of goodwill and innocent pleasure, but not in Whitechapel, where running had a very different meaning. It was outside Lord Rodney's Head that a police constable attempted to halt Hector's progress.

"Oi, stop!" he bellowed, stepping in front of what looked like a manic, ancient wereferret.

The bulk of the blue-clad man was brushed aside, leaving him tottering on his hobnailed boots to the great entertainment of the crowd. Hector did not even slow at the base of his stairs but ran straight up, leaping the flights, eventually breaking only at the normality of his own front door and his need to find a key rather than just crashing through it.

Inside he peeled off his coats and shirt and stood by the sink looking into the meagre mirror at a panting creature that he had never met before.

CHAPTER THIRTY-THREE

*T*he news from Germany was not good. The telegram soliciting help to remove or at least realign the military officers who had arrived and were making outlandish requests failed utterly. The answer was bitterly disappointing and blindingly simple. They must be obeyed. Whatever their request. Talbot called the guild together to announce the news. Krespka saw it as Talbot's own personal failure and stormed out of the room in a rage. The others just sat silently around the oval table and stared into the perfection of its polished surface.

Since the explosion in Essenwald the military had become suspicious of everybody. Guards had been doubled and a greater need to show their superior power was thought necessary. In the station, Sturmbannführer Keital and his men had already taken over. Nobody dared to argue with such uniforms. When the confirmation came from the guild that everything must be done to meet the Germans' needs, the operation was already under way; the train had different flatbed trucks attached, and the stored and spare replacement rails had been loaded, along with acres of sleepers. The rest would be cut from the living forest as soon as more steel arrived. But for now they had enough to make a productive start. Troops were arriving daily in heavy canvas-covered trucks. All was ready to extend the track and cleave the Vorrh, making a sensible route to the rest of the conquerable world. The entire workforce of the city was more than happy to help load the train and see the newcomers on their way. But not one stayed on the train when it started to move. Even though the officers were screaming commands and telling everybody to get on, nobody moved. They just watched the massively creaking carriages stunt and shudder forward as the engine strained against the weight, trying to find its purchase on the rails before it could move forward.

Gauleiter Plagge stepped down from one of the flatbeds in a crisp, even movement. He was a small man who looked like he had been born wearing his present uniform. He stepped over to the band of workers who had just finished loading the train.

"Get on, you are going with this cargo to construct the line."

Nobody moved or spoke. He came up close to one of the towering sweating men.

"Get on the train," he demanded. The man ignored him.

"Get on the train!" Plagge shouted, spittle flying from his mouth and onto the man's bare black chest. He looked back towards the engine and his commanding officer, who nodded loudly. Plagge fumbled for his holster while everyone looked on, frozen in the inevitability of the moment.

"On the train!" he screamed again, the barrel of his Luger in the man's face. He sluggishly obeyed the command, slouching sideways to mount the flatbed, followed by all the others who had been rounded up by the armed soldiers. A great mass of workers and station staff clung to the piled steel tracks and sleepers as the engine finally gained sufficient traction to move off. The troops scrambled onto the last two carriages as the train crawled out of the station. Talbot had been watching the event with Fleischer at a safe distance.

"This will all lead to disaster," he said and Fleischer nodded.

The first man jumped from the train as it entered the rim of the Vorrh. He was followed by almost all of the others, who preferred the risk of a broken neck to the certainties of brain death in the merciless forest. The soldiers had no idea what to do and most of the absconders had gone before they became aware of the mass exodus. One fired his machine gun into the speeding undergrowth. This alerted the officers, who had been enjoying the ride on the footplate of the roaring engine. They ordered Oswald Macombo, called Hoss to halt the train, which took a considerable time because of the weight, speed, and momentum of the load. By the time it grated to a halt, every man of the forced expedition had vanished, making their own slow way back towards the city and its outskirts, having no intention of going anywhere near the station or the lumber camp again. At least not until the Men Without Substance grew wise again. Retribution would be avoided this way, because the one thing they had learned about all the intruders was that they could not distinguish the difference between one black man and another.

After the soldiers had been screamed at by Plagge, the officers gathered to save some kind of plan out of their aborted expedition. There was no point in going on. Nothing could be achieved without an active workforce. They had of course heard about the Limboia, and that just made them even more infuriated and disgusted. Nothing in this ramshackle godforsaken pit of a town could be relied upon. There was only one option: to return and put the whole operation, including the train and the station, under martial law. They would bring in their own forces in bulk to make this venture happen. With this decided, they scolded Hoss into reversing the engine and driving everything back to where it had begun. They steeled themselves for the ridicule and laughter that would be waiting for them on their return, but were momentarily relieved to find the station and goods yards completely empty, as were most places they decided to go. The soldiers were marched back to their temporary barracks and the officers licked their wounds in the bar of the city's finest hotel and planned their next campaign. Meanwhile, the guild could have its pathetic train back to ferry the soulless men and the stinking wood. Hoss let the pressure down, slowly opening all the veins of the engine, and went home.

Talbot and Fleischer, with the blessings and the spurs of most of the Timber Guild, tried once more to reason with the officers. Troops had been arriving all week and the train station of the timber yard had become their centre of operations. Buildings had been requisitioned and tents erected around them. Metal rails were being ceaselessly manufactured in the company smithy, and the goods carriages added to the ever-increasing length of the train. Nothing would slow or stop their commitment to driving a track through the entire Vorrh. Even some of the guild members were beginning to believe it was possible, getting caught up in the impressive determinism of mechanical momentum. The fear of the Vorrh suddenly felt a long way off. It was obvious the Germans would not be swayed by tales of legend and myth, even if they had all been proven to be true. So the only thing the guild had to rely on was the indisputable truth of the malicious effects of the forest on human health and well-being. With medical facts they might change the course of the proposed line. They were told to wait outside of Keital's onsite office, the former stationmaster's room. To wait in the sun and watch the hectic flow of uniformed men, who were now the only workforce to be seen.

"Come in, gentlemen, I can give you ten minutes," said Keital, who was now at the door. "As you can see we are very busy."

Plans and other papers littered the desks that had been dragged together to form a central block in the middle of the room. Fleischer wondered if they might have a model train under all the paper to complete the reality of their proposal. He was quickly shunted out of his reverie by the sight of Plagge at the other side of the room tinkering with the controls of the heavy and ancient fan that languidly moved over their heads.

"So what do you want?" asked Keital in the most disagreeable way possible.

The two men looked at each other briefly, then Talbot began.

"To discuss the possible dangers to your men of a prolonged stay in the Vorrh."

Keital bristled and Plagge turned away from the troublesome controls and walked towards them.

"More nonsense," he said.

"No, Gauleiter, concern, our genuine concern about the health and safety of your troops."

Plagge made a deflated hiss and sank loudly into a chair.

"Continue," said Keital, standing behind the impressive table.

Fleischer took the baton and explained.

"There is indisputable medical proof of a condition that affects anybody who spends prolonged periods in the forest. It affects the nervous system and the emotional stability of the sufferer. Severe cases lead to permanent loss of memory and alarming dislocation of identity."

"You have it?" said Keital.

Fleischer was confused and assumed that the Sturmbann-führer was rudely suggesting that he was a sufferer.

"Have what?" he said defensively.

"The medical proof you speak of."

Fleischer did not know what to say and looked back at Talbot.

"Not as such, not on paper. But I myself have seen men grievously infected with this malady only after a few hours of exposure. Our own workforce is living proof of the long-term effect. If we might be permitted to bring them back to the slave house, then I can show you."

Plagge perked up. "You still have slaves?" He sounded impressed for the first time.

"No, Gauleiter, they are not slaves, but damaged workers, who—"

He was interrupted by Keital. "These are the ghosts who cut down the trees for you and work without pay?"

"Yes, Sturmbannführer," said Talbot, a glint of shame in his answer. "But they are not ghosts, they are real men who have been injured by the great forest."

"What, have trees fallen on all their heads?" Plagge jested. He and Keital laughed merrily at the image.

"No, their minds have been damaged by some miasma, some magnetic influence in the Vorrh."

"Oh, I see, the trees have brainwashed them." They laughed even more. "But that is not difficult, they are only Negroes."

Both men were besides themselves with glee until Talbot said, "Not all of them, and the same thing will happen to you and your men."

The laugher stopped and Talbot knew he had gone too far and their case was lost.

"You dare to compare us to that worthless scum?" barked Plagge out of a suddenly scarlet face.

"No . . . I—"

"You still want to divert the purpose of the Reich with infantile stories of lazy sick Negroes?"

"Again, you waste our time," said Keital, and sharply nodded at Plagge, who snatched the door open and used his chin to point at its exit.

Outside in the glaring sun they walked back into the city.

"We can do no more" was the only thing that Talbot said.

CHAPTER THIRTY-FOUR

*I*t had taken some time, but Ishmael realised that the Kin had never been into the forest before. They looked at things, touched them as they walked, and sometimes drew each other's attention to leaves or stones, the colour of lichen, or an animal moving above them in the trees. They made small noises as if conferring.

It occurred to him as he traipsed behind them that perhaps they had never been outside of Kühler Brunnen. Maybe never in the world at all. The thought reassured his pride; he might again become master here. After all, he was one of the most travelled men in the Vorrh: one of its survivors, his mind unscathed by its leaching effect. He was no ordinary man but something different, improved. Maybe he was a prototype, an original, just as Nebsuel had said all along. He should have listened more to the old man, stayed with him and kept his face unmarred. Perfectly other to the rest of humanity. Seth looked back over his shoulder to check on Ishmael's well-being and progress. They caught each other's eyes and made an assessment. Ishmael shaped the equation in his head and marvelled at its rightness. *If I master the Kin in this place, then I will have their support forever.* Perhaps there were more stored away in the house or crated in the warehouse that he tricked that fool Mutter into showing him. Maybe there were dozens: disciples. Or hundreds: a tribe. Thousands: an army.

They were walking deeper into the Vorrh on a path that was little more than an animal track. Ishmael was getting tired and hungry, and he asked them to find him some food. After their initial puzzlement and the explanation that they had no instructions, materials, or kitchen, they finally agreed to find fruit and roots. Seth started digging in the soft mulchy earth and Aklia climbed a tree. They had both retained some of the water from the pool somewhere in their heads or bodies and regurgitated it into Ishmael's open hands so that he could drink. When they returned, they watched him intently as he gnawed on colourless tubers and slobbered berries and a guava-like fruit. He demanded more water and this time, so as not to spill a drop, Aklia pumped it directly from her hard throat into his sticky mouth, like a bird feeding her young. After his repast he sat with his back against a tree and felt refreshed. He touched his face and found the socket closing its jagged lips, healing together.

"Where are we going?" he unexpectedly asked. His voice sounding strange and unneeded in the trees.

The Kin said nothing.

"How long are we walking for? I ask because if it's many more days, then I will need better food than this. You might have to think about hunting something."

A slight whirring chirp came from Seth, and Aklia moved her hand in a shape that was not a gesture.

"I will need proper sustenance for survival and keeping my energy levels high."

Still no words to his questions and demands.

"What's wrong with you, have you gone deaf and dumb?"

"No, we can speak and hear, but we have nothing to say," said Aklia.

"Just answer my questions," demanded Ishmael.

"We can't."

"Why not?"

"Because we don't know."

"We have no instructions," added Seth.

Ishmael stared at them in disbelief. As he did so a yellow butterfly landed on Aklia's hard brown chest, on the left domed bump that indicated that some part of her had been designated female. Aklia and Seth bent their heads to look at it, showing mechanical signs of what might be excitement in the lever actions of their limited facial expressions. Another butterfly landed on her shoulder, and they lost all interest in Ishmael. He started seething at their fickle attention and was about to speak again when the space between the trees changed colour and movement flickered there. A sound like rumpled paper filled the air, but softly, like the noise of snow landing. Yellow shimmered everywhere as a vast flock of butterflies came out of the forest. Tidal-waving between the dark verticals and falling in silhouettes against the bright sky that bobbed high in the canopy. Multitudes of butterflies arrived and perched on every inch of Aklia's brown body. Seth stepped back and Ishmael stood up. Aklia extended her arms and made a sighing sound. More and more came and balanced one on top of the other until they were up to five or six deep. Nothing could be seen of Aklia, her slender, tall form having been fattened out into a pulsing mass of manlike proportions. More and more flittered towards her and settled on the delicate mass.

Ishmael thought she looked like Bibendum, the Michelin rubber-tyre man that waved at him from the garage in town. He smirked at the ridiculous idea. More came until she lost all human form and the shapeless mass bristled yellow, absorbing every glimmer of sun. Their wings settled into unified flapping, making a pulsing murmur. They must have stayed like this for nearly an hour, mesmerised, before she started calling. A weird shrill blur that seemed to match, to resonate with the vivid colour, which was now swaying from side to side. Seth suddenly leapt at it, waving his arms like machetes inside the mass. He frantically tugged and shaved at the butterflies, plucking mangled handfuls away from the shaking form beneath. The smeared yellows were sticking to his shiny body as their numbers diminished into wet pulp. If he had been human, he would have looked at Ishmael for help. But he was not and thus he spared the humiliation and waste of time because the cyclops was bending and rocking, holding his chest in hysterical mirth, enjoying every second of the ridiculous pantomime that seemed to be staged for his entertainment. Finally, Aklia was back again, gleaming in the sunlight, her body covered with smeared wings and the yellow dust that was shed by them, now turned a murky ochre, mixed with their blood. She was trembling and moving from one foot to the other. It was the most human, childlike movement Ishmael had seen her or any of the Kin ever make, and he stopped laughing and came close to inspect her. Her jaw was chattering and Seth seemed to be imitating it while making gushes of what sounded like speech. All the words were chopped up in gnashing.

"What's wrong with her?" asked Ishmael, still smirking.

"I don't know. She seems disconnected or magnetised."

"Looks to me like she is scared."

"It might be the same thing."

"Then shake her out of it."

Seth grabbed Aklia's twitching arm and shook her body with great force. It seemed to work when he let go and she remained stationary. Then her jaw started jabbering again and her feet moved, putting her into a jolting shudder.

"Oh for God's sake, give her a slap," said the grinning Ishmael.

Seth thought for a while and then brought up his arm as if

reaching behind him. Ishmael ducked out of the way as the arm
and the outreached flat of the hand swung through space, hitting the doddering Kin firmly across the face and sending her
sprawling sideways. The sound of Bakelite on Bakelite was horrible and so shocking that it turned the cyclops's snigger into
a hiss. Aklia lay twisting on the earth, then sat up and looked
around.

"My God, it worked, it actually worked," said Ishmael. Seth
helped her stand and brushed her down. Ishmael was so stunned
by the accuracy of his advice that he let out another kind of
laugh, without the flavour of bile. Seth understood its difference and attempted to imitate it. The result was very wrong and
sent the cyclops back to his infancy with them, where once they
had all tried to join him in the mechanism, the performance
of laughing. It had terrified him and they'd had to promise to
never do it again. And now after all these years in these dire circumstances, Seth forgot. His vocalisation made birds flap away
from high in the canopy. It woke Aklia, who instantly tried to
join in. Her disconnected expression was still attached to her
yapping mouth. Ishmael clamped his hands over his ears, tears
running down his face, and screamed, "Stop it, stop it."

Which they did. The forest was silent with them until Aklia
regained the path and stumbled forward. The others followed
until their automatic bodies brought their minds back into the
steady pace of walking. Ishmael tried to question her about
what had just happened but got nowhere. Two hours later the
flies arrived and performed the same act of swarming over her
now-defensive body. But nothing would deter them. Thousands
upon thousands came until she wore a diving suit of their sandwiched bodies. All of the charm of the previous invasion had
been replaced by this writhing infestation of carrion-dipped
insistence. She screeched and warbled. Seth dug and paddled,

but nothing would stop them. There was even a queue in the trees waiting for their turn to attack and mass. At twilight they left and she lay between her companions, just her eyes and fingers moving. Then the mosquitoes came and there were a few in their many that were content to drink from their secondary target of Ishmael, while the horde blunted their hypodermic mouths continually on the smooth plastic hardness of Aklia. There must have been something in her that smelt of the sustenance of blood. She lay very still while the tide of insects found it to be a lie. Ishmael jumped and swatted and demanded a fire be made to smoke the beasts away. At dawn he finally slept, aching and itching all over.

They continued to walk later in the morning, this time with Aklia dawdling behind. Much of her energy had gone and she seemed aimless and wan.

"How much farther do we have to go?" mumbled Ishmael.

"I don't know. I hope we find one soon. She is running down to nothing," said Seth without turning to look at the questioner.

A few more steps and a few more jarred thoughts along the track, Ishmael said, "Find one what?"

"A charging frame."

It took Seth a few minutes to realise that he was walking alone. He turned and looked behind to the point where Ishmael had stopped, and Aklia, who hovered behind him, had copied his action.

"What's wrong?" Seth called, and getting no answer he mooched back towards them. "What's wrong?" he asked again.

"Charging frame?" said Ishmael. "We are looking for a charging frame here, in this?" He waved a sagging, heavy arm at the erect indifferent perfection around him.

"We need one to recharge. There is always one somewhere," said Seth.

Ishmael snorted loudly. "You stupid fucking machine. There's nothing out here, fucking nothing."

"But if we don't recharge then we will cease—"

Then, before the cyclops had time to scream or beat him, the beetles arrived. The first heavy black dot landed on Seth's face like an uncertain inkblot; then the air darkened in a clicking dry thunder of them. Ishmael slid down to sit in a heap and Aklia copied him. Seth stood black and shiny, trying to wait on his feet. But these creatures were much heavier than the others and after some hours he sank to his knees. A few landed on Aklia but seemed unimpressed and moved on. Two or three settled on Ishmael and he crushed their brittle carapaces in his much-bitten hand. After the chittering cloud dispersed, the three crawled into a huddle under the girth of a mighty oak.

Waiting for the visitation of the next plague was worse when still, so without conversation they agreed to go on, limping in the general direction they had been heading.

After a while they entered a shaved clearing where the atmosphere was different from anything they had experienced yet. Ishmael relished the open space; then he saw the frame. Seth saw it too in the far corner. It was undoubtedly man-made. The Kin rushed towards its angular uprights. Ishmael cautiously followed. It was a very simple structure made out of recently cut branches. Vines were tied into its corners and around the hollow where the head would sit. It was a mockery of the device that lived in the basement of Kühler Brunnen: a bush-crafted copy without the faintest trace of the power that the Kin so desperately needed. For the last fifteen minutes or so a low pulse like a drum had been coming from inside Aklia: a warning tone to alert them to her state of exhaustion. Seth touched the frame and its flimsy construction shook and started to come apart. Aklia approached and also touched it, her eyes seeking something in the others' faces.

"Perhaps we can fix it?" said Seth.

Ishmael had been pulling bits of skin from its surface and from under the vine ties.

"Fix it into what?" He groaned without looking up.

"Fix it for her," Seth answered.

Ishmael just walked away.

Near the centre of the clearing was a small raised hillock. A bump of human proportions. Ishmael poked about at its surface, dislodging some of the loose earth and fibrous plants. He pushed his hand into it and then started to reach inside. Its interior was hollow.

Seth had repaired the frame and placed Aklia in its constraint, tying her arms and legs and binding her forehead in a travesty of the power connection of the charging frame. She seemed to have brightened in her constriction, perhaps sensing familiarity in the ritual. The warning beat inside her had become faster and louder and they tried to ignore it.

Ishmael had found the entrance at ground level on the other side. He had pulled away the undergrowth and the circular stone that sealed it. He had started to crawl into it when he heard the charger start up. The low, unmistakable hum that fed the all-powerful Kin. He crawled back out expecting to see them standing over a camouflaged dynamo unit, concealed in the forest awaiting their foretold arrival. But none was there. The noise came from Seth, who stood behind the frame holding his hard hands to his mouth and imitating the hum from the basement. Aklia could not see him behind her as she lay, eyes closed, awaiting the first morphic jolt. The pulse from inside her was making a harmonic with Seth's imitation, and then the white ants came; a whispering stream like milk crossed the clearing and headed for the frame, twigs and fallen leaves pushed aside in its progress. When it reached the frame it climbed up its vertical form. Now less like milk and more like cream, its viscous flow moved in reverse, rising where it should be falling. Soon her body and the frame was a thickening, bubbling mass. Aklia started twitching, a long orgasmic sigh escaping beneath the thousands of writhing bodies. Her pounding had accelerated to pitch against Seth's cracking hum. The ants were also climbing his body, the vanguard already at his mouth, where he plucked at them and spat them away. The frame was shaking violently when the percussion ceased. She never cried again and it seemed as if she might have believed that Seth's hum was indeed the machine and the tide of ants the pulse of the current. When she ceased, the insects shrank back, the albino shadow draining out of the enclosure.

Seth walked away from the broken frame and stood next to Ishmael and the mound.

"What have you found?" he calmly enquired.

The cyclops greatly appreciated the Kin's complete lack of interest in the remains of his Bakelite companion. Nothing was there anymore.

"It's a cave, a man-made cave." They both crawled inside and found that the superstructure of the womb-like enclosure was made of roots, as if they had once grown over a solid space, now making a perfect hollow container. More a tent than a cave. They sat in the snugness that barriered them against the hostile vastness outside.

"How much energy do you have left?" asked Ishmael.

"Another day, I think," said Seth indifferently.

"There are no charging frames here, do you now understand that?"

"That was almost one."

"No, it was not, it wasn't even made by humans. I have seen one of those before. It was constructed to eat men from, the anthropophagi made it."

"Then men must be nearby."

"Not anymore."

"Will you make a charging frame for me?" asked Seth.

"I don't know how."

"No, neither do I," said Seth.

Ishmael suddenly realised that very soon he would be alone in the Vorrh. That Seth's warning sound would start to count off the hours towards his petering out. No one had ever been in the forest alone and survived. The prospect of being lost in its mournful tracks was terrifying and a long way from his vision of a dramatic return with an army of Bakelites at his side. The crouching cyst they now occupied seemed comforting against the endless openness of trees and all the shades that dwelt between them. Seth was picking at one of the twisted roots that made the veiny woven roof of the enclosure.

"Why did you bring us here?" asked Ishmael.

"To this place?" asked Seth.

"No, into the Vorrh, why did you take me from the house into the forest?"

Without a moment's pause Seth answered his question in plain, monstrous words: "We did not know we were coming here, it's where the water led us."

"Where did you think you were going?" asked Ishmael incredulously.

"Away from the child and the house, that's all."

"But why into the well?"

"There was no other place to go, no other opening out of the house. And the well has always spoken to our fluids."

"Explain more," demanded Ishmael.

"It tugs and shapes the fluid inside us, like the trees do here. It makes us like it by speaking inside. It is called 'turgor.' We learned it in two of your lessons, do you remember?"

The childhood days of the cyclops were far off and Ishmael's worldly experiences had mainly washed them away. He dug deep into the numbered cases of his remembered instruction.

"But isn't all the pressure of turgor contained?"

"The primal force, yes, of course. But so much constant might causes a resonate force outside of the cell wall, a bit like heat, static, and magnetic radiation being an external by-product of other forms of contained energy."

"And that is why you expected a sympathetic place here?" said Ishmael dimly. "And that is why you thought there would be a charging frame?"

Seth nodded and made a tiny whimper in the inner rings of his throat.

Farther into the forest the tracks were becoming uncertain. Ishmael was stopping and bending in pain, his stomach cramps unaltered by the handful of berries and the hard black root that Seth had given him. They had tried to catch a rodent-like creature that scurried past them on the diminished path but had failed miserably and spent a lot of energy in the process. They reached the end of the track and were confronted by a huge impenetrable wall of trees, foliage, and hanging vines. Their feet stopped scything the stiff grasses and they stood in the noise of everything else moving, which was quiet enough to let them hear the tattoo of Seth's warning beat pulsing inside him.

"I think we should go back to the clearing," said Ishmael.

Seth looked at him with complete emptiness. They turned and shuffled back, their footsteps automatically in time to Seth's alarm beat.

The clearing was exactly the same but brighter under the fiercer sun. The broken frame was empty.

"Where is she?" said Ishmael.

"Gone," was all Seth could manage.

The shadows raked the ground and they said nothing, trying to listen outside the moment.

"If I sit still, I probably have an hour or two," announced Seth.

"And then I shall be alone," bemoaned the cyclops.

"Not alone, the Vorrh is teeming with life, some of it almost human."

"I know that, I have met some of it and care not to again."

"The others might find you."

"Others?"

"The forever ones who composed us."

"You mean the men who made you?"

"Not men."

Ishmael stood up and grabbed Seth's stiff trembling arms. "You think they are here?"

"Some might be." The drumming inside him was louder now and parts of it escaped, sandwiched between his words. "But there are no charging frames, are there?"

"No," said Ishmael.

"Then I think you must eat me," said Seth, staring at the ground. "Before more insects come and before I cease. My fluid will become stagnant then."

"I don't understand."

"I think I am the last of the Kin. The last of your kin. I think I will not be recharged. So you must take some of me for your sustenance."

"But I am human," ventured Ishmael.

"Not completely," said Seth. "Some parts of you are like us."

Ishmael became agitated. "Is this more lies like you told Ghertrude, to keep her in control? Well, it won't work on me. I know I am human."

"Then why did we all have a single eye at the beginning?"

Ishmael halted, his mouth working without words.

"No, little one, we share similarity, and the truth of that will let you live longer." Seth walked over near the centre of the glade and selected a piece of fallen tree. He examined it like a carpenter, inspecting its contours and weight. He then carefully seated it on the hard soil and lay down with his neck resting on it, like an uncomfortable pillow. He beckoned Ishmael closer.

"Do not be alarmed by this, it is the natural way. You must drink of me. Do not waste a drop. I will concentrate it into my head. It will change you and keep you alive for some long days."

Ishmael got down on his knees to look into Seth's face.

"I hope they find you, little one," Seth said as he held his head in his long brown fingers and wrenched it backwards and to the side, across the raised edge of the old wood. The crack was like a whip or a pistol shot knifing through the trees. The arms hissed backwards as the body arched and the white creamy fluid pumped out of the jagged stump of his neck. His head was still clamped firm as if being held away from the ground and offered up like a chalice. Not one drop had been spilt from it. The dumbfounded cyclops eventually stretched out to prise it out of the still hands. The eyelids, nostrils, and mouth were clamped shut, giving Seth's head a mean, vindictive, supercilious appearance, the exact opposite expression of the act of sacrifice that he had just performed. Ishmael cradled the head to his chest like a precious child, careful not to spill a drop of the mysterious milky liquid. He lifted the neck stub to his lips and tasted it. It was at first bland, then like seawater, then it burnt and stung his teeth like citric electricity. Finally, it left an aftertaste of iodine. His gag reaction was quickly replaced by a savage thirst. He remembered the stream that ran close to the hillock of roots. He dashed to it, pushing his face into the warm mud. He sat back clumsily, looking like a dropped doll or a child's lost toy bear. The nagging hunger pains stopped and a warmth now sat in his churning guts. He lifted the head again and took a hefty gulp, being ready to douse his face against the nausea. But it never came and he only tasted iodine and a great sleepiness overcame him. He returned to the cave-like hutch and crawled inside, all his draining focus being channelled into the deliberate care of the Bakelite vessel that had once been called Seth.

The moon and the sun arched over the enclosure. Their shafting rays bent though the tangled mass where previously he had made holes. Heat and chill buffeted his numb body. Four or five days had passed while he slept in a kind of delirium. He thought that he had heard things moving outside, animals sniffing and brushing against his adopted home.

On what might have been the sixth day he crawled out, clutching the head. He blinked at the openness of the clearing and the absent space where Seth's body should have been. Then he saw the tracks. The prints were everywhere but were more compacted around his hutch. He had indeed heard animals outside, had heard their curiosity picking at his sanctum. But they had not been the softly hooved quadrupeds that he had hoped for. These prints were made by erect animals, and he knew what kind because they had pissed and stained their presence against the walls, and once smelt you never forget the stench of the anthropophagi. He held the head tighter and took a strengthening swig from the neck. Then he felt the eyes watching him and saw smears of yellow in threes. He had no weapon and there were dozens of them, probably all armed with the sharpened stick and wooden blades that he had tasted before. He bent down to pick up a fist-sized rock, fitting Seth's head under his other arm. So this was it. The final chapter, the revenge of the yellow eaters on men.

"Come on, then," he roared in a voice that he had never heard before. "Come on, let's be having you!"

Slowly they crept out from the trees, their piggy eyes watching him closely. He shook the rock and they stopped, some retreated. Ishmael had not seen his reflection for days. In his head he held his youth and attainment as his image. His mask, even though damaged, was a good face. The shining visage of the triumphant hero of the Vorrh nailed to the front of his skull. But that wasn't what the squat band of man-eaters were looking at. His hair had grown wild and matted, the fever and dirt dreadlocking it into jagged spikes and irregular tufts. Something in Seth's fluid had darkened him. The pigment in his skin had changed. His face was dark purple. The single eye burnt from the scar tissue, which was now jet-black. He had just gulped another mouthful from the hard neck and it had left an impression on his dripping lips, a white stain that highlighted his mouth like a fearsome mockery of a mockery, a black-faced minstrel from hell. As he shouted at them, white thick spit flew from his mouth like gooey sparks. The yellow creatures slunk back; they did not know what this was. They had seen and eaten all manner of long pig but had never seen anything like this.

"Come on, you ugly fuckers, let's end it here," Ishmael spat out and laughed.

They fell even farther back.

"You can't run, you owe me, you owe me my death now." And with screaming frustrated rage he threw the rock. Its velocity was astonishing and it hit the closest of the retreating horde, sending it squealing to the ground. Ishmael put Seth's head down and rushed at his emissary, stamping on its back until the squeals turned into grunts of painful breath. He kicked it over and hastily avoided the clashing bites of the hooklike teeth in the raging mouth. He kicked it again, his boot then holding the monster in place until he retrieved the rock and spun the creature round to receive three more blows just above its eye. It lay limp and shrivelled. Ishmael grabbed its clammy foot and dragged it back towards the woven hollow at the middle of the clearing. He meant to cut vines with the creature's wooden blade and weave them into a sinewy rope, to bind its hands behind its back and shackle its feet together. He meant to do all this and more, but his stomach cramped and the last rind of energy inside peeled away. He started to faint; his legs buckled and he fell painfully onto his knees, then flopped sideways into the scuffed footprints outside his sanctum, knowing that if he did not wake up first then he would only come to when his awoken bruised companion was eating him.

The eye of the beaten horror was staring into his when he finally awoke. He had the acute sensation that the lids of his eye had never closed. Something inside had closed down. The shutter between the lens and the brain. The horror was awake and sitting in a pool of its own stinking urine. They were both worn out: one from hunger, the other from injury. What went on behind their unmoving faces and bodies was impossible to tell. Only the rod of observation that joined their eyes showed any meaning. It became a tightrope of anything except communication, even though the cyclops had dreamt of or considered finding a way to speak to these disgusting creatures. Perhaps he had speculated there might be a way to join them, bend them with intellect, and nourish them in the warmth of his sensitivity. Show them how to live closer to more civilised animals. Perhaps even increase their evolution and lead them back in triumph into the world of men.

Ishmael unbent his stiff, numb leg and the horror twisted its face to keep their eyes aligned. It was in that moment that Ishmael crossed all known boundaries. Somewhere in the clawing concave of his hungry mind he had been fantasising at the disgust of cannibalism, or more accurately the devouring of humanoid bipeds, when the disgust somersaulted, inverted, and landed as a solution to all his woes. Repulsion and survival quarrelled in the cyclops's gaze. For a moment they might have both had the same thought. Then Ishmael changed it by using his superior brain. *Is this animal any worse than a pig in a sty? Is it sacred because it balances on two legs instead of four? Is its stink and filth any worse than mine?*

Later, as the sun vanished, impaled on the other side of the forest, Ishmael sat before a creaking busy fire, his stomach extended and his mind unhooked, bones and grease spread about him, and a sweet taste wedged into his teeth and endurance warming his blood. Tonight he would sleep in the woven hollow and watch the firelight flicker shadows and splinter warmth through his cage. Tomorrow he would go deeper.

CHAPTER THIRTY-FIVE

*C*yrena had written to Marais out of the blue and it had delighted him. Delight was rare at that time and his daily indulgences in morphine were increasing. She had suggested that they meet again: She could come and visit him or she could send a plane to bring him to her. He would have loved to see her again and bathe in her energy and grace, but the drug would not let him. Such a journey was now a terrible contemplation. He also did not want her to see what he had become. He still had enough dignity to prevent that. Better to leave things as they were, let them stay bright in both their memories.

Some weeks earlier, when he had been growing short of his limited supply of morphine, he had taken a fall. Fortunately in the confines of his own modest home. But he had ruined two shelves of his collection of objets d'art, which cascaded to the floor as he tried to grab something steady to hold on to. When he eventually found the will to clear up the mess, he discovered that he had accidentally broken the mud crown from the Possession Wars. A large piece of the clay had snapped off to reveal a shining interior. On further examination it revealed a structure of machine precision. So he continued to break the outer casing to find out what its true nature was. Midway he recognised the object as being very close to Cyrena's halo of insects. It would make an excellent gift for her and solve the problem about a meeting. A week later he finished the task.

And he was pleased with his letter to her and his shining gift of the halo of insects. He put the paper down and lifted the mechanical brass circle into his gaze. Its restoration and repair was the only dexterous manual task he had taken on for years. Something about the hands working to unpeel and clarify had come back from his student days. The revelation of the dissecting room. He had picked at and washed away the impacted mud to reveal the instrument beneath. He had cleansed and repaired the clockwork and the mirrors, so now it seemed perfect.

He looked hard into the glass lenses and their motors of action and saw for the first time the scratched writing on the inside of the crown. Not the London maker's marks he found before but crude yet elegant ciphers inscribed therein. These were charm signs, talismanic inscriptions written by its most recent owners thousands of miles from Europe, declarations of purpose that the original instrument had never known. He had casually put it on a couple of times, letting the mirrors whir a bit, the daylight dapple. It produced a mild optical soothing, which he liked, and he fancied it an expensive, amusing toy.

He stepped back from the table, deciding to add to his dosage to see if it heightened his clarity by softening his constant anxiety.

When he came back, he picked the object up and it had seemed to have shed some of its weight. He took it outside into the African sun, wound all its motors, and again placed it on his head, clicking the rotations of light into life.

There was no defence. No preparation. No understanding for what was shafted and wedged into his vision. The warm air still smelt of fecundity and promise. The sun on his skin still glowed in an optimism of another day. But both were without *Homo sapiens*. That supposed peak in the kingdom of animals was over. Every invention, idea, construction, and measurement of man had stopped and been disregarded. His eyes trembled as the cogs whirred; he faltered and sank to his knees. Vision upon vision unfolded before him, in vast explosions and waves of constant smoke or dust that stank of cindered bone. He saw pestilence and hatred married to genius and wealth. He saw governments and empires topple. Mindless conflict had been let loose without any containment. He watched and saw years of panic and hubris construct illness and machines. He saw every tribe and kingdom of mankind give up and become annihilated. He saw man try to burn the entire world alive and fail. After the smoke and noise had vanished and the long rains had cleaned away the ashes, he saw animals and plants creep back and then rove and entwine themselves into all the palaces and libraries and devour all evidence of the arrogance of humanity's faith that had finally taken its toll. All the fiction that *Homo sapiens* had told to their own species vanished. All the ideas about time and space, all the equations and microscopic details about animal life were eaten by the animals. Lichen and fungi swamped and paved human speculation, philosophy was besmirched and eradicated by worms. Measurements were eaten by ants and all the circuits were drowned.

The exhausted purpose was exposed, but before the brass clockwork had run down, he saw how this had happened and he'd had that conversation before. The forests had changed the air. Altered its composition over centuries, not as he had said once before by decreasing oxygen but by expanding it and denting it with other traces of more virulent gases. The trees had not starved and suffocated man, they had increased him. Force-fed the human brain to saturation. Making the two most powerful drives therein destroy themselves and all hope of redemption. Invention and territoriality had torn *Homo sapiens* off the face of the earth with tools of their own making. After some hours or days in a semiconscious torpor, Marais finally staggered to his feet and found his way back to the table where his letter to Cyrena sat, curling in a shaft of sunlight. He dragged the crown from his head, letting it fall beneath the table. He then left his home and made his last journey to the remote farm whose name in Zulu meant "the end of the business."

CHAPTER THIRTY-SIX

$\mathcal{H}$ector was horrified to discover that he had slept for an entire day or more. After his meeting at St. Paul's, of which he could remember little, and the run home, of which he could remember everything, he just slept. It had only been Solli's insistent knocking and calling that had hauled him out of the long dream of the long run. He staggered to the door, rubbing his bristled chin and bleary eyes. He undid the bolts and turned away from the door saying, "Come in, Solli, come in."

He heard them enter and close the door behind them as he shuffled towards the sink and the kettle. Then he heard their stillness and silence as they stood by the door, staring.

He turned. "What, what is it?" Imagining some auspicious or alarming piece of news had weighted them to the floor, transfixed them to the spot with the burden of its disclosure. "What?"

Solli was with the youth called Jerry, who lifted his hand to point at Hector. Their eyes were wide, their mouths stuck in imbecilic grins.

"Your hair, Prof, your hair . . ." Jerry said.

Hector remembered the wind and the imaginary mane, the stranger in the fragment of looking glass. He brought an unbelieving hand up to his head and touched the mass that grew there.

"You can see it?"

The thin, shrill question was answered by the men nodding in unison. Hector rushed at the mirror, lifting it from its nail and taking it to the window, where he moved it this way and that, steering the irregular glint of the shard and his astonished image back and forth. Causing an escaping dagger of reflection to bob and scurry over the walls and the ceiling of the room. For a moment it distracted Jerry's appreciation of the comic scene.

"I thought it was a dream. Only a dream," Hector muttered.

Out of the shadows and in the flooding illumination of the skylight, Solli and Jerry could see that it was not just the hair that had changed. Hector looked younger, something about his posture had changed. It had tightened and become more flexible at the same time. Solli did not like this kind of thing and recently there had been a lot of it centred around this strange old man. Best to ignore it. Impossibilities were for the real rabbis, not him; he had the muscle and the nerve of the street to deal with. He was not here to witness miracles.

"You're wanted across town," he said sharply.

Hector did not hear him.

"Uncle Hymie wants you over at Bedlam."

He heard that. It was not a request. Nobody could have ignored the urgent thuggery in the order. Even Jerry stepped back to look at his leader in surprise.

"I think you'd better get dressed, Professor," Jerry said, trying to calm the unpleasantness that was damaging the air.

"We'll wait downstairs, and I ain't got all day," said Solli, turning on his heels and gaining the landing before anybody else could move or speak.

"Better do what he says, Prof," said Jerry after a while.

Solli had started his second cheroot by the time Hector came down. He was leaning against the entrance, tapping his stick with irritation against the metal drain cover. There had obviously been bad words between the youths. Jerry said nothing and studiously looked in the opposite direction.

In an attempt to lighten things, Hector asked, "Are we going by boat?"

Solli looked at him as if he had asked for the crown jewels, and Jerry looked farther into his imaginary horizon.

"No, we fucking ain't. Ain't got the fucking time to muck about. Get a taxi," he ordered Jerry, who happily ran away from them towards the main road at the end of the street. Hector and Solli followed at a respectively brisk and artificially casual pace. Solli let the old man go in front so that he could scrutinise him with sideways glances. His walk had changed, both in rhythm and pace. It was brisker and more alert, closer to his own, which he did not like, and worse was the overall impression that the old man had grown taller. Solli aggressively chewed and puffed at his cheroot and clattered his cane at his heel like the teeth of a choke-chained dog. Jerry had the taxi waiting and they bundled in.

"St. George's Fields, Lambeth," said Jerry.

He had long since learned that you did not say Bedlam in front of Solli, or anybody Solli was with. He alone was able to use the B word, and when he did, you knew there was going to be trouble. They drove in silence, the cab full of smoke, the window tightly closed. Hector coughed and paddled at the window-release strap.

"Do you mind?" he said to Solli.

"Yes, I fucking do, it's too cold, keep it shut."

The matter was over and Hector tried to breathe in shallow gasps as they travelled the miles across London and over the Thames. Things got worse when they arrived at Bethlem Royal Hospital. Solli's hatred of the place and his uncle's captivity turned his gait into a begrudging swagger that seemed to increase in velocity without gaining speed. Nobody spoke until they reached the dormitory that Hymie shared with his "comrades." He was not there, but two of his pals were. Nicholas was standing next to a far bed spoon-feeding another man who sat propped up against the headboard. Hector was caught between a bristle and a smile at seeing the Erstwhile. Solli shouted across the room, making the man in the bed jump.

"Where's Hymie?"

Nicholas ignored him, spoke softly to the patient, and continued to spoon food into his bandaged head. Solli was dangerously near his cracking point. He sped across the room, seething in irrational aggression.

"I am talking to you, you fucking freak, where is my uncle?"

The bandaged man cringed, some of the food oozing out of his slippery mouth. Without turning around Nicholas put down the spoon and pointed one of his immaculately manicured hands towards Solli. He held it cobra-like about two feet in front of his nose and then made a repeated opening and closing of the fingers held together and the thumb below, imitating the head of a bird yakking. Solli reached inside his coat, his hand grasping the bone-slivered handle of his cutthroat razor. He was about to slash it out when Nicholas brought the index finger of his other hand up to his lips, making the sign of hush. The effect was instantaneous. All the air, acid, and violence drained out of Solli, deveining him until only a lost youth hung in the clothes that had been so stretched and threatening before. Nicholas returned to the dinner, picked up the spoon, and continued.

For the next ten minutes or so a great stillness filled the room. Only the soft pendulum of the spoon marked any passage in time.

"Have you had enough, Edmund?"

The bandaged man nodded and smiled.

"Very well, try to sleep now," Nicholas said, pulling the blanket up to the man's neck and setting his pillows at a lower angle. He then collected the plate and spoon and walked past the waiting men and out of the tall doors. He sat down on a broad bench in the corridor and briskly tapped the metal spoon against the china plate. Solli blinked and stumbled forward like a sleeper missing a step in a steep dream. Hector and Jerry also blinked back into action. All three came and quietly sat at his sides.

"Now, Solomon, you were asking about Uncle Hymie? He is in the treatment room receiving interruption like poor Edmund there."

"Treatment?" said Solli.

"Yes, they have come from Maudsley with interruptions, an invention from the colonies, as I understand. Something that stops the frowning, they say. But I think they are separating him, slicing away his visibility. The exact opposite of what I have been doing for centuries."

"Why are they doing it, Nicholas?" asked Hector.

"They said to stop the 'mood swings,' making them 'better' by tapping out the headaches."

"Tapping?" said Solli, stiffening back into his clothing, his skeleton of violence gleaming. He exchanged quick black glances with Jerry. "Tapping with what?"

"A spike and a hammer, I think Edmund said."

"Where?" demanded Solli, his rage back and doubled.

Nicholas extended a languid arm. "Treatment room B. Turn left at the end at the second corridor."

The words had barely left his soft grinning mouth and they were gone.

"Good, now we can talk alone, have you ever seen a mood swing? I think they must keep it in the gardens somewhere."

He paused for a moment as if his mind had wandered outside

to look for the allusive swing, hanging from a distant branch of one of the older trees in the walled grounds. He eventually returned, delighted to find his old friend still sitting at his side.

"Anyway, how are you, Hector?"

Hector felt ashamed about his previous behaviour to this extraordinary being. Now it all seemed so distant, with only his insulting language standing proud like an ugly rock in a quiet lake.

"I am very well, Nicholas, how are you?"

"Soho."

Hector ignored the possible mistake in language in case it was another invitation to join a scree of meaningless jokes. He had only just got over the last one.

"I must apologise for my bad language when last we met."

"Ah! You mean the Huns Toft," said Nicholas gleefully.

It was worse than Hector hoped for, he had actually remembered the words, or rather his version of it.

"Yes," he said very quietly. "I am sorry."

"But what does it mean, Hector? I have never heard it before."

The old man shrunk inside. "It's just bad language, that's all."

"But it must mean something, all words mean something."

He was not going to let go. Hector did not know if he was like a dog with a bone or a cat with a mouse. He secretly prayed for the former.

"It is the back end of an animal."

"What animal?"

"A dog."

"Ah! I see."

Patients and doctors were walking past. Each one acknowledged Nicholas and stared at his companion. They all seemed purposeful and busy and engaged in the serious business of real life.

"Is it its arse? Is that what you called me, a dog's arse?"

"No, not exactly." Hector was talking to his shoes again.

"What then?"

"Well, it's a female dog."

There was a silence while Nicholas stroked his chin and thought very deeply. Hector wanted to interrupt this and change the subject, but did not know how. And anyway it was nearly over, might as well brazen it through.

Three corridors down and at a right angle were the treatment rooms. Each with benches arranged outside. Little groups of men dressed in skimpy gowns sat waiting for assessment or treatment. Solli looked for Uncle Hymie among the vacant flock. There was no sign of him and he bit his lip in anxiety. Suddenly his attention was seized by a wheeled stretcher bumping out of the rubber doors of treatment room B. Its occupant did not look like the rest of the patients waiting. It looked like the spoon sucker he had just seen with Nicholas. He made straight for the trolley and held it fast in his small white hands.

The attendant stopped and sneered down at Solli. He was a large man, who had not bothered to shave that day.

"What you want?" he barked.

Solli looked into the patient's eyes, looked for a response, personality, or even life. What he saw changed the seething anger that he had carried all day, transmuted it by the violent application of fear. His eyes then found those of the burly attendant.

There are modes of communication that the superior human still shares with the animals that we deem to see as lower: expressions of dominance and power that are far more vital than all our words put together. Moments where the primitive must be trusted and obeyed. The large man was looking at one now and instantly knew that all his strength and size was meaning-less before the ferocity of the small man who was gripping the trolley.

"What happened to him?" said Solli in a voice that an ice-berg would be envious of.

"New treatment," said the attendant without a moment's hesitation.

Solli took one hand off the trolley and made a minute adjust-ment of his neck, his eyes never leaving the looming man.

"It's a Yank thing, they're trying it out over here, at the Maudsley. All hush-hush and now they are trying it here."

"In there?"

The attendant nodded and Solli was gone in a black-chromed blur.

"A bitch arse?" said Nicholas, very pleased with his deduction.

"Almost," said Hector, resigned to the humiliation of his exposure.

More occupants of the hospital passed them and stared, including a stern-looking nursing sister who had heard every word they'd said.

Solli heard Hymie's voice two rooms down the antiseptic-smelling corridor. A group of four men in surgical gowns and two nurses stood around a table talking quietly. Hymie's voice was corralled inside them. He was strapped to the table and his head was in a clamp. The authoritative tones of the most senior doctor could be heard above all others. A voice that had been trained by privilege, pampered with conceit, and smoothed by never encountering doubt. All attention was on him. Nobody saw or heard Solli enter the room and stand behind them. Hymie was equally ignored, talking to himself about this and that, a nurse occasionally shushing him when his volume interrupted the speech of the eminent man who was enjoying his audience and seemed to be conducting their admiration with a slim baton that he had in his hand and waved about in a casual manner. It looked like one of Mrs. Fishburn's knitting needles. Except that it was thicker at one end and tapered to a hard sharpness of gleaming steel. Mid-sentence the doctor gave a slight nod and the two nurses and one of the other doctors descended on Hymie, putting a gag in his mouth and a strap around his jaw, tightening his head in the clamp. The distinguished surgeon moved towards his patient, still talking, and Solli saw that in his other, inarticulate hand he held a hammer of stainless steel.

"I got it. A dog bitch's cunt. That's what you called me. A cunt of a bitch."

Hector grumbled agreement and Nicholas slapped his thighs and rolled about on the bench, guffawing and greatly savouring his new name.

"I shall wear it in the plural," he said, tears filling his laughing eyes.

"What is this plural you speak of?" asked Hector.

"It's when we sleep together again, as one. The great union of angel and man." He could barely hold the words together between his castanet-like outbursts of off-key braying guffaws. "It's what you have been sent for, so we can do it together and make a barrier, a ripple under the river." Tears were spraying Hector from Nicholas's hysterical head. "The bitch cunt and the Jew embracing eternity in the mud!" He slapped his thigh again and wiped his face on his sleeve.

Hector formed the next question in his mind and filled his mouth with the taste of it when the corridor suddenly turned into a cattle market. Something had grabbed him up by his arm and tried to do the same with Nicholas. It was Jerry, wide-eyed and frantic.

"We gotta go, now, quick, hurry."

There was the sound of a distant hand-cranked bell and a horde of running people. In its centre and moving quickly through the teeming mass was Solli, pushing his confused uncle in a wheelchair. The old man was wearing a loose-fitting smock, which refused to cover his sagging genitals and hairy knobby legs. When he saw Hector and Nicholas, he waved energetically, almost standing up in the chair. Solli put a blood-soaked hand on his shoulder and forced him back down into the fast-moving seat, dropping something shiny in the process. A snapped-off steel rod bounced brightly against the wooden floor.

"Come on, Prof, we got to go, scarper quick, like," said Jerry.

"But why?" asked the confused Hector.

"'Cause Solli's done a doctor."

Hector had no idea what was going on as he was gathered up in the tide. Nicholas refused to move, Jerry's hand having had no more effect than seaweed trying to push a cliff.

At the front Solli scooped his uncle up out of the chair and carried him down the front steps, the old man whooping with delight at such a game. Hector and Jerry followed, the young thug's eyes watching the retreating entrance for signs of pursuit. On the street they hailed a taxi.

"The Pavilion, Whitechapel," insisted Jerry. The cabbie, who had quite a lot to say about the motley passengers, their attire, and their comic destination, changed his mind when he saw Solli's eyes in his rearview mirror. Only Hymie spoke as they sped across town. Solli patted the old man as if in agreement, his fierce gaze locked on the passing streets. Hector attempted to follow the gushings of Yiddish cockney and not to look at Solli's bloodstained hand and sleeve, and Jerry closed his eyes and pretended to doze. They stopped outside the Pavilion and carefully helped Hymie out, who was ecstatic at being "home." Hector followed a few paces behind the hobbling uncle and supporting nephew. Jerry gave the cabbie a handful of scrunched notes and said, "Stumm."

The cabbie blinked, nodded, and was gone.

"What is happening, Jerry? Won't they come to take Hymie back across the river?"

"No, Prof, they won't come here and we can never cross the Thames again, Solli has burnt all our bridges. We are all here together now."

CHAPTER THIRTY-SEVEN

*C*yrena Lohr was sitting in her parlour when she heard that Eugène Marais had died, and that it was believed he had committed suicide. The news attacked a cherished, unlived part of Cyrena's life, the place where she had fantasised about a close relationship existing between them, where they would mutually guide and support each other in all the years that they had been separated. In the place where their meaning and ages were alike. Beneath that dream were the very real memories of her father and her childhood. That superstructure that formed the foundation of all her most reliable and enjoyable recollections. A suicide always hacks away at such supports. The rareness of Marais just made the cruel axe even blunter, more pointless. There was nobody to share her pain with. The grief and disbelief locked claws in her lonely heart in her empty house two thousand miles from where she last saw him. She climbed the staircase, stopping on each stair for a minute or two, her heels kicking the back of the step for reality. Her hand stroked the polished banister, feeling its firmness and the space between her grip and its surface. The view from each step she noticed for the first time. The difference, the uniqueness. How could he do it? How could he leave everything so unfinished? She moved through her favourite room touching things. Their temperature and texture imprinted them beyond sight in her innermost recess as if they were exotic, fabulous troves. She opened the glass-panelled door and smelt the city and the wilderness combine. A homeland that was suddenly more precious than any single person. For isn't it so for all that touches our animal brain? The old lizard mind notched just above the spine, surviving on a starvation diet forever. Then the meaning of the things in her room and the view from her stairs only found words to explain them. Their real sensations had crossed the chattering library of the frontal lobes without friction or a whisper. Their essence now uncapped as sign, direction, and pulse. She sat on her balcony and faced the Vorrh, closing her eyes and breathing it in. Seeking comfort without implication from its sultry, passionate indifference.

The next morning she decided to go to where he died. To see the place in which he faded.

Again she contacted Talbot. She hated playing the hurt and needy female, but she knew it was what he wanted. She explained her grief, isolation, and urgent need. She promised to explain it all to him on her return. Hinted at long evenings of intimate confession. The plane was waiting on the runway the next morning. It was the same as before but with a different interior, its skeletal furnishings extracted and replaced by plush, regular seating. Two other passengers were already seated. A wizened white woman and a tall black man dressed in a blue robe. He stood when she entered and the old woman winced, tutted, and looked away, staring out of the oval window. Cyrena smiled and took her assigned seat. Ten minutes later they were heading south, after circling over the Vorrh.

This time the journey was vague and numbed, the colours from above and below holding her and the plane in a blur of swaying, meaningless hugging. Before they landed for refuelling, the old woman moved into the seat next to Cyrena, peering back at the other passenger sitting at the rear.

"Disgusting," she said in a snarling hiss. "Disgusting that we have to share a compartment with that." She stabbed her thumb towards the back of the seat. "And how can 'they' get the money to buy a ticket? It cost me a fortune."

Cyrena took off her green Italian sunglasses, stared at the bitter harridan, and said, "He is my personal Obeah-man and his prayers will keep the wings attached to this plane. Please do not speak again or he will lose his concentration."

The old woman's mouth dropped open and she shrivelled back along the row of seats. Cyrena replaced her glasses over her magnificent eyes. On the next part of the flight there were only two passengers. It was somewhere over the sea of white sands that she first spoke to him. She had walked to the little bar counter at the back of the plane to stretch her legs and spine, balancing on the undulating thin carpet over the two inches of metal, over the vastness of blue vacant air. On her return she caught his modest eye. He said, "Thank you," without looking up.

"For what?"

"I heard what the other lady said."

Cyrena was surprised and mortified. How could anyone hear such a whispered conversation in the loud compartment of the juddering plane?

"Oh!" she said.

"The lady disliked me travelling with you."

"I think that lady would dislike travelling with anybody, including herself," said Cyrena.

The man grinned broadly through his troubled face. "Then, madam, you don't object?"

"Not at all."

The plane lurched in a pocket of swollen air. Cyrena stumbled backwards and then stopped, held in grip of crystal breeze, as if the interior oxygen of the plane had caught her and kept her from falling and guided her gracefully to the nearest seat. She was breathless and looked at three of her fingers held gently in the young man's sensitive hand.

"Are you all right, madam?"

"Yes, yes, thank you."

He let go and normality shuddered with the noise of the engines back into the cabin. He quietly sat next to her, offering a glass of water. She had no words to say, so she just sipped and slid into a remarkable and unexpected sleep. The stranger covered her with a blanket and adjusted her elegant spectacles that were pushed askew on her beautiful face.

When she awoke he seemed to be asleep in the next seat. She blinked and tried to remember the sequence of events that she knew was strange, but could not find them on the other side of her glowing sense of well-being. She had dreamt of the tree. The tree that Marais had guided her to, all those years ago. The tree where she had seen something wonderful that he seemed anxious or even scared about. She had been there again, bathed in a warm, overpowering light that was beyond vision and the irritations of sight. It had followed her into waking in the same way that it had waited for her in dream, and she knew that her fellow passenger had assisted in some way in the dissolving of the boundaries. She watched him carefully, looking for signs of recognition. There was a sense of ease about him that had nothing to do with contentment. Nor was it casual apathy. It was a positive known direction rather than a lack of feeling or interest. She had become an expert at recognising that, even if it had been a late and spiteful lesson in her essential optimism. Then, without knowing why, she stretched out her hand and moved it above the sleeping man. Moved it in a slow flat rotation as if caressing an invisible halo that floated around and over his gentle head. The steward came into the cabin and broke the intimate moment without dispersing the atmosphere of blessing. He announced that it was thirty minutes before landing and that it might be "bumpy" again as they crossed the last jagged ranges and flattened plains. The other passenger was concerned again about her well-being. She told him that she was more than fine and had enjoyed the flight in his company. He beamed openly.

"May I introduce myself?" he said cautiously.

Cyrena quickly nodded assent.

"I am called Seil Kor." And the name settled in a part of her mind that she did not know.

"I am Cyrena Lohr," she said, the name sounding rather detached in the space between them.

"I know," he said, and it seemed like the most natural thing in the world.

CHAPTER THIRTY-EIGHT

*I*shmael had been making greater and greater circles away from his woven dwelling, until it took him two days to return. He had been hunting small game and secretly hoped to bump into one of the ugly but nutritious yellow dwarfs who lived hidden in the trees. He was on the outermost rim of his orbits of discovery where the paths and animal tracks were at their most slender. The trees were stronger and more insistent here, their presence individually felt. Each of the giants had its own voice in the vast resonance of the forest. Even though the vines tangled and hid the contours of their singular semaphoric growth, the sound of their presence and age cut each a unique place of dominance to be respected. The shared external field around them was also highly charged and Ishmael could feel the ghost magnetism of turgor tugging at the thin salty waters of his brain. But still he had not suffered the outcome of all other men who dared to walk in the precincts of this leaching pressure. The walls of his personality cells had stayed intact. Not warped or broken or turned to mush like the brains of the Limboia. He shuddered at the thought of becoming one of them without knowing, and to reassure himself he clapped his hand against the solid trunk of nearest tree. This was more than just touching wood to fend off the bad luck of the horrible idea. It was a signing with the might around him and an agreement with its opposition to intruding man. A wish of union with the power of the place. He looked up into the high branches to see if his tap had registered, secretly hoping for a nod of acceptance in the tiniest of twigs. The distant sun spat and fingered through the canopy, churning the leaves and charming the sugars to rise. His isolation seemed complete against such everlasting forces. An exile in all living kingdoms.

An unprepared and vindictive recollection of Sholeh, Ghertrude, and Cyrena flounced back into his dismal ruminations. A flicker of the best of their company. Naked, laughing, and kind. Past pockets of contentment with each were exposed before him. He flinched at the warmth of the startling, vivid sentiment and drove the memory away with a whip of artificially inseminated spite. A vengeance lash against all those who had betrayed him and given him over to the executioners of that feeble city. He walked on, fuelled by the nightmare of blood that he would administer when next they met. He forgot where he was and the energy about him that had almost humbled his determination a few moments earlier. He swung noisily into a clearing where the absence of the tree that once held it was stronger than all the others' territories put together. The blast of its invisibility hurt. He stood dazed and dumbfounded, waiting for his senses to return. When they did he saw a bent figure at the far-off periphery of space, sitting over a hole in the ground, weeping. As his eye started working again and realigned to look outwards, he thought that it was wearing a coat made of porcupines, the same kind that he had seen scurrying away from him in the undergrowth. He lifted the spear he had made and crept around the rim of the clearing towards the back of the stranger. Then he saw the black pointed hands and a side-on glance of its face full of bristling quills. The creature was bigger than he, but looked old and fatigued. He dropped his small sack of possessions and took the spear in both hands and moved closer.

Without turning to confront his creeping visitor the being said, "I mourn my gentle brother who departeth this fair ground."

The voice sounded like it was spoken through layers of tin and desiccated grass. Ishmael watched the tears dropping into the hole where he imagined the newly deceased lay. He stepped forward for a better look, the burnt pointed end of the spear never leaving its aim at the being's broad back. The grave was shallow and empty.

"Behold the hollow that we were going to share. It's where he slept in preparation."

Ishmael knew that this must be an Erstwhile; he had finally come face-to-face with one. But it seemed pathetic and did not really notice he was there. He lowered his stick and crossed to the other side of the hole to get a clearer look at its strange and compelling face.

"Is he dead?" he asked, without knowing why.

For the first time it looked at him and its violet pupils rippled with a circular motion, as it cocked its head to one side like a curious dog.

"Have thee been dead yet?" it whisper-lisped. "Because thou canst have this hollow. It is made for sleeping, for our plural. Thou canst have it, it's not for the dead. It's for-spoken, I made it for him, he who believed himself to be totally Rumour. He has been sleeping and here for many seasons, becoming ready for our plural. He was mine, I found him, lost and forsaken. He had a name, you all have names, what is yours." The creature turned to look at Ishmael intently for the first time.

"Ishmael."

"That was not his name, not the same, he had two bites."

Ishmael remembered Nebsuel's distaste and distrust of the Erstwhile. He even indicated that they had grown mad, living with the centuries of guilt and failure.

The expression on Ishmael's injured face must have given the wrong signs because the creature continued, now animated by a greater need to protect and explain its nurtured hole.

"See its shape and the impression of our earthly forms."

It pointed one of its long black hands that looked like the tip of a raven's wing. "See the white roots there, threading their way from Etz haDaat tov V'ra to feed and meld the plural. But he woke too soon. Only rolling centums will unite." It looked up and straight into Ishmael's eye and seemed to be deeply sniffing at him. "He was needed for another, to make the plural on hard lands for hard gatherings of fire and stone. He is to plural with one that thee mated."

The tin and grass of its voice had become dryer and the eyes wider, more hectic, and baleful. Ishmael did not understand or know what to say. So he reversed and picked at the bones of his previous confusion.

"So was he like me, this one that was buried here?"

"No!" the creature spat out. "He was part us, but he did not know, that is why he had to dream backwards to become more like his father. Who was us."

"Do you mean that he was part human, part angel?"

At the word "angel," the creature covered its ears with its pointed feathered hands and let out a sound that was beyond description.

"I have learned language so as to never say or hear that name. Do not sound it."

After a grim and irritable silence Ishmael said, "I know nothing of you, I did not even know that you could speak."

The creature shuddered all over.

"I learned these sounds with Adam and much more since . . . eh . . . he . . . came . . ." It was again searching for the departed one's name. "He would speak in his sleep under the soil and plants and I would lie above him and listen, pressing my ears into the damp earth." Suddenly the creature elongated and shook its head. "Seilkor . . . Seil Kor! That was his name. His name when I found him lost."

The name meant nothing to Ishmael.

"He spoke much underground. I heard and learned much, and I could even hear the juice of Etz haDaat tov V'ra passing through him."

"What is Etzadatovfra?"

The being pushed his spiky head forward and lifted a hand to point menacingly into Ishmael's face. "You say tree of knowledge. Good and evil." It lowered the hand of accusation and pointed back into the grave. "Its roots worm and feed there. We suckled from it and it suckled from us."

They both stared into the hole without saying a word, until the being harshly broke the spell.

"You should sip of it." It stood up and extended its arm across the hole to take Ishmael's hand. For some reason it seemed the most normal thing to do and the cyclops raised his nervous paw on the strings of polite automatic response. The touch and the solid grip was totally unexpected as it guided him around the grave and back into the centre of the clearing. There was a shifting of temperatures in the being's hand that made the strangeness of its bristling dryness unimportant in comparison. The hand flushed from fever pitch to frostbite every half minute or so. It created a tactile pulse that seemed to bear no relationship to anything else in the world around it, but it began to create a similar rhythm in Ishmael, as if his heart were slowing to listening from inside his chest, trying to understand and match its beat, pushing its wet ear up hard against the dark cage of ribs. After an unbalanced and clumsy walk, they stopped. Before them was a raised disk of a gleaming black substance that glistened and shone like midnight chrome. It was ten feet across and nine inches above the smooth surface of the ground.

"Here was its above in the times of Adam, before all became Rumours." The being raised his other arm and extended it high above Ishmael's head. Ishmael looked up from the circular table-like stump and imagined the magnificence of a tree that once had this girth. The black surface shimmered under the shadow caused by its visitors, and both looked down again. The being had forgotten that one of his arms was still held up, pointing at the sky. The surface of the stump writhed, and Ishmael realised that it was not some kind of exotic polished ebony but a seething mass of thousands of black ants. They covered every inch of the ancient wood, capping its remnant form exactly.

"The tree is now below ground, an inverted plural, hidden, occulted, safe from all the Rumours." The being suddenly let go of Ishmael's hand, letting his heart fall back into the noise of its natural speed.

"Then why do you show me?" he asked, panting.

"Because I now know thou are not one of them, as well thou knows." He took his eyes off the cyclops to give him time to think, feel, and recall. And while he did the Erstwhile started clawing at the earth near the tree, digging scoops of it away with his long, pointed hands. He dug deep into the new trench and pulled up a pale colourless root as if he were unravelling a ball of twine or a reel of stubborn hose.

"Come, little one, come and taste."

Ishmael followed the request like an instruction, like a sleep-walker with a riot in his head. He knelt down close to the prof-fered root while the being chanted or whisper-sang a prayer over his hands. Its voice was drier than desert sand. A hooked green-ish nail or talon extended from one of its fingers and was sawing at the pale sinewy vein. It cut through with a slight gush as the pulsing liquid escaped, and the being raised its spiralling eyes to the cyclops, indicating that his mouth was quickly needed to suck at the sap of God's greatest gift to man. It tasted like the cream of the Kin, but much more alive. It too had the pulse of temperature change and again his heart shifted to its demand. He sucked into its throb as the fluid changed from a thin milk into a gel that drove deep into every tendril of nerve and capillary in his quaking body. It swallowed him in its wealth, all else dispersed and became transparent around him, except for the far-off voice of the Erstwhile.

It stood above him and was shouting: a sound like burnished metal being beaten with a stick. One of its hands was on Ishmael's head, the other still holding the root. It was trying to separate them, to prise the cyclops's manic suckling mouth away from the mangled root. But it was not working, he was not letting go. His mouth was ferociously clamped around the hard, shaking fibre. The being was using all its might to pull him off without snapping the root. It twisted his head against his neck and tugged at his hair. It became unbalanced with the effort, one of its feet slipping in the freshly dug earth. It fell, flailing, alongside the cyclops, now grabbing at anything to restrain him. Earth, twigs, and fallen leaves were thrown up in the kicking scuffle over the sacred site. Without either of the participants noticing, another movement flowed towards them. A mobile, glistening black stream aimed itself at them from the base of the stump. The being was now hitting the side of Ishmael's face, its long arms windmilling ineffectually, trying to hammer him away. Then it saw the brittle implacable river and shrank back, its feet kicking up dry earth and leaves as it fell over itself in a scrabbling to get upright again. The ants had reached their target and stopped to pool for a second or two before invading Ishmael's face. They came by the hundreds and covered his face and neck.

They came by the thousands and streamed inside his clothing to make a new skin. His mouth came away from the root, the sticky whiteness running down his chin. It was quickly gone, the black tide covering him without a single one of them tasting the fluid's joys. He felt no panic, it was soothing. He simply slumped into a sitting position like a fallen sack and let the infestation swarm. There was now a knotted black tributary between him and the stump. It pulsed with ants going back and forth, messages and commands carried on their twitching antennae. The Erstwhile flapped his hands at his side, his violet eyes bulging from their spiny sockets, watching Ishmael shudder under his umbilical joining to the living black circle, looking like a lost earthbound doll tethered to a pulsating nightmare balloon.

The throng moved over him for hours as they sat in the great circular clearing, which gave the clearest view of the heavens from anywhere inside the Vorrh. The Erstwhile had not moved, he just looked back and forth from Ishmael's seething black face to the calm of the night sky, seething with static stars. Eventually a greyness entered the dark, extinguishing the depth of the universe and painting in a single sky in preparation for the pink shadow of the rising sun. When it was high and the circular arena panted under it, the ants began to move back to the stump. Three-fifths of them returned; the rest remained on Ishmael's face, where they would live and breed forever. He stood up, brushed down his dusty clothes, and looked at the Erstwhile. As he did it his features shifted through different contours and profiles. At one moment looking Roman, the next African, then Asian, and thus through all the races of man. He beamed a great smile with his glistening ant lips and winked with his shiny black eyelid at his companion who appeared to be hanging in space, as if hoisted by its collar on some invisible hook, its limp arms dangling at its side. For all its wisdom and timeless horizons, for all it had seen come, go, and await to arrive, nothing had prepared it for this. This cyclops's head was outside of all evolution, including the mythical. When it spoke, its voice too had changed. Ishmael's vocal cords had been altered. His voice box had been breached and surgically changed. Specialised members of the insect tribe had nipped and cut, injected with formic acid, and bent backwards several delicate flaps of tissue, sealing them into a new form. There was still a rough edge to it, a soreness while it healed, but the clarity and oval sound could be heard below the pain.

"I will not speak for some days, and in the future never to men," he said. Another broad smile followed the statement.

A human onlooker would have wondered if the expressions of the new face were indeed a true readout of Ishmael's inner feeling or a surface manifestation of the combined will of the colony. It was impossible to know. His body language also gave nothing away, for now he moved with simple grace. Without hesitation or speed, impulse or doubt; a smooth linear action without a trace of meaning.

The Erstwhile, who had long since forgotten how to read the expressions of Rumours, accepted all that he was given and told by the new co-occupant of the place that had once been called the garden.

CHAPTER THIRTY-NINE

*L*utchen estimated that they had made only twenty or so miles in three days. The extended rest periods that Kippa needed after carrying his burden were slowing them down. The strength of the young man was not equally distributed throughout the day, so that he often used great bouts of energy early on, which generated fatigue towards the afternoon.

After each rest he would hoick up the flapping Wassidrus, who yelled at the shock, and went marching forward like an eager standard-bearer in front of a restless army. Kippa's instant enthusiasm lasted minutes, after which it sank into puffing resolute struggle. Sometimes his leaping ignition caused disastrous results, as when he thrust the pole too high and jammed the man-flag's head into a thick mass of overhanging branches. Wassidrus screamed for fear of his head being ripped off of his puffy neck, especially when Kippa yanked at the pole in a violent attempt to get it loose. If the girl hadn't shouted, Lutchen might not have moved back from his position several paces in advance before the decapitation had taken place, and Kippa would have marched ahead again unaware of the change to his dependent prize.

Lutchen tried to explain to the young man how he might save his strength, but it was a useless task. He just let him go ahead at the beginning of each stretch and then fall back until he could walk no more. So this became the shunting stop-start process of each day. It was in the middle of the fifth day that Lutchen realised that he hadn't heard Kippa's plaintive cry to tell them that he had fallen back to a complete standstill. He stopped and asked the girl if she had heard him. She shook her head and they turned and followed their tracks back the way they had come. Then suddenly jarred to a halt. Back along the beaten path stood Kippa, eyes popping out of his head, holding the pole still, its weight resting on the ground. All around him stood a horde of squat yellow manlike horrors, who stared up high at the Wassidrus, who was making odd coo-cooing sounds. There must have been about eight or ten of them, moving in and out the high, sharp grass. They had no necks, their cyclopean faces growing straight out of their chests. So to see the Wassidrus clearly they had to bend backwards in an uncomfortable manner. It was this that made them unaware of the approach of the priest and the woman. Some had pointed sticks, others had wooden knives. Lutchen drew out the massive automatic pistol that the Sea People had given him.

The babyish noises that spluttered down from above seemed to have the anthropophagi mesmerised, as did the swaying fragment of man that made them. The only movement that came from Kippa was the stream of yellow liquid that splashed down his trembling leg.

Lutchen loudly cocked the slide of the heavy gun. He had only ever done this once before, after assembling the damaged parts and test-firing it. The sound had been like mad intimate thunder and a flame had leapt from the barrel, tearing the bucking pistol away from its restraining binds. It had worked and remained in one piece. But now only his nimble hand held the faulty hand cannon in place, and without a trigger guard the naked automatic nuzzled impatiently.

"Aet mi now yu ugi fukkers," the Wassidrus said and laughed down at the mesmerised tribe of horrors. The old priest raised the gun and one of the horde saw it and let out a grating yell. Instantly, they all disappeared into the swishing undergrowth.

"Fukkers," bellowed the man-flag.

Over the next two days everybody was aware that the anthropophagi were nearby, following the motley band farther into the interior. Lutchen and Kippa were continually braced, awaiting the attack. Modesta seemed weirdly uncaring and moved between spasms of her previous fits and great lethargy. The Wassidrus seemed drunk with the idea of being eaten by the yellow tribe. He fumed and spat, roared and bumbled as his head lolled between the branches. It was during the tense next night, with the insects ragging loudly and forming incandescent balls in the dark foliage, that the old monk noticed that the girl and the man-flag were whispering together. He grew suspicious at the alliance and did not want to be isolated with the idiot youth, so he began to watch more closely for signs of collusion and treachery. That night his worst nightmare came to visit. He had noticed as the darkness got thicker that the luminous pulsing insects were coming together, their balls coalescing. He had dozed off watching their pulsing and was tipped into waking by the sound of Modesta again going into a fit. And then he saw it above her head and interlaced in the trees: a vast out-of-focus ball of light that changed between shimmers and shadow. He scrambled across the ground, tangling his feet in his sleeping sheet. The ball moved towards him; again it appeared to be attracted to his abject fear. It swarmed six feet from the ground, and its shifting circumference had reached eighteen feet and was growing. Out of the corner of his terror he saw the girl, who was sitting up and waving at it. A thin stream of ectoplasmic mucus-like gel swayed between the tips of her fingers and a tendril of insects that dangled from the ball. He tried to speak but his teeth were chattering and he feared biting his tongue. The Wassidrus and its keeper paid no attention to the manifestation as Lutchen slid back across the sinewy root-infested ground. All fear of the anthropophagi had left him. All doubts about his companions had become irrelevant. He just had to escape the suffocation of his terror. To his horror the young woman suddenly pointed her entangled hand towards him and said something that he did not understand. Utterly convinced that she was setting it upon him, he finally screamed out, "O merciful God, please, no."

She clapped her hands and the ball splintered apart, the millions of insects fleeing like sparks. The air resumed its usual buzz of night and nothing moved in the trees. The old priest stared at the woman, who was grinning at him. His heart was louder than anything around him except the words he had just said. They seemed to still be hanging in the air, displacing the monstrous ball. Under them Modesta lay down and pulled her sleeping sheet over her strange body, the grin never vanishing from her face. Even after she was sound asleep.

Lutchen finally surrender to rest, but soon Modesta was whispering inside his dream. She was telling him to wake up, they had things to do, somebody important to meet. He awoke and looked at her patchwork face of contrasting pigments and blinked.

"I have to make a special thing and I need your help. I don't have the strength in my hands to do it alone." She gave him the same smile as last night and he knew he dared not disobey.

She then told him exactly what she needed to make and why.

"But that's impossible, my child, we have no materials or tools."

She liked being called "my child," but he was finding it more and more difficult to say.

"We will use the trees and him," she said, pointing at the Wassidrus.

Lutchen did not understand and told her so, so she explained in great detail and finished with a smile. He felt sick and disgusted but knew that he dare not argue or see possible fault in her project. She told him that in some of the bags were strong knives and that she would construct the other instruments herself. While he collected them, she went back to the Wassidrus and whispered gently. A sound that was impossible to gauge could be heard, and Kippa came away frightened and shaking his head.

For the next four hours she searched among the roots and leaves, cut vines, and bled trees. She opened insects like snuffboxes and abstracted tinctures and essences from all around her. She then bound them together and spoke over their making. This was similar to the process that he had seen Tyc use, and he marvelled at the intricacies being known to one so young. When all the parts were made, she called the priest and the idiot over to the Wassidrus. He had been drinking some thick fluid that she had made the day before. She spoke to Kippa in his native tongue, telling him to use all his strength to hold his charge still. She placed a curved knife and a short stumpy saw in the old man's hands and demanded him not to shake or tremble. She took his wrist and guided him to the lower remnants of the Wassidrus, the fused section that clung around the pole and had once been legs. Together they toiled while the pole shook and whined and the night began to fall away.

CHAPTER FORTY

*A*s they parted at the gates of the airport, Cyrena and Seil Kor agreed to meet again before they left Pretoria.

She had arranged to stay in the same lodge as before, only this time it was thronging with visitors, all very excited and anxious to begin their various safaris. The puffy doctor who claimed to be Marais's friend sat solemnly waiting for her in the bar. They exchange pleasantries. It had been he who sent the brief letter to her saying that Marais had taken his own life and that he had left her something. He seemed surprised that she had come all this way and assumed it was to consult with him on why their friend had committed such a drastic action. He would have sent the parcel to her, the parcel that he now had by his side. When she explained that her purpose was to see the room where he passed his last few hours and minutes, the doctor became agitated. She saw it and thought that she smelt disdain on the man.

"It's not a morbid request," she explained defensively. "I knew he was unwell and in pain. I knew he relied on heavy dosages of analgesics to help him through. I have come to terms with his need to let go."

The doctor fidgeted and attempted to break her flow.

"We had often talked about other states of being. He had helped me discover new territories of understanding. I have no moral opinion about what he did. If the drugs ultimately softened his pathway and allowed him to escape, then I see it as a form of kindness. I just want to see where it happened."

All the doctor could say was "I don't think that would be a good idea." His face was agitated and disconnected. His hand movements were erratic and vague.

"I am not a child or a fainthearted girl."

"Yes, I see that," he stuttered. "But you don't understand."

"I understand that you are patronising me and attempting to prevent me spending a little precious time in his room." Cyrena was becoming angry. "If you won't help me then I will find someone who will. Someone who is prepared to understand our friendshi—"

"He did not die there," the doctor butted in with a hushed vehemence. "He did not die in a room and he did not die of an overdose."

Cyrena had suddenly gone cold.

"He died out in the bush at a godforsaken place called Pelindaba. He killed himself with a shotgun."

There was a long hard stillness before the tears choked her, sobbing up through her shredded repose. She wanted to tell him that he was lying, but she knew he wasn't. The horror of such a death, alone and in the wilderness, was overwhelming. The scholar's sleep in his pensive sad room was one thing. But the unmitigated violence of this act destroyed all redemption and, she feared, respect. The doctor awkwardly tried to comfort her, and between her sobs and her desire to leave, she thanked him for his honesty.

"There is this, he wanted you to have it."

He gave her the cardboard box and she took it absently like a sleepwalker.

"Thank you," she said again and left his agitated company.

She found her room, locked the door, and screamed into the pillow. All the futility that she had so studiously ignored gushed through her. All the dead and all the deceit wrecked her inside, ripping at the now-frail tranquillity. Each wrenching sob was abrading a layer of hope, a memory of joy. She eventually fell asleep in the chaise longue, turned inside out in a grey cold place where nobody lived.

Some hours later her dreams awoke her, the invisibility in the tree coming out to meet her and whisper into her blindness. She wiped the crushed tears and wetness from her face with the back of her hand and stared with red eyes into the empty room. It was the hour before twilight when everything begins to agree to its memory of the dying sun. Half the room glowed in it. The draining day and the approaching night met in a vector on the cardboard box that sat on the floor between the door and the window. She looked at it for a long while, trapped in a numb torpor. The kind that whispers: *If you keep very still, then all things might slide back to the way they were before.* The cobwebs of consistent dharma unbroken, the shocks and threats of the world ignored and wafted sideways in the bow wave of quiet continuance. But her restless agitation would not be hushed and offered a grudging negotiation of diminishing time in the form of a dripping clock, a burning fuse to her reentry into hateful reality. The sundial languidness of the moving shadow across the cardboard lid would time her awakening. She watched unblinking from the couch as the ungaugeable motion crept to the edge and evaporated, leaving the stiff rectangle grey and meaningless. She sat up, gritted her teeth, and retrieved it, pulling the knotted string from it without care.

Inside was the note.

My Dearest Cyrena,

Please forgive the circumstances of the arrival of this most accidental object. I meant to give it to you myself

*and explain its strange properties, but circumstances
have deflected my intensions. I do hope we can meet
again in person, but fear my health is not up to it at the
moment. So please accept this strange gift as a token of our
friendship.*

*It was only recently that I discovered the true nature
of this object in my possession and immediately associated
it with your description of a golden living crown that you
once told me of, from one of your dreams. So here it is. I
have no idea what its original purpose was.*

*Even stranger, I purchased it during my troublesome
expedition to the Vorrh. So it comes directly from your
part of this vast continent. I bought it from a trader who
had many artifacts from the time of the Possession Wars.
There was a story about the importance of its meaning to
a shaman of the True People, but sadly I have forgotten
it after all the years of struggle. I believed it to be a crown
of fired clay set and inlayed with metal amulets and
acquired it as such from a collection of many other quaint
and distinctive relics. Imagine my surprise when I finally
discovered its true mechanical properties.*

*As you know, my journey at the fringe of that
monstrous forest was a little traumatic. Your concern
about its malign energies seemed accurate after all. I was
fortunate to escape it completely intact. So my concerns
about my gathered cargo were, I am sad to say, totally
unimportant to me then. This object has sat forgotten on
shelves for many past forsaken years.*

*I fear I ramble, my dear. Please forgive an old man's
weakness.*

*I have cleaned this "treasure" and taken it apart, oiled
it, and reassembled its remarkable mechanism. It bears*

*the mark of a London instrument maker and must have
been made in the last century. Amazingly, after my little
labours, it all works and produces novel and mesmeric
effects when worn and operated. Do try it. God knows
what it was used for in the Vorrh, but its existence does
seem to have sympathy with your imagination. The roads
that we take and the tracks that others make crisscross and
exchange and are far beyond our little allotted time. I am
sorry not to be with you now. The rains have just started
and I seek the isolation of the bush for a short while. I will
have to wait to hear your impressions of this wonder when
I return.*

With my sincerest love,
EUGÈNE

She put her hand back into the box and touched the cold
metal detail. A faint whir vibrated against her finger. Startled,
she dropped it and the note. The crown rolled out of its container. It was made of brass, not gold or insects. A single circle
of engineered metal.

She felt no fear now and lifted it closer. A series of lenses
or mirrors were attached to spindles that lined its ring. Each
was joined to clockwork mechanisms with winding keys that
extended outwards from the crown. She marvelled at its intricacy and how different it was from her vision. She moved to the
luminosity of the window and turned it in her hands, admiring its weight and perfection. She wound the keys and found
the tight intensity of the constricted springs satisfying. She followed his suggestion and placed it on her head and released the
restraining trigger. It whirred loudly this time, spinning the circular reflections around her eyes and into her mind. The light

of the setting sun spun and amplified and she fell back into the place of the tree where the invisibility was waiting for her . . .

. . . A sound, a song from elsewhere, dragged her into the darkness of waking. She had been in deep communication, flooded by the yellow day of another place. All her fears and woes had been peeled away, broken off like the encrusted mud hiding the crown. The invisibility had entered her and explained sight and blindness and how she was to use them in the place of the tree, in a time so far off that she had to hibernate to reach it. The invisibility heard the song first and turned her to face it, the darkness of reality seeping into every pore of her being. She stumbled towards the window, the song was coming from there. She opened the partially closed shutter and the sound stopped all of her movements. Only her heart, which was now tiny and wrapped in the deepest layers of her meaningless meat, became excited. It tasted the sweetness of hope. She opened the windows that let out into a small courtyard. Seil Kor was sitting on a tiled well at its centre. He was singing to her and there was a luminosity about his blue robe and a light behind his clear eyes, as if they magnified a brightness within. The same yellow day that she had left before. All other sensations ceased. She had no awareness of what she had felt before or what she looked like now. Seil Kor stood up and walked towards her, taking her shoulders in his long dark hands. He guided her back into the room without ever missing a murmur in his rhythmic, undulating song. They glided towards the bed, where she fell back. He sat on its edge as she undressed while lying down, pushing the arcs of her body against the peeling clothing. Her eyes had rolled back in her head until the pupils disappeared. She lay naked in the sleepless sheets. He took off his robe and bent over her, the black angularity of his hard physic exaggerating the white richness of her curves. He cupped her mound in one hand to contain the breathing and closed the other over her mouth. Her perfect teeth set like pearls against his palm. He placed his wide mouth across her white eyes, stretching it to make a wet perfect seal. He sucked and blew until his lungs matched her heart. She pushed against him while his long sinewy legs held her twisting strength heavily against the mattress. She quaked and bucked into quietness. When he felt that she was totally still, he unfolded from her and collected the top sheet, wrapping her tightly in its swaddling. He moved her body across the bed and left her while he went into the little bathroom and washed from head to toe, all the time carrying his song just beneath his breath. When he came back he lifted her wrapped body from the bed and placed it on the floor, taking a seated position behind her. He carefully placed his long, curved feet on her shoulders and gripped her head in his equally long, curved hands. His song changed as his lungs filled with glowing air and his muscles rippled purple beneath his jet-black skin.

Before dawn the purring car waited outside. He carried her like a pliant mummy on his shoulders and placed her lengthways on the backseat. Next to the mechanical crown. The driver said nothing. The day was hot and the journey was rough. The city quickly vanished behind them in clouds of dust. The rainy season was over. During the journey he adjusted her heavy coma-like sleep so that she did not bruise or become burnt in the radiance of the slicing sun. At midday he started to unwrap her. With each unbinding Cyrena awoke. He washed her face with a scented damp cloth before she was fully conscious, combed her hair with his long ivory fingernails, and picked the loose cotton strands from her bare shoulders. In a place without an apparent name they stopped to let the engine of the old car cool in the ancient shade of the weird swollen majesty of a baobab. They were almost there, at the place of meeting and ends.

"We have arrived, Cyrena, the place you have been looking for."

Seil Kor spoke to the driver and took a shovel from the back of the car.

"We are here, my lady."

Cyrena completely awoke, her eyes eclipsing back into sight. She looked around her, at him and the implement in his hands.

"I will show you the exact spot," he said and took her hand.

As they stood motionless the car reversed and found the road, onto which it turned and drove away. Cyrena was looking at her nakedness under the white sheet, but was thinking only about the car. She was about to ask when it was coming back when Seil Kor answered, "It won't be coming back, there is no need."

They walked into the stinging grass for a few minutes and then he stopped and pointed. She looked at the stupid earth and he waited.

"Here?" she said.

"Yes, Cyrena, exactly here."

She slowly settled down, first on her knees and then curling in the grass, pushing her face into the earth where some essence of his blood must remain. Ants moved between her cheek and the soil, they multiplied as she tasted the earth, and Seil Kor began to dig around her.

He had taken his robe off and stretched it out on the ground nearby. She turned her head to look through the long filtering grass. To see him shovelling spadefuls of earth onto its once intense colour. She had a fleeting, flickering image of another naked man digging earth. It had been in the strange books of animal locomotion that she had seen so very long ago. In with the baboons and horses were men and women, children and deformed people, walking and climbing, going about their daily chores without a stitch of clothing. The one she now remembered was older than the rest. A bony white man with the beard and intensity of a biblical prophet. His muscular labours had seemed so very lonely, different from the rest. His simple task had become Sisyphean and tragically unobserved. There had also been a beautiful female dancer. The only one allowed a modest costume of an almost sheer classical dress, very much like the one that she was wearing now. Both of their statuesque bodies were as bright as polished marble and perhaps as heavy as hers felt. Seil Kor moved around her and started digging on the other side. He was six feet down in the trench when he hit stone with the sound of a cheap bell.

"Ground rock," he called out and continued digging around it. The entrance to the cave was farther down and clogged with earth and ugly root fibre. He clawed it away and hacked his way into the deep resonance of his growing hollowness.

"Cyrena, my lady, come see."

She stepped down carefully into the loose earth and peered into the lips of the access.

"Put on your crown and wait for me."

He then bounded up the steep loose banks of shovelled earth.

"Wait inside the cave," he called, and she ducked and squirmed in.

Seil Kor stretched up and grabbed the hem of his robe. Most of the dug earth sat upon it in a great heap. He tugged it and the drier earth fell around him. He jumped down, pulling the cloth after him. A great avalanche of gathered earth slid into the hole, its movement encouraging a landslide to follow. He crested a sliding mass of earth that rattled and hissed around his descent. He ducked into the hole of the cave as the carefully stacked hill slumped down from above. A great rain of dry darkness sealed them in.

"Make it work," he said.

And Cyrena fumbled at the brass switches on the crown that had once been William Gull's peripherscope. It fluttered into action, seemingly catching the subtle light that was escaping her luminous eyes. She placed it on her head, and it magnified and spun, sending silent splutters of blurred light darting about the stone walls.

They moved as sleepwalkers inside its tunnel of flickers, like pilgrims sheltering from an ancient and irrational rain. Time became obsolete as they spiralled lower and lower, occasionally stopping so that she could rewind the little motors. Each flicker of light that escaped her was replaced by a sugary darkness, peeled from the walls by exactly the same magnitude of luminescence. Cyrena was becoming drunk with so many hollows of shadow, her attachment to the surface forgotten. The path finished at a blank rock face with a manger-like recess cut into it.

"We are here," whispered Seil Kor.

"Here?" murmured Cyrena.

CHAPTER FORTY-ONE

*K*essler's pier looked different in the light of day, or rather in the luminous haze of the summer afternoon. Nicholas stood on the shaky wooden decking with Hector at his side. The time had come; they were to travel down to the estuary and find their place beneath the mouth of the Thames. Solli and Albi stood behind them, close to the alleyway. They had said their good-byes and it had been hard. Solli hated showing any emotion that was softer than rage. He had not spoken since Hector embraced him and wished him a good life. A cannonball made of tears sat in his throat and he turned his attention away from the water and stared back up towards the street and the hard, unflinching sanctity of his violent life. Hector stared into the swollen water. Nicholas pointed at the hanging tarpaulin that concealed the dented bugle.

"Call him," he said to Albi.

Ten minutes later the Cromwell could be seen heading towards them. It tied in against the jetty, the pilot's son and Albi tying the ropes. The passengers were stepping over the gunnels when the Patriarch appeared. He, like his boat and his pier, appeared totally different in daylight.

"Afternoon, gentiles," he said and then stopped speaking while he looked at Nicholas. Hector had seen the two men together before. Seen them ignore each other, on and off the boat. All that had suddenly changed. The Patriarch took one step forward and knelt, bowing solemnly so that his forehead touched the deck. Nicholas twisted his head around, making the gnashing sound that Hector was becoming used to. When he turned back, he was somebody else. He placed his hand on the pilot's yarmulke and whispered. Only the boat and the river moved.

Hector watched the pier with its sticklike figures diminish in the haze and the first slouched bend in the river. Then he turned to look forward, the chugging steamy throb of the Cromwell's heart beneath his feet. An insignificant momentum above the churning mass of the epic Thames, where deep down, the silt of Roman bones gritted with a pumice of wild oxen and the infinitesimal grains of gigantic mammoths. All ground down to form a shifting dim landscape, where older stains of petrified forests darkened the restless grey. In this curd, last week's murder merrily bobbed in its sunken slow motions of chains and concrete, alongside discarded prams and bits of nameless ships and all the dissolving tippings of the city. This was the pool bed and a long way from the soft sands that they were heading towards. It was also unlike the marshy ground of the upper Thames where Nicholas had been before. They were moving into wider bends that swirled across its mighty snakelike flexings. The entrances to the docks on each side were getting larger. Top-heavy vessels queued to be let into their labyrinths of canals and woodyards, warehouses and barges. The trepidation that sat like a constant bird on Hector's shoulders said nothing. It also stared out across the water and would have sleepily preened its feathers, if it had had any.

They were passing Greenwich when Hector started asking questions. Nicholas ignored the first attempts as if deaf. They were both at the front of the boat, the fresh wind buffeting their faces. Hector was quiet for a moment and then he decided to changed his tactic. They were passing a squat lighthouse on the north shore, which marked the entrance to the river Lea. Large spheres and huge cagelike cones leant at odd angles around the tower. Some were painted red. Men climbed over their imposing surfaces.

"Trinity Buoy Wharf," came the gruff tones of the pilot from behind them. "That's where they make 'em and repair the ones broken by the sea."

Hector grinned politely and turned his back on the information.

"Nicholas, tell me for one minute about why you are different from all the others?"

Nicholas turned and flattened his perfect hair with one hand and began his answer without repetition, hesitation, or deviation. "Because I have lived longer and escaped the forest earlier, having the opportunity to collect unused parts of fading men to gather myself and thus become as I am today."

"Will others come out and become like you?"

"Oh, I doubt it, it's far too late for those left behind, they should have slept their way out years and years ago." He suddenly slapped his hand over his mouth, saying, "Oh no, repetition of years."

Hector pushed on. "Will you get any older, ever?"

"That's a good question, but I don't know the answer. I know it's possible to get younger while sleeping, but don't know about the other way round."

"How do you get younger?"

Nicholas looked back at Hector, pointed, and laughed, twisting his head backwards over his stiff neck.

"You are so funny, Hector, both funny ha-ha and funny peculiar. I can never get younger. I was talking about the Before Ones, the ones that left the forest long before us, some of them were excavated as children. They have grown up as Rumour, lived so long as humans that they have forgotten what they are."

"Do you have contact with them at all?"

Nicholas stroked his chin and looked across the churning water, its brightness making him squint.

"Not really, I just know they are there." And then with a bolt of enthusiasm he continued. "Many of my kind will be making the plural. One of the old ones has been in your world for so long that she has forgotten what she is. So her plural is made with a fellow who is half Rumour and half Erstwhile, back in the old caves of Africa." He slapped his thigh and twisted savagely to gnash at his collar, his weird energetic giggling sending the pilot scurrying back into his wheelhouse.

The boat bobbed and its engine throbbed alongside the thin nailed-together jetty that looked like it had been made out of the charred, gnawed bones of ancient chickens. Hector's bad memories of another boating trip flapped back. The jetty shook with the vibrations from the Cromwell and Hector felt it in his hands.

"Is this safe to walk on?" he said in a voice that nobody heard.

The Patriarch was again prostrate before Nicholas, who had his soft hand on the old pilot's head.

"Honoured malokhim, will we ever see the likes of you or your kind again?" the old man asked, without ever raising his eyes.

"Bad pennies always turn up," Nicholas joked, removing his hand and walking to the gunwales and daintily stepping over onto the complaining, creaking structure.

"Come, Professor," he said, offering his arm to his hesitant companion. Seaweed peeled away beneath them, taking black gleaming muscles back into the salty water as they walked along the narrow boardwalk. Hector looked down into their ripples.

"Poor demented things," said Nicholas.

"Who?"

"Those sea mice, gone mad with the changing of the tides. Twice a day their world changes. One minute they're enjoying the taste of warm shit soup coming out of London. The next it's all cold, salty brine. Poor things, moon-cast like the lunatics of Bedlam."

The pilot and his son held on to the firm handrails and stared, transfixed. Nicholas remembered that they were there and called back over his shoulder, "Be careful not to miss your tide," and as if an afterthought, he said, "Take care of Hyman and young Solomon for me."

The skeletal wood became firm ground and Hector rushed forward, starting to breathe again. The engine changed tone behind them and the solid little boat slid backwards into the churning estuary. All the men waved, but the Erstwhile was already moving on, his interest in the past vanished. They walked into the broad evening of the open countryside, Nicholas taking exaggerated lungfuls of Kentish air as if he were back bathing in the limelight on the stage of the Pavilion theatre. Hector looked around him at the slump of marshlands on one side and broad cultivated fields on the other. They were walking on a slow downward gradient and any sign of the estuary vanished under the hedgerows. Hector became unsure why they were walking away from the water.

"Aren't we going in here . . . ?" he stuttered, facing back into the direction they had just come.

"Not yet, Professor, the tide is rising. That would never do, we would be washed back to Shadwell after taking the second step. Anyway, don't you want a hearty supper, condemned man's privilege and all that? They might even have the odd crust or a bone and a bowl of water for the cunt of a bitch." He chortled while Hector blushed under his scarf and new hair.

Eventually he said, "Who might?"

"The trusty publican of the Rose and the Crown."

"We are going to an inn?" His disbelief was lost amid the calls of a flock of gulls swooping inland.

"A pub, Hector, a pub. You are not in Baden-Württemberg now."

The old man still found this strange being's knowledge of his life unnerving, even after all their weird encounters.

"We must blend in with the locals tonight."

The idea of Nicholas blending in with any normal humans was difficult enough, but to merge with what Hector suspected would be ignorant yokels, of the kind that he had encountered in Southampton, was grotesque.

"Are we staying there?"

"Yes, of course, we have to change your dream shutters and your weight, that would have been impossible in London, wouldn't it?"

Hector had no idea what he was talking about, but nodded because it was the easiest thing to do.

"Are they expecting us?"

Nicholas stopped dead, beaming. He waved his hands about as if conducting the birdsong, making skipping motions on the rough road.

"Look about you, Hector, this is Hoo Allhallows. I don't think they have ever expected anybody."

They walked for another fifteen minutes or so, until the squat spire of the village church showed above the small bent trees and low-lying bushes, the humps of a few houses rising out of the seagrass and reeds. They tuned onto the rising path that skirted the wall of the cemetery, up into the crossing of a larger road where the Rose and the Crown sat stoutly at its corner.

"There she blows!" said Nicholas with glee.

They pushed open its solid door and stooped into the musky darkness that was constructed of the reassuring smell of log smoke, stale beer, and tobacco, with a distant hint of cooking to heighten the effect. Two customers sat at opposite ends of the room. The only sound was the fire dimly crackling and the drip of an unseen tap.

"Good eventide, gentlemen," said Nicholas theatrically.

The customers ignored him, but a shuffling could be heard behind the bar and a long-faced pinched woman appeared. She looked them up and down and then put her hands on the blades of emaciated hips.

"Yes?" she said through her long doglegged nose.

"We would like a room to share and dinner for tonight," Nicholas announced.

"Ain't got none. Out of season. No call for it now." There was no flow in her words, just chunks of statement that fell out of her large, thin-lipped mouth without effort or finesse.

"A front room overlooking the sea," said the angel as if he had not heard her previous emphatic statement.

"You deaf?" she said. "We ain't got none."

"But it must have one big bed, a dooble, so that we can sleep together."

One of the customers' chairs grated on the dark stone floor as he turned to look at these oddities.

"What?" she said, her mouth curling as if by the harsh application of sour invisible pliers.

"A dooble so that we can snuggle up."

Hector was now very embarrassed and had no idea why Nicholas was talking like this and why he was pronouncing things in a very strange way. The woman was speechless and both customers were looking over their shoulders.

"We are Germans, you see," added Nicholas, beaming.

The hag flushed and filled her scrawny lungs with rank air, ready to give what Hector had learned was called a "mouthful." But before she spoke, Nicholas placed two heavy gold coins noisily on the bar, very much in the manner of a conjurer who had just performed the conclusion to a lengthy and complicated trick. The sight of the gold stoppered her mouth and the pent-up air escaped through her shrill nostrils in a wet squeak.

"And this one is for you, my lovely," said Nicholas, advancing the third coin towards the baggy collar of her worn-out dress. But finding no cleavage there he daintily posted it in the slit of her mouth.

She instantly changed. Softened and unfolded. It was as if her bones had just inflated and a radiating warmth had suffused her body. An astonishing pulchritude reshaped her stance, pallor, and total demeanour. Hector involuntarily took a step back. She wiggled and blushed and started speaking in a soft befuddled manner, her words slurring over the gold. Nicholas pointed at the coin in her mouth and she retrieved it, flushed again, and curtsied.

"Just the one night, sirs?"

"Yes, my dear," said Nicholas kindly.

She whisked the coins off the bar and Hector noticed that the irregular disks had a portrait of a surly wide-headed man imprinted on them. Nicholas saw his curiosity and winked.

"Nero," he said.

Before any more could be said or choked upon, the woman was back with two carefully balanced glasses before her.

"Speciality of the house," she said.

Nicholas beamed and brought the dark red liquid to his lips.

"Ah! The blood, my favourite," he said.

"Blood?" said Hector peering into the heavy glass apprehensively.

"Port and brandy mixed like us, making the blood."

Hector sniffed the glass.

"Of the hero. Nelson's blood." He then turned towards the room and its gawping occupants. "To the hero, Britannia and death to all our foes abroad!"

The two elderly customers attempted to stand and raise their glasses, but before they could drink, Nicholas had quaffed his and returned to the attentions of the bar lady. At that moment another presence appeared behind the bar. A grim, unshaven man in an apron. He was just about to speak, his eyes fixed suspiciously on the strangers, when his wife grabbed his hairy wrist and opened her hand, so that the gold glimmered.

"Two more, please, patron, in our room," said Nicholas, and stepped past them through the bar and turned onto a broad wooden stair.

Hector followed, not wanting to be left alone surrounded by stares and unfriendly questions. He sipped the warming drink and followed.

The stair turned and narrowed on each landing; their room was in the eaves. It was tight and low-ceilinged with dismal furnishings in many different styles, the only common feature being the shared exhaustion and paucity of colour.

The bed looked overstuffed and Hector already knew that it was lumpy and squeaked.

"Excellent," said his elated friend, who had to stoop as he approached the wall to open the small squat window onto a view of the church and churchyard, and beyond it the gigantic far-off estuary. A purplish light smouldered from its waters laced with the shadows of clouds that floated under the glow of the setting sun.

"Magnificent," said Nicholas, who in his eagerness had torn the lace curtain aside and entirely dislodged both it and its string that had held it in the same place, undisturbed for years.

He shook it away from himself like an irritating cobweb, and again did more pantomime breathing. After they settled, he announced that they must make a few preliminary adjustments before eating.

"Please lie on the floor, Hector, after removing your shoes and jacket." His voice was without humour or warmth. In place of kindness was matter-of-fact abruptness, which Hector was sure that Nicholas had learned from all his years of listening to English doctors. So he did as he was told. Nicholas did the same and came to sit behind his head. He placed his socked feet on the old man's shoulder and wrapped his long elegant fingers around his jaw and cranium. He tightened his grip and Hector felt panic as he realised that his fragile spine was taut in this being's severe hold.

"Now, Hector Ruben Schumann, I want you to remember and see the first time you saw Rachel's beautiful naked body."

Hector instantly saw her, saw her before he had the chance to become outraged at the request and at the same time that Nicholas wrenched his head sideways and up. There was a crack like a pistol being fired as Hector's body was pushed hard away from his head by the angel's steel-hard pistoning feet. He then spun the body sideways, the neck crunching again, and a white sickening light hit him like an express train. Nicholas had twisted his own head backwards and fastened his teeth into the collar of his shirt. He looked like a skinned animal. All the curves and puffiness of gentle humanity had been extinguished, all the subtleties of expression instantly drained, the muscles knotted and the veins standing proud like strangling rope. His mouth had extended, unnaturally revealing row upon row of snarling teeth. The force he was exerting was enough to snap three men's necks. The inert mats and rugs of the room slithered across the gritty bedroom floor in alarming life as struggling feet kicked and hammered. Hector knew he was going to die, but not why, not now. Why like this? His legs were thrashing mechanically when the right impacted with the leg of the cast-iron bed and the left kicked a china bowl under the bed, sending it skidding and smashing against the wall. It was the last thing he saw and heard before a wave of deep black nausea snuffed him out.

Something was moving between a flutter and roll. It was also like a pendulum, only irregular and faint. He did not know if his eyes were open or closed. The white ghostlike stiffness could have been on either side of his sight, consciousness, or life. Gradually he felt his toes and fingers move and the white thing no longer was far away but was near and growing ordinary. He could make out the landscape behind it. A long plateau stretched for miles, grey-brown and unbroken by trees. A heavy dense sky kept the landscape compressed and stationery. Far far away he could see the irregular glimmer of shining domes set amid jagged mountains of precipices of ice. How had he gotten here? To this woebegone but exotic realm. He tried to move his head but it felt numb and limp. A breeze moved across his face; it smelt of seaweed and cinnamon, of oceans and stale infancy. The fluttering thing was moving in response to the breeze that gusted over and around everything. When it subsided it slowed to almost stillness. It was the lightest thing in all the surrounding darkness. It had words written upon it. Were these the words given at the gate of eternity? The fabled scroll of the Apocalypse? The utterance of final discorporation? He strained to decipher it and understand its meaning, hovering in the great plateau, willing his focus to pull against the flatness and endless distance before him. He read the words slowly in the darkness that flickered and nudged meaning into nonsense, and for a moment was reminded of the text of ants that he had never really seen. But as his eyes deepened again he saw that these were not that twitching scrawl. The letters were now as clear and precise as if painstakingly written by the hand of an ingenious and unskilled scribe.

He tried again to understand the esoteric meaning, which was written in the form of a request or command.

After what must have been hours, another light bloomed in the room and Nicholas said, "Ah! Awake at last, I thought you were going to sleep down there forever." Nicholas lit another oil lamp and the room flowed into order and logic. Hector was not standing up but was lying on his side, his head resting on a cushion and his body covered by the candlewick bedspread. He was staring directly under the bed towards the far wall where the china bowl had broken. This had been the landscape that he had so feared and pondered on for hours.

"Don't try to move yet, I will help you up in a moment."

A slight breeze made the lamps shudder and then settle. The flapping whiteness returned. It was a small handwritten sign that had been tied to the side of the bed. Somehow one of its strings had broken and now it dangled in the breeze by one. Again he read its erudition.

Will guests please refrain from placing the used chamber pot under the bed, because the steam rusts the springs.

Nicholas lifted Hector to his feet and guided him to a misshapen, difficult chair that felt as if it had been upholstered with bricks. He held one hand to the back of Hector's neck while moving him.

"How do you feel, my friend?"

"Tired. I feel as if I have been travelling for miles. What happened, why was I on the floor?"

"Oh, just resting before dinner. Are you hungry?"

"Yes, very."

A child and the flouncing woman brought their food to the door with a jug of dark beer. They ate in silence. Outside the night had closed in around the pub, making the room feel snug and the rest of the world dark, cold, and distant. A few warming sounds rose up through the floor, telling them that they were not alone. The chicken was perfectly cooked and the vegetables full of taste. So much so that Hector thought them the best he had ever eaten.

"What did you say the name of this place was again?"

"Allhallows on the Hoo peninsula. Allhallows at the end of the world."

"It's the best food I have ever tasted."

"It's not the place, it's your senses being reborn. It is happening in advance of our plural, tonight our sleep in this little hutch will complete the process."

The church bell sounded as Hector's eyes began to close uncontrollably.

"Time for the wooden hill," said Nicholas.

"What hill?"

"The wooden hill to Bedfordshire."

"You said Kent before."

"Bed. Bett, kleiner spatz."

Nobody had called him that in seventy years. Only his mother, so long ago. He stood and walked over to the bed, took off his shirt and trousers, and crawled in between the chilly sheets. He was asleep in seconds.

Nicholas washed in the room down the corridor. He was thinking about his radio and all the voices he would miss. The only thing he would miss. He carried the lamp back to the bedroom and looked at the man-child curled up under the blankets. Tonight, all night long he would hold him, locked on tight pressure points and speak the psalms of release: the charms of dispersal. Then the song of joining.

CHAPTER FORTY-TWO

*T*he bow she carried into the wilderness she had made from the man remnants of the Wassidrus. She used what was needed. He did not die but was sewn and sealed back into a less extended form that clung to the end of the long stained pole. Her skill with charms, drugs, and knives had been equal to her mother, Irrinipeste's. The bow was more perfect than the one her father had made. He had been totally human and therefore susceptible to all manner of uncertainties and vagueness. His bow had been made of faultless materials but was botched and mishandled in its construction. This bow had been made of vile and corrupt materials but was manufactured with dexterous and spiritual excellence, making it a far superior creature. Her parents' bow had been constructed for vision and transience. The gleaming purple weight in her hands now was crafted for protection and vengeance. She turned it in her sticky hands, feeling the heat of its silky glue against her skin. She then placed it in its drying place where no animal would dare approach it. She would start on the arrows tomorrow after a long and empowering sleep. She had dismissed the old priest, who had not spoken in hours, and collected all the scraps, shavings, and unused sinews, putting them in a tight bag so that after they dried Kippa might feed the titbits to his newly shaped, precious charge. All was done and she felt able to drag her bedding to the bow and curl around it. But the sleep was diverted by the queue of fits that waited to enter her body. She yelped and jackknifed as they took hold, while the solemn and hungry bow sat next to her. After thirty hours she passed out, exhaustion bullying its way ahead of the next string of convulsions. The old priest sat close and tried to mop her brow and put back the thin blanket that refused to cover her. She had tried to bite him and scratched out like a demented and restrained lynx, her hands and feet curled into talon-like claws.

When she came out of her spasms, her gaunt and hollow body was driven only by the purpose of getting the bow to work and using its homing instincts to take them farther into the Vorrh. She told him that the bow was to be gifted, that their meeting at the kernel of the eternal forest was the desired outcome of a great destiny. Lutchen said that this was not what he had been told by Oneofthewilliams. She looked into him as he spoke. Her dark, sturdy eyes carved away at his longing. As she took the meaning of his words in, he noticed that something had physically changed about her. He tried to look back more carefully, his enquiring eyes attempting to pass through the gate of her solid gaze. It was her skin that had changed, the pattern, form, and distribution of the patched areas of light and dark. The pigmentation had shifted, making new and different continents and smaller islands. He so marvelled at her new map and its ability to transform that he nearly forgot what they were talking about. She, however, continued in expressing her determination that the bow would be given to somebody that neither of them had met.

During the period they had to wait for the bow to season, they had been given offerings of food from the anthropophagi, who remained hidden while leaving them dead animals and crude bowls of mouth-numbing acrid mush. The smell of the dwarf horde was growing stronger each day, and Lutchen guessed their number was increasing. He did not know what they were or why they now followed. Did they wait as allies or disciples, or as cannibals ready to feed on their carrion? Their continual unseen presence agitated his already distraught mind and his peripheral vision, and the Mars pistol remained cocked.

When the bow was finally strung, it bled only a small stain of grime each time it was pulled. And when the Wassidrus had healed and stopped bellowing they moved forward, following the path of the arrows.

Modesta waited with each knot in the bow taut in her small hands. Waited for the fit that would spin her, dervish-like, while flexing the straining power. When the moment came upon her, she pointed the arrow skywards and released it from the resounding bow, sending it flying into the impenetrable forest. The sound that came from the bow stopped everybody in their tracks. It was a shudder of words, as if a muffled voice was contained inside the folded layers of bone and sinew. As the arrow fled its collapsing arc it seemed to ignite the voice inside its tension. Lutchen moved closer to Modesta's side and she glared at him.

"I want to understand what it's saying, to understand its meaning," he said.

"It is beyond your understanding," she hissed while selecting the next arrow. He shivered at the flutter of her power, as if she had walked across his grave, stopped, and looked through the earth and onto his impassive, skinless grin.

They hacked and tore their way through the undergrowth and resistant webs of hanging vines and creepers. With each arrow her determination grew and the old man's confidence diminished. He knew they were going in circles. He knew he must do something before her vision led them all to their demise. The power that radiated from her was thinning with every action of the bow, with every epileptic spinning and change of direction. The magic that kept them together and the anthropophagi at bay was vanishing. He knew that she was the direct descendant of the fabled Irrinipeste and that all beings on this continent would have been in awe of her had not her uniqueness been the direct cause of the Possession Wars. He watched the bushes, seeing the yellow men on the other side spying and attempting to talk about her. It was their fear and adulation that kept the wicked gnawing faces away from their necks. That, and nothing else. That's what he thought until the last arrow bisected the wound of the railway track. They had all heard the hideous sound squealing in the forest the day before and imagined the largest and vilest of beasts being slaughtered there.

➤→

The working half of the Limboia had been cutting and stacking trees for ten days. The train that was expected to arrive and take the timber away and replace them with the next shift of workers was late. But of course nobody noticed. Expectation did not exist for the Limboia. The train did not exist for the Limboia. Neither did the difference between day and night, waking and sleeping. It was only the overseers who demanded these constant changes, and noticed the levels of fatigue, and counted the days. The Limboia knew how to eat and shit, that was about all. Everything else they had to be shouted at to do. Back in William Maclish's time a doctor had conducted some experiments on them. A couple had died because of his curiosity, but he had proved the point that command was the only mechanism of direction in their existence. The operating commands were crude and elemental. Wake, sleep, work, and eat. They did not need to be told when to shit, they just did it while they worked and slept. This explained the condition of the slave house and why they wore loose-fitting skirts while labouring in the forest. The good doctor decided to test the power of command and had one of their number removed to a private room while he slept. He watched for more than five days as the creature faded and crawled towards death without ever leaving his bunk. Every time he began to show signs of waking a guard would bellow "Sleep" at the prone body. On the sixth day dehydration and malnutrition drained the last whimper of life out of him.

Three guards were standing around the timber station where the iron track ended. Two were talking and smoking cigarettes, gazing expectantly along the parallel lines that led back to Essenwald and pleasure. The other was standing by the huge mass of suppurating wood, keeping a wary eye on the massed group of workers, who had been ordered to stop work and eat. They were all squatting or sitting in the shade, eating their usual gruel from mess tins. It was not a pretty sight and the guard unfocussed his gaze from any real detail, which was why he did not see one of the vacant souls wander off from the edge of group and disappear into the forest. They always lost one or two this way, generally by them diverting away from the others but sometimes by what looked like choice. The will to vanish into the trees. It is of course impossible to discuss willpower in terms of the Limboia. Impulse seemed to be their only motivating force, and even that was unclear and paradoxical. Whatever it was that made them stray was beyond the understanding of their masters. The only thing that was known was that once gone, it was better to never find them again. The stories of those that had been discovered after a week or so were horrible, and one of the first things that any new employee was told. Madness in any human is a deeply disturbing thing to witness. But in those that already had lost most of their conscious mind it was appalling. Even worse, it seemed to be infectious. A prodigal Limboia put back in the work party or the slave house would induce manic raving in all the others in the space of a few short hours. Trainee guards were always told of the time when Maclish had to put one down to stop the entire slave house from becoming a writhing pit of hysteria. They were told how from the very moment that he was dispatched, or as Maclish would have it, "slotted," the others simply fell back into their normal torpor. As the sound of the shot faded, so did their cries and deafening shrieks.

This escapee lopped along the cut track farther and farther into the interior. When the cut track ran out, he followed a slender animal path. No one had commanded him to do this. There was no purpose in his action. He had moved on an impulse that had no name. A sound in the trees above made him stop and look up. Something was falling through the branches without the resistance of a bird or a monkey. It slowed above him and fell at his feet. It was a black arrow. He slowly picked it up and an ant of a memory crawled in his head.

The path ahead suddenly ran out, and he looked about him and discovered that he knew he was lost. He had no idea what to do, so he sat down.

The lost Limboia was rubbing his feet, having taken off the battered laceless work boots that he had been wearing. He did not hear the other being enter the trees and step quietly into his space.

"Arise," it said in a whisper from behind him, which he did, clumsily turning to look directly into the seething black face, and screamed. The guard by the woodpile heard the sound but did not identify it as human. The forest was brimming over with all kinds of cries, screeches, and barks. This was just another; some wild thing having engaged in mating or being ripped apart. They all sounded the same to him. But not to the Limboia, who all stopped eating and stood up and turned to face the same direction. This eerie concentration startled the guard, who telegraphed his dismay to his smoking comrade, who stood over the other man who had poured water on the hot iron tracks so that he could put his ear to it and listen for the train. He waved him over as he stepped forward to see if he could get a closer look at what had so galvanized the mindless ones. Then they started very slowly moving.

CHAPTER FORTY-THREE

*H*oss had been forced again into the Vorrh with his beloved train. The new Men Without Substance were highly skilled with their own equipment and petrol-driven trucks, but were incapable of controlling and taming the cantankerous ways of the guild's steam locomotive. It was said that at least three of the soldiers had been injured by the engine. Two by steam and one by the kickback from the heavy iron throttle lever—one of the little tricks of the old monster that Hoss had learned to anticipate and therefore master. So now he was needed and they escorted him with rifles from his home, where he'd had just enough time to find his braces and work trousers before being hoisted onto the cracked-earth road. He was trying to attach the buttons, hold up his trousers, and wave goodbye to his miserable wife, her mouth and arms resolutely folded in their crooked receding doorway as he stumbled hurriedly towards the timber yard and the obstinate hissing object of his desire.

The train was covered in soldiers. The flatbeds were loaded with rails and sleepers. They had even erected a crane on one of them. Machine-gun platforms had been added to the first and last truck, and Hoss wondered what they expected to encounter inside the Vorrh. There had been much talk about all the tribes of the Lands Without Substance going to war. It was even rumoured that there was not enough killing ground there, so they were bringing their battles here, where they could spread them wide and lonely. Perhaps that is what they hoped for once outside the city walls.

Hoss was very interested in the machine guns; he had never seen one before but had heard about what they could do. So once the steam was up, all the gauges checked and working, and the pistons and wheels greased and ready to flex their shining muscles, he put down his spanners and wiped his hands. He strolled away from the dripping, steaming mass towards the first carriage and the man in the dwarf tower sitting behind the svelte beast of the gun, its long barrel swivelling this way and that.

"That's a mighty weapon," he called up to the sweating soldier, who ignored him. "It must fire many rounds."

The gunner had no intention of starting a conversation with an ignorant black and rechecked the long belt of cartridges that ran through the articulated jaws of the breach. Plagge had been watching the pointless tableau and grew irritated in the process. He strutted up to the wide, dirty driver.

"Why have you left your engine? You must stay there, we will soon be ready to leave."

Hoss looked down at Plagge sweating in his tight, dark uniform and dragged the rag from his loose-fitting overall pocket and wiped his face with it.

"I was looking at this gun. I like machines, Bwana."

"I don't care what you like, go back to the engine and leave this soldier alone."

"What calibre is it?" asked Hoss, stretching up and touching the barrel.

Plagge stared at the impudent hand fondling the weapon. "Don't touch that ordinance," he snapped.

"Thirty millimetre?"

A sudden loud hiss from the impatient engine gathered their attention. Hoss was instantly drawn back, ignoring the diminutive Plagge as if he were never there. Whistles were being blown from among the hurrying ranks of soldiers. Officers were calling orders. Overhead birds were circling, some alarmed out of their trees around the station, others attracted by the bustle. So many humans always meant food. Higher under the thin sheeting of clouds, darker, larger birds wheeled in languid circles. Their fist-size eyes calculated the quantities of flesh.

Hoss was shouted at in his hot, oven-like cabin behind the gallons of boiling water and rigid contained fire. He had been given a soldier to stoke the fire. A man who never spoke to him once. Hoss touched his chest and then the picture of the angel, its broken frame wired onto the thick black steel. He opened the throat of the engine's shrill whistle and white steam shrieked through the dense humid air, like a razor through a pillow. He unwound the brake and eased the throttle forwards. A wet sensual power shuddered into motion, the piston hearts of the engine filling and discharging anticipation. The heavy length of the overladen flatbeds rolled forward, seeking the momentum sleeping in the rails. The soldiers, engineers, and officers braced themselves and began to enjoy the movement. This was to be a good outing, a logistic exercise in the vast forest that stretched out before them. Enjoyable and rewarding in contrast to the muddled battles and confused bloodshed that some of them had witnessed early in the year. The extension of the line through the forest was beneficial civil engineering, a gift in the tactics of invasion.

Twenty minutes later, and all sign and sound of the train had disappeared. The birds returned to the trees and the platform, seeking peace or scraps of food. The larger birds had moved off, following the trail of meat. One man remained in the fluttering space, now so devoid of humans. Anton Fleischer stood motionless as the last vibrations faded from the tracks.

➤→

The black face of the shapeshifter pulsed as he led the escapee back onto the broader path. If Ishmael was still under the heavy mass of gleaming ants, then he had changed. Even the walk of this man, if indeed he still was a man, was different: a quieter more unhurried gait, marked by a grace that had never been there before. The other Limboia approached and closed their eyes while Ishmael moved among them placing his seething hands above their heads. Each knelt until the whole mass of men were below him. A stillness moved through the trees, as if for the first time ever they had something to observe. The birds hushed and the breeze dropped and every leaf and whine seemed to feel its weight and cup it against the thin magnetism that holds everything together. Only the sound of arrows catching and falling in the branches could be heard.

Of course, the forest cared nothing about the flickering life of men. What had occurred was a moment of reflection. A refraction in the polished indifference of the Vorrh when the unearthly radiance of the soulless ones found a sympathetic index that agreed in its opacity. The Vorrh mirrored the transition perfectly with as much empathy as silvered glass feels for those who peer into it.

Two of the attendant guards followed the Limboia. The third stayed with his ear pressed to the track. The sight that greeted them confounded all their expectations: the kneeling Limboia were humming. A low moaning throb passed between. Ishmael stood at their centre, his black writhing hands holding his head, so that the ants could flow freely, making one mass out of the once separate parts of his anatomy. The guards looked at one another and unholstered their pistols, then turned and ran.

—▶

Modesta was moving fast ahead of her crippled party, still shooting arrows high into the canopy before her. Her bursting quiver of arrows was alive with ants. They were getting so thick that the mottled woman hesitated, not wanting to put her hands on the livid mass. The trees were very dense here with the sinewy vines heavily meshed between them. The way forward was becoming impossible.

"Kippa, come here," called Lutchen.

The mass of the grinning youth bumped into them as he stood behind their dwarfed backs.

"Can you clear some of this away and open the path?" the priest asked, pointing into the tangled mass.

"Kippa get," he said, leaning between them, almost knocking the slender woman over with his enthusiasm. He pushed his great fist into the vines and tore them savagely apart. "Kippa get."

They were all staring ahead when they heard it. A sound like an animal charging through the thick undergrowth, very nearby. They cringed, waiting for the boar, rhino, or worse to come crashing into their delicate space. Then they saw that it was not something arriving but something going. A great shrapnel of leaves, snapped-off branches, and yanked vines scurried and imploded a few yards away.

The Wassidrus was gone, pulled away sideways through the undergrowth at ground height.

"Quick!" shouted Lutchen without knowing why, and the three of them rushed at the shaking hole in the matted green. Inside its torn flutter could be seen the mass of his body and the top of his pointed head, moving quickly away, surrounded by yellow swags of movement and the overpowering stench of the anthropophagi. They were dragging him farther and farther into the impenetrable foliage.

"They are taking him!" shouted Lutchen, more to define his own amazement than to inform. But Kippa now understood and wailed out a terrible cry of defeat, and then sobbed up another and another, which almost drowned out the voice of the Wassidrus.

"Shut up," screamed the priest to the slobbering giant. "Listen . . ."

"They will eat him, eat him all up," Kippa blubbered.

"Listen."

Inside the noise of the snapping wood and the scuffle of earth there was another sound, a coo-cooing and the repetition of a single word trapped in the cradle of the aborted baby speak. It was faint but not uttered by a victim. Not squealed by a wounded quarry. It sounded more like a joyful egging on, an encouragement, an instruction, a spur. It said, "Purrradyce."

The undergrowth was quiet now, and the three survivors stood without words. There should have been a sense of relief, a thanking God for his departure, but none arose. In its place was shock and an icy dread. The act that had just occurred did not really have a name or a suitable description to pin it down and hold it sealed for cataloguing. It had been too fast and yet so obviously slow. The Wassidrus must have been speaking to them all the time. Planning what was beginning to feel like his escape. Could that be true? Was there enough vigour left in the freshly leaking wound of a man? The priest looked at the woman and asked the question behind his eyes. She seemed paler than normal, her thin limbs childlike and without expression or any of the strength that had so fervently held the bow. She stared at the ground where the arrow now lay, seeking some kind of resolution among the small stones and arid soil.

"Not eat him?" said Kippa in a very quiet voice.

Nobody answered because they did not know how to explain

or even say the words that filled their mouths. Did not know how to begin to describe the rage that had motivated and planned the escape. The rage that had always driven the man, kept the wreck alive, and now propelled the monster towards his place of healing. Lutchen began to tremble at the thought of what would one day return if that wraith found a way to repair its wrecked body. Modesta broke the circle and moved forwards.

"We must go on," she said, and the other two followed her.

They walked with their backs to the direction of the monster's departure, never wanting to see the low gash in the undergrowth between the trees again. There was no more expectation in their quest, they simply plodded towards what Modesta told them was inevitable.

➤→

Ishmael, or what had been Ishmael, was waiting for them. He was surrounded by half the Limboia, who were changed in a subtle and overwhelming way. They were no longer slaves. They all smiled gently and held their bodies in a calm ownership. The absence in their souls had been replaced, filled with a future that belonged to nobody. Because now they were all extensions of the Black Man of the Forest. Their bodies were his, his being and will filled them, and their energy flowed into him. Father Lutchen, Modesta, and the much-shrivelled Kippa walked into their presence without amazement. The journey and its horrors had robbed them of that and of the great purpose that had magnetically pulled them all this way. The sunlight was blinding in the clearing and Ishmael's partials of face made a wide smile to greet them. Kippa fell to his knees, instantly recognising the being from the ancient prophesies. The woman and the priest walked forward in a trance of unknowing, the bow held before them like an offering or a key. The black hands received it and the life between them became one. A radiance of shadows exchanged between the taut purple sinews and the insect-rippling grip. The Black Man of the Forest's face boiled, seethed, and undulated until finally settling into a composition of eyes, a head made of a great cluster of eyes looking in all directions and seeing nothing and everything. All the Limboia raised their hands above their heads and made the sign of a halo. Modesta fell to the ground in a fit that removed her memory, and Lutchen saw a vision of them all entering Essenwald. But not the city of hungry commerce, acting European in its tastes and controls, but another one overgrown and foreshadowed with young trees; the road between it and the forest seamless; the height of its sharp spires pulled out of focus by clinging vines and choking moss; its buildings vacant of white men and the birds and creatures of the trees nesting there; its streets hollowed by relentless growth, the warm wind of the Vorrh curling through its emptiness.

The Black Man of the Forest suddenly knelt before Modesta in a movement that flowed and had nothing to do with human anatomy. Modesta leaned closer and their faces touched. The ants swarmed over her, joining their heads into one shuddering mass. Her clothing was shredded in seconds and her mottled naked body became the same as his: an undulating blue-black writhing sleekness. The bodies folded to the moist ground and the Limboia turned away, encouraging Lutchen and Kippa to do the same. A pulse came out of their union that made the forest floor vibrate. It grew in intensity as they shifted and exchanged, slid, rocked, and shook in the shapes of all things. Before and after Adam and Eve had been a gleam in the universe's eye.

➤→

After the first fifteen hours the unprepared officers felt the full effect of the Vorrh, as did every article made of wood in their luggage. Hoss drove on. An intense uncomfortable apathy drained them as the train trundled deeper and deeper into the trees. A sullen nausea started to gnaw at the brightness of their purpose. They explained this to one another as the effect of the rickety carriage over a long period of time. The curling growths of limp shoots extruding from the varnished luggage rack they saw as being the result of inadequate cleaning by the idle native staff. It was near dawn when they decided to stop the train so that they might get some rest in the quiet of the forest without being rattled out of their stiff bunks by the violent pulse that was being felt in every inch of the train, which added to the sickening sensations of all the other unpleasant motion. They opened a case of wine to celebrate their wisdom. A soldier was sent to tell the driver to stop for an hour or so. He climbed along the side of train and fell into the driver's cabin, telling Hoss the plan. Hoss thought he misunderstood the shouted command over the noise of his engine. When Hoss finally did understand, he said no. Plagge was the next person to appear on the steaming footplate.

"Stop the train!" he bellowed.

"We cannot stop here, nobody ever stops in the Vorrh. We must go on," Hoss shouted back.

"We will stop to sleep for an hour and then continue."

"We must not stop here."

"Must not?"

"It is too dangerous."

Plagge considered the driver's advice for a second or two. He watched the black imbecile touch something in the cabin when he said the word "dangerous." Plagge moved inside the tight space to examine it. In the forge-like glow of the firebox and the swinging oil lamp and the first few weak rays of the sun, he could make out a foolish ragged picture of an angel bathed in a rainbow of celestial light. He looked up at the looming black man and then laughed and grabbed at the carefully wired frame, wrenching it from its sanctum, and threw it hard into the fast-receding darkness of the night.

"Now, you pig, stop the train!"

Hoss stared in outraged shock, his hand hanging on the regulator, which was set to full throttle. The other hand was bunched into a fist. He looked away from the little shouting man into the direction where his picture lay smashed and torn, somewhere back in the vanished darkness. He then took his hand off the controls and backed away, scared of the consequences if he got any closer to Plagge. He also knew that this foolish stranger had just committed an act of extremely bad magic and that the savage gods were now waiting to pounce.

"Stop the train," Plagge bellowed again as Hoss shook his head.

Plagge started to unlatch his holster as the two men moved around each other in the confined burning-hot space. Then he saw the lever. It was three feet long and painted bright red like the throttle. It was the only significant other control of the engine amid the writhing mass of dark pipes and sullen gauges, so it was obviously the brake. Plagge left the pistol in its holster and grabbed the massive lever, squeezing the clasp to release it from its locking ratchet.

"I will do it myself." He laughed and put the full force of his weight and strength onto the lever, pushing it all the way back.

Hoss screamed "No!" and scrabbled backwards onto the piles of coal, frantically clawing his way up. His panicked feet were kicking the slipping heap of coal, making a scree of it slide onto the footplate, where it rattled and bounced as a crunching

scream buckled through every inch of the engine. Plagge felt
the lever buck and shudder with such force that it started to
dislocate the joints of his fingers. He flew away from it as a series
of sharp metal cracks turned into deafening explosions. At the
back of the coal tender Hoss was wrapping empty sacks around
his thick neck and head. All the bolts and pins that held the
hammering thick steel rods that piston-spun the wheels sheared
and the massive rods came free. The scream from the engine
burst Plagge's eardrums and blood spurted from his nose. The
lever that he had so determinedly pulled was not the brake but
the reverser. At full speed he had just forced all the power of the
engine to run backwards against its own red-hot direction and
the tons of implacable momentum from the hurtling flatbeds.
His eyes bulged as he saw Hoss throw himself over the side of
the speeding train. For a moment he thought he had imagined
it, then realised that the insane driver had actually jumped. A
second later the rods flew in all directions. Those that spun outwards felled trees in a glance. Those that went inwards ground
wheels to earsplitting fragments of shrapnel and those that went
upwards penetrated the firebox and boiler with such force that
the violated steam held its breath in shock for a second before
it lacerated the night. The train was hamstrung in fifteen seconds, sent earthquaking death throes backwards into its carriages in twenty seconds, and was totally butchered in a minute.
Everything on the flatbeds slid backwards and the chains that
held the huge bulk of timber and steel snapped like uncooked
spaghetti. The soldiers were thrown off like rag dolls and the
officers were spilt and crushed in the enclosed carriage with
their furnishings and bottles. The rear gunner was wiped off
the last flatbed and onto the speeding track, and the front gunner was obliterated by flying coal and irregular steel blades.
His machine gun spat defiantly back at the peeling engine in

its cauldron of smoke and blistering steam. Plagge was caught in between and remained in one piece for just long enough to squeal for his long-dead mother.

In the clearing that had been called the garden, Ishmael and Modesta separated, slowly, and let the forest settle back into its rhythms of life. They were both jet black now and bathed in an immense powerful calm.

CHAPTER FORTY-FOUR

$\mathcal{A}$s Seil Kor said "We are here," the crown began to slow. Its clockwork motors unwinding for the last time. The only luminescence it was catching came from their eyes, and the reflections swam like lazy plankton around them. Marais's last crippling fear was unfounded. It had not inflicted Cyrena with the same vision that had seared his soul. She never saw Essenwald and Pretoria and every other city in the world become empty desolate husks, with all traces of humanity vanished forever. She had not witnessed the rotting books and the entire archive and memory of *Homo sapiens* disappear. Without a single smut or particle of the smoke of its extinction remaining. Her vision was seated before and after mankind in a world without human malice and invention.

"Here?" she asked as if remembering the meaning of words for the last time. Her vision had sealed her origin and her outcome into one. The words and meaning of her last questions sounded far off and made only for a ritual of leaving.

"Yes, the shelf of our embedding, where we become the long time of the plural. The Vorrh will grow and cover the world. The Rumour will vanish and we will return to the garden of beginnings."

"Like Adam and Eve?" she said absently.

"No, my lady, they were a mistake, we will start again and

another couple will guide us in God's good ways," said Seil Kor, gently removing the crown, which became silent and dark.

"I can see nothing now," she said and waited for his response that never came. Instead a great warm satisfaction rose up inside her body. A tide of all-embracing blindness, guided by the invisible from the foliage of the distant tree of her trance. She understood everything. It had always been so clear. She laughed without sound as she dissolved in it. Nothing more was said and he helped her climb into its recess and began to fold her breathing, guiding her in farther where she stretched out and he snuggled in beside her. It was pitch black and the hewn stone felt warm and impossibly soft. There was no barrier of self or body between the inner and outer darkness, and everything settled to the same temperature. He put his arms around her as they drifted into what would become the longest sleep of containment, while above all manner of human conflict raged in all manner of violent light and heat in a growing open land of ignorance.

CHAPTER FORTY-FIVE

$\mathcal{T}$he Vorrh had been changing the composition of its transpired gases over the last two years. Gradually shifting and increasing the components of the new air. Its effects were beginning to become obvious to all but its chosen target: the occupants of Essenwald, who had become the guinea pigs because of their proximity. Both old and recent citizens were becoming more angry and dissatisfied. Restless and self-obsessed. Minor conflicts had taken on a more brutal and unrelenting quality and the major conflicts had been swallowed live by the military infestation. The division between the tribes had worn itself raw, and all defensive gates between the black and white had fallen. Families with younger children were already leaving the township. Omens of disillusion and contempt were found in the entrails and stars of prophecy. Stories of new sicknesses were rife. It had even been said that the despicable plague called "the Touch" had returned: a contagion that had swept through Essenwald before, causing terrible injures and blights and producing paranoia and suspicion in all its citizens.

No one even notices that the Limboia were slowly waking from their somnambulism, which had been so convenient to their masters for so many years.

Now all the remaining Limboia had left the slave house and made their determined passage into the Vorrh. They followed the railway lines until they became torn up and dangerous. Uniformed bodies of dead and dying men were strewn everywhere. One of the officers was gathering the less maimed and able-bodied, constructing stretchers, and generally trying to make some order out of the wreckage. When he saw them approaching, he barked orders, telling them to gather here and begin to help carry the lame and dying men back to Essenwald. They all ignored him, as they did everything else. The officer shouted again, spitting blood, insults, and deformed German because all of his teeth had been broken. He choked in a coughing fit as the Limboia just walked past without registering him or the plight that surrounded him. The engine was still steaming, its torn hot steel festering in pools of drying water. It looked as if it had been stamped on, like a tin toy under the foot of a careless adult.

Sturmbannführer Heinrich Keital ran out of words as the blood dripped onto his uniform. How could this be, what was it about this accursed forest and this impossible country that insisted on defeating him? He could not let this happen again. He would get the wounded back to Essenwald and start again, only this time he would not bother trying to make sense out of their antiquated railway. He would build a road, tear up their tracks and build a road. He would burn down every tree if necessary to open the route from the estuary to the edge of the Congo. It would have his name stamped upon it. He planned this and said it out loud, spraying blood in his epistle. He would bring in more troops from the coast and they would break the barrier of this place. Nothing would stand in his way. There was no one or no thing that could quench or halt his determination and his path. Most of his living audience were in too much pain to hear it, but it attracted the attention of a small interested party who found the sound of vigour and the smell of his blood most attractive. They sidled along the blind side of the torn wagon that he was using as a podium. Their faces oozing with saliva that made their yellow skin appear bright and optimistic.

Closer to the garden and picking through the shredded track was a much taller figure that had no interest in the Limboia's approach and they had none in his. His body was covered in long bristling spikes. His hands were pointed and looked as if they had been structured from the torn-off wings of ravens or some other large black carrion bird. He was shaking his bristled, quilled head from side to side and lamenting over a ripped picture in a mangled frame. He had heard about such things that lived outside the forest: permanent reflections made by Rumours of what they thought he and the other Erstwhile should look like. He looked at the mangled print of one of William Blake's bright angels that had once graced the cabin of Hoss's prized engine. To have one of these mirrors meant that he might become it: the looking going both ways, the light shared. It might even mean that if he left the forest then he could take his visibility with him, rather than have it follow on later. God in his wisdom had made that separation so that the attendants of the tree might not become distracted by the outside world or any notion that they could become part of it. The only way to ever escape was hibernation. The shattered picture he held might allow him some dimension, even though it was spoilt, its perfection ruined. His hands were incapable of repair, even if he knew how. Only Rumours had those skills. For a second he looked up at the passing Limboia and thought about asking them to mend it. Then he saw their eyes and did not bother. As the Limboia passed, each made a sign to the tall being before continuing their journey to find their own mirror of perfection. Then he saw another Rumour among the wreckage staring at him. As it approached, he saw that its gaze was not on him but on the broken picture he held. The Rumour was covered in blood and grey ash; it held out its damaged hand and started to cry. The tears dissolved the ash showing the wet black skin beneath, making two straight parallel lines down his large face. The Erstwhile had no choice but to give the picture up, he would have to find his conversation of reflections elsewhere. He gave the picture back to its owner. Hoss took it and held it close to his chest and then moved away, limping back to Essenwald.

➤→

The guard at the slave house had fallen asleep. Now he awoke to see the door had been open. There had never been any need to lock it; the Limboia had no place to go and no reason to find one, until now. He looked inside to find it empty. They had gone. In a panic he grabbed the rope of the fire bell that hung outside at the edge of the building. No one had ever used it. No one had ever tried. He tugged at the rope and pulled a muffled clatter out of it. He tugged again and a spindly translucent creature cascaded down, landing on his shoulder and the back of his head. The almost exhausted partial diagram of the half-alive archaeopteryx dug its brittle pencillike bones into the guard to prevent itself from falling any farther. It had flapped and crawled its way from the river and back through the forest floor, seeking the tranquillity of the warehouse where it had lived in gentle silent stone for so long. The bluish haze that had so animated it was growing dim and weak. It had gotten only as far as the slave house on the outskirts of the city before fatigue and transparency made it stop and hide. Its longing to be petrified back into nothing had not been supported by the flickering energy that was running out. It had found the old bell and climbed the rope and nested in the cobwebs, hanging upside down in the protection and density of the thick red-painted brass.

The guard danced and squawked as he pulled the clinging

Urvogel off his shoulder, his other hand still tugging at the now-resounding bell. He did not know what it was, this thing that was gripping him, but was aware of all the disgusting and lethal animals that lived in the bush. Also of the vermin of the Scyles and the legendary horrors that thrived in the Vorrh and occasionally crawled out to inflict wounds and malice on innocent workingmen. It flapped weakly in his hand as the bell rang and the Limboia dispersed without paying it any attention. Wirth appeared at the door of his house.

"What's going on?" he barked up to the dancing guard.

Amadi was not with him; she was attending to some matter in the breeding rooms on the other side of the enclosure. He turned his blind eyes back into the house and shouted, "Domino."

The guard had finally plucked out all of the Archaeopteryx's spiky holds and was now trying to shake its clinging web off his hand. He let the bell rope go to peel it off with his other hand. Domino was at its master's side, ready to take on any who dared approach. It looked around and sniffed at the emptiness of the compound. Then it saw the guard and his huge flapping hand. Its grimy nugget of a brain calculated this was the only possible assailant that it had been called to chastise. It looked at its master, then back at the dancing man and remembered the sweet taste of human fingers. Target and delight ignited in its huge bony head. Wirth, having no idea what was happening, sensed only discord and possible personal danger, so when the hyena growled and thus indicated the imminence of his fear, he gave the command that unleashed the beast's fury.

"Seize," he said and backed into the house.

Domino leapt from the porch and hurtled towards the slave house. The guard had finally shaken the Urvogel off his hand and onto the plank boardwalk, where he now stamped it out under his feverish hobnailed boot. The white blur saw its target divide and decided to take out the big one first. What was already mangled would be going nowhere, and she could lick that up after feasting on the jumping man, who was now curiously still.

➤→

The Timber Guild had broken apart. Its esteemed senior members gathered everything they could and left Essenwald to its own ends. Only Talbot and Krespka held on to a belief of salvation and renewal: Talbot because of his inflexible faith in organisation and command, and Krespka because he could not face the reality of living anywhere else, where the horrors of respectability were pinching and severe. He was too old to grow a moral code now; he knew where and how he was going to die, and what kind of pleasure he was going to indulge and saturate himself in during the process. But that was before he had seen those creatures of the forest at the edge of the city.

Most of Krespka's family and friends had already deserted Essenwald, and he was down to his last two whores, whom he paid to be drugged and were without any meaning except to him. And one ancient servant who brought him daily news and gossip about what was happening on the other side of his locked and bolted doors. It was he who proclaimed that the forest had grown into the ends of the northern streets and the trees there were not saplings but fully grown. Krespka grew sick of all this nonsense and decided to go and see for himself, taking a large-calibre pistol for protection, just in case. He walked fast for the first five minutes then sagged into his normal puffing pace. By the time he had reached the beginning of the northern streets he was fighting for breath and needed to take pauses in his slow progress. The air had changed. It was almost dark when he saw the shadows of the forest overwhelming the end of the street. He swore at its impossibility, imaging it to be some kind of optical illusion until the overhanging vines caught in his hair and scratched at his face. His bleary eyes widened and he stared in openmouthed disbelief. It was true, it was all true. He rubbed his eyes violently, and as he did, other eyes lit up in the darkness of the forest. First only two, then four, and then hundreds. Eyes that contained their own illumination, which was growing in a fearful intensity. The first four eyes moved forward, revealing themselves as two humans, a man and a woman, he thought. He was about to scream abuse and command at their black glistening bodies when they melded into one form. Then the other eyes gathered about them, giving the impression of a shapeless but solid knot of vast sentient power. He was frozen to the spot until something moved in front of the them, something on all fours, a dog or worse. He remembered Wirth's savage pet hyena and what it had done to Fleischer. He fumbled for his pistol but his hands were shaking too much, and he dropped it into the dense grass that concealed his shoes. The naked animal on all fours looked up and Krespka turned white, seeing total insanity in the eyes of what had once been the Reverend Father Gervasius Lutchen. His wild tangled hair and beard had lost all colour. His teeth, toenails, and fingernails had grown into sharp and broken fangs and talons. His naked body was mottled and broken by a network of knotted veins that writhed beneath his peeling skin, which was also laced with vines and crumpled leaves. Without any warning the Lutchen-beast sprang at Krespka, climbing up and over his body, forcing the old man backwards, screaming in pain and fear. Then it ran off into the dark, empty streets.

Krespka was sobbing when he turned his back on the depth of the forest and all those that had come to its new perimeter to look at him. He felt their eyes on him as he tried to escape. He was halfway down the street when somebody punched him hard and low in the back, just above his kidneys. It took the wind out of him. Now he was prey and each abuse would shrink him further. He did not look around to confront his attacker, he just continued to plod and stagger on and away. But with each step he felt something move inside him, an indigestion of spiteful proportions becoming a pressure of blind gnawing. Then the tip of the arrow passed through his intestines and pushed through the fat and skin of his bloated belly and tore out of his sagging shirt. His eyes bulged and his terrified hands fluttered, unable to touch the instrument of torture as it slowly revealed itself. With each step the arrow shaft exited more and more until the fletching caught in the exit wound and torn cloth and the arrow dangled like a starved pendulum that swung jollily with every stagger of his draining life.

➤→

When Talbot heard about the destruction and humiliation of the German garrison, he demanded to know why all of Fleischer's promises had failed. Somebody had to be named to relieve his embarrassment and possible repercussions back in the fatherland. Talbot's normal icy composure had boiled over into a teeth-clenched attack on the worthlessness of Fleischer, who stood in grave humiliation while Talbot paced and spat. Fleischer did not know where to look and dared not lift his eyes into his superior's rage. Then he saw the long maroon arrow lying on Talbot's impeccable desk. It was totally out of place, which helped form an enigma to stanch the outflow of the young man's pride. He left his superior's immaculate office defeated and exposed. But with a need to extract payback from somebody else. By the time he was in the hot street he knew who was to blame, and he would suck every pleasure from the sweetness of revenge.

All of Fleischer's plans had come to nothing. The breeding parlours, the supply of fleyber, meant nothing now. The blind criminal and his whore who had perverted his noble schemes were to be held directly responsible for this disaster. With the military hoard already leaving the city with its tail between its legs and the Timber Guild in confusion, he chose his plan with cool, determined menace, an experience he had never savoured before. The stupid death of Urs, the duplicity of Hoffman and Maclish, the price that he felt he owed Maclish's impressive widow, all this joined with his humiliation of losing the validation of finding the Limboia the first time, his triumph given to a common criminal. This time the victory would be his and only his. The heat of his plan twitched and burnt his mangled hand. Every time he looked at it he became ill with remorse. How could he have let Wirth and his filthy beast get away with this? Why in God's name did he ever trust him in the first place? Every day that man existed was an affront to Fleischer's carefully structured life. The short-term, apparent success of his control over the Limboia had only made things worse. Well, now that was over and he would take everything away from the blind leech who had been vampiring his confidence and pride.

Fleischer poured himself a drink to quieten the trembling that had so excited his body. He had started picturing the demise of his enemy and the butchering of his disgusting hyena. Then there was Amadi: Wirth's Masai sphinx, who had the ability of looking right through him, of reading every motive that bubbled within him, the intoxication of her beauty and strength that so exhilarated him. He wanted her power and grace at his side. He had fantasised about them panting together, sweating through the long dark nights. The crescendo of his dream was always dispersed by the sound of Wirth's crude laughter; the two of them talking about him, the blind man guffawing, his hand clamped on her body, she tittering behind her immaculate hand, the other reassuringly touching Wirth's scarred arm. Perhaps the best thing to do was to kill her too. Best to put her down and cleanse all memory of her existence.

He sent word that he needed loyal mercenaries: top-dollar hunters to obey his commands. In two days he had gathered a pack of the worst and the best available. He met with them in a tin hut on the far side of Essenwald and explained his plan. Even this gang of war-weary veterans was surprised at the basic savagery of his need.

"Let me get this right," said the veldt man, "you want us to wipe out a blind man, a woman, and a dog?"

"I want two shooting teams to shred them in the cross fire."

"Shred?" asked the mercenary.

"You heard me. I want them torn to pieces and finished with bayonets."

"But that's a job for one man, not all of us," he said, looking at the gathered congregation in disbelief.

"You don't know these three. And it isn't a dog. This is what it did to me in a few seconds." Fleischer pulled back his sleeve and thrust what was left of his once-delicate hand into the hunter's face.

"I have seen them do worse than that. Some say they eat human corpses to steal their voice and then circle a house at night, calling their victims out in a man's tongue," said a darker-skinned man from the back of the pack. He was called Fillip and had ruined his life in the Tirailleurs Sénégalais. His accent indicated education, but his caste and what he had just said was a denial, and the other men ignored him.

Fleischer was fazed for a moment and then snarled, "Do you want the job or not?"

The eight men agreed that they did and the plan was confirmed by a shaking of hands. Most ignored the unoffered hand of Fillip, but Fleischer insisted on shaking it using his mangled claw that had just been trivialised. Before they left, he drew their attention to a small crate that had been sitting ominously on a chair. He was beaming as he opened it, peeling away the oiled paper and taking out the objects as if it were Christmas morning, giving each man one of the three-foot-long bayonets. Some took them, grinning like old friends; others held them as though they were snakes.

"You might have to adapt your weapons to accommodate these," said the gleeful Fleischer. "I will of course pay for any such modifications."

A bald man who wore the khaki shorts and jacket of a plains hunter was examining the triangular section of the blade.

"Jesus, man, you must really hate these fuckers to use these pig stickers on 'em."

"Yeah, and a woman too," added the veldt man.

"You have reservations?" snapped Fleischer, his smile wiped away by a sneer. "I will be the first to use these on them, if you have doubts about this, then—"

The bald man interrupted, "No doubts, boss, we are all in."

At dawn the nine men split up and approached the slave house from different directions. Fleischer had told them about the hidden runways that connected to the warden's house and how they might be used as possible escape routes. He told them that Wirth, his whore, and the hyena slept together somewhere in the warden's house and that his plan was to lure them all out onto the front porch. That was to be the killing ground. Each man had his own trusted rifle: heavy-bore hunting guns with sights and triggers shaped by use into perfections as individual as signatures. The bayonets looked out of place on some of them, but all were firmly attached. The shooting team lay in the scrub grass facing the porch, angled so that their bullets would intersect, crossing trajectories near the door.

As the sun rose the sightless boy was heard on the road tapping his way towards the house. Chalky had been begging in and around Essenwald since the age of five. He knew every inch of it and everybody knew him. He could be trusted to carry messages and deliver small goods. As he reached his tenth year, he was beginning to dream of a worthy business moving news and objects about the city and giving up begging entirely. The parcel he carried today was the fanciest thing that he had ever felt and he did not understand why it smelt so strongly of meat and some other sweet thing that he could not name. Smooth, silky paper was held in place by a bow of velvety softness. He carried it very carefully in his sling. When he reached the porch he put his stick down, took out the parcel, and carried it up the three steps. He placed it gently on wooden floor. His instructions had been very clear: *Do not take the parcel to the door. Leave it by the top step, knock on the door, then walk away. When you are on the road run back to collect more money for your work.* Chalky was proud at being trusted. He knocked at the door, turned, and walked softly down the stairs, almost tiptoeing so as not to spoil the magic. When he retrieved his stick he noticed that his hands were wet. The parcel must have leaked. This worried him as he paced along the path towards the road. He did not want to get this delivery wrong, to be blamed about the leakage. He was frowning as he passed through the long grass and heard or sensed something move near, something that was hiding. This was not right. Nobody ever hid from the blind. He stopped and waited, listening for potential danger, fearing that it might even be his father spying on him to discover how much money he was really making. The door to the house opened and Amadi stood there totally naked. Behind her the head of Domino could be seen. Chalky turned, smelling the hyena and knowing that he was in grave danger and that running now would be the worst thing he could do. Amadi looked at the parcel and the boy and called back into the house. The sound of sharp metal crickets clicked around Chalky as nine safety catches were unlocked. Domino saw the boy and prowled forward. Near the parcel it smelt the fresh bleeding meat inside and lost interest in the boy. It grabbed the paper in its vast jaws and shook the parcel apart, devouring the meat in one mouthful. There was enough cyanide in it to poison an army. Amadi stepped up behind Domino and affectionately ruffled the spiky white fur of her collar and neck, while she bent down and picked up the blood-soaked velveteen ribbon. Another figure appeared behind her in the shadows of the doorway. Fleischer screamed, his excitement and joy tainting the word: "Fire!"

Chalky dropped his stick and covered his ears as the first volley sounded around him. The second roared a moment later and made sure that his hands stayed there. There were two more, then the grass erupted and he heard the sound of running feet. These were mixed with the squeals of an animal, or was it a woman, maybe a girl? There was a hammering sound as if somebody was pounding the porch with a blunt chisel. Then it quietened for a long time before men began talking.

"Where's Wirth?"

Up on the porch eight of the men stood over the carcasses of the albino hyena and Amadi. Lying back in the doorway was another woman whom nobody recognised and never would, because her face had been ripped apart by high-velocity bullets. It had not been Wirth standing behind Amadi when Fleischer gave his command. It had been a visitor, a passing innocent.

"Where is he?" shouted the distraught Fleischer. "Search the house."

Three of the hunters moved inside while Fleischer staggered over to the balustrade to support himself. He slipped on the blood and kicked noisily against Domino, swearing loudly. The hyena's pink eyes had swivelled wildly, giving it a comic expression.

One of the men who was searching the house came out and blandly said, "I think he's in the tunnels."

"What?" bellowed Fleischer, wiping his face with the back of his sleeve, smearing blood like a trophy across his face.

"There's a kind of banging shuffle coming from the wall . . . Eh! There's no more hyenas, are there?"

"Only the one," he said dimly, regaining himself and moving to listen to the flap at the tunnel's entrance. After a moment he said, "It's him, he is crawling away. Spread out and find him."

The men stepped onto the rough wooden structures that extended from the back of the house and connected to all the other buildings. They moved in haste and did not notice that Fillip was holding back. When they had left the veranda he quickly stooped and cut out Domino's eyes, which were in fact stones that one Nebsuel would pay well for.

They were walking all the lengths of the planked-in structure, listening below their boots for sounds in the tunnels. A tall thin man started waving and pointing beneath him.

"He's in here, I can hear him moving."

Two more men climbed up onto the walkway on top of the tunnel and three climbed over it to the inner side.

"Bayonets," said Fleischer.

The cheap wooden panelling gave no resistance to the unbending steel. All nine men took long twisting stabs into the splintering timber. They quickly found their mark, forcing their victim to crawl away while screaming for mercy, only to be punctured farther down the tunnel. They tightened their attack, concentrating the impaling until the begging voice coughed into silence and the caged kicking and shuffling ceased and blood flowed freely out of the broken holes. The bayonets were sucking up squirts of it every time they cleared the splintered wood. One of the panting men standing above said, "That's enough, man, he's dead. Nothing could survive that."

After they had gone Chalky stood up in the long grass where he had been hiding. He did not understand what had just happened but knew it was bad and that he was part of it. It was the parcel he carried that caused all this shooting and screaming, the strange-smelling gift that felt so beautiful. Whatever demon had been inside it was ferocious and without pity. He had heard about boxes like that before. Dangerous locked boxes that imprisoned genies. He turned his back on the house and tapped his way to the road. Perhaps, he thought, perhaps begging was safer. He had never met a demon on the road or in the alleyways of the city. Occasionally people put bad things in his open hand, sometimes they hit him, but nothing like this. The business of boxes was a dubious affair; he would have to think it over carefully. He was chewing his finger in concentration as he walked. Behind him he heard the high shrieks of carrion birds arriving at the house. He thought again about hyenas and boxes, about the taste of almonds and the day he and his sister had eaten them. About how her face felt when she smiled . . . and then he dropped his stick. His wet finger had changed. The almonds had become bitter and alive. His little heart shrivelled and his mind thickened to a standstill as the effects of cyanide took him. He fell dead and kicking in a small circle of dust on the empty mud road.

Fleischer's mercenaries collected their money and made their way out of the city, except for Fillip. He sent word via a bird to Nebsuel that he had a fresh pair of eye stones taken from the hyena, and that he would sell them to the old shaman or one of his emissaries. He named the cabin where he would wait, smoke hashish, and watch the nomadic passage of tribes and the inevitable retreat of all the white Men Without Substance. He could already hear the great drumming that was building from below the Scyles and to the west of the crumbling city wall. Another caravan of painted men was passing through or announcing the arrival of their encampment. As the bass pulse deepened, lighter echoing talking drums trembled and nailed the vastness of countryside and the closeness of unknown men. Campfires appeared, snake-charming black strings of smoke rose into the breezeless air. More and more ignited on the perimeter of the city, looking like fallen scattered coals from a looming, far-off volcano. The sombre drums added to this, making everything sway to their unseen percussion that greeted the swaying night. The Men Without Substance closed the windows and shutters of their dwellings as the black people opened all of theirs. The scent from the campfires perfumed everything as every grain of sand wanted to melt in the intoxication of the drums, melt and become glass so that it could at least reflect the stars in an attempt of gratitude. Three men died that night and no attempt was made to justify or apprehend the culprits. Such acts seemed to blend into the disjuncture of the city. The ligaments of control and alignment were slipping apart or fracturing under the pressure of the Vorrh. Even the stiff verticals of the German building was breaking down or softening with tendril vines and substantial growths of lichen.

CHAPTER FORTY-SIX

Cyrena had disappeared, vanished from the face of the earth. Ghertrude could not believe it. The world without Cyrena's presence was unthinkable. Things between them had been difficult and strained. A distance had grown, but only a momentary one, only a gap in which her love for Thaddeus might be understood. It was never meant to be like this. She had last been seen near Pretoria in the cape. A friend of her uncle's had spoken to her about the poet's death. She had seemed greatly disturbed, he said. Then nothing. No trace. All her belongings and personal things were left scattered in her lodgings. Cyrena did not behave like that, something terrible must have happened. Weeks went by without any word and Ghertrude became more distraught with their passing. Thaddeus comforted her the best he could without disclosing the ugliness of his hypocrisy, because in his good heart lurked a glee about Cyrena's exodus. From the moment he heard, a flutter of joy erupted. Of course, he quickly suppressed it and kept it securely caged over the progressing weeks, but it was there grinning inside him daily. He knew what Cyrena felt about him and never shared Ghertrude's confidence that her dear friend would "come around" to understanding and see the love that bound them together. She had become his enemy and there was no way of resolving it without Ghertrude's being hurt in the process. So when the news came, he could not believe his luck. She had been swallowed up hundreds of miles away. Hope of her survival was fading fast. She had not slid away on some caprice or spent her wealth on a travelling indulgence without telling her friends. She was simply gone. Devoured. Ghertrude had visited Talbot to ask for help and returned in angry tears. The loyal and doting friend had changed. At best he seemed indifferent and irritated by her questions. At worst, rude and dismissive. He said he had not heard a single word from her since he had gone to the trouble of arranging her expensive flight, and that after her disappearance he had of course made enquiries and found nothing "of consequence." When pushed, he reluctantly told of some accounts of her travelling with a native black man. Talbot's face was sour and rigid as he gave Ghertrude the details. No trace of this man could be found. The name on the ticket was fictional and his whereabouts unknown. Wherever they had vanished to, it was obvious that they had vanished together. Talbot could do no more. Cyrena had made her own decisions and it was not his business to pry. He suspected that she had fled the continent, but where was anybody's guess.

As he showed Ghertrude to the door of his elegant, stark office he had added spitefully, "Anyone who has 'gone native' cannot expect to find sympathy in their homeland or from those who consider themselves her friends."

Meta was reading a book about ferns when she heard something being dropped through the letter box of 4 Kühler Brunnen. She carefully put the book down and retrieved a small box with her name written on it. Inside was a little stone and a folded note that read:

What has been taken from you can again be found in the camera. There is a wooden tongue hidden in its base. Put this stone under it.

Meta climbed the stairs towards the tower and the camera obscura, the stone in one hand and the paper in the other, her heart confused. A strong wind was buffeting the open window in the high room; leaves were being tossed and fluttered in the wide distance outside and a few fell to rest near the humming strings. Meta carefully placed the stone on the white paper of the letter, which she had smoothed flat and floated like a pure island in the shadows of the tall space. She sat and watched its inert concentration, some part of her hoping that it might give a sign or become activated without her essence being its catalyst.

Below, the ailing city limped about, performing what duties it could find to occupy it now that all the major industries had closed. The sky smouldered and shaped vast cloud furnaces, being fed by the late-day sun. Swallows stitched the distance and proximity together. To the north the Vorrh was approaching in a stealth of magnitude that was unobservable to the few remaining citizens who moved at normal human speed. But the camera obscura gazed openly in a different time and saw everything. Meta knew the lens was already open and had been casting images to itself all that afternoon. She gathered the stone and the paper and went to do its calling, making herself comfortable on a low stool, looking at the device, trying to see it objectively. It occupied almost all of the room and the small space around it gave no means to stand back. Her back was touching the wall and her sandaled feet brushed the wooden planking of its circular base. Beside her were the stone and the paper. She put her hand under her skirt and began to feel the plump curves that had hardened over the last few years.

The curved bowl of the obscura was above her eyeline. She did not want to see the outside world and did not want it to see her. Instead she set her dark eyes on the motes of dust that spun and spiralled in the projected beam. Twilight was near, and the soft dove light had relinquished its heat. Soon it would be dark and the camera would hold only invisibility and project that into its nude concavity. Her abuse in the warehouse had removed every trace of what had been her budding sexuality. Vengeance and care had taken its place and they had now both been satisfied. There was no hollow in Meta. No longing to fill and no absences. Her heart and her veins were full. So to have to invent this seemed unfair and backwards. Then something stirred in her memory. It was an overheard conversation between Ghertrude and Mistress Cyrena. They had been talking about Ishmael. It was not in Meta's psyche to eavesdrop or linger around other people's conversations, but in this case she'd had no choice. She had been in the adjoining room when they began in earnest. There was no escape without declaring her presence and she was already too embarrassed to do that, so she waited until they were finished and then left, feeling flushed and guilty. The Ishmael of their talk had little or nothing to do with the monster that was so implicit in her father's death. And it was possible to visualise the one they spoke of without any reference to the condemned murderer. Ghertrude had started the conversation by belying the qualities that had so beguiled both women. They laughed together to exorcise their foolishness. They grew cross and spiteful at his deceits, then during a pause Cyrena mentioned his lovemaking. During the next whispered fifteen minutes each woman goaded the other to give up or share the intimate details of their couplings. There was some laughter, much sighing, and a little disbelief bordering on jealousy. They both agreed on the remarkable nature of his stamina and appetite. They were less verbal about his unique anatomy. The spiral barrel of Ishmael's penis and its ability to extend and twist with his heartbeat still was beyond detailed discussion. Much of what they had said Meta did not understand. But something about their tone, the catches in their voices and hoarseness in their throats made her tingle and melt.

She twitched in her core. Before she could contemplate what was happening, the first shudder made her feet scuff hard against the base of the camera while her hips twisted and the muscles in her legs clenched. A whisper of the drums spilt into the chamber. She clasped her hand to her mouth as the deeper wave hit, making her cry out. She was now in the total power of the orgasm and it made her body sing and scream, retreat and embrace, wrapped around her automatic hand as she was thrown adrift in the violently bobbing tide of her resounding body. Then the drawer slid open. She saw it out of the corner of her eye and one part of her went to examine it in triumph. The rest remained static around the root of her hand and the shudders of her breathing, and the pulse that filled the dimming room. Finally, out of anxiety that the drawer would vanish again, she withdrew her hand and combed back her consciousness. She arose and straightened her eyes. There it was, the wooden tongue in the tray of the drawer. She cautiously examined it, lifting it gingerly and touching the damp cleft beneath. There was an odd scent about. When she felt sure that she knew as much as possible about its simple but mysterious structure, she retrieved the stone and slotted it into the recess, letting the tongue lay back across it. She looked at the projected city fade as the drum of her aorta pulsed in time with the enclosure outside. The drawer slid back into hiding and the surface of the white disk changed forever.

➤→

Nebsuel had made that delivery to Meta and now had one more task to complete before he could return to the solitude of his leprous island. He took the other plum-coloured stone that came from the hyena's eye to the coast, arriving at the Sea People's home in the estuary just after dawn. There had been a ceremony the night before and many people were still asleep on the beach or outside their low huts. There were no guards to question him, so he found his way to what was obviously the most important dwelling in the village and sat down outside and waited. Hours later a vast ancient woman staggered out of the doorway. Her body was covered in tattoos and her hands were covered in blood. She glared down at the old shaman sitting cross-legged, calmly drinking water from a goatskin bag. He lifted one hand and rotated it above his head as if describing an invisible crown.

"I have come to meet Oneofthewilliams," he said.

After the formalities had been performed and his credentials established, he was taken inside a more modest hut nearby. It was dark and smelt of seashells and cinnamon. Propped up against a wooden structure at the room's centre was the holy being himself.

Nebsuel spoke a few words in the language and then switched to a rare and obscure form of English.

"Sacr'd being i has't cometh to gift thee a most wondrous treasure. but in its giving i might not but touch thee. shall thee allow this and bid thy people hither yond t might not but beest so?"

A weird textured atmosphere began to fill the small space. Not unlike bromide coarsely woven into seaweed and melancholy. Oneofthewilliams's arms then lifted and made sweeping gestures that attracted the fast attention of a young man who held one of the offered hands, the fingers of which wrote and

sliced touch into the translator's hand. He then thought carefully and spoke clearly so that all might understand. They looked
at Nebsuel and he nodded that it was right. Further discussion
took place in the same manner until Tyc came and tugged the
old shaman forwards, within reach of the collapsed bundle that
lifted itself towards him on strong white arms. Nebsuel held out
his hand and it was taken. Oneofthewilliams gently lurched forward, allowing its entire weight to fall across Nebsuel so that
the arm and hand were free to communicate. The intimacy and
strangeness of his gesture greatly pleased Nebsuel and greatly
disturbed him.

The head sack of Oneofthewilliams flopped to one side and
came to rest tucked in near Nebsuel's armpit. Its veins, sinews,
and nerves were tied together, twisting with each breath from
both bodies until they worked in unison. Nebsuel then spoke
slowly in many languages while the sun crossed the sky. At twilight Nebsuel asked to move his body, to rearrange his arms and
let his back rest for a while. This was gently done by Tyc and her
acolytes. Food and drink were given and the conversation began
again in the moonlight. Finally Nebsuel reached into his pocket
and brought out the plum-coloured stone. He then spoke to Tyc
directly and she came to stand close, already chanting deeply
from her solar plexus. Her wrinkled nimble fingers undid the
tie of Oneofthewilliams's head sack and showed a gap that was
large enough. Nebsuel quickly dropped the stone in, where it fell
to nestle in the pink folds of the loose brain. Tyc then tied it back
to close its containment. The deed was done. The ceremony was
over. Nebsuel was treated with great care and dignity while he
waited for the first vision to come to Oneofthewilliams. It then
took the translator four days to be able to say it to the old shaman in a language that he might understand.

"There are two beings who stand at the edge of a great forest.

Who stand in a garden where they will always remain. Around them are the chosen ones who will tend that garden and will work for all that grows straight and sound. They look out but cannot see an empty city in an empty world. Because the great forest has grown and overtaken all. Every mile below the mountains is covered by it. The seas of memory have agreed to this and a balance has been made between the salt and the sweet. God's spirit has again moved over the face of the waters. The trees have grown gigantic in this understanding and the animals in them have multiplied. Only a few of the gardeners exist now in the balance they were meant for. All the stories and equations, objects and sounds they made for themselves have vanished or been lovingly eaten by everything else. The great forest finally has reached its divine purpose and this telling of it like all others will be nothing but dust in the time that cleans and the winds that balm."

➤→

After a year Cyrena Lohr was officially declared lost and presumed dead and her will was read. The business and properties were of course handed over to her brother. Servants and charities received wet-eyed handouts and a significant bequeath was given to Rowena for her education and future travel abroad. Thaddeus spat under the thank-yous. Even in her death the pious witch had extended her hand into what he now considered to be his family. To adjust and control and to wrench apart. To remove Rowena from the love of her mother, his steadfast guardianship, and the warmth of the home that they had made. Hadn't the child been through enough without snatching her away and shipping her off to some foreign land, where she might learn how to be as snobbish as her benefactor? There were quarrels about the money and possible futures.

Meta stayed clear, refusing to take part or give an opinion. She was living with her mother and Berndt, her younger brother, caring for their needs. She would move back into Kühler Brunnen only after her mother's death, and the lonely Berndt was relocated to an uncle and aunt in America, where it was considered he would benefit by being removed from the pernicious influence of the war in Europe and its inevitable effect in Africa.

Meta was spending more and more time in the high rooms of the attic and the tower, finally deciding to live up there. There was no dissuading her after she made up her mind. Turning down the much more comfortable rooms offered by her mistress and her brother, whose gratitude and affection never faltered, but she was set and determined on inventing her new home in and around the Goedhart device and the camera obscura.

Meta was only nineteen and she knew that she had seen too much, already experienced more than she was ever supposed to, and had acted well and with significance in it all, even the bad things.

The fleeing sounds of departure had faded. All the mechanical noise had gone, allowing the breath and utterance of the Vorrh to invade the streets and alleyways.

As the years went on, Meta would watch the hushed city grow thicker with sleep and trees. She had first noticed the encroaching green after she installed the stone under the wooden tongue. It appeared around the edges of the circular porous dish that received the city in bent light from the lens and mirror above. She would recognise individual people growing old on the curved dish under the inspection of the long lens. She often hummed or sang to herself while gazing into the dish, and that's when she saw them look up at her as if they had heard her small voice or as if they could see the camera watching them. So she sang more and more every day. Her voice, which was now part of the resonance, could be heard all over the house: faint and overwhelmingly sad. Sometimes she sang with the wires in the middle of the night, when the fierce stars insisted. Or with the summer winds or the storms that came with salt from the sea. She sang for the seasonal swallows who circled the roof and nested under her protection. But mostly she sang for Rowena, especially after her parents faded away to kind ghosts who forgot about life.

Thaddeus was Rowena's father, because her mother told her so. And it had been clear all her life that his care and presence were constantly meant for her. Ghertrude never stopped watching her daughter for signs and likenesses of Ishmael but found none. As the child grew older, Ghertrude tried to convince herself of the happiness of this proof but found only that its shadow of disappointment was becoming stronger. She had banished all thought and speculation of her own conception. What the Kin had told her had never been truly explained, but she had an unflinching hope that they would return, explain everything, and be with her on her deathbed. Meanwhile she ran Kühler Brunnen the way a good wife and mother should. She kept Rowena close, never letting her go away to school. Tutors and scholars had come to the house to teach her and Cyrena's name had been constantly mentioned in those formative years after Ghertrude had found a loophole in the exact wording of her friend's generous wishes for Rowena, and they were all happy to pass through it, especially Thaddeus, who used his long backwards hands to part the way.

Ghertrude started to significantly fade a year before the crate arrived. She had been becoming less and less involved in the world outside and had now started to forget the names of those closest to her. During her last days she became agitated and demanded that all the doors of Kühler Brunnen remained unlocked, night and day. She also demanded that Thaddeus kept all the cellar rooms open. In her final hours she wept her way towards extinction. Bitterly disappointed that the Kin never came back to be at her side to explain the world to which they had told her she belonged, she made Thaddeus swear an oath that he would go and find them, even if they were in the Vorrh. Saying that her soul would never rest until somebody, especially him, understood everything and prayed the truth at her grave. He of course tried to dissuade her. Using Rowena as the excuse for his staying at home and never taking on such a mission.

But she would not have it. The last of Ghertrude Tulp's iron resolve was set on this task being achieved and she would have it no other way. "Meta would take better care of Rowena than her Thaddeus ever could," she had lashed out when sealing her determined command. *Thaddeus must go and find them.*

So in a blistering hot wind two days after her funeral, he did. With tears and dust in his eyes he walked out of the almost ghost town of Essenwald. Never to return.

On the day before the crate arrived, Rowena had a dream that disturbed her and she could not wait to tell Aunt Meta. She carried the breakfast tray to the top floor and put it on the polished table next to the wooden windlass in the wall. She wound it energetically and the flap in the ceiling opened and a cage on the rope descended. Her father had made this, so that food and other things might be ferried up into the attic without the need of a precarious balancing act on the attic ladder. She loaded the tray into the cage and winched it back up, then climbed after it.

She and Aunt Meta made an odd pair as they sat in the glow of the shafted light with the sound of the wind and birds buffeting in around them. Her aunt had always been compact, solid proportions held in a smaller than normal framework. Now she was denser, her weight more profound. Rowena was willowy, she had grown long and narrow, her womanhood and natural beauty favouring the vertical. Her hair was like her mother's and it glinted as it was caught by the warm breeze.

As she told of her dream, she nibbled toast. "The tree in my dream was full of shadow, but the shadows were all white, like snow."

Meta devoured her words in silence while buttering the crumbling bread.

"I have a picture of snow and it was just like that, white where the darkness should be."

Meta began to munch her toast noisily.

"There was a tingly feeling about and it woke me up."

Meta appeared to have more interest in the bread.

"Aunt Meta, what do you think it was? Does it mean something?"

She put the crust down and looked at the young woman. Something of her old ability to see before and after things stirred.

"It is a sign of God's wisdom on earth and that you have been touched by it."

Rowena looked startled at such a large answer.

"Imagination is a gift, prophecy a curse." And with that, Meta again munched into the bread.

Rowena said nothing while she pondered the meaning of what she had just been told.

The second crate arrived two weeks later. They had ignored the first one, hoping it was a mistaken delivery, being so near the gate and all. Rowena told her aunt about the new one. This time it stood near the stables.

"Where could it have come from, who could have delivered it?" she asked.

Meta was very clear about what to do but never answered her questions. "Do not open them. Ignore them, pretend that that they are not there."

"Will you come and see, Aunt?"

"No, child, I will never leave the attic now. You will have to do all things below."

The third crate was found standing against the far inside wall of the courtyard. The crates were all the same size, just a little taller than the long-limbed Rowena. She stood on tiptoe when she examined the oblong box.

"It's the same size as me," she told Meta. "I could stand up inside it."

"Are there any labels?"

"No, Aunt, nothing."

"Mmm . . ." said Meta.

"I am going to watch to see who brings them, and find out who else has a key to our gate."

Her aunt said nothing and averted her eyes. She thought she knew who was bringing the crates. She had waited for so long for Mutter's ghost to come. To beg forgiveness and see him again. She had tried to force every particle of longing into his shape, his presence. But nothing materialised and she exhausted herself trying. And now this. Why would his ghost still perform such hard, menial tasks? Where was he dragging the boxes from? The warehouse was rubble and ashes, she had seen to that. She imagined him puffing across the courtyard, standing the crates up on their end, and then retreating to the stables. She had been there many times, touching the workbench, the harnesses, the rusting tools. She could still smell him there: the dense acrid warmth of his cigars lacing the straw and the scent of the horses. Why had he not returned this way? The absence of her father had untethered her from the world. It had only been the act of vengeance in the rescue of Rowena that had saved her from being lost forever. She looked back at the girl and lit a smile in the darkness of her hurt.

"Will you tell me everything you see, or think you see?" she said softly.

"Yes, of course, Aunt."

Rowena left her and went downstairs, not really understanding the look in Meta's eyes.

There were now eighteen crates in the overgrown courtyard and Rowena was still watching from her upstairs windows, a vantage point that she discovered was best for overlooking the courtyard. This was the next best way to catch the culprit red-handed. But her sentry duty was becoming more difficult because of the continual fast growth of trees in the courtyard. She had tried to hack the persistent vegetation back, but it was a losing battle, and sometimes when she was down there, tools in hand, she felt as if she were being watched by someone or something. She had her mother's curiosity and wanted to rip open the crates, but would never go against her aunt's wishes. She then went once again to confront the actual boxes. The wind outside was warm and damp; it blew leaves about the cobblestones, where they stuck in the grass and weeds that were growing in the cracks between them. The hard, polished appearance of the yard that she thought she remembered was being softened, smoothed out of focus by the new tufts of green that now seemed everywhere. Even the walls were tinged with it, a haze of moss growing over the surface. She walked to the nearest box, the second one to arrive, and pushed against it, feeling the weight of its resistance. She hammered on its surface with her long slender fist. It was not empty. She knew she was tempting her curiosity to greater needs and that she had to stop. Perhaps in the changing weather the wood might fatigue and a glimpse of the interior would become exposed. Perhaps the wind might tip one over and . . . and . . . and . . .

She told her aunt about her thoughts and Meta felt a snatch of envy. It was what she so wanted to do. To communicate with her dead father. She once believed it could only have been Mutter haunting the courtyard and stairs. Bringing the crates and boxes again. Didn't ghosts always perform what they did in life, seeking recognition in continuance? She even listened for the sound of his horse and wagon on the cobbled streets outside. But nothing was heard. No wagon or cart moved in any of the streets of the dead city. A blank, unmoving silence was enveloping everything. She told Rowena of her desire and how she had first thought that the manifestations of the boxes in the yard was a sign of Mutter's restless spirit. Now of course she knew it was not. The growing number of upright crates was a very different kind of haunting. Rowena saw the anguish in her kind aunt's face and wished that she could have summoned the old reprobate for her, even for a moment, a fleeting second to soothe the sadness that lived in Meta's heart. A few days later another crate appeared in the unkempt yard. This time the girl did not report it. Better to leave it unsaid. But she guessed that Meta knew when the pendulums sang again in the eaves. At such times Meta always went to the strings or the camera obscura for consolation. Always expecting to see Mutter somewhere in the square.

Then it happened! At first she thought it was her abused channels of perception weakly coming back, then she realised it was a scent, a smell. It was his tobacco somewhere nearby, somewhere in the house. She had vowed never to leave her eyrie again, but this once must be an exception. She descended the wooden ladder onto the upper landing and the smell dispersed to nothing. How could this be? If he was not wandering the house, then it meant that he was in the attic with her. Surely she would have felt him before, sensed his presence nearby. She paced the landing and looked down the long stairs. Only a trace of the distinctive tobacco was there. She turned and climbed the creaking, excited ladder back into the active twilight. Yes, it was stronger here. He had been here. Her heart was overjoyed. She knew that in life he hated climbing all those stairs and especially the ladder with its small portal that he had found so difficult to squeeze through. But he had done it now, done it to comfort her, to settle the wounds and lace together her hopes. Even if this had been his only sign, then it had been enough.

The song Meta and the strings played had such emphasis and mode that it stopped Rowena, who had been busy in the kitchen, and she climbed through the resounding house to see what Meta was doing. She called from below the ladder and then climbed up, putting her head and shoulders into the singing air. Meta stopped and came over to her; the strings continued holding on to her voice, which they had tuned themselves to.

"He came, Rowena. He came to tell me that everything was right."

"Your father?"

"Yes, Poppa came, up here, just for a moment to tell me."

"Did you see him?"

"No, but he was here, here somewhere smoking those stinky cigars that only he liked."

Rowena looked around the room in a rather theatrical manner.

"Don't worry, child, he has gone now. He just came back to say that he was his old self."

Rowena had nothing to say and in the dim light she seemed to flush and hesitate. Meta saw this and felt as if she had overburdened the girl with her emotion.

"I am so happy, Rowena. Forgive me for saying too much, please come back later when I am more settled."

"Yes, Aunt," the girl choked out as she hurried down the steps, not stopping until she had reached the first floor, where she stood panting, her eyes brimming with tears. She did not mean her little act to have become so significant, so devastating to her aunt. She did not really know what she had done or why she had done it. And now it had turned into something that must remain untellable between then. The only thing in the world that she must always lie about. The responsibility outweighed the guilt but nevertheless left a stain.

When she had found Mutter's cigar in the stable, she'd had no purpose for keeping it safe. She had not intended or planned to tiptoe up the ladder and puff the horrid smoke into the attic room while Meta could be heard moving elsewhere, in the tower of the camera obscura. She did it on impulse, expecting only a little wonder for her sad aunt. Never the overwhelming meaning and total joy that she had just witnessed. She sniffed and walked back to her sentry post at the upper window, which she opened slightly to clear the air and let its freshness drive out her culpability. In the courtyard the knee-high patches of grass waved in the slight breeze. The scent of foliage and trees was everywhere. Now that the mills and rubber works were silent and a great majority of the citizens had left, all the human-manufactured odours had flattened or dispersed.

She had heard some say that the Vorrh had walked into Essenwald to reclaim it for its own. And she imagined that outside the stout wall of Kühler Brunnen the city was changing, with roots, trunks, branches, twigs, and vines embracing everything. The crates looked oddly part of it now; they had lost their new-wood blankness. Lichen and moss began to write over their surfaces as they stood there waiting to be opened, stood there like sentinels or statues of emperors and poets from some long-forgotten empire in some long-forgotten ruin in its overgrown garden. Rowena knew that one day after Meta had gone, she would be alone with the crates. When the courtyard had given up its meaning and all the cobblestones had been overturned from beneath by verdant, insistent growth, she would be left standing among the fully grown trees, crowbar in hand. She was held in this thought for a moment until a gust of wind from the Vorrh shook the glass.

She lowered her eyes and looked out into courtyard below; she was just about to leave when she saw a small movement. It was not somebody moving into view or passing but rather something moving out of sight—a going.

EPILOGUE

And as the rose is felt by his odour and as the fire is seen in his sparkles . . . For the virgins shall have the crown that is called aureole . . . after the feast of All Hallows he should establish the commemoration of all souls.

—*The Golden Legend*

LONDON, 1940

$\mathcal{B}$reakfast was set for them in the bar, which smelt stronger than before, the stale beer and tobacco wrestling with the astringent disinfectant.

"Ah, England," proclaimed Nicholas, looking around the empty room. Outside the sun was tugging between green and yellow. Rain or shine.

The child of the house brought steaming bowls to a recently washed table and indicated without a word that it was for them. Hector was ravenous and dug into the inert volume of the thick grey paste before him.

"This is very good. What is it?"

"Porridge, I think," said Nicholas.

"Remarkable," said Hector, emptying the tiny cracked sugar bowl into his dish.

This was followed by thick slices of undercooked bacon and runny fried eggs.

"Delicious," said Hector, forgetting all of his years of astute table manners and speaking through his mouthfuls of food. "What is this?" He waved the bacon rind on his fork in front of Nicholas.

"Pig," he answered without interest. "Swine flesh, I think you call it."

Hector stared at the impaled fat for a difficult time, then devoured it, saying, "Delicious."

"Enjoy it, my friend, it's the last you will taste for a very long while."

Hector did not hear it. His tongue had overcome his ears in wallowing delight.

An hour later they were walking back through the tall grasses where the summer morning had won in earnest over the shadow of rain, its warmth bullying its way past the initial chill. The brightening light and vastness of sky was making everything shine and sharpen each particle of its existence in the world.

They reached a high, lopsided gate that had been repaired and remade many times.

"A chronicle of the parish," said Nicholas as he stretched up to lift the black iron chain, whose weight held all in place like a sleeping necklace.

On the other side and farther on they climbed over a step in another fence and then halted and sat there for a while, silently smelling the sea getting closer. To their right was a rolling corn-field that glared with optimism, exchanging yellows with the unfettered sun. Hector watched a far-off grey steamer sail slowly through it, the boat seemingly floating across the hushed sway-ing waves.

"It is time to go," said Nicholas, who stood up and looked out towards the lolling sands, their colour shifting between the descending water and the ascending light. The beauty of the morning was flooding every space around them. Birds filled the air, calling against the vanishing clouds; gulls wheeled in their freedom and starlings massed in smoky swirling flocks. Soon the swallows would arrive. The sea had withdrawn, drank itself into a trench between the jutting rocks of land, snuggled into some hollow a thousand fathoms deep. The fresh water of the hills had been pulled down into the sluice of London's gritty aorta, sucked out towards salt in the estuary's million tributaries and veins. You could hear all the tricklings as one, whispering over the breathing mud that was popping, gulping, and letting go, sighing as it resigned itself again to ponderous gravitation.

"It's a fine day," Nicholas called out, more to the birds and the brightness than to Hector, who sat bundled and unsure, tightly wrapped in his overcoat on a plank that bisected an old wooden fence. Nicholas had called it a "stile." Hector's hat and scarf obscured his face. His gloves, shoes, and the cuffs of his trousers were patterned with sand and splashed mud. His eyes had been watching the glittering water subside and the long beaked waders paddling against the speed of its flow. The turmoil that had been his understanding had also drained away. A major dose of God's "kindness enzyme" had been delivered during his sleep. He found no fear ahead, no trepidation of what lay beneath the waters. After all, this was at least his third life. He had given himself up to death by colourless filtration in the Rupert the First all those years ago in Heidelberg. He had played out his demise in its constant temperature and the settling of all his memories and little achievements into one of the many sleeps to nothing that the home had been made for. There was no one there to mourn or even notice his departure. His enjoyable exercises in irritation might be missed by Capek in the form of relief, if indeed he outlived him. The way things were going back in the fatherland meant that all the rules had changed, even the elemental ones that controlled and conditioned life and death itself. Nicholas had been right to prevent his return. The spitting poison that he had heard in the Erstwhile's cat's whisker radio had all come true. He would never see the Germany he had lived in for so many years again. A curlew laced the morning sounds and Hector turned his head to try and locate it, bobbing out and back of his thoughts, which were vanishing one by one as he moved on to the next. Anyway, that Hector would have never dreamed of the London adventurer: the hunter of madmen and angels, conversationalist of corpses, raconteur of villains. Had all that been true? So much life instigated by so much long-term death. All compressed in a few short years. He grinned under the woolly scarf. So much fun. It had been beyond his wildest dreams. So much greater than his anaemic youth, made cumbersome by books and saturated in oily pride. What would he have made of Solli then? Let alone talking scarecrows.

Only his time with Rachel remained untarnished or dimmed by the London escapades. Her face never vanished, and often he found that explaining all this strangeness to her helped him come to grips with its impossibility. In the last few years she had been with him high above the streets of Whitechapel. Ever since the phenomena on the first floor, since his attack and what Nicholas had disturbingly called "his enlightenment," she had been more and more vivid to him. But he knew she was not here now. The next transaction was reserved for him and Nicholas alone. The thought did not sadden him, because she was deeply enfolded in him and not in his attic room, which was now a very long way away.

"We should begin," called Nicholas, and Hector arose and

took off his overcoat, gloves, and hat, his long lustrous hair falling around his ears. He hung the garments over the fence and put his foot on the crossbar of the stile and started to undo the lace.

"What are you doing?"

Hector twisted his head back towards the estuary.

"Taking my shoes off."

Nicholas laughed and clapped his hands together.

"Hector, you are a caution, extra points for that one. We are here to invest the plural. To lay ourselves down to make a protection, not to go paddling."

"But I thought . . ." muttered Hector.

"You'll be wanting a bucket and spade next."

Hector just grinned back, holding out his arms and hands, palms up, and shrugging. "What do I know?"

"Nothing, nothing yet, my dear friend, but very soon everything." He held out his hand and Hector walked over to join him, one shoelace drawing a swaying, skittish line behind him in the placid mud.

As they set out across the yellow-grey flanks of smooth sand and mud, Nicholas started stamping on the surface and in and out of the puddles, building up a regular rhythmic stomping motion forward.

"Why are you dancing like this?" asked Hector, who was merely shuffling behind.

"I am testing the strength of the surface, in case of gullies and crevasses."

Hector nodded earnestly as if he understood.

"It's my Ghost Dance," Nicholas said.

"I read about those once, a long time ago. Is it part of the ritual of the plural? Are we summoning our ancestors to help us stand against our foes? Should I be dancing too? To make the calling better."

They were up to their calves in water and Nicholas sloshed over to his friend, who was beginning to move from one foot to the other. He put his hand gently on his shoulder.

"You make me laugh, Hector, extra points for that. I meant my Ghost Dance at the Pavilion, when I was in the chorus of Indian braves. I didn't only play cowboys, you know! It's only pretend. But it does test the firmness of the mud. Let's dance together." He took Hector's arm and they stamped forward until they were up to their knees and then their waists.

The sun was high and its brilliant reflection dappled and swam energetically in the water, casting rippling light upwards into their faces. They were getting near the middle and Hector suddenly stopped, a look of loss and emptiness filling his face. He stared at Nicholas. Fear started to bloom in his vacancy. Nicholas put his hand over Hector's head, held it flat, and made the circular sign of a halo over his sleek, shining locks. They spoke a few words that could not be heard because they coincided with a squadron of raucous geese arguing midair with several laconic cormorants.

Hector regained his composure and purpose and strode on ahead of Nicholas, sinking an inch or two with each step. The Erstwhile halted him before his chin touched the water. He was at least a foot and a half taller and the returning water had not yet reached his armpits.

"We should do this bit together," he said. "I don't want you to be afraid once we are below. We still have a long way to go, and if we hold each other tight, then we won't slip or be washed back up."

Hector nodded at the obvious sense of Nicholas's statement. They linked arms and moved ahead and downwards with great caution and deliberation. Just before the salty sea and the earthy Thames covered his mouth, Hector said, "Thank you, Nicholas, for selecting me. Thank you and the other ones for giving my little life such a purpose." The last words were spluttery because the water was over his nose and he had to stretch to say them. "Thank you for letting me help save foolish humanity."

And then he was gone, the water closing over him, his hair rising like a slow-motion anemone, flowing under the surface, and Nicholas's reply, which of course he never heard, even though the Erstwhile's mouth was also disappearing below the choppy dazzling surface when he said, "Oh, Hector, it's not for the Rumour. We are doing this for the Vorrh."

ACKNOWLEDGMENTS

Multitudes of thanks again to my brilliant editor, Timothy O'Connell, whose wisdom, skill, and enthusiasm so shaped this book. And to his team at Vintage.

Great thanks also to Mark Booth and his team at Hodder & Stoughton.

And to my brave agents, Jon Elek and Seth Fishman.

And a special thank-you for all of my first test readers who made sure I was not writing "All work and no play makes Jack a dull boy. All work and no play makes Jack a dull boy." And made the first edits and corrections on my long path to literacy. Giving confidence and direction inside the Vorrh:

Iain Sinclair, Flossie Catling, David Russell, Sarah Simblet, Rebecca Hind, and Honest Publishing.

And thanks to those whose generous and critical support drove the manuscripts on:

Alan Moore, Ray Cooper, Terry Gilliam, Michael Moorcock, Tony Grisoni, Geoff Cox, Anna Sinclair, Jo Welsh, Caroline Wirth, Tom Waits, Peter Jewkes, Stuart Kelly, Phillip Pullman, Jeff VanderMeer, Alex Preston, and Roddy Bell.

And for the solid ground of the Ruskin School of Art and the Pitt-Rivers Museum, University of Oxford.

Printed in the United States
by Baker & Taylor Publisher Services